The Bloodline Code

Bloodlines of Power Series

Book One: The Bloodline Code
Lucas Brandt inherits more than an empire. He inherits a legacy of secrets too dangerous to keep… or expose.

Book Two: Dust and Empire
When truth collapses an empire, the dust doesn't settle—it chokes. And the past comes hunting.

Book Three: Echoes in the Ledger
Memory becomes a weapon as apartheid-era secrets rise from the vault to fracture the future.

Book Four: The Clean Hands Coup
Power rebrands. Justice is staged. Lucas is framed in a media coup—and Zara strikes back.

Book Five: The Inheritance Clause
The clause that crowns the next Brandt ruler. Lucas must choose: burn it all, or become what he hates.

Book Six: Redemption Protocol
Final moves. Final betrayals. A coded legacy, a buried truth—and one last shot at redemption.

For future releases and series updates:
sandtonpublishing.com
sandtonpublishing.com/newsletter

THE BLOODLINE CODE
Book One of the Bloodlines of Power Series

JOHN BUCK

SANDTON PUBLISHING
Sunshine Coast, Australia

FIRST EDITION, 2025

PUBLISHED BY SANDTON PUBLISHING
An imprint of John Buck
Buderim, Australia

Cover design by Sandton Publishing Design

ISBN 978-1-923581-01-2 (paperback)
ISBN 978-1-923581-00-5 (ebook)

For more information, visit:
www.sandtonpublishing.com

For Lea-Anne, my constant, my calm, my compass.

For my children, Jane and Patrick—the future is yours.

For everyone who ever refused to stay silent.

Table of Contents

Author's Note

Power doesn't die with its architects—it adapts, finds new hosts. Growing up in post-apartheid South Africa, I witnessed how systems of control rebranded themselves as progress while preserving their machinery. Fortunes built on extraction didn't vanish with democracy; they simply learned to speak the language of transformation while keeping the grammar of exploitation.

The Bloodline Code was born from a question: What do you do when your inheritance is complicity? When the wealth that educated you, the connections that elevated you, the very name you carry are built on foundations you cannot defend but cannot escape?

The characters are fictional, but the moral terrain is real. In a country still learning the difference between reconciliation and justice, the hardest battles are fought not in courtrooms or parliaments, but in the human heart—where loyalty and conscience wage their quietest wars.

This is a story about choosing who you become when everything you inherited tells you who you should be.

— John Buck

SANDTON
PUBLISHING

BRANDT

Note to Readers

The Bloodline Code takes place in contemporary South Africa, against a backdrop of historical reckoning, corporate corruption, and generational legacy.

Throughout the novel, you may encounter local expressions, acronyms, place names, and cultural references unique to South African life and history. While context will often guide meaning, a **Glossary** is provided at the end of the book for readers who wish to explore deeper understanding.

No prior knowledge of South African politics or geography is required to enjoy the story. But for those curious about the forces shaping the novel's world—from the ANC to Sandton, from muti to the TRC—the glossary may offer additional insight.

An *'essential'* glossary is provided on the following page.

— John Buck

Essential Glossary

A complete glossary of South African terms and references appears at the back of this book.

Sandton

Johannesburg's financial hub, often called *"Africa's richest square mile."* Gleaming towers, luxury malls, and corporate headquarters define its skyline.

Rosebank

A vibrant Johannesburg district known for its hotels, offices, and shopping precincts. A common meeting place for business and politics.

Hartbeespoort

A dam and mining region in North West Province. Site of industrial tragedies and cover-ups referenced in the Brandt family's past.

Muti

Traditional African medicine, ranging from herbal remedies to ritual practices, is often woven into both rural and urban life.

TRC (Truth and Reconciliation Commission)

South Africa's post-apartheid tribunal (established 1995) that heard testimony on politically motivated crimes from 1960–1994 and offered conditional amnesty. **Historical; not an active investigative body today.** Its reports (1998–2003) still inform public debates and cases.

Chapter 1 – Funeral for a King

Lucas stepped off the plane into Johannesburg's assault of heat and memory.

The terminal's air conditioning fought the African sun and lost. Humidity clung to his skin like an accusation. His pulse matched boot-strikes on tile.

The air tasted of dust and jet fuel. An old Johannesburg welcome. Twelve years in London's polite distance, and the city still recognized him. It watched him with the same patient malice that had exiled him over a decade ago.

Up on the mezzanine, a man in a cap leaned against the railing. Too still for the hour. Lucas clocked him once, dismissed him as a traveler killing time. Only later, on the street, when the same figure surfaced closer—paper cup in hand—was he harder to ignore.

Passengers flowed past, glances lingering just long enough to catalog him.

Expensive suit. Careful posture. The taut stillness of a man returning to a place he'd tried to forget.

On the mezzanine, a teenager lifted a phone and filmed the arrivals sweep. Recognition rarely announced itself here. The city watched.

The customs queue inched forward. Lucas slipped a hand into his coat pocket and felt the brass key under his fingertips—cool, deliberate, impossible to mistake. The letter had arrived three days after the funeral announcement, slid under his London apartment door like a confession someone couldn't bear to deliver in person. Anton's handwriting, unmistakable even in death—the same careful script that had signed school reports and tuition transfers before signing contracts that moved mountains and buried secrets.

If you're reading this, I'm gone and you're still running. Stop running, son. Come home. There are things you need to understand about why I let you go.

No date. No signature. Just the words and the key taped to the paper. It had weight now, not measured in grams but in force. A private gravity. The stamp thumped; his passport slid back across glass.

"Next." The immigration officer had a weathered face and institutional patience. He scanned the passport, eyes flicking from the page to Lucas, then to the screen with the look of someone who read newspapers and remembered headlines.

"Business or pleasure, Mr. Brandt?"

"Family obligations."

The stamp landed with mechanical finality. "Welcome home."

****

Home followed him down the concourse and into baggage claim. Duty-free's perfume drifted like staged innocence. Lucas moved past with his carry-on rolling behind him like a reluctant witness. He'd packed light.

Habit from years of moving between airports and conference rooms, a life built on the theory that geography could absolve genetics.

His phone had found the local network. Missed calls: Helena ×3. Funeral director ×2. Two messages stacked on the lock screen.

The first from Helena: DO NOT SPEAK TO ANYONE UNTIL YOU SEE ME. PHONE OFF IN CAR. The second from Zara Mokoena—an investigative journalist, and once his closest confidante—sent before takeoff: Call me when you land. There are things we can't put in a message.

He deleted Zara's text. Some conversations were dangerous at any distance.

Outside, the heat hit like judgment—inescapable. A black sedan idled at the curb where the letter had promised. Driver in a gray suit that guaranteed discretion.

"Mr. Brandt." The man's voice carried forty years of navigating Johannesburg's complicated maps. "Welcome."

7

"The estate," Lucas said. He slid into leather that smelled faintly of cigarettes and other people's secrets. He watched the terminal glass recede. The man in the cap had drifted down to street level and stood with a paper cup, too casual. Eyes on the car, body angled to avoid the cameras he didn't want to be in. Lucas felt the key in his pocket and forced his gaze forward.

The airport perimeter fell behind them.

The highway unfurled—billboards promising mobile data and immaculate dental work, razor-wired walls protecting nothing as carefully as they protected the illusion of safety. Tin roofs crowded against stucco mansions. The new towers in Sandton gleamed ahead, clean lines and quiet money. Somewhere in the weave of traffic a dark SUV matched their speed for three exits, then dropped back and returned at the next merge. Long enough to notice persistence, not plates.

"Election security," the driver said, nodding toward a convoy of military trucks heading the other way. In the truck beds, soldiers sat with their rifles at that particular angle that meant *not yet*. "Tense since the mining strikes."

London had offered Lucas a different vocabulary. He'd helped write anti-corruption frameworks—clean code meant to restrain the very kind of power the Brandt name had practiced for a century. Every compliance clause had been a private act of rebellion.

The irony was never lost on him: he made his living building cages for men like his father while carrying a key to a door he had never opened.

He'd once told himself that integrity could be rebuilt one framework at a time, but London had begun long before the frameworks.

He'd left South Africa the year the inquiry convened. Not because he was named, but because he wasn't. Anton's lawyers had polished the record so clean it reflected nothing, and the absence sickened him more than any accusation would have. Cameras flared on the courthouse steps; pundits called it a master class. Helena had said Anton was proud—

his son had shown judgment, put an ocean between himself and the noise.

London wasn't absolution. It was distance that photographed well. When the first offer arrived—a compliance role that promised clean language and measurable ethics—he took it before dawn. He told himself he was choosing work; what he chose was quiet. He learned to write frameworks that looked like fences and to live with the knowledge that he'd fled the field where damage had been done in his family's name.

Leaving wasn't atonement. It was surrender arranged to resemble virtue.

The city blurred past the window, new towers rising over old ground as if reinvention were an architectural trick.

Talk radio bled into a news bulletin. An anchor rehearsing the eulogy of an empire—philanthropy always mentioned before offshore accounts, handshakes before wire transfers. The phrases were familiar and meant to be. Legacies were stories sculpted in public; the numbers lived in private columns.

"Mrs. Brandt asked to keep the phone off," the driver said without turning. "We'll be at the gates in twenty-five."

"Keep to your route," Lucas said.

The city slid past. Palms, jacarandas, bougainvillea spilled like wine. The boy who'd believed this landscape belonged to him had died some small death on a Christmas visit, standing in Anton's study with a file he wasn't supposed to open. Shell companies with names like poetry. Transfers that read like policy. A ledger you could put your fingers on and feel the heat.

His mind reached for a memory to soften the edge and found one intact. He was eight, in a too-stiff shirt, feet not reaching the carpet from one of the study's leather chairs. Anton had knelt to tie his boy's tie—no staff for this part— thumb pressing the knot flat once, twice, until it sat perfect. He'd leaned back and appraised the result the way he appraised a proposal.

"Things must hold, Lucas." The cologne was warm tobacco and pepper. "If it comes loose when you need it tightest, it was never properly tied."

For years, the line had lived as fatherly advice. Later, it read like operational doctrine.

***

The sedan turned off the highway, took a private road lined with indigenous trees and European nostalgia. The fence came first—landscaping until you were close enough to see the barbs. At the gatehouse, a guard examined IDs, consulted a list printed in a font that signaled authority, pressed a button that retracted steel with hydraulic precision. The dark SUV did not turn in. It drifted slow past the entrance and continued up the road as if it had always belonged to another destination.

"There may be protests," the driver said, the apology built into his cadence. "Especially this week."

Lucas nodded without looking at him. Expectation didn't blunt impact. You can know a fire is lit and still be surprised when the heat reaches bone.

The house revealed itself gradually—imported stone and European lines shipped whole and assembled against African sky. The circular drive curved under jacarandas heavy with purple bloom. Pollen dusted the marble steps like a confession no one would admit to making. Security moved with precision designed for cameras: visible enough to reassure, discreet enough to suggest there was nothing to see.

He heard the voice before the car stopped.

"Murderer! You think marble can wash blood clean?"

A man stood beyond the fence—gaunt, sun-bleached clothes hanging off a frame used to going without.

He held a cardboard sign with handwriting more precise than rage usually allowed. A small group lingered with

10

him—two women, one boy of twelve maybe, camera phone raised with a hand that didn't shake.

"Hartbeespoort!" the man shouted. "You remember Hartbeespoort, don't you?" He didn't wait for an answer. "Twenty-three men buried alive for your father's gold!"

The name worked under Lucas's ribs like a surgeon's hand. Hartbeespoort, 1994, a dam town an hour northwest of Johannesburg, where miners' families had blockaded the highway with burning tires—a collapse ruled an accident on paper that had since yellowed into official memory. He remembered whispers from junior inspectors whose careers died after they whispered, a draft report that went missing, payments filed under euphemisms, the way silence could be notarized.

He pushed open the car door. Heat swallowed him whole.

"He's not wrong," Lucas said to the driver.

The sentence settled like a weight he'd been carrying by mistake and had finally recognized. The heat pressed its hand on his chest.

***

Helena Brandt—his mother, as formidable as ever—opened the front door before he could lift a hand to knock. Black dress that admitted mourning without conceding ground, pearls that scattered light across the clavicle like a gathering laid out for auction. She moved forward with precision that suggested rehearsal, spread her arms, and gave him an embrace calibrated to look maternal and cost her nothing.

"You came," she said. As if his presence were victory rather than obligation.

"You'll stand where the cameras can see you," Helena said, voice smooth as poured oil. "Grief is wasted in corners. The world must see a son devoted to his father's memory."

"Or to your version of it," Lucas said. But Helena was already adjusting his tie as if it were punctuation in her speech.

The foyer stretched, designed to intimidate anyone who didn't already belong. Carrara marble floors—Michelangelo's saints recast as geometry—arranged to lead the gaze toward portraits that told a single story for four generations: Brandt men who stared at artists until the artist got the eyes right. Wilhelm, who crossed an ocean with expertise and moral elasticity. Frederick, who learned the rhythms of governments the way a miner learns a seam. Anton, captured at that careful age where power reads like certainty.

"The resemblance is stronger than I remembered," Helena said, following his glance up the wall. "Especially around the eyes."

For an instant he was ten again, standing too straight under a gaze designed to measure. The remembered click of a fountain pen cap, the sound that meant a decision had been sealed. The way approval always felt indistinguishable from relief.

"Anton's study is ready," Helena said. Her heels clicked like a metronome as she led him inward. "There are things you should understand before tomorrow."

They moved through rooms built for theater: a dining salon where crystal threw light across a table that had hosted ministers who liked to be entertained before they were convinced; a smaller room with two low sofas facing each other, a geographic arrangement perfect for a private argument that needed to look like a conversation; a library bearing first editions under glass and white papers in an unassuming binder that mattered more than the glass.

"Funeral arrangements are complete," Helena continued, the efficiency that had been terrifying in his childhood now trained like a weapon. "Dignitaries confirmed. The minister of mining will speak. We've allowed limited press access— I've approved the pool photographers."

"Of course," Lucas said. "And the questions."

"Succession," she said, with a half-smile that didn't reach her eyes. "Stewardship. Continuity. Our people have prepared talking points."

Our people. The phrase slid in like an old acquaintance and took a seat as if it were invited.

They reached the study door—oiled oak carved with designs a Brandt would recognize and a visitor would mistake for family pride. The motifs were stories. Knots that suggested continuity without revealing how the rope frayed; tools that never appeared in photographs with faces.

"Twelve years," Helena said, pausing with her hand on the brass handle. The nails were painted in a shade that signaled grief with taste. "You've been away, practicing that talent you have for choosing to be elsewhere."

"I didn't choose away," Lucas said. "I chose different."

She laughed, a small exhale with edges. "Choice. Such an American idea for someone who grew up with continental maps. As if bloodlines were outfits that could be swapped when fashion shifted."

Anton had called it the bloodline code—obedience dressed as duty. The syntax changed with each generation: silence traded for stability, guilt converted into policy, favors recorded as philanthropy. Lucas had spent twelve years pretending distance could rewrite it.

She turned the latch and stepped back.

***

The study exhaled the ghost of its former occupant— pipe tobacco and leather-bound certainty, the accumulated scent of decisions made in rooms where consequences were theoretical and profit was not.

Books lined the walls to the ceiling—legal systems and geological surveys, biographies of men who had made their names by naming what already belonged to other people. The desk commanded the center of the room the way certain people command attention without moving. The

13

sunlight came in at an angle that implied it had been negotiated.

On the desk: Anton's Montblanc, black with gold trim. Next to it, a brass key, old-fashioned, the teeth worn smooth by use. Lucas could feel the twin to it in his pocket answering like a tuning fork.

"In the third drawer," Helena said, voice neutral. "He said you would know when to use it. He said your background would help you understand the implications."

The key turned without resistance. The click wasn't loud, but he felt it along the nerves in his forearms. Inside, nested in blue velvet like an apology arranged for later, lay a black USB drive without markings, except for a single word etched in Anton's hand: CYPRESS.

"What is it?" Lucas asked, though some part of him already knew the answer. His job for a decade had been reading between lines.

"Insurance," Helena said. She moved closer, not touching the desk. "The kind your father specialized in. The kind that outlives men."

He took the drive. It weighed too much for plastic and silicon. He put it in his pocket and felt the weight settle next to the letter key. Weight recognized weight.

Through the study windows, the garden had become a performance—two groundsmen shaping a hedge into the idea of a hedge, a woman kneeling with a brush to clean pollen from the base of a marble urn. The estate had always welcomed news cameras as if they were mirrors.

Helena opened a different drawer with the same ease. She produced a manila folder thick enough to whisper when it moved. "Financial records. Accounts that will transfer. Responsibilities that will not."

He flipped the cover.

The first pages were bank statements from institutions that promised discretion until public pressure made them promise cooperation. Figures with too many zeros and footnotes with too few words. Then the names. Some he recognized from parliamentary committees and charity galas;

others from boardrooms where votes were counted differently and never recorded at all. The euphemisms did what euphemisms do: CONSULTANCY FEES. ADVISORY RETAINERS. COMMUNITY PARTNERSHIPS.

Lucas closed the file halfway, hands braced on the cardboard as if holding a door. He could feel the architecture of it without reading every line. This wasn't record-keeping. It was a map. A network. A way to make a phone ring in a minister's pocket at midnight and have the minister answer it.

"Some of it will require action," Helena said, as if discussing spoilage dates. "Some of it will require interpretation. Your father left… notes."

"Where?" He didn't look up.

"In the safe," she said. "But the principles are the same." She glanced toward the portraits visible through the open doorway. "Leverage is leverage, whatever you call it."

He let the folder close. The air in the room felt denser. People talked about paper trails as if they were routes out of a forest. This was a maze. He felt a memory rise—Anton's hands tying a knot until it held—and wondered when the lesson had shifted from cloth to country.

"How long have you known?" he asked.

"Since the beginning," Helena said. Her face didn't move. Only her voice lowered half a register, the way people do when truth is close by and should not be frightened. "Someone had to manage the details while he managed the vision. Someone had to translate between proof and power."

"I used to think you hosted," Lucas said, glancing toward the rooms they had crossed. He remembered her body angled just so in photographs, the way she had learned to be the light men arranged themselves around.

"I did," she said. "And I managed."

Silence flexed between them. He stared at the Montblanc and thought about all the decisions that had been signed where he stood. Men liked to imagine their crime scenes were elsewhere.

"Tomorrow," she said, moving toward the door, "the house will be busier—caterers, security, logistics. The press has been given a route and a time. The minister has been given his lines." She paused, hand on the handle, eyes on him. "Tonight is for remembering—and for deciding what kind of man you are willing to be."

She turned the handle but didn't open the door yet. "Your father used to say power is like gravity—no one sees it until something falls." Her expression didn't change. "Things are going to fall tomorrow, Lucas. Be the one to choose where."

When she left, the click of the latch sounded smaller than it felt.

***

He went to the window and watched the groundsmen stand back from their work to assess a line of box hedge as if its perfection could change the news ticker. The protester's voice carried in memory more clearly than through the glass: *You think marble can wash blood clean?*

Lucas set the folder on the desk and opened it again, this time reading with the discipline that had made him useful in London. Numbers became transfers, transfers became obligations, obligations revealed the pressure points they had been designed to sustain. On a separate sheet, a list of projects labeled with innocuous names—the kinds no one would object to: water, housing, schools. Off to the side, in his father's exact hand, the smaller words that explained the actual purpose: PACIFY, CONTAIN, REFRAME. The handwriting had always been neat, even when the content was not.

He came to a set of scanned emails between foundation staff and a deputy director in a provincial office—meeting minutes sanitized into bulleted lists, and an expense line that read TRANSPORT SUPPORT with an amount that would have purchased a clinic wing. A marginal note, again in Anton's hand: *No more than this.* There was a second note below it, lighter, written over the first at a later date: *Except when necessary.*

He breathed out and let his eyes blur a second to stop the paper from vibrating.

The phone buzzed on the desk, face down. He didn't have to check to know it was Helena; she had grown proficient at timing. He flipped it anyway. A single sentence: *Remember your discretion.* Below it, a second message arrived, then was recalled—deleted before his eyes. The system registered a notification and then corrected itself, like a body swallowing on reflex.

He put the phone face down. Behind him the Montblanc sat where it always sat, at the angle Anton had always favored when stepping away to consider. The pen was an instrument of performance: it turned decisions into signatures, made power legible. The USB drive in his pocket was the opposite. It would make power portable.

He thought of calling Zara. He imagined her voice—steady even when angry, skeptical even when kind. He imagined telling her about the man with the sign, the way the groundsmen's shears made that *shk-shk* sound against tender growth, the way language could be trained to mean two things and pay for both.

Instead he slid open a side drawer and found what he knew he would: a ledger bound in black, its edges burnished with oil from years of being moved and opened and consulted. The first page wasn't labeled CY anything. It carried a different word first—Foundations—with the plural underlined, and below it an index written in a precise hand. Cypress appeared on page 11 and again on page 27 with a separate arrow he recognized as a private notation: *If broken, break.*

He read, and the room stayed the same as rooms do when you learn things in them that the room already knew.

****

After a time that could have been an hour or the length of a single careful decision, he closed the ledger and looked up at Anton's portrait hanging in the corridor beyond the open door. The painter had been hired to catch a gaze that held two expressions depending on how far back you stood. From the threshold, Lucas saw the one he had grown up with: calculation that presented as control. When he stepped closer to the doorway, the expression shifted, almost imperceptibly, into something that could be mistaken for pride if you weren't the person it was pointed at.

The day's heat began to drain into evening. Across the lawn, a woman in catering black wheeled in a silver cart as if laying out grief for inspection. Somewhere beyond the fence a car horn sounded, then another. Sirens braided together and moved past, searching for a different address.

He took the USB from his pocket and set it on the desk next to the Montblanc. Two instruments, two grammars. One wrote the world down in a way that could be framed. The other could pull at the wires behind the frame and make the picture stutter.

He considered, for a foolish moment, slipping the drive into his shoe the way he had once hidden a contraband coin at school to see if smuggling felt like bravery. He put the drive back in his pocket and pressed it flat. He set his thumb on the brass key until he felt his pulse in the metal.

When he finally left the study, the house had changed key. Staff voices moved in the hallways in that efficient hush particular to practiced households. A tray had appeared on a side table without being visible in transit: three bottles of water condensed with beads, two glasses dry, a napkin with the family crest folded into an absurd little castle.

On a console near the stairs, a photograph he had never noticed before caught his eye—Anton on a boat, a rare candid. He was younger there than Lucas was now, wind lifting his hair, eyes squinting against the light as if he weren't sure whether to smile. Lucas touched the frame the way you touch a bruise to confirm it exists, then pulled his hand back as if etiquette were a form of first aid.

He went to the front steps and stood in the heat gone thinner. The protest group had dwindled to two. The boy was gone; the man with the sign sat on the curb, elbows on knees, the sign resting against his shins. The woman beside him scrolled through the day's footage with her thumb, pausing occasionally to zoom on a frame and shake her head, not in disbelief but in the rhythm of people who catalog because they must.

The guard at the gate glanced over as Lucas lifted a hand. It wasn't a wave and it wasn't a truce. It was acknowledgment—of attention paid, of a ledger that existed outside drawers. The guard didn't nod back. He looked beyond Lucas, up the drive to the house, and then away again, as if attention were a resource he'd been ordered to conserve.

Behind him, the door opened. Helena's voice, close as a shadow. "Don't wander."

"Watching," he said.

"Then learn something while you do," she said. The door eased shut without a click.

He stayed until the protester stood, until the woman with the phone put it in a bag that didn't close properly.

He stayed until the light stained the marble steps the color of old bruises and the security lights clicked on with a certainty the sun had not been able to provide all day.

When he went back into the study, the USB in his pocket felt warmer from his hand. He set it on the desk again, this time on the velvet in the open drawer, and closed the drawer softly, feeling the spring catch. He took the brass key and turned it once more just to hear the sound, to know the lock would receive him again if he asked.

He sat in Anton's chair and picked up the Montblanc. For a moment he let it hover above a legal pad. The pen was full. The lines it would write would be crisp and dark and persuasive; the signatures it produced would pass scrutiny. He put it down. He took out his phone and typed a message he didn't send: *Zara, there's a drive. Name on it is CYPRESS. Do not...* He deleted the draft letter by letter until the screen was blank as if nothing had been thought.

Voices in the hall again, footsteps, a door closing in a room two turns away. Somewhere upstairs a tap ran for three seconds and stopped, as if someone had begun a thing and thought better.

Lucas leaned back and stared at the ceiling's plaster work, angels so gently rendered you could forget their wings were muscles. He could feel the pattern settling around him—the arrangement of events one might mistake for fate. But he had written frameworks; he knew the difference between inevitability and design.

Tomorrow would be for public rituals. A parade of acceptable sadness, a series of microphones, a distribution of sympathy and suspicion according to rank. Photographs of a son at a podium beside a widow whose restraint would be measured as virtue. The minister's eulogy printed in papers nationwide, translated into multiple languages, edited twice by people on the foundation payroll. The questions afterward about legacy and leadership, about what comes next.

Tonight was for choosing the language he would use when the questions arrived.

He looked again at the drawer. He didn't open it. He didn't need to. He could feel the pull of the little rectangle from across the desk, the way some metals tug at a compass mind. It wasn't calling him. It was reminding him of a fact: he had carried one gravity to another.

He stood. Turned off the study lamp. Left the overhead light on, because darkness was a kind of performance too and he didn't feel like performing it. He paused at the doorway and looked back—at the velvet edge just visible when the drawer was closed but not locked, at the pen at its practiced angle, at the chair that remembered the weight that had sat in it longest.

Then, on impulse—or maybe caution—he crossed back to the desk, slid open the drawer, and pocketed the drive. No point leaving temptation behind in a house full of ghosts.

Helena's last words traveled across the room clean as glass. *Be the one to choose where.* The word choice was a shape she could live inside.

Lucas touched the brass key one last time and felt—clearer than comfort—how little the metal cared about what it opened. Keys didn't contain ethics. They offered access.

He put the key in his pocket and closed the door behind him with a soft click that felt precise enough to be a promise.

The brass nameplate on Anton's coffin bore the family crest—scales of justice in one quadrant seeming to watch him with metallic indifference. Lucas had always assumed they represented the family's commitment to fairness. Tonight, he wondered if they represented something else entirely.

Tomorrow would bury Anton. That would be the ceremony the world understood.

The real inheritance—the code that determined where gravity landed—had already changed hands.

Chapter 2 – The Empire's Cracks

The morning after Anton's funeral, Lucas stood in the lobby of the Brandt Building, its glass walls reflecting a city already restless with whispers. The elevator's brass buttons felt cold under Lucas's fingertips as he pressed 23. Each ascending number marked distance from the funeral, but the burden remained lodged between his shoulder blades like an unreachable knife. The mirrored walls showed him in fractured pieces—dark suit wrinkled from morning ceremonies, eyes hollow with the exhaustion that came from burying family secrets along with family members.

When the doors slid open with their muted whoosh, he stepped into a reception area that treated him like a stranger in his own inheritance. The lobby had been gutted since his last visit in the early 2000s, every trace of Anton's personality surgically removed and replaced with corporate sterility that could belong to any multinational anywhere.

The Brandt Building sat in the heart of Johannesburg's central business district, its glass facade throwing back the financial district's morning rush hour like a mirror angled to catch the city's restless energy. Walking inside always felt like crossing a border between two cities that pretended to be one.

The transformation was so thorough it felt malicious—as if his father's ghost had been exorcised through interior design.

Light here was surgical—white and merciless across glass panels and polished stone. Its glare erased every shadow, every hint of depth or history. Where Anton's mounted hunting trophies had once declared conquest—horned beasts against dark wood paneling—abstract paintings now hung like colorful bandages over old wounds.

Ovals of tangerine bleeding into cobalt, rigid black lines slicing through canvas. Corporate art designed to offend no one and inspire nothing, but here they felt deliberate: victory recast as innocuous geometry, history neutralized into décor.

Lucas paused at the threshold, hand hovering near his coat pocket where the Cypress drive sat like a ticking bomb. The air smelled manufactured—like a new-car showroom where every surface had been wiped of fingerprints and memories. No tobacco bitterness from Anton's cigars, no coffee staleness from late-night strategy sessions. Just filtered air and fresh carpet fibers, the scent of erasure designed to make visitors forget there had ever been anything worth remembering.

At the front desk, a woman sat behind white marble veined with gray, her expression as unsullied as the stone. Her smile was perfect—dentist-perfect, rehearsed like a recorded greeting that had been focus-grouped to death. Everything about her seemed calibrated for maximum inoffensiveness: hair styled to suggest competence without character, makeup applied with the precision of someone who understood that personality was a liability in corporate spaces.

"Mr. Brandt." Her voice was detached, reading from an invisible script. The way she pronounced "Brandt" made it sound like a historical curiosity, something clipped and held at arm's length. Her manicured fingers moved across the keyboard with slow deliberation, each tap echoing beneath the antiseptic hush of the vents like coins dropping into a collection plate.

Lucas leaned against the desk's edge, feeling marble's chill seep through his palm. He studied her face—the tight skin around her eyes, the rigid set of her jaw. The smile was professional armor, and there was no warmth beneath it. She might have been beautiful once, before the corporate machinery had pressed her into this shape.

"Good morning." His voice carried in the cathedral silence, bouncing off the stone walls like a dropped pebble in a tomb.

She blinked—a precise, measured movement—and slid a sleek tablet across the marble slab. "Please sign in."

On the screen, his name appeared in a visitor's list he'd never authorized. He tapped it, watched a green light blink confirmation, and imagined his presence spiraling into the company's digital nervous system like a virus. She didn't offer directions or small talk. Simply watched him with the detached interest of someone observing a museum exhibit—curious but careful not to engage.

The lobby stretched before him, vast and empty of soul. No trophies glinting under spotlights, no sepia photographs of Anton shaking hands with presidents or mining barons. Nothing to root these walls in real blood and sweat and history. Just white expanses that absorbed every footstep, every whispered conversation, every trace of humanity like silence made architectural.

Between two large canvases of pastel meaninglessness, he spotted something that made his chest tighten.

A small silver plaque mounted flush against the brushed-metal wall, so understated it was almost missable. He stooped low to read the elegant engraving:

ANTON BRANDT
Pioneering Entrepreneur
Tireless Innovator
A Legacy of Integrity

Lucas tasted bile. "Legacy of Integrity." He almost laughed. The man who built Brandt Mining had been many things—brilliant, ruthless, visionary—but integrity wasn't among them. Anton had been brutal when necessary, efficient always, unforgiving by nature. A merciless god in a tailored suit who'd built an empire on other people's bones. The sanitized language made Lucas want to tear the plaque from the wall and replace it with something honest: "Built on blood, backroom deals, and broken promises."

Instead, he stood in the antiseptic glow, breathing shallowly and feeling his father's ghost laughing at the whitewash. Someone had spent considerable effort transforming Anton Brandt from predator into saint. The question was whether they'd done it to honor his memory or to hide his crimes.

A sharp knock echoed behind frosted glass. Lucas straightened, muscle memory from childhood making him automatically compose his expression. Through the glass, he saw movement—a shape approaching with the purposeful stride of corporate authority, each step measured and inevitable.

The door slid open with mechanical precision. A man stepped through wearing a charcoal suit so perfectly tailored it looked painted on. Every hair was in place, his tie knotted with mathematical precision. He extended his hand before Lucas could fully register his appearance—a practiced gesture—the kind perfected across countless encounters, each one identical in its professional warmth and underlying calculation.

"Mr. Brandt. Tobias Cole, chief operating officer." His voice was smooth as aged whiskey but twice as calculated. The handshake was firm but distant, the kind used to seal mergers rather than greet old friends. His palm was dry, controlled—the hand of someone who never perspired under pressure.

Cole's handshake lingered a moment too long, his palm carrying the faint ridge of an old scar—the kind that came from learning to hold more than pens and presentation clickers.

"Tobias." Lucas studied the man's face for tells. Cole had ageless corporate handsomeness that could be thirty-five or fifty-five, maintained through expensive dentistry and careful living. His eyes were pale blue, intelligent, completely without warmth.

"Please, follow me." Cole gestured toward a corridor flanked by glass panels that turned the hallway into an aquarium for ambition. "I trust the service was... appropriate?"

"Adequate." Lucas didn't bother to soften the word. He wasn't here to make friends, and Cole's casual reference to his father's funeral felt like a test disguised as courtesy.

Cole's smile flickered—a micro-expression that confirmed Lucas's suspicion that every word was being weighed and cataloged. "Your father was respected by many.

His vision shaped this company, this industry." The past tense hung in the air like smoke from an extinguished blaze.

Lucas noted the careful distance, the way Cole spoke about Anton as if he were already a historical figure rather than a man who'd died only days ago. They passed workstations where employees hunched over screens, their faces pale in the blue glow. He caught fragments of conversation—shipping manifests, regulatory compliance, environmental impact assessments. The language of legitimate business, but something felt rehearsed about it all, like actors performing their roles for an invisible audience.

"Impressive renovations." Lucas gestured at the sterile perfection surrounding them. A woman in a navy blazer glanced up from her computer, met his eyes briefly, then looked away with the practiced indifference of corporate survival. Her reaction seemed automatic—the kind of reflex developed by people who'd learned not to see too much.

Cole's smile tightened almost imperceptibly. "Your father believed in evolution. Adaptation to changing markets and regulatory environments. Though he always insisted we preserve the substance—the foundation of relationships and understanding that makes everything function."

"Understanding can change." Lucas noted how Cole's jaw tensed at the words. The response was involuntary, unguarded—the first genuine reaction he'd seen from the man.

"Can it?" Cole stopped at a conference room door, his hand resting on the brushed steel handle. "I suppose we'll discover the answer to that question soon enough."

The conference room beyond was a shrine to corporate anonymity—black leather chairs arranged around a table that gleamed like an obsidian altar. The space felt designed to intimidate through its very neutrality, as if personality itself was a form of weakness. Cole tapped a hidden control panel embedded in the wall. The glass walls shimmered from transparent to opaque—the world beyond dissolving into merciful mist.

"Please, take the head chair." Cole gestured to the seat that would position Lucas with his back to the only door. A power move disguised as courtesy, the kind of subtle manipulation that had probably been refined through countless similar meetings.

Lucas remained standing. "I prefer to see the exits."

Something flickered behind Cole's eyes—surprise, perhaps, or calculation. He smoothly gestured to a side chair instead. "Of course. Your father always said paranoia was just pattern recognition in disguise." The quote sounded rehearsed, as if Cole had been waiting for the right moment to deploy it.

Lucas settled into the leather, testing its give, noting how it was positioned to face the windows—another subtle psychological maneuver to make him feel exposed. The conference table's surface was so perfect it looked liquid, reflecting their faces like a black mirror that distorted everything it touched.

Cole positioned himself at the opposite end, leaning casually against the wall with studied nonchalance. His posture suggested relaxation, but Lucas caught the tension in his shoulders, the way his fingers drummed silently against his thigh like a pianist practicing scales.

"First, my sincere condolences on your father's passing." His voice dropped to that practiced register used for condolence calls and bad quarters. "News of his heart attack shocked everyone who knew him."

Lucas watched the performance with detached interest. "Did it? He'd been having chest pains for months. Helena mentioned it during one of our rare conversations."

Cole's composure flickered—just for an instant—before reassembling itself. "Yes. Well. Anton was... private about his health concerns. Very much in character." The admission sounded reluctant, as if Cole hadn't expected Lucas to be informed about family details.

"He was private about a lot of things." Lucas leaned back, feeling the Cypress drive press against his ribs. "Speaking of privacy, I noticed some interesting changes to the access protocols on my way up. New security systems, different clearance requirements."

"Standard upgrades." Cole's voice carried a defensive edge. "We've implemented comprehensive digital security measures across all operations. Your father was very concerned about industrial espionage in his final months." The explanation sounded practiced, refined through repetition.

"Industrial espionage." Lucas let the words hang in the air like smoke. "From whom, exactly?"

Cole's smile returned, but it didn't reach his eyes. "Competitors, regulatory agencies, journalists looking for scandal. The mining industry attracts attention from many quarters, as I'm sure you're aware." Each category sounded like an entry in a threat assessment matrix.

"Some attention is warranted." Lucas studied Cole's micro-expressions—the slight tightening around his eyes, the way his breathing had become more controlled. "Transparency isn't always the enemy of profitability."

"Your swift involvement in the transition process—" Cole hesitated, gauging Lucas's expression before continuing. "—it's quite admirable, really. Shows real commitment to continuity."

Lucas arched an eyebrow. "I'm not here to step in, Tobias. I'm here to understand what I've inherited."

Something shifted in Cole's demeanor—surprise giving way to wariness like sunlight disappearing behind clouds. He cleared his throat delicately. "Of course. Understanding is crucial. Given the circumstances of the transition, we've prepared a comprehensive strategic review: brand positioning, organizational realignment, stakeholder mapping. It's what we do best."

"You've 'positioned' other companies in other sectors." Lucas's voice carried just enough edge to draw blood. "Mining operations in Botswana, logistics firms in Mozambique. Now you want to reposition what's mine."

Cole's professional mask slipped another notch. "We deeply respect the Brandt legacy—its history, its impact on the region. But we also believe firmly in modernization: operational efficiency, regulatory transparency, sustainable practices. That's precisely why we've updated the physical environment, restructured the leadership hierarchy." The words came faster now, as if Cole was trying to build a wall of corporate speak around something fragile.

Lucas allowed himself a slow nod, tasting the corporate speak like soured wine. He could smell the whitewash, the effort to sand away every rough edge Anton had left. "Tell me about the board. The real board, not the public-facing version."

The mask cracked completely. Cole's posture hardened, his shoulders squaring as if preparing for impact. "They've been thoroughly briefed on the transition parameters. Extremely loyal people, of course. Understand the complexities of the business." Each word was chosen with surgical precision.

"Do they know I'm here? Right now, I mean."

Cole shifted his weight from one foot to the other—the first genuinely human movement Lucas had seen from him. "Not officially, no. We thought it prudent to allow you time to assess the organizational landscape before any formal announcements." The admission carried the weight of decisions made without consultation.

Lucas's expression darkened. "Sounds like you wrote the entire script without bothering to consult the author."

"Continuity, Mr. Brandt." Cole's smile returned, more genuine this time but somehow more unsettling. "Smooth transitions require careful orchestration. Your father understood that better than anyone."

"Continuity." Lucas let the word roll around his mouth like a sour confession. Anton had built this empire on disruption, on deals that blindsided competitors and regulators alike. The idea of "smooth transitions" would have made the old man laugh until his ribs cracked. "I'll keep that in mind."

"Excellent." Cole inclined his head with satisfaction. "I'm confident that once you've had time to review our strategic recommendations, you'll see the wisdom in maintaining established protocols." He checked his watch with practiced precision, the gesture signaling their discussion was approaching its predetermined conclusion. "You'll have the paperwork by evening."

Lucas stood slowly, his spine a bar of wire drawn taut before the day had even begun to move. His movement was deliberate, calculated to project authority while betraying none of the uncertainty gnawing at his chest. "I'm sure you've put considerable thought into those recommendations."

"Indeed we have." Cole moved toward the door, his hand hovering over the control panel like a conductor preparing to end a symphony. "I'll let you get to your other appointments."

"I have what I need—for now." The qualification hung in the air between them, a promise and a threat wrapped in diplomatic language.

Cole's fingers danced across the panel, and the glass walls shimmered back to transparency. The world beyond materialized like a magic trick—employees at their workstations, the distant hum of legitimate business, the careful stage-management of corporate life resuming its eternal performance.

They walked back through the corridor in silence that felt loaded with unspoken threats. Lucas noted details he'd missed on the way in: security cameras positioned at every intersection, keycard readers that seemed to track each employee's movements, the way conversations stopped when they approached and resumed only after they'd passed. The surveillance was comprehensive but subtle, designed to feel protective rather than oppressive.

At the lobby, Cole stopped by the exit, his hand resting on the brass door handle like a guard at a checkpoint. His smile had returned to its default setting—professional, warm, completely empty of genuine emotion. "Remember, Mr. Brandt—everything here is under careful management. Your father built something remarkable, and we're committed to preserving that legacy."

"That's exactly what worries me, Tobias."

Cole's smile never wavered, but something cold flickered behind his eyes—a glimpse of the calculation that lurked beneath the corporate courtesy. "Perhaps we should schedule a proper follow-up? A full board presentation, stakeholder introductions, comprehensive overview of our strategic initiatives?"

"Perhaps." Lucas moved toward the exit without committing to anything beyond his immediate escape.

"I'll be in touch." Cole's words carried weight beyond their surface meaning, the promise of future contact that sounded more like a threat than professional courtesy.

"I'm sure you will."

"We're very easy to find, Mr. Brandt. Always available when you need... guidance." The pause before "guidance" was barely perceptible, but Lucas caught it—the suggestion that his independence was temporary, conditional, subject to revision based on factors beyond his control.

Lucas stepped into the elevator alone, jabbing the ground floor button harder than necessary. As the doors closed, Cole's smile remained visible through the narrowing gap—perfect, professional, and utterly without warmth. The image burned itself into Lucas's retina like a photographer's flash, leaving afterimages that would linger long after he'd left the building.

***

The plaza surrounding the Brandt Building pulsed with midday energy that felt orchestrated rather than organic. Lucas emerged into brilliant sunshine that made him squint after the building's artificial twilight. Security cameras pivoted. Uniformed guards stood at strategic positions, their presence both reassuring and ominous—protection or surveillance, depending on your perspective.

This was Darren's domain—a carefully staged theater where power lunched with influence under Italian umbrellas. Marble tables dotted the space in geometric patterns that looked random but weren't, each positioned to maximize both privacy and observation opportunities. The fountain at the plaza's heart sent crystalline arcs into the air, their spray catching the light like scattered diamonds and providing just enough ambient noise to frustrate electronic surveillance.

At a corner table positioned for maximum visibility and escape routes, Darren Katz lounged with the casual confidence of someone who owned not just his seat but the entire theater. Even from fifty feet away, his posture radiated controlled authority—shoulders relaxed but ready, head tilted at the perfect angle to survey his domain while appearing completely at ease.

"Lukey!" Darren's voice carried over the fountain's hiss and the low murmur of a dozen conversations in three languages. He stood with fluid grace, smoothing his blazer lapel—a gesture so automatic it seemed choreographed. "You actually made it. I was starting to think London had made you soft."

Lucas approached with measured steps, each footfall deliberate on the heated marble. Darren pulled out the opposite chair with theatrical flourish, his grin wide enough to sell insurance or hide murder. "Sit. You look like death warmed over and served on the good china. Always serious, Lucas. Some of us learned levity at your father's table."

"And some of us learned not to stay for dessert," Lucas said.

Lucas lowered himself onto the surprisingly cool stone seat, feeling heat radiate off the table's surface in shimmering waves. The umbrella above provided blessed shade, but the air still tasted of exhaust fumes, expensive cologne, and the metallic tang of surveillance equipment humming just beyond the range of conscious hearing.

Darren signaled a waiter with the subtle hand gesture of someone accustomed to immediate service—two fingers raised, a slight nod toward Lucas. The young man appeared instantly, as if he'd been waiting for the summons. His uniform was pressed to military precision, his smile as rehearsed as the receptionist's upstairs.

Darren never looked at the waiter. "Drinks for us. A coffee for me. Rooibos tea for my friend here—he's feeling delicate."

The waiter nodded and disappeared into the controlled chaos of the service area. Lucas watched him go, noting how other staff members tracked his movement, how conversations paused and resumed in his wake. Even the waitstaff were part of the surveillance network, their eyes trained to see everything and report to whoever paid their salaries.

"You look..." Darren paused, studying Lucas with the calculating gaze of a sculptor examining flawed marble. "Familiar. But different. Older, obviously. More serious. London was good to you, wasn't it? Gave you that cosmopolitan polish."

Lucas shrugged, not particularly interested in small talk that wasn't actually small. "You're not the only one who's changed, Darren. You've acquired some interesting new accessories since I left."

Darren's laugh was genuine—a warm sound that seemed oddly out of place in their sterile surroundings. "True enough. Last time I saw you, you were fresh-faced and nervous as a virgin in a whorehouse. Now you've got that thousand-yard stare that comes from seeing too much." He leaned forward conspiratorially, lowering his voice. "So what really brings you back? And don't feed me therapeutic bullshit about closure."

Lucas folded his hands on the table, feeling the sun's heat penetrate his jacket and the weight of the Cypress drive against his ribs. "Curiosity. Obligation. Maybe a little of both."

"Curiosity killed the cat." Darren's observation carried weight. "But satisfaction brought it back. Which version are you hoping for?"

They fell into momentary silence—the kind that stretched between old friends who'd shared too much history to need constant conversation. But Lucas caught the undertones: Darren's breathing was controlled, his posture relaxed but ready. This wasn't a casual reunion. It was an interview, carefully staged to look like coincidence.

The waiter returned with Darren's espresso in a delicate white cup that looked like museum porcelain. He set it down with meticulous care, the china ringing softly against marble, then turned to Lucas with the practiced deference of someone used to expensive tastes. "Your rooibos, sir."

"Man of consistent tastes." Darren's observation carried no mockery, but Lucas caught the emphasis—a reminder that Darren had been paying attention to details others might dismiss.

"I remember when you used to live on energy drinks and corporate ambition."

"Simpler now." Lucas watched the fountain's spray catch the light, creating momentary rainbows that appeared and vanished like promises. Around them, tourists snapped photos while executives conducted business in carefully modulated voices. The whole scene felt choreographed—a performance of normalcy that couldn't quite mask the undercurrents of tension.

"Speaking of aging—" Darren's tone grew carefully casual, but Lucas caught the shift in his micro-expressions, the way his shoulders tensed almost imperceptibly. "How does it feel being back? Really back, I mean. South Africa's changed since you left. Different rhythms, different rules."

Lucas met his gaze over the rim of his mug, tasting the tea's familiar comfort against the day's bitter revelations. "Heavy. Everything feels heavier here. The air, the history, the weight of expectations."

Darren nodded with what might have been understanding or calculation. "Family legacies have that effect. Generational weight pressing down until you can barely breathe. Your father understood that better than most." He leaned closer, lowering his voice to barely above a whisper. "He had real vision—no question about that. Genuine vision for what this country could become. But the board's been... unsettled since his passing. Politics shift by the hour in this business. Everything's up for grabs."

Lucas kept his expression carefully neutral, but his pulse quickened. "You always did love a good gamble, Darren."

Darren's grin was predatory now, showing too many teeth and too much satisfaction. "And I always win. That's what makes it interesting."

The admission hung between them like smoke from a fired gun. Lucas sipped his tea, letting the silence stretch until it became uncomfortable. Around them, the plaza continued its elaborate dance of commerce and surveillance, but their table had become an island of tension in the carefully orchestrated flow.

"Your father left you more than just company stock." Darren's voice dropped to a register that wouldn't carry beyond their table. "There are assets. Arrangements. Relationships that extend well beyond the mining business."

Lucas felt his chest tighten. "What kind of arrangements?"

Darren reached into his jacket with deliberate slowness, the movement designed to broadcast non-aggression to whatever watchers were tracking their conversation. He extracted a thick white envelope that seemed to pulse with potential energy, sliding it across the marble surface with the casual precision of a dealer distributing cards.

"Account details." His voice was barely audible above the fountain's spray. "Offshore holdings your father accumulated over the years. Swiss accounts, Cayman structures, some cryptocurrency wallets that predate most regulatory frameworks. Complex stuff, but portable. Liquid when it needs to be."

Lucas stared at the envelope without touching it, feeling its gravitational pull like a black hole made of paper and possibility. "Why bring this to me?"

"Because the vultures are already circling." Darren's expression grew serious, the playful mask dropping to reveal something harder and more calculating underneath. "Regulatory authorities, rival mining companies, journalists looking for scandal. Your father's death created a vacuum, and nature abhors those. I figured you'd want first access before someone else decides to fill the gap."

Lucas tucked the envelope into his coat, feeling it settle against the Cypress drive like twin pulses. The juxtaposition wasn't lost on him—evidence of his father's crimes pressed against evidence of his father's wealth. Two sides of the same tainted coin, both carrying enough weight to crush him or set him free.

"You sound like him." Lucas studied Darren's face for micro-expressions, noting the slight tightening around his eyes, the way his breathing had shifted to a more controlled rhythm. "Anton always talked about portfolios and contingencies when he meant blood and betrayal."

Darren rose in one smooth motion, straightening his lapels with the same unconscious precision he'd displayed as a teenager preparing for school photographs. "Take that as a compliment." He dropped a business card next to Lucas's mug—heavy stock paper with only a phone number and a small logo. A compass rose with one point conspicuously missing.

"Think about it." His voice carried undertones of urgency despite its casual delivery. "That roadmap might guide you through some very interesting territory. Territory your father spent decades mapping."

"Toward what destination?"

Darren's smile was sharp enough to cut glass. "That depends entirely on how far you're willing to travel. And what you're willing to leave behind."

With a nod that somehow managed to be both dismissive and inclusive, Darren melted back into the crowd with the practiced ease of someone who'd spent years disappearing when convenient. Lucas watched him go, noting how other pedestrians unconsciously created space for his passage, how conversations shifted to accommodate his movement.

Left alone with his tea and his doubts, Lucas remained seated while the plaza performed around him. The fountain's crystalline arcs fell in predetermined patterns that reminded him of his family's rise and fall. Children laughed somewhere in the distance. Life continued its relentless forward motion while he sat suspended between past and future, holding secrets that could reshape both.

The business card lay next to his mug like a chess piece awaiting his next move. Lucas picked it up, studying the compass rose logo. The missing point might be north, south, east, or west—or the only point that mattered: the direction away from everything he'd ever known.

***

Night descended like smoke settling over the city, painting the Johannesburg skyline in shades of copper and shadow. Lucas walked streets that felt familiar and foreign simultaneously—old brick facades pressed against gleaming glass towers, the city's architectural DNA revealing layers of ambition and compromise that stretched back to the first gold strikes. At each intersection, he paused to watch traffic lights cycle through their eternal sequence: red, amber, green. Order imposed on chaos, but only temporarily.

His phone buzzed against his ribs with the urgency reserved for family summons. Helena's message was characteristically brief: "Dinner at eight. The Observatory. Don't be late." No please, no explanation, no option to decline. Just expectation disguised as invitation.

He pocketed the device and continued walking, the envelope from Darren weighing against his ribs alongside the Cypress drive. Two secrets, two paths, both leading into darkness he couldn't yet fathom. The setting sun stretched his shadow across cracked pavement, making him look taller and more substantial than he felt—a distortion that seemed appropriate given the day's revelations.

The Observatory Restaurant occupied the forty-second floor of the Johannesburg Stock Exchange building, its floor-to-ceiling windows offering a panoramic view of the city's sprawling nervous system. Lucas arrived precisely at eight o'clock, still wearing the same dark suit from the funeral. It felt like armor now, protection against whatever ambush Helena had orchestrated for their reunion.

The maître d' recognized him instantly, though they'd never met. That was the power of the Brandt name—it opened doors and triggered memories even when you wished it wouldn't. The man's expression carried the particular deference reserved for inherited wealth and inherited danger.

"Mr. Brandt. Mrs. Brandt is waiting at the usual table."

Our usual table. As if he and Helena were regular dining companions instead of virtual strangers bound only by blood and shared trauma. The man led him through a dining room that hummed with the quiet energy of serious money—crystal clinked against crystal, conversations murmured at frequencies designed not to carry, and every surface gleamed with the kind of cleanliness achieved through constant vigilance and unlimited resources.

Helena occupied a corner table with her back to the wall—a position that allowed her to survey the entire dining room like a general reviewing troops before battle. She'd traded the sobriety of the funeral for something sharper and more predatory: midnight blue silk that caught the city lights beyond the windows and threw them back like accusations. Her jewelry was minimal but expensive—pieces chosen for their ability to catch light and attention in equal measure.

"You're prompt." She didn't rise to greet him as he approached. No kiss, no embrace, barely even eye contact. Just acknowledgment that he'd met her minimum standards of punctuality. "I was beginning to wonder if London had taught you to be fashionably late."

"You taught me well." Lucas settled into the leather chair that probably cost more than most people's monthly salaries. The view beyond the windows was spectacular—Johannesburg spread out like a circuit board made of light and ambition, each pinprick representing lives and decisions that would never reach this rarefied altitude.

A waiter materialized with the practiced invisibility of expensive service, his movements so smooth they seemed choreographed. Helena ordered wine without consulting the list—something South African and undoubtedly expensive, chosen as much for its provenance as its taste. Lucas considered his options carefully.

"Whiskey. Single malt. Whatever you think appropriate for the conversation we're about to have."

The waiter's expression didn't change, but Helena's eyebrow arched slightly. "Expecting something unpleasant?"

"I've learned to expect the unexpected where our family is concerned."

The waiter retreated, leaving them alone in the amber glow of carefully positioned lighting. Through the windows, Johannesburg sprawled below them like a living organism—arteries of light pulsing with traffic, clusters of illumination marking centers of commerce and power, dark spaces where the city's underclass lived beyond the reach of electricity and surveillance.

"How was your visit to the office?" Helena's question sounded casual, but Lucas caught the steel beneath her measured tone—the way her fingers drummed silently against the tablecloth, the slight tension in her shoulders.

"Sanitized." He chose his words carefully. "They've scrubbed Anton's fingerprints from everything. New paint, new furniture, new corporate philosophy. It's like he never existed, except for that ridiculous plaque in the lobby."

Her lips curved into something that wasn't quite a smile. "Progress has its requirements. Sometimes the best way to honor the past is to move beyond it."

"Is that what we're calling it? Progress?" Lucas loosened his tie slightly, feeling the day's tension settling into his shoulders like concrete. "Or just erasure of inconvenient truths?"

The wine arrived with ceremonial precision—a ritual that Helena observed with the solemn concentration of a priest taking communion. She tasted it with closed eyes, nodded her approval, then watched as the waiter poured two glasses despite Lucas's earlier order. When they were alone again, she raised her glass with deliberate ceremony.

"To new beginnings." Her voice carried undertones he couldn't quite decipher.

Lucas stared at his glass without lifting it, noting how the wine caught the candlelight like liquid rubies. "Whose beginnings would those be?"

Helena's eyes narrowed almost imperceptibly—the first crack in her composed facade. "Careful, Lucas. Cynicism ages poorly, and you're already carrying more years than you should at your age."

"So does blind loyalty." He countered, finally lifting his glass but not drinking. "But I suppose we each have our particular burdens to bear."

She set down her wine with the precise control of someone who'd spent decades practicing emotional restraint in public spaces. "Nothing about this family has ever been blind, Lucas. Every decision, every alliance, every sacrifice— it's all been calculated for maximum strategic effect."

Lucas studied the wine in his glass, watching how it captured and refracted the restaurant's ambient light. "Darren gave me something today. Information about offshore accounts Anton maintained. Details about assets I never knew existed."

Helena's expression didn't change, but her fingers tightened on the stem of her glass—a minute tell that spoke volumes to someone who'd learned to read her micro-expressions in childhood. "Did he now? How... generous of him to share such sensitive information."

"You knew about it."

"I know about everything that matters." She leaned forward slightly, her voice dropping to barely above a whisper. "The question isn't what I know—it's what you plan to do with whatever knowledge you think you've acquired."

Lucas studied her face in the candlelight, searching for traces of the woman who'd read him bedtime stories and kissed scraped knees. She was still there, buried beneath layers of calculation and compromise, but accessing her would require archaeological excavation. "That depends entirely on what else I discover in the process."

"And if you don't like what you find?"

"Then I'll have to decide whether the family business is worth preserving, or whether some legacies are better left to die natural deaths."

Helena's laugh was soft but dangerous, like silk wrapping around a blade. "You still think you have a choice in this, don't you? After everything, you still believe in the luxury of moral options."

"Everyone has choices, Helena. That's what separates us from the animals and the machines."

"Do they?" She gestured toward the windows with fluid grace, where the city sprawled below like a living organism. "Look out there, Lucas. Every light represents someone who thinks they're making independent choices. But they're all following patterns laid down by people like your father, like me. Infrastructure, Lucas. Systems. Power isn't something you choose to inherit—it's something that inherits you, whether you want it or not."

Lucas followed her gaze to the lights below, each pinprick representing lives and families and futures that would be shaped by decisions made in rooms like this by people like them. The weight of that responsibility pressed against his chest like a physical force, making it difficult to breathe the rarefied air.

"Maybe that's the fundamental problem."

"Or maybe—" Helena raised her glass again with ceremonial precision. "It's the only solution that actually works in the real world."

This time, Lucas drank. The wine was indeed excellent—smooth and complex, with undertones of earth and smoke and something darker that he couldn't identify.

Like everything else in his family's world, it was beautiful and surely carried a price he hadn't yet been asked to pay.

"There's a board meeting tomorrow." Helena's tone shifted to business with the fluid efficiency of someone accustomed to managing multiple agendas simultaneously. "Emergency session. They want to discuss succession planning, corporate restructuring, the future strategic direction of the company."

"Without consulting the heir?"

"They're consulting you now." She signaled for menus with a gesture so subtle Lucas almost missed it—two fingers pressed briefly against her water glass. "Through me, of course. Just as they always have, just as your father intended."

Lucas set down his glass with deliberate precision, the crystal ringing softly against marble. "So you're my voice in these proceedings? My representative in matters concerning my own inheritance?"

"I'm your mother." For the first time all evening, her voice carried genuine emotion. "And I'm trying to protect what your father built from people who would destroy it for short-term gain and ideological satisfaction."

The waiter returned with leather-bound menus that probably cost more to produce than most people spent on groceries. They studied the options in silence—Helena with the focused attention of someone for whom dining was a form of diplomacy, Lucas with the distracted air of someone whose appetite had been murdered by revelation and replaced with something more urgent.

"Order something substantial." Helena's voice carried the authority of someone accustomed to being obeyed. "Tomorrow's going to be a very long day, and you'll need your strength for what's coming."

As they made their selections—Helena choosing the kudu with the confidence of someone who'd never questioned her right to consume whatever she desired, Lucas opting for linefish in a gesture toward something that might once have swum freely—Lucas felt the weight of both envelopes in his jacket pressing against his ribs like competing heartbeats. Darren's offshore accounts and Anton's Cypress drive. Two different maps to the same dark territory, two paths that would probably converge at a destination he wasn't sure he was prepared to reach.

The waiter departed with their orders, leaving them alone again with their wine and their carefully maintained emotional distance. Helena leaned back in her chair, the city lights beyond the windows painting her face in shifting patterns of shadow and illumination that made her look alternately vulnerable and predatory.

"You know—" Her voice was softer now, almost human. "Your father was proud of you. More proud than he ever knew how to express."

Lucas looked up sharply, caught off guard by the unexpected vulnerability in her tone. "Proud of me running away? Proud of me abandoning the family when things got complicated?"

"Proud of you surviving." Her voice carried the weight of genuine emotion—the first he'd heard from her all day. "He always said the smartest thing you ever did was leave when you did. Get out before the consequences caught up with you, before you got so deep in the machinery that extraction became impossible."

"Then why call me back now? Why drag me back into whatever web you've been weaving in my absence?"

Helena's smile was genuinely sad for the first time since he'd returned—an expression that transformed her face and reminded him of the woman who'd sung him lullabies and taught him to tie his shoes. "Because sometimes, Lucas, even the smartest choice turns out to be the wrong one. And because some debts can only be paid by family, some problems can only be solved by blood."

Outside the windows, Johannesburg continued its eternal dance of light and shadow—beautiful and brutal, wealthy and desperate, a city built on gold and bones and the dreams of people who'd never lived to see their ambitions realized. Lucas stared at those lights and wondered if he was strong enough for whatever was coming, or if strength was even relevant to what his family was asking of him.

The wine's warmth spread through his chest, and for a moment, he allowed himself to imagine that this was just dinner—a son and mother sharing a meal and catching up after too many years apart. But the weight of the drives in his jacket, the careful neutrality of Helena's expression when she thought he wasn't watching, and the way her eyes constantly scanned the room for threats reminded him that nothing in his family's world was ever that simple.

Tomorrow would bring choices he wasn't ready to make. Consequences he couldn't yet imagine. Tonight, he would drink expensive wine and pretend that the past could be outrun and the future negotiated. But beneath the table, his hands trembled slightly, and he knew that the boy who'd fled this world was about to discover whether the man who'd returned was strong enough to survive it.

Chapter 3 – Ghosts of the Gold Line

The neon above Katz's townhouse fluttered, more warning than welcome. Intermittent shadows fell across the razor wire along the perimeter fence. Lucas stood at the gate, his breath visible in the winter air, security cameras tracking him with machine-precision accuracy.

The Cypress files in his jacket pocket grew heavier with each passing second—digital ghosts demanding attention, their presence a constant reminder of the choice he'd already made simply by being here.

Committed now—no walking away. The decision settled like a lock clicking shut.

He pressed the intercom button. The speaker crackled to life with distant music and laughter bleeding through electronic static. The party had been going for hours already, judging by the cars lined up along the street—sleek German sedans mixed with armored SUVs, the kind of automotive display that screamed new money trying to look established. The winter air bit sharper here, edged with the smell of petrol and overwatered lawns.

"Lucas bloody Brandt." Darren's voice emerged from the speaker, slightly slurred but still carrying that familiar edge of amusement that had never quite masked the predator beneath. "Thought you might chicken out."

"I'm here." The words carried more weight than their brevity suggested.

The gate buzzed open with a mechanical whine. Lucas stepped through into the courtyard. Imported marble gleamed under security floods that turned night into harsh artificial day, while indigenous plants struggled in geometric planters that looked more like sculptures than gardens— beautiful, expensive, and lifeless.

Everything about the space screamed Darren's aesthetic: expensive, precise, hollow at its core. As if the gold line itself had simply changed dress code—designer suits, champagne in hand.

The front door swung open before Lucas could knock, revealing Darren in his element: white linen shirt unbuttoned just enough to show the gold chain beneath, designer jeans that probably cost more than most people's monthly salary. That predatory smile had once unsettled their classmates at Redhill High—the country's most exclusive school, where old money mingled with new and future leaders were born.

Time had treated Darren like a shark—edges sharper, appetite intact. But Lucas caught something new in his old friend's eyes, a hardness that hadn't been there in university. The look of someone who had learned that idealism was a luxury he could no longer afford.

Between them, the years seemed to telescope—old trust narrowing to a blade's edge.

"The prodigal son returns." Darren spread his arms wide in mock benediction, the gesture theatrical enough to suggest an audience beyond Lucas. "Come in, come in. You look like you've seen a ghost."

Lucas stepped inside, immediately hit by the wall of sound and sensation that seemed designed to overwhelm rather than welcome. The music pounded—traditional rhythms layered over electronic beats, expensive and hollow.

The air reeked of cologne, smoke, and money burning—the scent of wealth that never learned the difference between cost and value.

The interior had been gutted and rebuilt—transformed from colonial mansion into an oligarch's fever dream. Black marble reflected chrome fixtures, abstract art replacing family portraits. History erased. Expensive emptiness.

"Drink?" Darren was already moving toward a bar along one wall—an altar to excess, his movements carrying the fluid confidence of someone completely at home in his own constructed reality. Behind it, bottles priced like cars caught the light.

"Whiskey. Whatever's open."

Darren laughed, the sound sharp and genuine in a way that made Lucas's skin crawl. "Nothing but the best for old friends. Besides, after what you've been through, you deserve the good stuff." He paused, hand hovering over a bottle of Macallan, and for a moment his expression softened with something that might have been regret. "Your father said I had expensive taste and cheap principles. Turns out he was half right."

He poured from a Macallan Lucas pegged at R5,000 a bottle. The amber liquid caught the light like liquid gold. The casual reference to Anton carried weight—decades of shared history compressed into a single, bitter observation.

Lucas accepted the glass, noting how Darren's hand trembled—a tell he usually buried under polish. Darren had always been good at hiding his tells behind bravado and expensive distractions, but Lucas had learned to read the spaces between the performance.

"Anton kept promising me a seat at the real table." Darren's voice dropped to something more intimate, more honest. "Twenty years of being the promising protégé, the bright young operator who'd inherit the kingdom when the old king stepped down." He took a long sip, eyes distant with memory. "Funny how promises change when succession becomes more than theoretical."

***

Near the windows that overlooked the city's sprawling expanse, Lucas spotted a cluster of foreign faces—Chinese businessmen in perfectly tailored suits that spoke of Beijing's new influence, American consultants with the posture of men from places that didn't officially exist, Europeans who carried themselves with the quiet confidence of old money learning new tricks.

New players taking their angles in the latest 'transformation' play.

A commotion near the main entrance drew their attention, cutting through the artificial atmosphere like a blade. Security guards in expensive suits were escorting someone out—a young Black woman whose press badge identified her as working for one of the independent newspapers that still bothered with actual journalism.

She wasn't going quietly. Her voice carried the kind of authority that came from believing in something larger than herself.

"The people have a right to know." Her words cut clearly across the room despite the music, each syllable delivered with the precision of someone who had learned to make every word count. "You can't hide behind charity galas and art collections forever."

Lucas recognized her immediately—Zara Mokoena, the investigative journalist who had once been his closest confidante and was now making waves with her coverage of corruption in the mining sector. She was a match in a velvet room soaked in gasoline, dangerous not because of what she might do, but because of what she might reveal.

"Ah." Darren's voice was tight with barely controlled irritation, the mask of hospitality slipping just enough to reveal the steel beneath. "It seems we have a party crasher." He watched the security guards with professional interest, then added quietly, "Your father would have handled this differently. More... permanently."

The words carried the weight of shared knowledge, of operations Lucas had never been privy to but had always suspected. Darren's tone suggested not just familiarity with Anton's methods, but a certain nostalgia for their brutal efficiency.

"Let her go." The words escaped Lucas's mouth before he'd fully processed the decision, emerging from some deeper place that his conscious mind hadn't yet accessed.

He kept his tone even, careful not to push—yet the words still landed like a strike.

Darren turned to him, eyebrows raised in genuine surprise. "Excuse me?"

"I said let her go. She's not hurting anyone." The lie felt heavy on his tongue—they all knew journalists hurt people, but only by telling the truth.

"She's a journalist, Lucas. One gets in, and the whole colony follows. They don't just report—they burrow until they hit bone."

But Lucas was already moving, pushing through the crowd toward the security team with a purpose he couldn't fully explain to himself. He could feel Darren's eyes burning into his back—not just anger, but something like calculation. As if Lucas's intervention was being cataloged, filed away for future reference.

Conversations paused as people registered what was happening—the Brandt heir challenging security at a party hosted by one of the most connected men in Johannesburg, breaking the unspoken rules that kept their world functioning.

***

"Gentlemen." Lucas reached the guards, his voice carrying the quiet authority that came from generations of inherited power—a birthright he'd never wanted but couldn't entirely escape. "I think there's been a misunderstanding."

The lead guard—a thick-set man with the weathered face of someone who'd seen combat in places that didn't make the news—hesitated. He clearly recognized Lucas, but wasn't sure how to handle the conflict between his employer's wishes and the potential political ramifications of manhandling a Brandt.

Power's math was complex. Mistakes at this level could be fatal.

"Sir." The guard's words were measured and diplomatic. "Ms. Mokoena was not on the guest list."

"And now she is." Lucas's assertion carried more confidence than he felt. He turned to Zara, their eyes meeting across a decade of silence and the weight of shared secrets that had never been spoken aloud.

"Hello, Zara." The familiarity in his voice cut through the formal atmosphere like a blade. "It's been a long time."

For a moment, something flickered across her face—surprise, perhaps, or recognition of the boy who'd once trusted her with alibis that could have saved his life. Then her professional mask slipped back into place, but not before he caught the flash of something deeper: the memory of midnight phone calls and whispered conspiracies against the adult world that had tried to shape them both.

"Lucas." His name on her lips carried the weight of shared history—late-night conversations about justice and corruption, dreams of changing a system they'd been born into but never chosen. "Still playing the white knight, I see."

The barb hit its mark, carrying echoes of their last real conversation twelve years ago, when he'd chosen exile over confrontation, leaving her to fight battles he'd been too afraid to face. Her eyes held the accumulated disappointment of someone who'd once believed he might be different from his family.

"Some habits are hard to break," he replied, the words carrying layers of meaning only she would understand—an acknowledgment of old promises, old failures, old debts that time hadn't erased.

Darren approached through the crowd, his face a mask of controlled fury that transformed his features into something predatory and cold. Behind him came a tall, elegant woman with the kind of bone structure that suggested both African heritage and European finishing schools—a living embodiment of the continent's complex colonial legacy.

His expression shifted when he saw Lucas and Zara together, a flicker of calculation replacing anger. "Well, well. Look what the cat dragged in. The old neighborhood rebels, reunited at last." His voice carried a note of amusement that didn't reach his eyes. "How touching."

"Lucas." Darren's voice carried a warning that seemed to lower the temperature in the immediate vicinity. "What exactly are you doing?"

"Catching up with an old friend," Lucas replied, though they all knew friendship was too simple a word for what had existed between him and Zara—too clean for the mess of loyalty, betrayal, and unfinished business that stretched between them like a wire under tension.

"Actually—" Zara's voice cut through the tension with professional precision, her tone shifting back to the journalist she'd become rather than the girl who'd once covered for him. "I'd like to ask Mr. Katz a few follow-ups on my Nkomazi series. I want an on-the-record comment about your relationship with certain mining operations in the Free State."

Lucas felt the familiar chill of recognition—the same fearless curiosity that had once made her willing to lie to Anton's driver, now turned toward enemies with far more dangerous resources than teenage curfews.

***

The terrace overlooked Johannesburg's sprawling expanse, the city lights stretching to the horizon like a galaxy of earthbound stars that spoke of millions of lives being lived in the shadows of power games they couldn't even see. The winter air was sharp and clean after the claustrophobic atmosphere inside, carrying the scent of jacaranda blossoms and diesel fumes in equal measure—beauty and corruption intertwined like lovers in an old song.

Lucas breathed it in, unsure which scent would linger longer.

Darren closed the French doors behind them, cutting off the sound of the party but not the watchful eyes of the guests inside. Through the glass, Lucas could see people pretending not to stare while straining to read lips and body language.

"So—" Darren lit a cigarette with a gold lighter that caught the security lights and threw back miniature suns. "What exactly do you want to know, Ms. Mokoena?"

Lucas caught the deliberate formality in Darren's address—a pointed reminder that whatever teenage alliances had once existed were now buried under layers of adult complications and conflicting loyalties.

The lighter was new, Lucas noticed—engraved with initials that weren't Darren's. A gift, or a trophy. Another piece of the puzzle that was his old friend's transformation from idealistic student to whatever he'd become.

Zara pulled out a small digital recorder with the practiced efficiency of someone who had learned to document everything, setting it on the stone balustrade between them like a gauntlet thrown down. "I want to know about the Nkomazi Border Post. Specifically, about the customs arrangements that allow certain shipments to pass through without inspection."

Lucas felt his blood chill. The name hit him like a physical blow. Nkomazi was mentioned in the Cypress files, part of a smuggling network that stretched from Eastern Europe to the ports of Mozambique like a spider's web of corruption.

The same fearless directness that had once made her willing to challenge Anton's authority now aimed at targets with far deadlier resources. Some things never changed—including her talent for walking straight into danger.

If Zara was investigating that operation, she was walking into a minefield that could terminate careers and end lives—including her own.

Darren took a long drag from his cigarette, exhaling slowly as he considered his response. The smoke curled between them like incense at a funeral. "I'm afraid I don't know what you're talking about."

"Really?" Zara's voice carried a note of skepticism sharp enough to cut glass. The same tone she'd once used when calling out lies in their teenage circle, though the stakes had grown exponentially deadlier. "Because I have shipping manifests that suggest otherwise. Manifests with your company's name on them."

"Manifests can be forged." The woman accompanying Darren interjected, her voice carrying the kind of casual dismissal that came from years of practice in making inconvenient truths disappear. "It's a common tactic used by disreputable journalists looking to make names for themselves."

Lucas watched Zara's jaw tighten—he'd seen that expression before, usually right before she did something that got them both into trouble. The protective instinct that had once made him step between her and Anton's driver stirred again, stronger now and far more dangerous.

"The manifests are genuine." Her voice stayed steady despite the odds stacked against her. "I have sources inside the customs service who can verify their authenticity."

"Sources who might find themselves transferred to less desirable postings." Darren's observation was mild, his tone carrying the kind of threat that didn't need to be explicit to be understood. "The civil service can be very unforgiving of disloyalty."

***

Before the tension could escalate further, the French doors burst open and one of Darren's security guards stepped onto the terrace, his face grim with urgency. Lucas could see the outline of a concealed weapon beneath the man's jacket, a reminder that they were all balanced on the edge of violence.

"Sir." The guard addressed Darren, his voice tight with controlled alarm. "We have a situation inside. You need to see this."

Through the glass doors, Lucas could see confusion spreading through the party like ripples in a pond. Conversations stopped mid-sentence as guests clustered around someone's phone. Their faces were pale in the device's glow, expressions shifting from curiosity to alarm to something approaching panic.

Whatever they were seeing had shattered the evening's careful facade of celebration and success.

"Breaking news, sir. About the Hartbeespoort mining accident. Someone's leaked classified documents."

Lucas felt the world tilt beneath his feet. Gravity became unreliable as the words hit him like a physical blow. Hartbeespoort was one of the operations mentioned in the Cypress files, a mine where a supposed accident had killed twenty-three workers—men with families, dreams, futures that had been snuffed out for the sake of quarterly profits.

The official investigation had blamed faulty equipment, but the real files told a different story—deliberate negligence, safety corners cut to maximize profits, warnings ignored until it was too late.

"What kind of documents?" The elegant woman demanded, her composure cracking for the first time, revealing something raw and desperate beneath the polished surface.

"Internal memos, ma'am. Safety reports that were never filed. Communications between management and... certain government officials."

Lucas caught Zara's expression shift—the same look she'd worn as a teenager when she'd caught wind of adult secrets, except now her hunger was professional, sharpened by years of chasing stories that powerful people preferred buried. He recognized the dangerous gleam in her eyes, the one that had always preceded her most reckless decisions.

"Which officials? What did the communications say?" Her questions came rapid-fire, the instincts that had once made her relentless in pursuing neighborhood gossip now laser-focused on corruption that could topple governments.

But the guard had already said too much, his training warring with the urgency of the moment. Darren grabbed him by the arm, pulling him back through the doors with barely controlled violence. "Not here. Inside. Now."

Lucas saw Zara take a half-step forward, as if to follow—the same impulsive movement he remembered from their youth, when she'd never known when to leave well enough alone. Without thinking, he caught her arm, the contact sending a jolt of memory through both of them.

"Don't," he said quietly, his voice carrying the weight of shared understanding. "Not like this."

For a moment, their eyes met, and he saw the question there—whether the boy who'd once run from fights had finally learned to pick his battles, or if he was still the same coward who'd chosen London over taking a stand.

By morning, the Hartbeespoort story had vanished from front pages, buried under a flood of distraction headlines Darren's media allies pushed onto the feeds.

As they disappeared into the party, Lucas found himself processing the implications. The Cypress files contained information about both operations—the border smuggling and the mining corruption.

If someone was leaking selected portions of that information, it could only mean one thing: someone else had access to the files. Someone with their own agenda.

"We need to leave." He turned to Zara, the urgency in his voice cutting through whatever resentment still lingered between them. "Now."

She studied his face, reading something there that made her nod—not agreement, exactly, but recognition that he knew more than he was saying. The same intuition that had once made her trust his warnings about which teachers to avoid, now applied to threats with far deadlier consequences.

But through the windows, he could see unmarked vehicles pulling up outside the gate, their occupants moving with the purposeful efficiency of law enforcement operations.

The party was over. Whatever investigation was beginning would sweep up everyone in its path like debris in a flood.

***

"This way." Zara grabbed his arm with the same decisive authority she'd shown as a teenager—the girl who'd always known which routes avoided the security patrols, which back gates stayed unlocked after hours. Her grip carried muscle memory from years of navigating dangerous territory, both as kids dodging adult attention and now as a journalist avoiding far deadlier consequences.

They pushed through the crowd of panicking guests, heading for whatever exit Darren's security hadn't already sealed, moving through the chaos like swimmers against a riptide. Behind them, Lucas could hear shouting as the front door exploded inward, armed figures in tactical gear flooding into the foyer with military precision.

"Just like old times," she muttered as they ran, and Lucas knew she was thinking of the night they'd fled through the gardens of his family's estate when Anton's security had nearly caught them listening at study windows. The same quick thinking, the same sure instincts—only now the stakes were life and death instead of groundings and lectures.

They reached Zara's battered Honda just as the raid began in earnest. The engine coughed to life on the third try. They careened out of the alley onto the main road, tires squealing as she took the corner too fast, both of them pressed back into their seats by forces they couldn't control.

"Where to?" Her question hung in the air between them, loaded with the weight of choices that would determine whether their shared past meant anything or if twelve years of separation had made them strangers.

Lucas hesitated for a heartbeat—trusting her meant crossing a line he'd spent a decade avoiding. But the girl who'd once lied to Anton's driver to save him from a beating was the same woman now risking everything to expose the truth about his family's empire.

"The estate," he said finally, the words carrying more weight than simple directions. "There's something I need to show you."

Something flickered in her eyes—surprise, perhaps, or recognition that the boy who'd once run from confrontation might finally be ready to fight. "Your father's house? Lucas, if they're monitoring—"

"They're monitoring everything already," he cut her off. "And there are things hidden there that make tonight's raid look like a parking ticket."

Whatever was happening was bigger than a simple corruption investigation. Someone was playing a deeper game, and he needed to understand the rules before he became another casualty in a war he barely comprehended. More than that—he needed someone he could trust, and despite everything that had happened between them, despite twelve years of silence and the weight of his family's sins, Zara was the only person who'd ever kept his secrets when it mattered.

****

The estate felt different in the small hours of the morning. Shadows stretched longer and more menacing than he remembered from childhood visits that now seemed like scenes from someone else's life. Lucas slipped through the service gate just after the guards rotated, boots silent on wet gravel as motion sensors swept the darkness three meters to his left—the same route he'd mapped as a teenager, though the consequences of discovery had grown exponentially deadlier in the intervening years. Zara moved beside him with the quiet familiarity of someone who'd navigated these halls before—late-night adventures when they were teenagers, sneaking through corridors that had seemed less ominous then. He led her through the main house to his father's study, past portraits of stern ancestors watching with institutional disapproval— generations of Brandts who had built their fortune on secrets and maintained it through silence. "Still creepy as hell," Zara murmured, glancing at a particularly forbidding portrait of his great-grandfather. "I used to have nightmares about that one." "Wait here." He descended into the cellar where the real family business had always been conducted.

The hidden compartment was exactly where Anton had shown him years ago, concealed behind a false wine rack that moved on hidden hinges with the smooth precision of Swiss engineering. Inside, wrapped in oilcloth and sealed against moisture and time, were the documents and drives his father had accumulated over decades of careful planning—insurance policies against enemies and allies alike. But it was the USB drive labeled *Cypress* that made his blood run cold. Anton's looping script was barely legible in the accumulated dust of years. He realized then that the drive he'd carried in his pocket for weeks had only ever been a copy—Anton had made duplicates of everything, one to protect the secret and one to expose it. He held the master up to the dim light, feeling the weight of secrets that had hollowed his father long before his heart gave out. A part of him wanted to believe this was a warning— another part feared it was an invitation to join Anton in whatever hell the dead occupied.

Lucas climbed back upstairs to find Zara examining his father's desk, her journalistic instincts overriding social niceties as she processed the room like a crime scene. The same careful observation skills that had once helped them map the household staff's routines, now applied to evidence that could topple governments. She looked up as he entered, her eyes immediately focusing on the drive in his hand with the laser intensity of a predator recognizing prey.

"Is that what I think it is?"

Lucas's thumb hovered over the drive. He had sworn never to let anyone else see what Anton left behind. Trusting Zara was a risk, maybe the worst one he could take. She had lied for him once, years ago, when Anton's driver asked why Lucas had come home after midnight. Zara's alibi had spared him a beating then. Now, when the stakes were ruin instead of curfew, he leaned on the same instinct. The girl who'd risked Anton's wrath to protect him was now a woman who'd risk everything to expose the truth—but the core of who she was, that stubborn loyalty mixed with fearless curiosity, remained unchanged. If he fell, she'd fall too. He studied her face—calculating, relentless, but not cruel. If she betrayed him, she'd burn too. He slid the drive into place, hating the tremor in his hand.

He plugged it into his father's computer, watching as folders of evidence filled the screen—first photographed documents, then digital files, then video recordings—atrocities catalogued with bureaucratic calm. The scope was breathtaking and horrifying in equal measure.

Shipping manifests, transfers, comms—Nkomazi and a lattice of schemes across the continent like a web of corruption that touched everything and everyone.

Zara breathed, leaning over his shoulder to read, her proximity filling his senses with the scent of her perfume mixed with adrenaline and fear. "All those years we suspected, all those whispered conversations about what your father really did—we never imagined it was this extensive."

Lucas nodded, feeling the weight of inherited responsibility settling on his shoulders like a burial shroud. His father had died protecting these secrets, but Lucas wasn't sure protection was the right choice anymore.

Maybe it was time to burn it all down and see what grew from the ashes.

"The question is—" His voice carried the weight of decisions that couldn't be undone. "What do we do with it?"

***

Outside, Johannesburg's horizon bled from black into a flat gray light that painted the study in shades of compromise and consequence. The city stirred without ceremony, as if even the sun was reluctant to rise on what was coming. Somewhere in the city, Darren was probably explaining himself to investigators while his elegant companion called in favors to minimize the damage.

The old order was cracking, but it wouldn't fall without a fight—and the fight would be bloody.

Zara pulled out her phone, scrolling through contacts with the practiced efficiency of someone building a story that could change everything. "I know someone who can help. Someone with the resources to get this information out safely."

"And what happens to us?" Though he already knew the answer.

She looked at him with eyes that had seen too much truth for one lifetime, aged beyond their years by exposure to the machinery of power. "Remember when we used to plan our escapes? Back when the worst consequence we could imagine was your father finding out we'd been reading his files?" A bitter smile played at her lips. "This is the grown-up version."

"We disappear, if we're smart. Find somewhere to hide while the world burns down around us."

Lucas thought of the comfortable exile he'd built in London, the quiet life he'd abandoned to return to this chaos like a moth drawn to flame. The same exile Zara had once accused him of choosing as cowardice—running instead of fighting. Now she was suggesting the same path, and he wasn't sure if that made him vindicated or damned. There would be no going back now—the moment he'd intervened at Darren's party, he'd chosen a side in a war he barely understood.

"You know I won't run again," he said quietly. "Not this time."

Something shifted in her expression—recognition, perhaps, that the boy who'd fled to London might finally be ready to stand his ground. The only question was whether he'd live long enough to see how it ended.

"Then we better get started." He copied the files to a secure drive with hands barely trembling, then photographed each document methodically before downloading everything to multiple encrypted locations. "Because I have a feeling we don't have much time."

As if summoned by his words, his phone buzzed with an encrypted message from an unknown number, the text appearing on his screen like a death sentence:

You have something that belongs to us. Return it, or join your father.

Lucas showed the message to Zara, who paled as she read it, the color draining from her face like water from a broken dam.

"Too late for second thoughts." Her voice carried the fatalism of someone who had always known this moment would come. "Looks like you're finally going to get that fight you always avoided."

"We're committed now," she added, and he heard the echo of all their teenage promises—the vows to change the world that they'd made in whispered conversations, before life taught them how much change could cost.

He deleted the message and powered down the computer, erasing traces of their access with the methodical thoroughness his father had taught him. The original drive went into a safety deposit box whose location he memorized but didn't write down—information that existed only in his head, where it might die with him.

Before they left, he handed Zara a duplicate—an encrypted copy of the Cypress files. "Insurance," he said. "In case I don't make it to the deposit box."

Whatever happened next, the truth would survive— even if they didn't.

Standing in his father's study for what might be the last time, Lucas felt the ghosts of the gold line pressing close, whispers of the dead mixing with the morning air that filtered through windows his ancestors had looked through while making decisions that shaped a continent.

Generations of Brandts had stood in this room, making deals that determined who lived and who died, who prospered and who suffered. Now their heir was about to tear it all down, armed with nothing but conscience and the stubborn belief that some truths were worth dying for.

The same stubborn belief that had once made a teenage girl risk everything to cover for him, now transformed into something that might finally be worthy of her faith.

He carried the legacy now—but not its code.

The sins of the fathers would end with him, one way or another.

Chapter 4 – The Journalist's Ledger

The apartment door clicks shut behind her with the finality of a coffin lid closing. Zara leans against the scarred wood, breathing through her mouth to avoid the familiar cocktail of stale cigarettes, instant coffee, and the mustiness that clings to spaces where someone lives alone and sleeps too little. Her hands shake as she turns the deadbolt—not from fear, but from the peculiar exhaustion that follows adrenaline's retreat, leaving behind a body that feels borrowed and unreliable.

The Honda's engine ticks in the parking lot below. Metal contracts in the cool night air after their desperate flight from Darren's compound. Through thin walls, Mrs Mthembu's television murmurs in Zulu. Some late-night talk show pretends the world makes sense when viewed through studio lighting and careful editing. The sound offers an illusion of normalcy that makes Zara's chest tight with something between longing and contempt.

Grace Mdluli, whose leak started all of this, would have laughed at the irony—hiding from truth-seekers in a building where everyone pretends not to see what happens in the corridors. Grace believed transparency could disinfect anything. Grace, who was murdered for that faith. The apartment's stale air seems to echo with her voice, soft and certain, speaking words that still burn in Zara's memory.

****

The memory strikes without warning: Grace eight months before her murder, sitting on the concrete steps outside the Department of Home Affairs during her lunch break. Not the scared woman from their final coffee meeting, but the Grace from before, when she still believed the system could be fixed from within.

"You know what's funny?" Grace unwrapped a sandwich from brown paper with the precision she applied to everything. "My daughter asked me yesterday if I help bad people. She's seven, right? Sees me in my uniform, thinks I'm like the police officers on TV who always catch the criminals."

Zara joined her on the steps, balancing her notebook on her knees while Grace's colleagues streamed past. They headed to lunch spots that served better food than brown-bag sandwiches and regret. "What did you tell her?"

"That sometimes helping good people means stopping bad people from doing bad things." Grace took a small bite, chewing thoughtfully. "But I'm starting to think she's smarter than I am. Seven years old, and she already knows that uniforms don't make you good."

The laugh that followed was tired but real—the sound of someone who hadn't yet learned to be afraid of her own conscience. Grace pulled out a manila folder thick with photocopied shipping manifests she'd risked her job to obtain. She set it between them like an offering.

"Container MSKU-7749356." Her voice carried quiet certainty. "Cleared customs Tuesday with a manifest listing mining equipment. But the weight's all wrong—too light for drill bits, too heavy for safety gear. And the shipper..." She pointed to a company name Zara didn't recognise. "Shell corporation registered in Mauritius last month."

Zara felt the familiar electric thrill of a breaking story. But, studying Grace's face—the dark circles carved beneath her eyes, the way her fingers trembled as she turned pages— she sensed something else. Responsibility. This woman with a seven-year-old daughter was risking everything to hand over evidence that could finish careers, end lives, reshape the country's understanding of its own corruption.

"Grace. You don't have to do this. There are other ways—"

"No, there aren't—" Grace's voice carried absolute certainty, the tone of someone who'd already calculated every alternative and found them wanting. "I've been watching these containers for six months. Different manifests, same pattern. Same weight discrepancies, same shell companies, same officials who just happen to be off duty when the suspicious shipments arrive."

She closed the folder and handed it over, their fingers brushing. Grace's skin was warm, calloused from years of manual labour before the customs job. Entirely human in a way that made Zara's chest tighten with something between admiration and terror.

"Promise me something." Grace stood and smoothed down her uniform skirt with movements that spoke of pride in work honestly done. "When you write this story—and you will write it, I can see it in your eyes—promise me you'll remember that the people moving through that port aren't just numbers on shipping manifests. They have families. Children who ask questions about right and wrong."

That had been Grace's tragedy—not naïveté, but clarity. She'd seen the human cost of institutional silence and found it unacceptable, even when acceptance would have kept her safe.

Zara kept the promise. The story ran two weeks later on the front page of *The Continent*—Grace's six-month pattern analysis intact—and the injunction threats began within days. But by then, Grace was already targeted—transferred to "administrative duties" that existed only on paper, her access revoked, her questions reclassified as insubordination.

The daughter who'd asked about helping bad people never got to see her mother honoured as a hero. Grace Mdluli was murdered for refusing to stay silent, her death disguised as a heart attack, another casualty in the war between truth and institutional power.

Zara read the forged death certificate twice—then a third time. She heard the silence between the lines—the kind of silence only power could purchase. Grace Mdluli had not died by chance; someone had paid for her elimination.

***

Zara drops her bag beside the door. She notes how the strap has worn a groove in her shoulder, a permanent indentation that speaks to years of carrying evidence weighing more than paper and hard drives should. Her jacket follows, landing in a heap that releases the scent of Darren's party—expensive cologne and political tension.

The bathroom mirror reflects a stranger back at her: hair plastered to her scalp by humidity and stress-sweat, mascara smudged beneath eyes that wear thirty-two like it had been lived twice. Cold water runs between her cupped palms, still trembling with residual shock. She presses the liquid against her face like a baptism that might wash away what she'd witnessed.

But water can't cleanse the memory of Lucas standing in his father's study, cradling those secrets like communion wafers. Can't erase the moment she'd watched him choose between comfortable lies and uncomfortable truth, his hands shaking in a way that reminded her of Grace's final days—when the weight of knowing became too much for one person to carry alone.

In the kitchenette, the corner where a hot plate and mini-fridge huddle like survivors, she finds the bottle of Jameson tucked behind expired medications and unopened bills. The whiskey burns with deliberate purpose—a small violence against the numbness creeping up her fingertips.

Grace never drank. Said it clouded judgment, made you miss details that could save lives or end them. But Grace also believed in backup plans and safety protocols, and look where that precision got her—murdered without a trace, the story dying with its source.

The glass finds its way to the window overlooking Hillbrow's array of lights. Each point of illumination represents a life proceeding without knowledge of what she's uncovered. People sleeping peacefully in their ignorance while she stands sentinel over secrets that could reshape their understanding of their own country.

Her laptop waits on the small table that serves as both dining room and office. Its screen is dark but somehow expectant. The Cypress drive sits beside it like unexploded ordnance, its black plastic surface reflecting the room's single overhead bulb. Hours now she's carried it, sensing its weight like a malignancy that feeds on secrets.

***

The laundromat's hum was steady, a mechanical lullaby masking conversation. Detergent and heat hung in the air. Zara sat beside a row of empty dryers, coat folded across her lap, watching the reflection of her contact in the glass door opposite—middle-aged, nervous, uniform shirt still bearing the customs patch he hadn't removed.

"You said you weren't followed?" she asked softly, eyes fixed on the tumbling linen.

He shook his head, then hesitated. "I shouldn't even—"

"You're not giving me anything," she said. "Just helping me understand a pattern."

The man rubbed his hands together, eyes darting to the CCTV camera above the change machine. "If they trace it—"

"They won't."

She slid a small prepaid phone across the folding bench, its casing wrapped in a paper bag from the corner café. "Use it once, then break it. You'll get nothing from me after tonight."

He studied her, uncertain whether to trust the calm in her voice. She met his gaze just long enough to steady him, then glanced away. The trick was never to hold a man's fear—just absorb enough of it to make him believe you could carry both your secrets.

"The containers," he said finally. "They're marked for reinspection, but no one opens them. The system flags them—then deletes the record an hour later."

Zara nodded once. "Names?"

He looked at the dryers, at the circular glare of the heat lamp, then whispered. She memorized each syllable, committing them to the same internal ledger where she kept Grace's warnings and every other fragile truth someone had risked to tell her.

When she stood to leave, she didn't offer thanks. Gratitude was dangerous—it made people feel complicit. She simply placed her coat over her arm, left the prepaid phone on the bench, and walked out into the wet-brick night, the hum of the dryers chasing her like static.

***

This is what Grace died for. Not the plastic and silicon but what lives inside—proof that the comfortable lies propping up the new South Africa are built on the same foundations as the old one, just painted in different colours.

***

The whiskey glass sweats rings onto wood scarred by years of similar nights—other stories, other revelations, other moments when the weight of hidden truth threatened to crush the messenger beneath its mass. Tonight carries the gravity of finality—doors closing behind her that will never reopen.

Fingers steady now that work offers structure to replace shock. She plugs in the drive. The laptop's fan whirs to life, and with it comes the familiar scent of warming electronics—ozone and possibility mingling with the apartment's stale air. She queues Grace's voice notes and forwards the key clips to Lucas over encrypted chat, the sound of that steady voice an anchor against the night.

Files populate the screen like a digital autopsy—each folder an organ system in the corpse of Anton Brandt's empire. Financial records. Shipping manifests. Correspondence threaded with the casual cruelty of people who've learned to discuss human suffering in the language of profit margins and operational efficiency.

DURBAN_ROUTES. One click, and the folder opens to reveal an assembly of data points that map the corridor Grace had died trying to expose. Port schedules coordinated with customs rotations. Bribery payments disguised as

68

consulting fees. Container numbers corresponding to shipments that officially don't exist.

Each document lands like a body blow, another slice of the world's innocence fed to the machine of greed. Methodical reading follows, journalist instincts forcing professional distance even as her stomach churns with the implications. Officially, twenty-three workers died at Hartbeespoort, the dam town about an hour northwest of Johannesburg, because safety equipment cost too much. Border guards bought for the price of their children's school fees. Government ministers whose signatures appear on documents approving operations they publicly condemned.

Grace's voice whispers in her memory: *Follow the money, but don't let it follow you back.* Too late for that now. The money has teeth, and it's hungry.

The pattern emerges slowly, like a photograph developing in chemical baths. Not just corruption—that's the ocean South Africa swims in, familiar as gravity. This is systemic, engineered, a machinery of exploitation so sophisticated it requires institutional participation at every level.

Her hands hover over the keyboard. Muscle memory wants to begin, to turn evidence into narrative. Something stops her—a recognition that traditional journalism isn't equipped for what she's uncovered. This isn't a story that can be contained within newspaper columns or television segments. It's a reckoning that demands transformation rather than mere exposure.

Grace understood that. In the end, that's what killed her—the realization that some truths are too big for conventional channels, too dangerous for normal procedures. Some truths require martyrs, not journalists.

Names scroll past, some familiar from years of investigative work, others shocking in their prominence. Cabinet ministers. Supreme Court justices. CEOs of companies that advertise their social responsibility during commercial breaks. The web of complicity stretches so far that tugging a single thread threatens to unravel the fabric of institutional power.

Another sip of whiskey. The burn reminds her that she's still alive, still capable of sensing something beyond the intellectual horror of documentation. Grace's face materialises in her peripheral vision, young and earnest, believing that evidence and moral clarity could triumph over systems designed to absorb and neutralise both.

***

Six months ago. The coffee shop on Pritchard Street that served journalists and activists with equal suspicion, its windows fogged with steam that provided convenient cover for conversations that couldn't be overheard. Even the air tasted different that day—charged with the electricity preceding thunderstorms or confessions.

Grace sat across from her, fingers wrapped around a mug that had seen better decades. Steam rose between them like incense in a confession booth. Even then, Zara had noticed the changes—the way Grace's eyes darted toward the door every few minutes, the careful modulation of her voice that suggested performance rather than normalcy.

"They know." Grace's words fell between them like stones into still water. "About the containers. About the route changes. About us."

Zara leaned forward, journalist instincts sharpening despite the fear that lived like a constant tremor in her chest. "How much do they know?"

"Enough." Grace's smile carried the sadness of someone who'd realised their death had already been scheduled—they just hadn't been informed of the timing. "My supervisor asked me about my 'hobbies' yesterday. Wanted to know if I was still interested in extracurricular activities."

The euphemism hung between them, loaded with threat and possibility in equal measure. Extracurricular activities—

as if exposing government corruption were equivalent to joining a book club.

"We can protect you." Zara had insisted, knowing even as she spoke that protection was an illusion, a story journalists told themselves to sleep at night. "Transfer to another department. Change your contact information. Go underground until—"

"Until what? Until they lose interest? Until they find other sources to silence? Until you get bored and move on to the next story?"

The accusation stung because it was true. Zara had built her career on exposing corruption, then moving on when the public's attention shifted to newer scandals. The sources who'd trusted her often disappeared into bureaucratic reshuffling or strategic reassignment, their lives rearranged to accommodate journalism's appetite for revelation without consequence.

But this was different. Grace was different.

"This is bigger than anything we've uncovered before. The evidence is—"

"The evidence is meaningless if we're dead." Grace stood abruptly, chair scraping against linoleum with a sound like fingernails on slate. "I'm done, Zara. Find another source. Find someone who hasn't figured out that truth doesn't protect you from bullets."

That was their last conversation. Two weeks later, Grace Mdluli was officially transferred to a clerical position in the Department of Home Affairs. Unofficially, she was murdered—her silence sealed by a forged death certificate filed as heart failure. On paper she had simply been transferred; in truth, she had been eliminated to prevent her testimony from destroying careers and governments.

***

Back in her apartment, the whiskey glass empty now, Zara stares at the Cypress files with Grace's warning echoing in her memory. *The evidence is meaningless if we're dead.* But

Grace had been wrong about one thing—the evidence wasn't meaningless. It was dangerous precisely because it had meaning, because it connected dots that powerful people had spent decades ensuring remained unconnected.

The cursor blinks, waiting. Grace's story wants to be told, needs to be told. But more than that—it demands to be finished. What Grace started, what Grace died for, what Grace believed in despite everything.

A new document opens. Not for the investigation, not for the exposé, but for the only audience that matters now. The dedication materialises on her screen without conscious decision, fingers moving across keys worn smooth by years of chasing truth through bureaucratic labyrinths.

For Grace Mdluli, who understood that some stories are worth risking everything to tell.

The words stare back at her, their weight settling into her bones like lead poisoning—slow, cumulative, ultimately fatal. Grace's death hadn't made headlines. People who are murdered officially don't generate news coverage when their deaths are disguised as natural causes. Heart failure brought on by stress, according to the falsified death certificate that appeared weeks after she was eliminated. Natural causes, they called it, as if there was anything natural about a twenty-six-year-old woman being murdered for refusing to stay silent.

The phone rings, sharp and sudden in the apartment's careful silence. Lucas's name appears on the screen like an accusation. The device rings through to voicemail, and she plays the message in the darkness.

"Zara, I know you're processing everything from tonight. I know I don't have the right to ask this, but I need to know you're safe. The people we're dealing with—they don't leave loose ends."

His voice carries exhaustion that mirrors her own—the weariness of people who've stared directly at power and seen the machinery of violence that keeps it functioning. But beneath the fatigue, she hears something else—an uncertainty that sounds like someone still discovering the weight of his own choices.

No callback. Not yet. Grace taught her that patience was a weapon, that rushing into contact could compromise everything. Grace, who was murdered because someone was impatient, someone couldn't wait for the proper moment.

***

Instead, she returns to the files, diving deeper into the documentation Grace died to obtain. Bank records showing payments to customs officials whose salaries couldn't support their lifestyles. Shipping logs detailing the movement of containers that bypass normal inspection protocols. Correspondence between Anton Brandt and government ministers discussing human lives in the language of profit and loss.

Each document unfolds like a small death—another piece of the world's innocence sacrificed to greed. But collectively, they form something larger: a pattern that reveals the true architecture of power in post-apartheid South Africa. Not the Rainbow Nation promised in speeches and tourism brochures, but a system where freedom exists primarily as a marketing slogan while the real work of exploitation continues in shadows maintained by institutional silence.

Grace had seen this pattern before anyone else. Had traced its edges, mapped its connections, understood its implications. And for that clarity, for that courage, she had been murdered as efficiently as a typing mistake.

The clock on her laptop shows 3:47 a.m. In a few hours, the city will wake up and go about its business. Millions of people navigating their daily routines without knowledge of what she's uncovered. They'll board taxis that run on roads built with mining profits. They'll work in buildings whose construction involved materials shipped through the very corridors Grace had died exposing. They'll vote for politicians whose campaigns were funded by money

73

extracted from communities that will never see those profits returned as infrastructure or opportunity.

Ignorance is its own kind of safety, she realises. Knowledge carries obligations most people can't afford to shoulder. But journalists don't have the luxury of ignorance—they're paid to stare directly at what others turn away from, to carry the burden of institutional violence so that society can pretend its hands are clean.

Grace knew that burden. Carried it without complaint, without expectation of reward or recognition. Carried it until they killed her for it.

Her reflection stares back from the laptop screen, superimposed over documents that detail the systematic murder of twenty-three miners whose only crime was showing up for work on the wrong day. The expression she wears belongs to someone who's seen too much to ever sleep peacefully again, aged by hours, not years.

But something else lives in that reflection—purpose. The same quality that had burned in Grace's eyes during their final meeting. The recognition that some responsibilities transcend personal safety.

***

The cursor blinks in the empty document, waiting for her to begin the story that will transform evidence into accusation, documentation into revolution. But the words that want to come aren't meant for publication—they're meant for Grace, for the conversation they'll never have, for the apology that can never be adequate.

I told you to wait. I told you to be careful, to let me handle the dangerous parts. I thought I was protecting you, but I was just protecting my own conscience. I made you expendable so I could feel brave.

The confession stares back at her, brutal in its honesty. Delete. Type again. Delete again. Some truths are too sharp to exist outside the privacy of her own guilt.

Outside, Johannesburg settles into the deepest part of night—that liminal space between yesterday's sins and tomorrow's reckoning. The distant hum of the city shifts, traffic thinning to an occasional whisper of tyres on asphalt. In a few hours, she'll need to decide what to do with the evidence Grace died to obtain. Whether to publish and risk becoming another casualty in the war between truth and power, or to bury the files and let Grace's death join the statistical void that swallows people who ask inconvenient questions.

A new document opens, and she begins to type. Not as a journalist crafting an exposé, but as a friend keeping a promise to the dead.

The truth about the Hartbeespoort mining disaster begins with a lie—the official investigation that concluded twenty-three workers died due to equipment failure when they actually died because Anton Brandt decided their lives were worth less than the cost of proper safety measures.

The words feel like blades being forged in real time. Each sentence cuts through the comfortable fiction that justice exists in South Africa for anyone willing to pay the price of challenging power. Through the darkness she writes, forging an indictment that encompasses not just individual crimes but the systems that make those crimes inevitable.

But more than that, she writes with Grace's voice in her head. Grace's conviction in her fingers. Grace's refusal to accept easy answers or comfortable compromises. This isn't just her story anymore—it's their story, the story of two women who chose truth over safety and found that choice had consequences neither of them had fully anticipated.

By dawn, she has written Grace's epitaph in the form of the story that will either honour her sacrifice or transform Zara into another name whispered in newsrooms as a cautionary tale about the cost of staring too directly at power.

***

The city begins to stir outside her window. Five million people wake up to a day that will be fundamentally unchanged by her revelations. But change, she's learned, doesn't come from single stories or isolated acts of courage. It comes from the accumulation of small truths that eventually overwhelm the machinery of lies.

Grace understood that too. In her final weeks, when the surveillance had become obvious and the threats explicit, she kept working. Kept digging. Kept believing that the truth would find a way to survive even if its messenger didn't.

Multiple encrypted drives receive the saved document, each one hidden in a different location across the city—in safety deposit boxes and trusted contacts that span the informal networks journalists have built to survive institutional hostility. If they come for her—and they will come for her—they won't find all the evidence in one place. Grace's murder will not be rendered meaningless by the silencing of the only person who remembers why she died.

The city brightens under harsh, colourless light. Light falls on glass and concrete with no promise of renewal. But in the apartment that smells like solitude and secrets, Zara sits with truth that will transform everything it touches. Writing the story that Grace Mdluli died to tell.

The war between truth and power continues, and she is no longer content to be a correspondent. She has become a combatant.

Chapter 5 – The Devil's Terms

The following night, the engine coughed over the potholes in a forgotten corner of Johannesburg. Sandton's skyline flickered in the mirror—glass towers reduced to distant pinpricks—another man's heaven.

He flexed his fingers on the worn steering wheel. Leather cracked beneath his grip. Those towers—Brandt Tower included—had once been his domain: boardrooms where champagne sealed multimillion-rand deals with the efficiency of men trading lives for margins. Now they glared back with street-lamp indifference. Tombstones of a life he could never reclaim.

A battered Ford pickup roared past. Its axle spat small-caliber stones. Lucas flinched at each impact, his body conditioned by weeks of looking over his shoulder, sleeping with one ear tuned to footsteps that might herald his final reckoning. In the fading taillights, he caught his reflection—hollow-eyed, unshaven, paranoia fit tight as an undershirt.

Detective Mahlangu stepped out of the ruin, all purpose and restraint. Even in silhouette against the sunset's dying blush, he radiated authority born of years walking the razor's edge between justice and survival. A brown leather satchel hung heavy at his side, its surface warped and scarred by evidence runs through townships where truth was a luxury few could afford. Each mark told a story of compromise—necessary evils justified by impossible choices.

He approached the passenger door with deliberate steps, scars flecking his forearms—thin white lines from older wars. The door creaked, quiet, wary. He slid inside with fluid grace—someone accustomed to invisibility, to becoming part of the landscape until action was unavoidable.

Silence pressed between them—dense, oppressive, alive with unspoken accusations. Through the cracked windshield, half-lit windows in distant tenements stared back like sockets in a skull picked clean by scavengers.

Lucas leaned forward and retrieved a brown folder from beneath his seat. Corners sharp enough to cut, heavy enough to matter.

"You'll want to read this." His voice was carefully measured to mask the tremor beneath, fear threaded through every syllable.

Mahlangu's eyes flicked to the folder, then back to Lucas's face, reading something that made him fold his hands like a barrier against contamination.

"No, I don't," he said flatly, each word carrying the weight of collapsed truces and idealism murdered by experience.

But after a moment—the pause between self-preservation and duty—he uncurled his fingers and accepted the file.

Lucas exhaled slowly, shoulders sagging as tension drained. Relief was a lie—thin and temporary.

"Names. Dates. Money trails. Every signature, every transfer, every handshake that turned justice into a commodity. Everything you need to understand how deep this runs."

Mahlangu thumbed through pages with methodical precision. His brow knotted with each revelation like a man reading his own death warrant in installments. Shell companies that existed only as P.O. boxes. Shipping manifests documenting cargo that never existed. Photographs of men in expensive suits shaking hands in rooms that officially did not exist—back-room negotiations where the future was auctioned to the highest bidder.

Finally, he closed the folder, knuckles white against manila.

Mahlangu's radio crackled. A burst of coded numbers made him pause mid-sentence, hand automatically moving to silence it.

"Sorry," he said. "Never really off duty."

Lucas caught the lie in his eyes. Some duties, apparently, took precedence over others.

"You think I don't know the Brandt story?" Mahlangu's voice carried bitter acknowledgment, resignation threaded with contempt. "We've all memorized it. Learned to speak around it in the careful language of institutional amnesia. The question is what you expect me to do about it."

Lucas's jaw tightened. The familiar weight of his surname settled across his shoulders like a yoke designed by generations of careful criminals.

"What I didn't know—how badly you wanted to die."

The words hit Lucas like a blow, knocking the air clean out of him. His head snapped up, eyes glittering with anger and the ghost of hope.

"I want to live—with the truth. I thought that's what you wanted too. Justice. Accountability."

Mahlangu's shoulders sagged with decades of impossible choices. For a moment Lucas glimpsed the man beneath the badge—tired, worn down, longing for simpler compromises.

"I want my wife back. My pension. Sleep. But you don't get truth and safety here."

"Then make it safe," Lucas pressed. "File it. Log it. Archive it in records they can't erase."

Mahlangu shook his head, weary certainty in his eyes. "You can't make this safe. This doesn't threaten safety—it kills it. Evidence like this can only be buried completely or set alight so it destroys everything it touches. There's no middle ground."

Lucas rubbed his temple, headache pulsing with desperation. "This is your job. Make it work. Turn evidence into justice."

Mahlangu's response came with icy calm. "I could arrest you right now. Theft of evidence. Interference with an investigation. Possession of classified material. You brought this to me; that means you own it now. You've made yourself part of the conspiracy."

Lucas met his gaze, pulse hammering. "Are you charging me?"

Mahlangu shrugged—the gesture casual but loaded with institutional indifference. "No one pays me to keep you out of jail—and you might be safer inside than with this file burning holes in your pocket."

Defiance flared in Lucas's chest like a struck match in a room full of gasoline. "So you'll do nothing? Just let them bury another investigation?"

A forced smile flickered across Mahlangu's face— uneasy truce between contempt and necessity. "I'm doing you a favor by not arresting you, son. Push harder and don't expect the law to protect you. These people don't end careers; they erase lives."

Without another word, he opened the door and stepped into the dust-thick air. He slid the folder back across the seat as he stepped out—refusing possession as if it might burn him.

Lucas watched him go, settling dust drifting through the halogen glow of the petrol station's security lights. As Mahlangu's figure vanished into darkness, Lucas felt the full weight of his isolation press around him.

He stayed in the idling Toyota long after Mahlangu vanished. Watched the station's halogen lights pulse like exhausted stars. A dog nosed through a torn rubbish bag by the curb, carrying off a cracked polystyrene clamshell like he owned the block. Two teenagers drifted past on a scooter, helmets unbuckled, laughter brittle and reckless as if safety were only ever someone else's problem.

Lucas cracked the window and let the night in. Smell of petrol. Warm bread from a bakery that shouldn't be open. The sweetness of jacaranda sap, faint but insistent, a scent he had always associated with the first lie told in spring.

He pinched the bridge of his nose and tried to breathe past the nausea that had arrived with adrenaline's retreat.

On the passenger seat, the folder waited—heavy as an accusation. He thought of a ledger he had once seen in Anton's study: a column for profit, a column for loss, and nowhere a line for the cost of being human.

What did you call the numbers that measured what a man became by surviving his family?

His phone blinked: three voice notes from Zara—Grace, calm and unafraid. He played the first through the car speakers and let her cadence slow his pulse.

He turned the key and the engine coughed awake. Somewhere down the block a security siren started—that rising, falling howl the city used instead of confession.

Lucas pulled into the empty road and let it chase him, a reminder that even when you moved, nothing was really behind you.

***

Across the city, *The Continent* newsroom felt like a mausoleum at this hour. Fluorescent lights hummed a funeral dirge over abandoned desks and coffee cups that bore the lipstick stains of journalists who had learned to survive on caffeine and stubborn hope. The walls breathed stale failure and the accumulated disappointment of stories that had died before reaching print.

Zara stood in the editor's cramped office. Towers of cardboard boxes teetered on creaking desks like monuments to ambition defeated by compromise.

Each box was stuffed with shredded drafts and abandoned headlines—half-finished stories sacrificed on the altar of endurance. Truth had weight here—too heavy for the paper to carry. A faded map of Africa hung crooked behind the editor's chair, its edges curled like pages left too long in the rain.

Ronald Mthembu, editor-in-chief, slumped behind a battered oak desk, wood scarred by decades of desperate journalism. The overhead lighting flickered, casting pallid bars across his lined face. Financial reports were scattered across the desk like evidence from a crime scene—testimony to the paper's slow strangulation. His eyes, red-rimmed and hollow, carried the look of a man forced to measure truth against solvency every day—and losing.

"You can't let them shut us down." Zara's voice stayed steady but carried the exhaustion of someone who had been fighting this battle too long without reinforcement. "We're *The Continent*. We survived apartheid, state capture, the Zuma years. We don't bow to corporate pressure."

"Not anymore." His voice barely rose above a whisper. "Back off, Zara. While you still can."

Her jaw firmed—that stubborn defiance that had made her dangerous to powerful people. She pictured the newsroom beyond this office—that warren of desks, each one representing half-finished stories and half-formed hopes for justice. "I won't back off. Not now. Not when we're this close to exposing something that could change how this country understands its own history."

Behind him, front pages trembled in the draft from a cracked window. Bold headlines now ghostly reminders of victories from better days—stories that had brought down ministers, exposed corruption, changed laws.

He leaned back in his chair, upholstery groaning with the sound of something old giving way. "I know it's important. But so is keeping the lights on. So is making sure our remaining staff don't end up like Grace Mdluli."

The name hung between them like a blade drawn in daylight. Zara's face hardened. Her voice dropped to a whisper. "Grace was murdered, Ron. We both know that. And if we don't publish what she died for, her death means nothing."

Mthembu's hands trembled as he reached for his coffee mug, the liquid long cold. Grace's murder had changed everything—transformed theoretical threats into proven realities, academic discussions of press freedom into obituaries written in advance.

"Whose threats?" His voice carried the weight of a man who had been cataloging them for weeks. "Government? Corporations? Give them faces."

His gaze fell to the unopened mail stack beside his computer—bills, legal notices, probably more threats wrapped in official letterhead. He kicked at the pile with his foot, a gesture of futility. "Does it matter? Pressure comes from above, from the side, from places you never even knew existed. Any misstep, any excuse, and we pull the entire investigation. Those are my orders."

She crossed her arms, chin lifted in defiance. The fluorescent hum felt oppressive now—light itself seemed to hold its breath. "We can't. This story is bigger than the paper, bigger than any one of us. Grace understood that when she handed me those documents."

Mthembu rubbed his temples with both hands, trying to massage away lines etched by years of impossible choices. Finally, he pushed a battered file box across the desk, its edges worn smooth like old bones.

"Every threat we've received in the past six months. Every lawsuit. Every intimidation attempt. We've lost four freelancers—two to better offers, two to hospital beds. I can't lose you too, Zara."

She opened the box with the reverence of someone handling trial evidence. Inside lay unanswered emails on cheap paper, veiled warnings printed on expensive letterhead. Each envelope looked as menacing as bullets in a display case. Her chest tightened, but her voice remained calm.

"No one else is touching this story. It's mine. It always has been—ever since Grace handed me that first document and was murdered for it."

Mthembu closed his eyes. Years of accumulated weight pressed down on his shoulders. When he spoke, it was nearly a whisper. "You've got a name and a future ahead of you, Zara. International recognition—book deals—speaking engagements. Don't let them take both your story and your life."

She stood abruptly. The office suddenly felt smaller, air pressed thin as the walls closed in. In the dim light filtering through dirty windows, she turned back one last time. "We're not just targets in this war. We're leverage. And I intend to use every bit of it."

The door swung shut behind her with the finality of a verdict being read.

Zara slowed at the threshold of the bullpen. Desks slept beneath their clutter: mugs with inside jokes, dog-eared style guides, a map pricked with pins that had once meant field reporting and danger and awards no one could afford to collect. She reached out and straightened a crooked frame— a front page from a decade ago when the paper had toppled a minister and everybody here had believed in oxygen.

In the reflection of the glass she saw herself the way her enemies preferred her: tired, alone, another woman with an unwise sense of proportion. She pressed her palms into the small of her back until something clicked—a cheap trick to make the ache shut up. Then lifted her phone and scrolled the day's messages. Half a dozen "be carefuls." Two unsigned threats. One note from a freelancer in Limpopo: "Heard they're asking around about your brother."

She pocketed the phone and looked again at the map. The pins had colors—red for stories published, blue for stories killed, white for stories no one would touch. Too many blues.

She took a pen and circled Johannesburg because superstitions were just another way of insisting the work mattered. Then she killed the lights and left the room to dream its old, loud dreams.

***

Helena Brandt's heels clicked against polished marble with the precision of a metronome marking time before an execution. Each sound was swallowed by cathedral hush, bouncing off oil paintings that lined the walls like witnesses to centuries of power—portraits of tyrants and lovers lost to history, landscapes scorched by ambition. The silence itself seemed curated, designed to intimidate through beauty rather than threat.

Fresh varnish mingled with Helena's expensive perfume, layered over the faint hum of climate-control systems that strained to preserve millions of rand in art—pieces purchased with money that remembered violence. She moved through the gallery as though it were a confessional, each measured step acknowledging sins preserved in gilt frames.

Darren Katz stepped out of a shadowed corridor like something materializing from Helena's darkest thoughts. His silhouette rigid against the crystal glare of chandeliers. A security guard swiveled, cataloged him as authorized personnel, and turned back with the indifference of someone long accustomed to power's rituals.

"Too long since we've spoken, Mrs. Brandt." Darren's voice carried cultured tones honed into a weapon. "How is your boy adjusting to his new circumstances?"

Helena paused beneath a painting of a windblown plain, canvas rippling with unseen storms. She studied it a moment before replying, her voice cool as marble touched by winter air. "Growing up. Finally. And remembering things that perhaps should have stayed forgotten."

"An artist must maintain proper distance." Darren moved closer with calculated refinement. "Close enough to observe the truth, far enough away to survive the revelation."

Helena turned to face him fully. The chandeliers caught her earrings, scattering prisms across her face like stars reflected in ice. "Your friend Lucas was sloppy. Too close to the flames to be either effective artist or surviving witness."

Darren's smile was all shadows and sharp edges. "Emotional men make poor artists. And even poorer corpses when the cleanup begins."

Her gaze was surgical. "We had a deal, Darren. A very specific arrangement with very clear parameters. I intend to see it honored."

He shrugged, gesture encompassing the cavernous space—its priceless canvases, its manufactured silence. "Deals change as circumstances evolve. Fortunes rise and fall with political tides. Surely you understand that better than most."

Helena's eyes drifted to a blank canvas positioned in the corner—its emptiness alive with infinite possibility, drenched in everything endured to reach this moment: every sacrifice, every compromise, every necessary evil. "This space isn't empty; it's saturated with history. What we've survived to stand here."

Darren stepped closer, voice dropping to a register reserved for conspiracies. "There's a time to erase the past and a time to remember it selectively. The art lies in knowing which moment requires which."

Helena didn't blink. For the briefest instant she saw her mother's face, lips pursed against a lifetime of silence, the lesson carved into her bones: doubt is weakness, memory is leverage. She buried the flicker before it reached her eyes.

"Never complete erasure." Her tone was unyielding. "History, even bloodstained, is leverage over the ignorant."

"Knowing that blood has been spilled before," Darren said, voice hardening like cooling metal, "is accepting that it will be spilled again when circumstances demand it. But if you can keep the present stains from showing, I'll see the cleanup is thorough."

She nodded once, iron certainty in her eyes like light flashing off a blade. "Lucas is unpredictable, which makes him dangerous. But he's my son—blood of my blood. No more violence, Darren. Not until I've exhausted other options."

Darren's laugh was soft and hollow, echoing off the marble like the sound of something dying in a beautiful space. "Maternal sentiment is a luxury we can't afford. Blood relations are useful only so long as they serve our purposes."

Helena's expression didn't change, but something hardened in her eyes—the look of a mother who had spent decades balancing love and survival in impossible proportions. "Lucas is indispensable for maintaining our façade. His exposure would unravel everything we've built. I'll handle him my way."

"I'll send you a *catalog of alternatives*." Darren's voice carried the weight of threats wrapped in courtesy. "In our world, choices are always few—and inevitably grim."

He receded into shadow as smoothly as he had emerged, leaving Helena alone among ambitions and regrets preserved in oil and varnish. She stood

before the blank canvas, seeing in its void all the stories still waiting to be written.

The guard coughed into his fist and pretended not to watch her. Helena stayed with the blank canvas a moment longer, feeling the muscles in her jaw harden around an old habit: never let the first emotion be the true one. Her mother used to say power is a kind of fasting—you go without until appetite becomes obedience.

She moved to a smaller painting, all knives of light over dark water, and studied the artist's signature—initials only, crisply withheld. It pleased her that someone else understood the value of leaving a name off a thing. Names belonged to the living. The living made mistakes. Legacies required fewer witnesses.

Her phone buzzed. A single line from a number with no country code: "He's moving." No subject, no honorific, not even the discipline of punctuation. She typed nothing and deleted it twice—once for the room, once for propriety.

On her way out she paused beneath the windblown plain. Somewhere out there—beyond the frame, beyond the walls that curated remorse—men were digging holes for truths that refused to stay buried.

Helena squared her shoulders. Art conserved the surface. Her job was the preservation of myth.

***

Miles away, in a very different kind of space, Zara's flat felt like both sanctuary and prison. Its mismatched furniture bore witness to the compromises of a life lived on the margins of power: a coffee table scarred by cigarette burns from late-night interviews with nervous sources; a sagging sofa patched with duct tape where the foam had surrendered under exhaustion and adrenaline crashes.

A single lamp cast uneasy amber light, creating small islands of illumination that were swallowed by shadows pooling in corners like silent observers. She poured a measure of whiskey—cheap stuff that burned going down but quieted the voices in her head—and watched the liquid ignite in the lamp's glow.

On the coffee table, her recorder blinked a steady green eye, daring her to press play. The air thickened as she finally did. Static hissed, the white noise of surveillance pushed past its limits. Then a voice emerged—rough, uncertain, vibrating with equal parts fear and conviction.

"The land deals. The gold. You think anyone's clean in this? You think there's anyone in government or business who doesn't have blood on their hands?"

The walls seemed to contract as the words spilled into the room. Her chest tightened, the voice trembling with the knowledge of its own risk.

"Not even your boy, if he knows what's good for him. Not even Lucas Brandt, if he's smart enough to know when he's in over his head."

Zara's eyes closed. She was back in that cramped interview booth that reeked of sweat and desperation, the kind of place where truth came out because there was nowhere else for it to go. The tape crackled, splintered, then one last burst: "The Brandts. The President. They're all—"

Click. Sudden stillness, heavy and absolute, like a vault door slamming shut.

The recorder sat mute, its light now seeming to mock her with electronic indifference. She pressed a palm to her chest, feeling her heart hammer in syncopation with the silence. Then she grabbed her phone, thumb trembling slightly despite her best effort, and opened the voice memo app.

"Lukey." Her voice was low but resolute, carrying the weight of decisions that couldn't be undone. "They've shut us down. Editor's scared shitless. This is bigger than the paper, bigger than any one story. We're not just targets anymore. We're leverage—and they're getting ready to use us."

She hit send. The message spiraled into the digital void where loyalties shifted like sand and allies could become enemies with a single call.

She sank back against the duct-taped sofa, whiskey burning a warm path down her throat as the recorder's green light blinked its indifferent eye. Tomorrow she would have to choose—retreat into safety or push forward into darkness, following a story that might consume everything she had built.

The ice cracked in her glass like a distant shot. She let the sound settle, counting backward from ten. Inhale on even numbers, exhale on odd. By five the panic softened into something she could name. By one it was only a fact: she would move forward, and they would try to stop her.

On the windowsill a fan of printed photographs gathered dust: Grace framed by fluorescent warehouse light; a clipboard; a smile too careful for someone not yet thirty— taken weeks before they murdered her. Beneath that, a snapshot of Zara and Victor on a beach in KwaZulu-Natal, wind eating the edges of their laughter. She touched the corner of that one and felt the grit of old salt, proof that a day had existed in which no one wanted anything from them but joy.

The recorder's light kept blinking. She rewound the tape three seconds and pressed play again, listening only to the breath between words—the place where fear lives when grammar runs out. It told her enough: the source was tired, practiced, the kind of person who knew to check a door twice before saying what could ruin everyone.

∗∗∗

The grandfather clock in Anton Brandt's study had been ticking for forty-seven years, marking time through coups and elections, the rise and fall of apartheid, and the painful birth of what some optimistically called the Rainbow

Nation. Each tick was a heartbeat in a house that had witnessed more history than most parliaments, more conspiracy than most libraries.

Lucas moved through the room like a ghost haunting his own past, footsteps muffled by the thick Persian rug that had seen more secret meetings than a dozen ministries. As a boy, he had been told it was a gift from a grateful arms dealer—its intricate patterns hiding bloodstains no amount of professional cleaning could entirely erase.

Floor-to-ceiling bookcases bowed under the weight of leather-bound tomes—law, economics, strategy, political theory—the collected wisdom of men who had built empires on the suffering of others and called it progress. The scent of yellowed pages and polished oak lingered in the air like incense in a secular cathedral, mingling with the ghost of Anton's pipe tobacco and the must of secrets sealed for decades.

A dust-coated globe stood in the corner, its antique brass tarnished by time. When Lucas was a child, Anton had spun it to show how power flowed not through armies but through shipping routes, trade agreements, and careful relationships. Influence mapped across oceans like invisible veins.

Lucas placed the manila folder on the mahogany desk, feeling the wood's residual warmth from decades of late-night plotting. The surface bore scars: pen gouges, ring stains from whiskey glasses raised to toast deals never written into law. Beside the folder he set a USB drive, its blue LED pulsing with the steady rhythm of a digital heartbeat.

His gaze drifted to the black-and-white photograph given pride of place: Anton beside the president-elect on the day after the first democratic election, both men smiling for cameras while privately calculating profit. Surrounding it were smaller snapshots: a mine collapse site where accidents had been arranged, boardroom dinners where legislation was bought and sold like commodities.

He traced a note he had once scribbled in the margin of a ledger: *Truth is flotation; legacy is weight.* The contradiction throbbed in his mind. Would exposing the rot free him—or drown him beneath consequences as old as the family name?

The air in the study grew colder as a draft slipped down the chimney, carrying with it Johannesburg's midnight whispers. The city exhaled its toxins as if corruption wasn't an aberration but its organizing principle.

A sudden crack shattered the silence—a gunshot echoing through the night, rattling windowpanes, vibrating along the beams. Lucas froze, nerves screaming, body recognizing the sound even as his mind struggled to process its implications. Distant yet intimate, the shot carved its question into the dark: How far would they go to protect their secrets?

He pressed his back against the bookcase, history's weight at his spine. The shot had come from the direction of the main gate—too close to be random street violence, too precisely timed to be coincidence. Security lights blazed to life across the estate grounds, their harsh illumination sweeping across manicured lawns like searchlights hunting for escaped prisoners.

Lucas moved to the window, staying in shadow as he watched uniformed guards emerge from their stations, radios crackling with urgent exchanges. The head of security—a man Lucas recognized from his childhood, someone Anton had trusted with family secrets—barked orders as his team deployed across the perimeter.

A patrol vehicle's engine roared to life, headlights cutting through the darkness as it raced toward the estate's northern boundary. Through the static of radio communications, Lucas caught fragments: *... single shot ... no breach ... likely a warning ...*

The message was clear. They knew he was inside. They knew what he was doing. The gunshot wasn't random violence—it was communication, a reminder that his father's security apparatus had evolved beyond Anton's death into something that served newer masters.

But Lucas didn't recoil. He let the commotion fade, watching as the guards returned to their stations, their search revealing nothing because there had been nothing to find. The violence had no direction—just a reminder that danger was permanent, even here in his father's sanctum.

When the estate settled back into its artificial calm, Lucas returned to the desk. He lifted the USB drive, its blue light pulsing defiance against the shadows. Compressed into circuits smaller than a coin, heavy enough to shift the balance.

Regardless of the cost—blood or tears, reputation or soul—he would free the truth. Tonight he chose revelation over silence, justice over loyalty, the uncertain possibility of redemption over the inherited certainty of complicity.

The grandfather clock struck midnight, solemn and final. The LED blinked like a beacon, announcing a war he had already chosen to enter.

He didn't move at first. Let the clock count three more seconds, like a notary's stamp on a document no one sane would sign. Through the window the lawn rolled down into trees, and beyond that the road kinked toward the city—a vein feeding everything he was about to poison with truth.

Lucas set the USB on the ledger and opened the bottom drawer where Anton had kept—among cufflinks and passports—an index card in black ink: CONTINGENCIES. Beneath the title, five names and one instruction: *Call only if necessary.* Two of the numbers were dead. One belonged to a judge who now confessed on television for cash. The fourth rang once and resolved into silence. He didn't try the fifth. There are people you call only when you've chosen violence; tonight he'd chosen witness.

He slid the drawer shut and listened to the house. Pipes ticking. The faint, restless thrum of the refrigerator in a kitchen no one cooked in. The particular hush of expensive emptiness.

He tucked the USB into his inside pocket and felt its hard geometry against his ribs, proof that the past could be made small enough to carry but never light enough to forget.

When he finally switched off the study lamp, the window threw his reflection back at him in perfect black glass—a man shaped like the ghost of a dynasty, walking toward the city that ate better men and called it order.

The devil's terms had been offered and accepted.

Chapter 6 – The Portrait and the Ledger

3:17 a.m. The study held its breath. The lamp's hard white pooled across mahogany, making an autopsy table of old wood. Every nick. Every coffee ring. A small confession. Lucas sat on the edge of Anton's chair, not quite claiming it. The cushion exhaled in a tired, human way.

The air was thick with what the room remembered. Varnish baked into paneling. The faint bite of fountain-pen ink. A ghost-thread of Anton's pipe tobacco that clung to books like inherited prejudice.

The uncapped pens had crusted at their mouths—tiny scabs where words had dried mid-sentence. Beside them, half a tumbler of The Macallan caught light and turned it amber. Dust drifted on its surface like patient thoughts. He lifted the glass. Medicinal going down. Punishing, after.

There had been nights, growing up, when that same smell meant safety. Anton home. The predictable gravity of his presence holding the house in orbit. Now the scent only made the walls lean closer.

The shelves rose around him in courtroom rows. Leather spines announcing a discipline the family practiced only in public. *Principles of Corporate Governance. The History of Mining in Southern Africa. Constitutional Law and Human Rights.* Books kept for their posture. Lucas knew, as any son raised to stage a life would know, which titles to lend visiting board members. Which to leave in view.

He could hear Anton's voice in the cadence of those decisions. Baritone, patient—never hurried. Always certain.

The books had taught him early that appearance was its own kind of truth. Anton had taught him that the kind that mattered was the kind other people believed.

A moth tapped the rim of the lampshade and whirled out of sight. Blind orbit around heat. It kept returning—small skull against white. A metronome for sleeplessness. Lucas rubbed his eyes. The day had unspooled too far.

Hours, now, were thin and treacherous, the kind that let old logic back in.

He had told the world the truth.

It hadn't changed what the house was. It hadn't uncarved Anton from the furniture or opened the walls to daylight. Outside, Johannesburg lay dark and latched. A city that knew how to keep secrets. Inside, the study was a diagram of a man—drawn to scale.

He should have slept. He'd tried the guest room, the one he'd used when Helena wanted distance presented as decorum. But the silence there made him feel like a tenant in his own past. In the study he at least understood the terms. He set the glass down and let his fingers map the desk's scars. Reading them like Braille: deals struck. Threats delivered. Forgiveness postponed.

The waiting haunted him.

This room had been a place where men waited for Anton to decide who they were.

A photograph lay on the blotter—one of the loose casualties from the toppled drawer. Lucas and Darren, teenagers in borrowed confidence. Squared to the camera with that mean, private joy young men wear when they think they've invented the future. Darren's arm slung across his shoulders. Lucas thinner then, smiling in spite of himself.

The background was unmistakable: Sandton—Africa's richest square mile. Glass towers rose beside luxury malls. Reputations were made or destroyed over lunch. Behind them loomed the Sandton City cinema, its banner shouting releases they hadn't been old enough to see. School blazers unbuttoned. Ties loose. Postures daring the world to stop them.

They'd called it *Operation Matinee.* Their own dumb spy code for slipping the leash. Darren even forged hall passes once, signing with the flourish of "Principal Mandela." A joke that had seemed hilarious at fifteen. Felt sacrilegious now.

He hadn't thought about that day in years. They'd been dropped at school in separate cars, separate gates. Lucas had waited behind the library block while Darren slipped out the far exit. Collar up. Backpack slung like a deserter's kit. Together they walked up Grayston Drive, keeping to back streets where the cameras were older. Hedge-lined sidewalks where no one expected heirs to vanish.

"Shit—C-Class," Darren hissed once, ducking low. "Might be your uncle."

Lucas had snorted. "He drives a BMW."

Sandton City was nearly empty that morning. They rode escalators. Bought snacks. Dared the world to notice them. For a few hours they weren't Brandt and Katz. Just boys high on caffeine and the sensation of having outwitted their guardians.

They were queuing for a movie they weren't quite old enough to see when the air shifted.

"Lucas Sebastian Brandt."

Helena's voice. Cold. Surgical. The kind that made strangers turn before they even registered her face. He remembered the precision of her heels on tile. The way she reached for his collar and pulled him from the line with a grip that didn't bruise. But promised it could. The walk back through the mall had been conducted in silence weighted like ceremony.

And Darren—arms folded, expression unreadable—until he smiled.

Not smug. Not mocking.

Just delighted.

Lucas turned the photograph facedown. He didn't need to see it again. Darren still wore that smile. Only now it was sharper.

And aimed.

The lamp hummed. The moth tapped again. Somewhere in the house a pipe ticked as it cooled, the sound like a foot on a stair. He slid the photograph away and let its silence press into the wood. The ledger pages— Anton's—sat in a shallow stack at the corner of the desk. Edges feathered from handling.

His stomach knotted at the sight.

He wasn't ready yet. There are doors you do not open without a witness.

Through the window, security lights swept the estate grounds in their automated patterns. The same pattern that had blazed to life after the gunshot hours earlier. The memory of that single shot still echoed in his mind—too precise, too timed to be random violence. It had been a message, clear as a telegram: we know where you are.

We know what you're doing.

The estate's security system had responded exactly as designed. Guards deployed. Perimeter checked. Radio chatter documenting the all-clear. But Lucas understood now what the guards themselves probably didn't: they weren't protecting him.

They were monitoring him.

Every motion sensor, every camera, every patrol route fed data to someone who wasn't necessarily interested in his safety.

He stood and moved through the room the way he used to as a boy. Tracing the perimeter without touching anything. Pretending the rules he didn't break meant he was good. The portraits along the far wall caught his eye the way traffic catches a driver's. The kind of unavoidable.

Anton three ages of himself: the young lawyer with the skeptical mouth, the middle-aged patriarch in a suit that did too much, the late-life grandee with hands on the back of a chair. As if on a throat. The painter had done something to the eyes in the last one so that they followed you softly. A painted kindness that felt like surveillance.

A thin fissure ran through the varnish near the right edge of the frame. Barely a hairline. The kind of flaw a varnisher would curse and a son would learn to ignore. Lucas didn't step closer, not yet.

Let the crack wait.

He looked instead at the glass-fronted cabinet where Helena kept the things she said were "for guests." Gifts given back to themselves: medals in velvet, commemorative coins, a pen presented by a bank whose ethics statement read like a confession. The cabinet door's lock had always been stubborn. He could hear the tiny scrape now in memory as Helena coaxed it at parties. Laughing because a woman who unlocked things was irresistible in certain rooms.

He was ashamed of the thought. Ashamed he had learned an entire taxonomy of what women were allowed to be in this house.

But Helena had always been different from the other women who orbited Anton's world. She wasn't a wife acquired for decoration or alliance. She was Lucas's mother. The woman who had shaped him from infancy. Whose blood ran in his veins. That biological connection had given her a power in this house that no mere marriage could provide. Anton had trusted her with secrets he would never share with a spouse chosen for convenience.

He returned to the desk and forced himself to sit. When he had been a teenager and the silence grew dangerous, he would write things down. A practice Helena encouraged, saying the mind cleared when the hand worked. Tonight the notebook that had followed him from apartment to apartment lay closed. Elastic band dogged around it like a tourniquet.

He took a pen from the blotter. Shook it. Pressed it to the page.

Nothing came.

Words felt like trespass. The room did not want confession. It preferred minutes.

He let the pen rest and thought instead of Grace Mdluli; Zara's forwarded voice notes still lived in his ear with their patient defiance. Truth never wins outright—it only outlasts the lies. She had believed that and it had cost her everything. Not just the soft parts of life, but life itself. Grace was dead, murdered for the documents she'd tried to preserve. Lucas carried the weight of that knowledge like a stone in his chest.

Her death wasn't from the "heart attack" listed on the falsified report. It had been an execution—clinical, calculated—disguised as injuries sustained in custody. Designed to silence her permanently.

He wondered what his belief had cost other people. The house waited, patient with him the way a parent is patient with a child who refuses to be taught.

Another orbit of the moth. It stumbled in the light's heat and righted itself, stubborn. Lucas watched it land on the shade and cling there. A small dark punctuation at the edge of brightness. He had the sudden, unhelpful sense that he was being asked to read something correctly.

And would fail.

He looked again at the photograph he'd turned face down. Beneath it, a second, thinner photo had slid out—a shot of the study from years ago. Candids from the anniversary party when Helena had insisted on a string quartet to domesticate the night. In the shot, the painter was adjusting Anton's cuff. A gesture of tenderness that made the stomach turn.

He slid both photos back into the drawer and shut it carefully. As if something living were inside. The ledger stack waited. He lifted the top page with two fingers as if testing temperature. The paper had a clean, matte tooth. Anton had chosen it for how it took ink, not for how it looked.

A list of dates and names. Figures and annotations in the narrow hand that had made boys cry in depositions. The tidy cruelty of numbers. Lucas read a line and then another. After the third line he placed the page back down.

He was not going to open the door without deciding who he was on the threshold.

He took a second mouthful of amber, smaller, and lowered the lamp's dimmer until the room slid a half-step toward dusk. Enough to see. Not enough to be seen. The house at night had always recalibrated him. Stripped the performance from the day. Made him count only what he could carry in silence.

In that honesty there had been comfort.

Now it felt like being measured for a suit he didn't want.

At the edge of his hearing: a tap, then another, spaced like thought. He turned his head. The fissure in the varnish by the portrait had widened in the low light into a suggestion. A seam the eye wanted to follow. He stayed where he was, unwilling to be lured by the idea that the house could still surprise him.

Nothing in this room changed without permission.

The crack hadn't asked.

"Not tonight," he told the room, and his voice sounded like a borrowed instrument. The moth lifted, made another slow arc, and landed on the ledger stack. As if to mark the last page his father had touched. A tenderness rose in him that he hadn't expected. That he did not trust.

He placed the glass aside. Folded his hands as if in prayer. Let the tenderness harden into something he could use.

He thought of Helena's insistence on beauty. Darren's false innocence. Grace's murdered dedication to truth. His father had paid duty's cost in other people's currency—and Grace Mdluli had paid the ultimate price for refusing to accept that transaction.

Lucas flexed his fingers.

"I will write it," he said. "But I will read it first."

The pen moved—grudgingly—as if persuaded by resolve. He wrote a date, then a sentence about the room, setting the record to face him instead of the world. The words came slow but clean. Like water bled from a stubborn pipe. He did not describe Anton so much as inventory him: the chair, the scent, the books—facts that did not flatter or accuse.

On the page, he could bear the weight of what he knew.

In the room, he was small.

When he lifted his head again, the moth had vanished into the shade's hollow. The house sounded like a sleeping thing. The ledger stack seemed to breathe, faint curling at the corners where warmth meets ink. He closed the notebook. The crack at the portrait waited in his peripheral vision. Not a summons yet, merely a possibility.

He stood, finally, and the chair sighed again, relieved. On his way past the shelves he let his fingers brush a spine—*Constitutional Law and Human Rights*—and felt foolish. As if it might bite. He smiled despite himself. In a different life, a saner life, he would have been the kind of man who read what he kept.

In this one, he was the kind who learned too late what the keeping meant.

At the door, he paused. The room did not release him. It never had. "Tomorrow," he said, to the portrait, to the ledger, to whatever the crack wanted. The lamp threw his shadow up across the books in a neat, rectangular absence. He crossed back, lowered the dimmer once more until the moth's orbit disappeared into the dark.

And left the study with the knowledge that he would come back.

If only to prove the room wrong about him.

***

The corridor received him like a vein in a sleeping body. Dark walls pulsing with the faint hum of electricity. Through tall windows, streetlight fractured into shards, staining the striped wallpaper burgundy and cream. The pattern had been chosen by Helena's decorator to simulate inheritance. An old-money signal for guests who didn't know how recently the family had learned to look respectable.

Lucas paused at the threshold. The study's gravity clung to him like tobacco smoke. The leather chair behind him exhaled as though grateful to be empty. Out here, the air was colder. Perfumed faintly by polish and silence. The kind cultivated to keep family secrets from echoing beyond the walls.

He stepped forward. Floorboards shifted beneath his Italian shoes. A hidden orchestra of groans and sighs announcing every movement. The house documented him the way Anton once had—without mercy, without pause. Motion sensors stirred awake with nearly inaudible clicks.

Feeding his progress into systems Helena had insisted were essential for safety.

Had always felt more like surveillance.

After the gunshot earlier, Lucas understood those systems differently. They weren't just recording his movements for security. They were creating a record for someone else. Every pause, every hesitation was being cataloged. Analyzed. Reported. The estate that should have been his sanctuary had become his most sophisticated prison.

He imagined the data points forming a dossier: each hesitation flagged for review. Even here, in the supposed sanctuary of family, there was no such thing as privacy. The weight of that awareness pressed against his shoulders. As real as a hand guiding him down the hall.

At the base of the grand staircase, Lucas let his palm drift along the banister. Mahogany polished to mirror-brightness reflected a fractured silhouette. Above him, the chandelier dangled like a relic of Versailles. Crystal prisms splintering the weak streetlight into cathedral tones— sapphire blues, crimson reds, golds too heavy for sunlight.

The foyer glowed with the palette of stained glass.

More mausoleum than home.

The paintings watched him from their frames. Each portrait was a sermon on power—faces arranged in generational procession. The earliest canvases showed men with hands thick from picks and shovels. Eyes carrying the feverish hunger of prospectors clawing wealth from earth. By the next generation, the hands had softened. Nails manicured. Eyes sharper with calculation.

By Anton's era, the gaze was entirely predatory.

No hunger left. Only entitlement.

Lucas stood in the cathedral light, dust swirling around him in slow motion, and felt like a congregant waiting for judgment.

On his right, Anton's hat stand rose like a totem of absence. Oak, massive, stubborn. It carried coats with the reverence of a shrine. The black wool overcoat still smelled of cigars and winter rain. Lucas could see the faint bulge of a cigar cutter in its pocket. Untouched since Anton's last use. Beside it, the hunter-green field jacket sagged at the elbows where Anton had leaned against Range Rover doors during morning shoots.

Back when hunting still required leaving the house.

Each garment hung in its ordained space, never disturbed. Helena had insisted the arrangement remain exact, calling it "a living memorial." Lucas recognized the truth: she had curated absence as though grief were another performance for society pages.

But more than that—Helena's preservation of Anton's effects revealed something deeper about her connection to him.

This wasn't the devotion of a wife maintaining her husband's memory. This was a mother preserving the legacy she had helped create. The empire she had birthed alongside her son.

Opposite the hat stand, the Brandt crest dominated the archway. Carved in mahogany and inlaid with mother-of-pearl. A shield divided into quarters told the official story: mining tools crossed with rifles, a lion devouring a snake, scales of justice weighed against bags of gold. And, at the center, a crown that had never been earned.

Had always been assumed.

He remembered tracing those lines as a child. Helena explaining their supposed meanings in her lecture voice: tools for honest labor, weapons for protection, the lion for courage, scales for fairness, crown for natural leadership.

All lies. Each more exquisite than the last.

The tools had dug graves as often as mines. The rifles had defended stolen land. The lion hadn't eaten snakes—it had devoured villages, forests, entire cultures in its path. The crown was no gift of nature. It was theft burnished into inevitability.

Lucas's reflection in the polished crest stared back at him. Warped by the convex curve of the shield. For a moment he thought he saw Anton there, faint and overlapping. As though the carving had absorbed more than polish over the years.

He turned away before the illusion could settle.

He moved through the house as though haunting it. Doorways opened on memories rehearsed so often they felt staged. The dining room where Helena had drilled him in etiquette—forks, knives, posture—while Anton explained over soup why certain people deserved their seat at the table.

And others deserved none at all.

The library where Lucas recited poetry while men in suits discussed which communities would be displaced for the next round of extraction. The music room where Helena once insisted he practice piano for guests. Each note another rehearsal in the choreography of civility.

Every room was a classroom.

Every lesson bent toward power.

The hall narrowed into the gallery, its walls lined with portraits like a tribunal of the dead. Military uniforms glinted with medals earned by others. Women draped in pearls strung from profits no obituary had ever mentioned. Their painted eyes tracked him. Centuries of judgment painted in oils. Frozen but unyielding.

Lucas slowed at Anton's official portrait. Commissioned the year he took his seat on the mining board. It showed a man leaner than Lucas remembered. Eyes softened by the artist into something approaching benevolence. His father's hand rested on a stack of legal documents. Sunlight slanting through painted windows onto his face.

At fifteen, Lucas had thought the portrait regal.

At thirty-six, he saw what the artist had disguised: the faint curl of cruelty in the mouth, the calculation veiled as kindness, the predator dressed as patriarch.

He stood beneath it, dust motes orbiting in the chandelier light, and felt the weight of a gaze that even varnish hadn't dimmed. For all the grandeur, the portrait whispered one thing only: this house, this family, was built— not on foundations but on concealments.

The longer Lucas stood beneath the painted tribunal, the more he sensed the house holding its breath. Anton's portrait—varnished into permanence—had always unsettled him. Tonight it pressed harder. As if daring him to question what it concealed.

His gaze snagged on the right-hand edge of the frame. A hairline crack, so fine it could have been an accident of settling plaster. Glimmered in the dim light. Yet once noticed, it was impossible to ignore.

Dust hung in the air like ash after confession.

He reached up, fingers tracing the seam with the tentative care of an archaeologist brushing dirt from a fossil.

The wood gave a fraction more than it should have.

His pulse quickened. Anton had believed in hiding things in plain sight. Counting on spectacle to shield the truth. Of course he'd conceal something behind the family's most public symbol.

Lucas pressed harder. With a low, reluctant groan, the massive frame swung outward on hidden hinges. Its weight balanced by mechanisms buried deep in the wall. The air that escaped smelled faintly metallic. A cold exhalation that had been sealed away for decades.

Behind the portrait gleamed a safe: steel-faced, keypad glowing with quiet insistence.

Six empty squares blinked at him. Patient. Waiting.

He froze, breath shallow. What sequence would Anton have trusted? His father had never been careless. Never sentimental in the way ordinary men chose birth dates or anniversaries. Each possible code swam before him— founding date of Brandt Mining, their wedding anniversary, even Lucas's own birthday.

Each felt too obvious.

Then memory struck with the force of something long buried rising to the surface: Helena's birthday. February 14, 1957. She had called it her "real independence day," reminding him every year that it mattered more than any anniversary or boardroom triumph. Anton had mocked the sentiment at the time. But Lucas remembered the glint in his father's eye—mockery masking respect.

That date had always been sacrosanct in this house. Shaping rituals no one dared break.

Valentine's Day. A cruel irony, or the most deliberate of all ironies. The birthday of the woman who had been Anton's partner in everything—not just marriage, but the entire enterprise of building and maintaining their empire. Helena hadn't just been his wife. She had been his co-architect. The mother of his heir. The one person whose bloodline was inseparable from the family's destiny.

Lucas's fingers hovered over the keypad. He could almost hear Anton's voice: "Legacy isn't what you build, son—it's what survives when the builders are forgotten."

Six digits. A cipher. A dare.

A curse.

He entered them one by one, each beep reverberating like a hammer on steel: 1-4-0-2-5-7.

For a moment nothing happened. Then the lock disengaged with a soft electronic chirp. A sound indecently loud in the museum hush of the gallery.

The door swung open.

Inside, treasures more dangerous than jewels waited.

A leather-bound ledger sat atop a manila envelope. Both positioned with Anton's trademark precision. No stacks of cash, no gold bars, no family heirlooms—just words and images. The currency Anton had always trusted more than metal. Lucas reached in with both hands, bracing for weight. What he felt was heavier than paper: the gravity of accumulated secrets. The mass of decades compressed into objects no larger than a school exercise book.

The ledger smelled faintly of leather polish and ink. Like a church hymnal rewritten for darker worship. Beneath it, the envelope sagged with photographs.

Evidence. Not keepsakes.

Lucas set them on the table beneath the chandelier's fractured light. His hand lingered on the ledger's cover.

Fingertips absorbing the quiet menace of Anton's handwriting embossed into the leather. He hesitated, struck by the intimacy of the moment—his father's secrets in his grasp. The truth offered not by confession.

But by discovery.

He glanced back at the portrait, still swung wide like a door into a vault of hypocrisy. Anton's painted eyes stared at the space his concealment had occupied. As if the artist had known even then what lay behind the smile.

The house around him seemed to retreat into silence. The motion sensors ticked and clicked, registering his stillness. Dust spiraled in the chandelier's colored light. Lucas realized he was standing inside a tableau Anton himself would have admired: the son uncovering the father.

Inheritance stripped of illusion.

His fingers tightened on the ledger.

He opened it.

The handwriting was Anton's—precise, unemotional, familiar from report cards and signed contracts. Each line carried the weight of empire: dates, initials, amounts, notes in shorthand only a participant would decode.

Lucas skimmed the first page, his stomach knotting. Money paid. Favors granted. Silences purchased. It read less like a ledger than like scripture for a church built on complicity.

He set the ledger aside, pulse rising, and reached for the manila envelope. Photographs slid free in a fan across the table. Black-and-white and grainy. Each image another incision into memory. Men in parking garages. Briefcases exchanged like communion wafers. Anton shaking hands with faces Lucas recognized from newsprint obituaries.

Darren. Even Darren. Stepping out of government buildings with a briefcase marked by the same cryptic symbol etched into Anton's other dealings.

The room tilted. Lucas gripped the edge of the table, nausea mixing with rage.

The safe hadn't held valuables.

It had held the truth.

And now the truth was his to bear.

***

The leather creaked as Lucas opened the ledger wide. Pages falling to reveal Anton's handwriting marching in columns—precise, unwavering, a script that had once signed school notes and birthday cards. Now that same hand charted something colder.

Dates lined the left margin. Next to them: names reduced to initials, amounts in tidy figures, and brief annotations that sounded bureaucratic until their true weight registered. Anton had always been exact. The ledger was no different.

Each entry was a blade dressed as a pen stroke.

March 15 – N. Langa – R 2.5 million – Pipeline clearance.

March 22 – D. Mahlangu – R 800,000 – Evidence suppression.

March 29 – T. Sibeko – R 1.2 million – Witness relocation.

April 3 – H. Brandt – R 5 million – Clean-slate protocol.

April 7 – D. Katz – R 1.8 million – Media management.

April 12 – Z. Mokoena – Surveillance/containment – ongoing.

Each line was initialed with Anton's sharp "A.B." Stamped with a small scales symbol—the same justice scales from the family crest. But rendered hollow.

Mocking.

Lucas had seen this mark on offshore banking records and Cyprus shell companies.

He read them twice, his mind refusing to accept what his eyes made plain. This was no business ledger. It was a payroll of silence. A balance sheet of corruption masquerading as administration.

The entry for Zara stopped his breath.

Surveillance/containment—ongoing.

His throat tightened. They had been watching her long before he returned. Long before their lives intersected again. His return had been a trigger, not a cause. He thought of every conversation with her—every café meeting, every late-night call—and wondered how many ears had been listening in the dark.

How many of her sources had already been compromised.

How much of her safety he had gambled by letting her stand near him at all.

And then there was Grace. Another entry, earlier in the ledger, that made his blood freeze: G. Mdluli – Permanent solution – R 750,000 – Executed. The clinical language of murder, documented like any other business expense. Grace hadn't died from her injuries.

She had been executed. And her execution had been budgeted, approved, and filed away in Anton's meticulous records.

And Helena. H. Brandt – R 5 million – Clean-slate protocol. His stomach lurched as if the floor had tilted. Helena, the matriarch who had preached that justice was the only inheritance worth defending. Five million rand to erase the past. Or worse—to erase the people who carried it.

"Clean-slate protocol." The words landed like a sentence.

Lucas closed his eyes, gripping the desk until his knuckles paled. It was one thing to suspect Helena's complicity. Another to see it cataloged in Anton's meticulous hand. The woman who had raised him, shaped him, orchestrated his manners and his morals—written into the ledger as a transaction. A contractor in elimination.

His mother. His flesh and blood. Had been a paid participant in systematic murder.

And Darren. His name leapt from the page like a brand. Media management. R 1.8 million. Suddenly, the photographs in the envelope made sense. Lucas tore it open, spilling the contents across the table.

Grainy shots. Black-and-white. Their compositions accidental but devastating. Men in underground parking garages. Suits cut sharp against fluorescent gloom. Briefcases changing hands with the solemnity of communion.

One frame caught Lucas's breath: Anton beside Johannes Kamp, the mining minister whose "suicide" had been treated as the unfortunate end of a compromised man. In the photo, Kamp extended a hand to receive an envelope. Anton's expression taut with satisfaction.

The timestamp was three weeks before Kamp's death.

Another photo struck deeper: Darren exiting the Union Buildings in Pretoria. Briefcase in hand. Expression grim. Not a boy. Not a friend. An operator.

On the briefcase's corner was the same white sticker. The same hollow scales symbol—the mark of Anton's network. Justice perverted into its opposite.

Lucas staggered back, bile rising. The smile Darren had worn the day Helena caught them at Sandton City—Lucas saw it now for what it was. Not embarrassment at mischief. But the quiet pleasure of a plan unfolding.

How long had Darren been reporting?

How much of their friendship had been surveillance disguised as loyalty? Every confidence shared, every in-joke, every secret confided—what if all of it had been filed away in some report stamped with those scales?

His vision swam. He dropped into a dining chair, photographs spilling around him like shrapnel.

Rage and grief battled in his chest until they felt indistinguishable.

He forced himself back to the ledger. Later pages spread wider arcs of corruption, mapped with Anton's unfailing neatness. Shell companies nested inside others like Russian dolls. Money flowing through jurisdictions the way water finds cracks. Payments to journalists for "editorial alignment." Bribes to regulators disguised as "expedited fees."

Contributions to opposition politicians labeled "strategic diversity."

One section carried the heading Narrative Management. Names of PR firms, think tanks, universities. Each marked with sums designed to purchase scholarship and respectability. Studies were commissioned to praise the industry's "commitment to sustainability." Articles planted to brand protestors as radicals. Donations made to schools that would hang plaques with Anton's name.

Another section was titled Community Outreach. Lucas read the numbers with growing nausea. Payments to traditional leaders. To ward councilors. To municipal officers. Money buying silence, or at least acquiescence, when the bulldozers arrived. Villages had been relocated. Rivers diverted.

Graves disturbed—all smoothed over by signatures purchased in advance.

Then came the final photograph, tucked at the back as though Anton had known its weight. A conference room lit by harsh fluorescents. Around the table sat men Lucas recognized from the Truth and Reconciliation Commission—the very body meant to heal the country. At the head sat Anton. His posture that of a man presiding over inevitability.

Lucas's vision blurred. The TRC—the country's fragile attempt at cleansing its wounds—bent and manipulated by Anton's hand. Testimonies silenced. Evidence buried. Narratives rewritten before they could be spoken. The nation had believed it was reconciling.

Anton had been reconciling the balance sheet.

He sat back, chest hollow, eyes burning. Every hope he'd carried for reform, every belief that the country could heal if only the truth were told—undermined by the evidence in his father's careful script.

The ledger shut with a sound like a coffin lid. Lucas gathered the photographs, hands mechanical, mind numbed. The safe gaped behind Anton's portrait, ready to reclaim its secrets.

But he knew now they could never be hidden again.

Inheritance had always been a chain.

Tonight, he realized it was also a weapon.

***

The photographs lay scattered across the table like evidence before a jury. Their grainy surfaces refusing to be ignored. Lucas sifted through them with hands that no longer felt like his own.

Faces looked back at him—ministers, executives, men he had seen shake hands at board dinners. Men who had smiled at Helena's garden parties. Each caught mid-exchange of envelopes and briefcases. Every gesture a sermon on complicity.

One image held him captive: Anton seated at the head of a fluorescent-lit table. Surrounded by officials Lucas recognized from history books. Commissioners sworn to shepherd a nation through its reckoning. Their role to exhume wounds and allow healing. Yet in the photograph they were co-conspirators. Leaning forward as Anton spoke.

Their expressions were not the faces of truth-seekers.

They were administrators of silence.

Lucas flipped the photo over. Anton's script slanted across the back with surgeon's precision: "Testimony suppression protocols agreed. Commission cooperation secured. Truth contained. Alternative narrative prepared for public consumption."

The words hit him harder than any bribe recorded in the ledger. The TRC—once sacred in his imagination, a promise that the new South Africa would not repeat the old sins—exposed as another stage-managed performance. The nation had gathered to witness contrition. Forgiveness. The fragile possibility of a future not built on denial.

But in parallel rooms, his father had negotiated which testimonies would vanish.

Which stories would never scar the official record.

He pressed his palms against his eyes until white heat burst behind them. The ledger had been damning.

These photographs were annihilation.

When he lowered his hands, the chandelier light fractured the images into shards of color. As if the house itself wanted to disguise what he'd found.

But the truth was indelible now. Stamped into him with the same brutal permanence as Anton's signature.

The past had not been reconciled.

It had been purchased.

***

He carried the ledger and photographs back to the study. Each step heavier than the last. The safe still gaped open behind Anton's portrait, waiting to swallow the evidence again. But Lucas knew there was no going back. Secrets once read could not be unread. They clung like smoke to the lungs.

On the desk, the moth still circled the lamp. Wings translucent now. Exhausted but relentless. Drawn to a light that promised warmth.

And delivered only death.

Lucas sank into the chair, the leather sighing beneath him, and watched it spiral. His inheritance was no longer wealth or name or monument.

It was conscience.

And conscience, he realized, was the most dangerous ledger of all.

Chapter 7 – The Founder's Ledger

Lucas stepped across the threshold. The air thickened. Light knifed through blinds, striping furniture, cutting his shadow into ribs. The scents hit immediately: leather, polish, Anton's cologne lingering—authority disguised as civility.

Anton's desk dominated the room. Too big for practical use, a slab of carved wood better suited to admiration than writing. Its surface gleamed darkly, reflecting only chosen light. Behind it stood the leather chair, empty yet warm with memory. Lucas could almost see his father's shoulders impressed in the cushion—the indentation of command no one else had been permitted to occupy.

He set his palm on the brass knob of the top drawer. Generations of Brandt hands had smoothed it to satin. He let it rest there, unwilling to open it yet, as if touch alone could tell him what lived inside.

The Persian rug muffled his steps. Its intricate pattern was a geometry of discipline. Lucas remembered being told as a boy not to spill anything here. That was the only warning given, but it carried an unspoken threat—a single stain would expose him as careless. Unworthy.

Even then he had known this rug did not merely cover the floor—it measured obedience.

The weight of last night's discoveries pressed against his chest: the gunshot that shattered midnight silence, the security team's choreographed response, the ledger hidden behind Anton's portrait—each revelation peeled another layer. Illusion gave way to anatomy.

Now, returning to this study in daylight, Lucas felt like an archaeologist revisiting a dig site, knowing that each artifact would only deepen the horror of what lay buried.

He moved through the study with careful economy—someone who had learned to obey in order to survive. His fingers trailed the bookshelves. Their spines announced respectability with suspicious loudness: Constitutional Law and Human Rights. The Principles of Governance. Mining in the Modern Economy.

None had cracked spines. The gilding on their titles still shone. He doubted any had been opened past the first page. They existed not to be read but to signal depth, gravitas, legitimacy.

Lucas did not trust surfaces. Men who built empires rarely told the truth at eye level. They hid important things exactly where people expected to look—behind the illusion of civility, between the pages of decorum.

He pulled open the desk drawers, one after another. They slid silently, conditioned by years of rehearsed use. Inside—legal pads in precise stacks, pens aligned like soldiers, a sterling letter opener with a Namibian dealer's crest etched into its blade. Business cards too, bound in leather, names embossed in gold leaf—as if their purpose were not communication but intimidation.

Everything here was immaculate.

Neatness, Lucas knew, is theater. It leaves no fingerprints where they matter.

His eyes moved back to the shelves. He let his fingers brush along the row, reading the weight of each book rather than its title. One felt wrong—not dramatically so, only the subtle imbalance of something that did not belong to the harmony of the shelf.

A single off-note in an otherwise rehearsed chord.

He pulled it free: Mining Law Compendium, 1962. Its cloth cover was faded at the edges, but the weight was uneven—hollow. Lucas felt his throat tighten as he tested it. He smiled without meaning to—a small, brittle thing. The kind a man gives when pantomime masks slip and stage props are revealed.

The book was a vessel. Its pages had been glued together, hollowed, and lined with red felt. Nestled inside, wrapped in oilcloth, was a ledger bound in cracked leather.

Lucas set it on the blotter. His pulse ticked too loudly in his ears. He unwrapped the oilcloth with the care of someone unbinding a wound.

The cover bore his father's handwriting.

Brandt & Co., Engineering and Rail—Ledger of Accounts, 1932–1939.

Below that, in smaller script: For the eyes of family only. History belongs to those brave enough to write it.

Lucas ran a finger across the words. The ink had faded but not weakened. Anton's hand had always been neat, precise—a surgeon's confidence, a banker's calculation. Even here, the script radiated authority.

He opened the book.

At first, it seemed ordinary—lists of bridges, rail lines, waterworks. Contractors' names, costs, timelines. The language of nation-building. Lucas felt a small flare of hope that perhaps this was all—the record of legitimate construction projects, the arithmetic of empire, but not its conscience.

But then, at the edges, the ink shifted tone. Notes appeared in Anton's distinctive shorthand: Mistral Project— dual-use authorization. Transit Route 9—unmarked cargo. The sums beside them dwarfed the legitimate entries.

Each entry ended with a small triangle—Anton's private symbol of righteousness, now recast in Lucas's mind as a brand of guilt.

Lucas turned more pages; the handwriting darkened. Phrases appeared that once had been taught to him as puzzles or jokes—games of code between father and son: Silence buys freedom. Complicity is currency.

He remembered laughing at them—the way children laugh when adults let them glimpse the world of secrecy. But now, translated by context, they were doctrine.

Another turn. Infrastructure blurred into influence. Legitimate projects became shells for transactions that pointed elsewhere. Accounts opened in neutral jurisdictions. Numbers that weren't numbers—codes. Offices that had never existed hosted rivers of capital.

Names he had known surfaced in black ink: Malan, Du Plessis, Naidoo. Men who had attended dinners, patted him on the head, called him promising. He saw them now as shareholders in silence.

The ledger did not confess—it instructed.

It was a manual on how to make a country bend while convincing its citizens they still stood upright.

Lucas sat back, his hands trembling. His father had not merely profited from the country. He had bought the language that made profit lawful. Each entry was another mortgage of trust, another reputation traded like a commodity.

At the back lay a later note, the ink darker: The vault isn't a diary. It's a loaded weapon. Use it well—or it will turn on you.

Tucked behind the cover, a photograph—two men standing before a low compound ringed in razor wire. Anton, younger, in a posture that read like permission. The other in fatigues, his insignia deliberately blurred. Heavy machinery crouched in the background like waiting predators.

On the reverse, five words in Anton's hand: We built what they couldn't control.

Lucas stared at the photo until the edges blurred. The room seemed to tilt around him, its order rearranging itself into accusation. The rug beneath him no longer muffled footsteps—it recorded them. The shelves no longer signaled respectability—they threatened silence.

He rewrapped the ledger in its oilcloth. The fabric rasped beneath his fingers like bandages binding a wound too dangerous to expose. The book was heavier now, though no weight had changed. It carried the mass of understanding—of lineage clarified into weapon.

The study's calm deepened. Lucas sat with the ledger pressed against his knees, the words of his father's doctrine echoing louder than any memory:

Legitimacy   buys   time.
Silence   buys   freedom.
Complicity buys influence.

And for the first time in years, Lucas felt the cold realization—inheritance was not about bloodlines or wills. It was about carrying forward structures built to outlast the men who made them.

***

The door clicked against its frame, soft as breath. Lucas looked up, startled, though he had half expected her. Zara stepped into the study without hesitation—the kind of entrance that suggested she had already decided the room owed her answers.

Her boots made little sound on the Persian rug, but her presence was weight enough. She carried herself differently in spaces like this—shoulders square, gaze sharp—the air of a woman who had walked through too many corridors of power to be awed by one more.

Still, her eyes moved quickly across the room, taking in the polished desk, the shelves of unread books, the faint authority that clung to air like smoke.

"How did you get past security?" Lucas asked, though part of him already knew the answer. After weeks of surveillance and that warning gunshot, no one should have been able to simply walk onto the estate.

Zara's expression was grim. "The same way I always have—through the service entrance. Your mother gave me the code years ago, when Grace was still alive and feeding me information. Helena wanted insurance, someone who could get close to the story if things went wrong."

The words hit Lucas like a physical blow. Helena had been playing a longer game than he'd imagined, positioning pieces on the board with the same methodical precision Anton had used. Zara hadn't just stumbled into this story— she'd been guided into it. Shaped into a weapon Helena could deploy when the time was right.

"Insurance." Lucas tasted the word—bitter, inevitable. "Insurance against what?"

"Against the possibility that the truth might actually matter," Zara said. She moved closer to the desk, her gaze falling on the oilcloth bundle in his hands. "Helena knew Grace was getting too close. She knew someone would have to clean up the mess. She just never expected that someone to be you."

Her eyes fixed on the oilcloth in Lucas's hands. She didn't ask what it was. She didn't need to.

"Not a cache," she said at last, voice level, eyes on the object. "An archive."

Lucas exhaled. The word pressed into him like a key turning in a lock. "You already knew it would be something like this."

"I guessed," Zara said. She moved closer, studying the oilcloth with surgical care. "Anton Brandt wasn't the kind of man who relied on memory. He cataloged. He curated. He built systems."

Lucas unwrapped the ledger and let her see. She leaned over the desk, her fingers hovering but never touching—as though proximity was dangerous enough. She read quickly, lips tightening as the coded phrases revealed themselves.

Legitimacy buys time. She repeated the words under her breath, as if tasting them. Silence buys freedom. Her mouth pressed into a hard line.

"It reads like scripture."

Lucas swallowed. "That's what I thought. Except scripture pretends to be for salvation. This is doctrine for control."

Zara's hand hovered closer, not touching, but as if steadying the page. "Scripture is just a manual for power. Anton was honest about that much."

He flipped farther into the ledger, showing her the entries where names appeared—familiar men recast as conspirators: Malan, Du Plessis, Naidoo. She absorbed them with her usual calm, her journalist's mind already sketching networks, cross-referencing possibilities.

Lucas wanted her to be outraged—to break the silence with anger that matched his own. Instead she was clinical, calculating. Her eyes moved with precision across the handwriting, extracting structure from rot.

"You thought this was about inheritance," she said finally, looking at him, not the ledger. "It's about architecture. Your father didn't just build an empire. He built a framework anyone could inhabit. He made sure corruption was modular—replaceable parts, permanent design."

Lucas felt the words cut. "And now it's mine to carry."

"No."

Zara's voice was sharper than he expected. "Don't mistake blood for ownership. You're not condemned to wear this."

He blinked. "But it's in my hands now. His handwriting, his instructions, the doctrine…"

"It's evidence," Zara interrupted. "Evidence doesn't belong to heirs. It belongs to the world it describes. You're holding a blueprint for systemic capture, not a family heirloom."

The ledger weighed heavier in his lap. Her words made sense, but the conditioning of childhood was stubborn. The Brandt name was a cage built from expectations, its bars polished by legitimacy.

He ran his fingers over the photo tucked at the back— Anton younger, standing with blurred soldiers and blurred machinery. "He even left images," Lucas said softly. "Visuals to match the ledger. He wanted posterity to see what he built."

"No."

Zara corrected him. "He wanted posterity to admire what he built. That's why he called it history. That's why he wrote, for the eyes of family only. But you and I both know—history isn't family property. It's public record waiting to be claimed."

Her words steadied him in a way outrage never could. He had expected her to recoil, to accuse, to cast him in the same shadow as his father. Instead she turned the ledger into what it was—not a Brandt relic, but a map.

Lucas closed the ledger, his hand trembling. "If this is architecture, then the foundations are still here. This house, this study, the vault he hinted at—"

"—is the rest of the blueprint," Zara finished. Her eyes were already moving across the shelves, cataloging possibilities. "The ledger is metadata—a preface. The vault is the full manuscript."

Lucas looked at her, startled. "You're talking like he designed this to be found."

"Maybe he did. Or maybe he designed it to be hidden in plain sight. Either way, the act of recording means he believed in control through knowledge. And control leaves residue."

Lucas almost laughed, though there was no humor in it. "You make it sound inevitable. As if we were always going to stand here, reading this."

"Not inevitable," she said, voice steady. "But predictable. Men like Anton don't build empires without planning for succession. You were meant to inherit the façade. He left the archive in case anyone ever needed the instructions."

Lucas sat heavily in the leather chair behind the desk. It sighed beneath his weight, exhaling old air. He pressed his palm against the blotter, feeling the indentations left by years of Anton's handwriting.

He hated that even paper could remember.

Zara circled the room slowly, her journalist's gaze cataloging props—the books, the polished wood, the curated impression of gravitas. She stopped at the blinds, parted them with two fingers, and glanced out at the estate. Floodlights illuminated the fever trees in the distance, their shadows long and skeletal against the wall.

"Rooms like this exist everywhere," she said. "Pretending to be about governance, about stability. But really they're mausoleums of power."

Lucas lifted the ledger. "Then this is the corpse."

"No."

Zara turned back to him. "This is the autopsy."

Her words landed with surgical precision. For a long moment, neither of them spoke. The study's silence pressed in—no longer patient but expectant.

Finally, Lucas asked, "So what do we do with it?"

Zara's expression hardened into something resolute. "We decide whether to treat it as a wound to bind, or a weapon to fire. But not here. Not yet. Helena knows I'm here—she's probably been tracking my movements since the moment I set foot on the estate. We need to move this conversation somewhere she can't monitor."

Lucas nodded, though the weight of the oilcloth felt immovable. He realized he had been waiting for her verdict—not because he needed permission, but because he needed to hear the ledger named for what it was.

Not inheritance. Not confession.

Architecture.

And now that it had been named, he knew he could not unknow it.

***

Lucas rose from the desk as if pulled by gravity older than choice. The ledger sat wrapped on the blotter, heavier than anything its size had a right to be. He crossed to the shelves on the far wall, his steps measured, the rug swallowing their sound.

"This one," he murmured. His fingers traced the spines until they found the groove. Muscle memory, learned as a boy, surfaced unbidden—the way Anton had forbidden him to touch these shelves, the sharper-than-necessary reprimand, the fear that came from realizing some rules mattered more than others.

He pressed: a click, a sigh. The shelf yielded with the slowness of something that had waited too long to be moved. Hinges whispered. Dust lifted in a faint breath as the case slid inward, revealing a narrow stair spiraling into cool darkness.

The air that drifted up was different—not the stale perfume of memory that filled the study, but something filtered, mechanical—like air scrubbed of history itself.

Zara stepped beside him, her face unreadable in the half-light. "So it wasn't just ledger entries. He built a catacomb under the mausoleum."

Lucas swallowed. "He called it a vault. Said it wasn't a diary. Said it was a weapon."

The word weapon lodged in the air, heavy and metallic.

They stood at the threshold, listening. The stairwell breathed. Somewhere below, machines hummed with patient regularity, each note too precise to be mistaken for chance.

Lucas descended two steps.

Concrete walls glistened faintly, paint sealed to gloss.

The sound ricocheted back, magnified—as if the stairwell wanted to remind him: trespassing.

He stopped.

Below, in the dim, he could just make out the outlines—filing cabinets lined in military rows, server racks glowing with pinprick LEDs, the faint geometry of a wall crowded with paper and photographs. Threads stretched between them like veins across a body. It looked less like storage than like a circulatory system—something alive, even in stillness.

Zara's breath caught, soft but audible. "This isn't storage," she whispered. "It's an archive."

Lucas knew she was right. He felt it in the back of his teeth, in the marrow of his bones. The ledger upstairs had been preface.

This was the manuscript.

He placed his hand on the nearest rail. The metal was cold, clinical, as though it had been designed to resist any warmth. He imagined drawers filled with names, transactions, deaths disguised as accidents. He imagined photographs pinned in assemblies, maps marked with pushpins, audio files humming with his father's voice.

His stomach turned. Every instinct screamed to move forward, to seize what lay below, to know—and yet another voice whispered just as urgently: Not tonight. Not yet.

He felt Zara's eyes on him, steady, waiting.

"This is what he wanted me to inherit," Lucas said. His voice shook in the hollow shaft. "Not the estate. Not the company. This. A cathedral to secrecy."

Zara's tone was sharper than the air. "And what you inherit, you can also refuse."

The words struck, clean as glass. He turned toward her. "You think it's that simple?"

"I think nothing about this is simple," she said. Her gaze stayed fixed on the dark below. "But I know this: archives are only dangerous when they're unacknowledged. Once you decide to see them, they lose their ability to haunt. The question isn't whether you open it—it's when."

Lucas stared down into the half-lit space. The temptation was strong, like leaning over a precipice that invited him to fall. But falling now would mean never climbing back. Never pausing to breathe before the plunge.

"Helena will know we've been here," he said. "The security system will have logged our access to this room, the time we've spent here. If she's monitoring the estate as closely as you suggest, she'll know we've found something."

Zara nodded grimly. "Which means our window for action is closing. She'll move to contain this before we can expose it. The longer we wait, the more dangerous this becomes—not just for us, but for anyone else who might know pieces of the truth."

He thought of Grace Mdluli, murdered for exactly this kind of knowledge. Of the gunshot in the night, the security teams that served masters other than him. Of Helena's patient manipulation, stretching back years, positioning him as the unwitting heir to a throne built on corpses.

He stepped back. The stair creaked under his retreat.

"Not tonight," he said, louder this time, as if the room needed to hear it. "But soon. Tomorrow. We need to document everything before she can destroy it."

Zara looked at him, searching his face. Then she nodded once. Not relief, not agreement—just acknowledgment.

They closed the shelf. The hinges groaned softly, then the bookcase clicked back into place, sealing the stairwell. The study resumed its familiar stillness: leather, polish, dust.

But the silence was altered, charged. It knew what lay beneath.

So did they.

Lucas picked up the ledger again. The oilcloth rasped against his palm. The words inside pulsed like a heartbeat he couldn't silence.

For years he had believed inheritance was a chain, a set of expectations binding him to his father's will. Now, standing in the room that pretended to be permanence while hiding a vault of corruption beneath, he felt something shift. Inheritance was no longer a weight dragging him backward.

It was a summons, urgent and unavoidable.

The study pressed in around him, portraits watching from the walls. Anton's eyes, captured in oils, seemed almost amused. Lucas stared back.

For the first time, he did not flinch.

But as they moved toward the door, the faint vibration of his phone broke the silence. A text message, sender unknown: Your guests have overstayed their welcome. Some invitations cannot be withdrawn.

Lucas showed the screen to Zara. Her face went pale.

"Helena," she whispered.

A beat.

"She knows exactly what we've found."

Chapter 8 – House on Fire

This was not the intimate townhouse gathering Darren had staged weeks earlier. It was spectacle. He'd brought it to the Sandton penthouse—one more set in his portfolio of homes.

The lift opened on marble polished so fiercely it held the city upside down. Chandeliers hung like captured constellations, each prism splitting light into marketable brilliance. Beyond the glass, Johannesburg spread fifty floors below—arteries of sodium gold, tower lights blinking red like instruments left running.

Electric fences sparkled along suburban edges, and two hundred guests drifted through the rooms like managed currents. Ministers in tuxedos, heirs with watches heavier than municipal budgets. A judge the newspapers still called independent, laughing too loudly at a donor's joke. The arrivals corridor was a gullet of flashbulbs—photographers shoulder to shoulder, catching the manicured handshake, the practiced pause.

Screens the size of cinema walls cycled Darren's slogans in sharp white type: *Building Tomorrow. Resilience. Integrity.* Below them, hashtags rolled like river chorus, curated to look spontaneous.

Theater pretending to be politics.

Champagne moved through the crowd like infantry. Canapés were engineered to be elegant but forgettable. A jazz quartet played with all the dissonance shaved off. The skyline was backdrop, the guests were cast, and Darren— somewhere near the dais—was the director who insisted on starring in his own production.

Lucas stood at the window and let the city's reflection cross his face. A flute of champagne in his hand.

Untouched.

He was here because absence, in this world, was guilt. Darren understood the moral economy of missing chairs. He could weaponize a refusal better than most men could weaponize a speech. The weight of the past week pressed against his consciousness like a physical burden.

Seven days since Anton's funeral had set everything in motion.

Seven days since he'd first discovered the key that led him to the ledger, to the safe behind Anton's portrait, to the vault beneath the study. In that compressed timeframe, his entire understanding had been destroyed and rebuilt. Family. Inheritance. Identity.

Zara appeared at his shoulder in the reflection. Her dress black, simple—a line drawn through indulgence. Among sequins and silk she looked like intent in human form. Precise. Unornamented. Built to move quickly if the floor collapsed. She didn't turn her head.

"Grace's documents went live twenty minutes ago," she said.

The words landed inside him like a key clicking into place. He lowered the glass to the sill.

"Which set?"

"Nkomazi. Customs. Offshore accounts. The lot." Her gaze scanned the crowd, exits measured with animal reflex. "It wasn't one of ours. But it's everywhere now. Mirrors, torrents, overseas desks waking up."

No way back.

Lucas thought of Grace Mdluli, murdered six months ago for exactly these documents. He pictured her in what must have been a cramped hospital room, knowing they were coming for her, knowing her death had been ordered and budgeted like any other corporate expense. All at once or not at all. Whole truth, or the system would bleed it slow and call the stain an accident.

"She died for this," he said quietly.

"And now her death means something." Zara's voice was steady steel. "If there's still a cost, it lands on people like us."

A waiter passed with oysters balanced on ice. Somewhere laughter spiked into a shriek before falling back—one sound masquerading as the other. Outside, the jazz quartet counted time while the city below kept the brutal beat of sirens and late-night freight.

Darren was three rooms away. Hand resting on a minister's shoulder, his face turned toward a lens. He had perfected the candid angle: within fifteen degrees of any camera, his jaw could read as sorrow or determination, depending on the headline.

Even relaxed, he radiated readiness.

Lucas's skin prickled. Beneath the polish, the building had a pulse. Air systems thudding somewhere in the bone. Elevators climbing like thoughts. Shutters folded invisibly above doors that could close at command.

The penthouse was a body with nerves. Darren was the brain.

Lucas raised his chin, scanning. Not drinking. The truth had already escaped into the night.

Now he waited for the response.

***

The first warning was so subtle that Lucas almost ignored it: a thin, whistling note under the polite thrum of jazz and glass.

It threaded through the room like a filament stretched to breaking.

The alarm descended—sudden, absolute. A blade of sound. Chandeliers trembled on their chains, scattering frantic light. Red strobes burst from the crown molding, flattening faces into masks.

The building's voice overrode all others—contralto, without urgency but with terrifying certainty:

Please evacuate the building in an orderly fashion. Please use the nearest stairwell. Do not use the elevators.

For three seconds, the party pretended nothing happened.

Geometry collapsed.

Conversations broke. Bodies turned. The crowd surged.

Lucas gripped the sill, steadying himself. This wasn't random. Grace's documents had just been detonated across the internet, and whoever had triggered the alarm meant for it to bleed into panic. The timing was too perfect. Someone had been watching. Waiting for exactly this moment.

Zara's hand found his sleeve. Her lips barely moved. "Service stairwell. Behind the kitchen. Back corner."

He nodded.

The quartet had stopped playing—bows lay across music stands like picked bones. Anchors who had been filming intros now shouted into live feeds, their microphones swallowing the alarm and spitting it back as breaking news. Cameramen wrestled with tripods, abandoning etiquette for survival.

On the dais, Darren appeared with a cordless mic. His smile too wide for the emergency strobes. His voice cut clean through the noise, polished by the sound into certainty.

"Ladies and gentlemen, remain calm." He lifted his hand, palm down—the gesture as effective as the voice. "This is a coordinated harassment campaign. They think chaos substitutes for evidence."

He angled himself to the cameras, offering the half profile vetted by focus groups.

Instruction, disguised as poise.

"You are safe here."

Less a man than an instruction manual for how to look unafraid.

The floor shuddered. Not dramatically—just enough that the chandeliers clicked like ice shifting on a lake. Somewhere below, a door surrendered to a breaching charge. The tremor translated up the walls, a concussion disguised as architecture.

Zara's voice brushed his ear: "They're not here for the guests."

Lucas didn't argue. He already had the map of the building in his head from childhood parties, back when the penthouse still belonged to Darren's family. He knew where staff corridors split from guest routes, where stairwells hid behind unmarked doors. He tugged Zara with him, moving through the churn of sequins and tuxedos.

They passed a woman in diamonds jabbing at her phone, her fingers trembling too badly to dial. A junior minister's security detail shoved ineffectually against the tide—realizing they were the wrong kind of protection for this kind of night.

A man in evening shoes fell. Cufflink spinning across marble before being swallowed by the crush.

The kitchen was a furnace of abandoned heat. Trays of lamb chops congealed under silver domes. A chef's knife lay mid-sentence on a chopping board. The service door yielded under Lucas's palm. He pushed it open to a corridor of concrete painted with gloss that reflected the red of the alarms.

The stairwell yawned before them.

Narrow. Echoing. Each step a swallowed breath.

"Long way down," Lucas said, his breath already sharpening.

Zara stripped off her heels. Carried them in one hand like weapons. Her bare feet whispered against the concrete as they began to descend.

By the twenty-first, they overtook a knot of waitstaff huddled together, clutching each other's jackets as though fabric might stand between them and fate.

One raised terrified eyes at Lucas. Silently asking: fire or war?

He didn't answer. The truth had no meaning here.

Eighteenth.

The stairwell thickened with bodies. Guests clung to railings, gasping, their gowns and tuxedos wilting under the heat. A man slipped, tumbling three steps before catching himself—his cuff stained with blood where he had skinned his palm. Someone prayed in Sesotho. Another cursed in Afrikaans.

Zara kept their pace steady. Weaving through the press. Her hand hovering just behind Lucas's shoulder—not touching, but magnetic.

By the fifteenth, voices bled into the stairwell: clipped commands over radios, codes and numbers that spoke of weapons being checked.

The tactical teams were already inside.

"They're coming up," Lucas whispered.

"Then we go faster," Zara said. Her tone stripped of panic. She was calm in the way only people who had run before could be.

They pushed harder. Lungs scraping. Sweat slicked Lucas's collar. His hand brushed the wall, leaving a dark smear that looked like a signature.

The tenth floor: a sobbing child pressed into her mother's sequined shoulder. The mascara on the woman's face cut rivers down her powdered skin. Lucas met her eyes for a moment and saw not complicity, not politics, but a human being who had been dragged into Darren's theater.

He kept moving.

On the eighth floor the stairwell door burst open. Hinges screaming as boots hammered downward—an avalanche of discipline.

"Garage," Lucas gasped. "Visitor section."

Zara's jaw tightened. She adjusted her grip on her shoes, as if she might need them as blades.

***

Fluorescent tubes hummed overhead. The air reeked of oil and rubber, old water pooled in corners. Zara's Honda Civic waited in a visitor bay—so ordinary it looked almost invisible beside the polished SUVs.

She had the keys in hand before he could speak.

The engine coughed, then roared alive. Headlights cut the concrete.

"Move!" she snapped.

They dived in. The car jerked forward as the stairwell door clanged open behind them. Voices spilled out, sharp with authority, followed by the metallic clatter of rifles.

The Civic shot between rows of sedans. Tires screamed as Zara wrenched it into a turn.

The exit ramp corkscrewed upward.

Headlights appeared in the rear mirror.

Two. Four. Six.

Moving with precision.

"They're organized," Lucas said, twisting to look.

"They're paid to be." Zara's knuckles blanched against the wheel.

At the top of the ramp, the barrier stood lowered. For an instant Lucas thought she would stop.

Instead, Zara pressed harder.

The Civic hit the bar with a crack. Splinters scattering. They burst onto Sandton's streets—neon lights glaring, music spilling from rooftop bars. Pedestrians froze at the sight of a battered Honda pursued by a convoy of headlights moving without sirens.

Without pretense.

Zara took the first corner too hard. Hubcap sparking against the curb. Lucas braced against the dash, lungs burning.

"Left," he gasped. "Two blocks, then service road behind the medical center. We can lose them in the lanes."

She obeyed. The Civic skimming past parked cars, mirrors barely clearing. The headlights followed— unwavering, disciplined, moving in intervals like choreography.

No sirens. No announcements.

Just pursuit.

Lucas stared into the mirror. He could already hear what those lights meant, even if no one had said it aloud:

We are here. We know where you're going. You cannot outrun us forever.

But for tonight, they kept moving.

***

The Civic rattled into silence beneath the fever trees of the Brandt estate. Gravel cracked like bones under the tires. Floodlights cut the house into hard relief—every brass fitting polished until it reflected starlight.

Lucas sat forward in his seat, breath still raw from the chase. The ledger pressed against his ribs like contraband. They had only glimpsed the vault the night before, and already it had gnawed at him, whispering through every moment of Darren's theater, every second of the stairwell descent.

Tonight there was no more postponing.

Zara killed the engine. The cooling tick of metal was the only sound for a moment, until the estate's insects claimed the silence.

"Are we safe here?" she asked.

"Safe enough," Lucas said, though the words tasted like a lie. Helena's surveillance systems would have logged their arrival, cataloged their approach, fed data to whoever was monitoring the estate. But the vault called to him with an urgency that overrode caution.

They crossed the lawn in shadow. They slipped past the main entrance to the service door hidden beneath the third flagstone. Lucas pressed, felt the stone shift.

The key was still there.

Some rituals of this house outlasted reason.

The mudroom exhaled polish and dust. Rows of boots lined the wall, leather gleaming in disciplined order. Coats hung stiff on hooks. Portraits watched from the corridor, eyes painted to follow.

Zara's gaze flicked to one of the oil paintings. "Your family?"

"Three generations," Lucas said. His voice echoed faintly in the hush. "But Helena turned it into a fortress after she married into it. She didn't want a home. She wanted something that couldn't be erased."

"It feels like a mausoleum now," Zara murmured.

He didn't argue. She was right. Helena had spent years curating the house like a monument to Brandt power. Every detail calculated to project permanence and authority. It was the work of someone who understood that symbols mattered as much as substance.

Perception could be as valuable as truth.

They reached Anton's study. The air was thicker here—the scent of leather and whiskey clinging like an old verdict. Lucas crossed to the shelves. His fingers found the hidden catch.

The bookcase sighed inward.

The stair yawned open.

This time they did not stop at the threshold.

The stairwell swallowed them, concrete sweating under the pulse of alarms still faint from the city. The air was dry, filtered, stripped of time.

They descended into the belly of inheritance.

The vault greeted them with cold light. LED strips flickered alive one by one, revealing the full extent of what had only been hinted at before.

The space was vast, carved from stone with paranoid precision. Filing cabinets marched along the walls in ordered regiments.

Server racks hummed, lights blinking like patient heart monitors.

And dominating the far wall: the evidence board. Photographs, maps, contracts pinned in compilations. Strings stretched between them like veins, connecting power to profit, influence to violence. At the center hung Anton's portrait, a faint smile playing on his lips—as though he had orchestrated even this unveiling.

Zara froze at the threshold. Her phone already in her hand.

"This isn't a cellar," she said softly. "It's a command center."

Lucas felt the truth of it lodge in his chest.

The house above had been mask. This was the face.

***

134

Lucas crossed to the central desk. The computer sat dormant but not dead. He slid Anton's fountain pen aside and inserted the Cypress drive he had carried like a stone.

The machine awoke with a cheerful chime. Grotesquely out of place.

Folders populated the screen in sober rows: *Consulting Fees. Transport Support. Clean Slate Protocols.*

Zara leaned over his shoulder, breath sharp. "My goodness."

Lucas opened *Consulting Fees.* Spreadsheets bloomed, line after line of transactions. Euphemisms for bribery disguised as scholarships, road maintenance, education funds. Ministers' names coded as alumni references. Money balanced to the cent. Moral rot disguised as symmetry.

He clicked *Transport Support.* Shipping manifests masqueraded as medical cargo. Serial numbers that, cross-referenced, belonged to surveillance equipment and worse. Photographs of containers moving unchallenged through customs—inspectors' faces ghosted in the margins, deliberately looking away.

Zara filmed in bursts. Steady. Controlled. "Scope first," she muttered. "Then examples. Don't drown in detail."

He opened *Clean Slate Protocols.*

His stomach tightened.

Flowcharts described the choreography of elimination: isolate, discredit, remove. Media playbooks. Prosecutorial missteps engineered to sink cases without fingerprints. Travel incidents arranged in jurisdictions with weak forensics.

Then the grid of profiles appeared. Each name tagged green, amber, or red.

Lucas scrolled until he saw it.

G. MDLULI, GRACE—Status: TERMINATED. Authorization: H. BRANDT. Fee: R750,000. Method: Hospital intervention. Cover: Natural complications.

The cursor blinked.

Notes, clinical: Subject refused final offer. Media risk unacceptable. Permanent resolution implemented per Clean

Slate Protocol 7. Timeline: 72 hours post-authorization. Status confirmed: 15:47, March 12.

Lucas whispered the words aloud.

The room contracted around them.

Zara filmed, her jaw tight. She didn't speak Grace's name, but Lucas heard it in the silence. They had the proof now—not just that Grace was murdered, but that Helena had personally authorized it. Paid for it. Supervised its execution.

"Helena's signature," Lucas said. "My mother ordered Grace's death like she was ordering catering for a board meeting."

He clicked away and opened the folder marked *Audio*. A private dining room appeared on screen. White tablecloths, curtains softening sound.

Anton's voice filled the speakers. Calm. Deliberate.

"The transition must be seamless. Lucas has qualities we can use. He believes himself moral, and that belief can be harnessed."

A second voice, deferential: "And if he objects?"

Anton's reply was mild, almost amused: "Then Helena will handle him like any other problem. She has the stomach for necessary corrections that I sometimes lack."

A third voice—unmistakably Helena's—cut through the recording with surgical precision:

"Lucas is my son. My blood runs in his veins. That gives me certain advantages in managing his idealism."

Lucas shut the file.

The words cut deeper than any ledger. His biological mother, the woman who had shaped him from birth, discussing his potential elimination with the same clinical detachment she'd brought to Grace's murder.

Zara touched his shoulder. Lightly. Not comfort, but brace. "You wanted to know why the vault mattered. Now you do."

He nodded. He could barely breathe.

They moved faster now. Draft contingency statements prepared for ministers, executives, family. All written in advance, blanks left for dates. *This is the act of a rogue element. We are shocked and dismayed.* The language of denial rehearsed before the crimes had even been committed.

Lucas's hands shook. "They had scripts ready for every lie."

"Every empire does," Zara said. "They just rarely write them down this cleanly."

He searched for a mirror. A folder lit: *Mirror – Offsite.* Endpoints listed across jurisdictions.

Keys waiting.

Of course Anton had redundancy. Of course he had built for survival.

Lucas began bundling directories: Cypress-A, Cypress-B, Cypress-C. Progress bars crawled. Zara toggled her phone to secure channels, uploading through encrypted tunnels, seeding copies across borders where injunctions arrived too slowly to matter.

"Legal risk?" Lucas asked—the phrase absurd in the vault's stale air.

"Total," Zara said. "But speed is protection. If it's everywhere, they can't stop it without shutting down the world."

When the first bar ticked complete, Lucas felt his chest tighten.

Not relief, but finality.

Choice narrowed into a single line. He was walking it.

He typed the statement Zara demanded:

I am releasing these materials because the story of my family cannot be allowed to stand in for the story of a country. This is evidence of a system that took public courage and converted it into private wealth. My mother authorized the murder of Grace Mdluli for trying to expose these crimes. If I am part of that system by accident of birth, then my only act is to make the evidence public. Decide for yourselves what these files show. Do not let anyone decide it for you.

He hated the last sentence. It read like a slogan.

But sometimes the slogan was true.

Zara skimmed, changed nothing, and hit send.

The progress bars climbed. The servers blinked faster—a second heartbeat filling the vault.

Lucas stood, unable to sit any longer. He crossed to the evidence wall, eyes raking over photographs: ministers, generals, CEOs, Darren with his hand possessively on Anton's shoulder. Every face a node in the web. Every smile a transaction.

"Once it's everywhere," he said, voice low, "this house becomes a museum."

"It already was," Zara said. "We just turned on the lights."

The fans whirred. The mirrors seeded. The vault hummed like a living thing.

Lucas pressed his palm against the glass of a high window. Outside, the sky had begun to pale—the first bruising of dawn over Johannesburg. The city was waking, and with it, the reckoning his father had never believed possible; his mother would wake to something worse.

She would discover that her greatest weapon had turned against her—truth, carried by her son, aimed back at its maker.

By dawn, the paper's site would be offline, the first injunction served before they even woke.

Conscience was the only ledger that couldn't be balanced.

Chapter 9 – Choreography of Shadows

The safe house exhaled instant coffee and the molecular weight of exhaustion; scents had settled into cheap furniture like testimony from sleepless nights.

Lucas sat at a folding table, watching news feeds multiply across Zara's laptop screens, viral replication in pixels and bandwidth. The vault data had been live for two days now. Sixty-seven countries. Fourteen languages. Mirrors spawning faster than Darren's people could kill them.

But the choreography had already begun.

Helena stood in the Brandt Foundation's atrium, flanked by scholarship recipients whose faces had been selected for maximum redemptive impact. She wore charcoal gray—the color of penitence seasoned with authority—and spoke in measured cadences that transformed confession into resurrection. Light fell through the glass ceiling like a benediction designed by committee.

"The documents released by my son," she said, voice carrying the weight of maternal disappointment married to institutional responsibility, "represent a profound failure."

The reflex rose—throw, break, bleed—then died in his throat.

"Not just of oversight," Helena continued her eyes finding the camera with the directness of someone who understood that the nation was watching her choose between family and duty. "But of the very systems we trusted to safeguard our democracy's transition."

The journalist—handpicked, he was certain—nodded with the grave poise of discovery staged as live.

"Lucas has always been troubled by the moral compromises necessary for systemic change." Helena's pause was perfectly calibrated. "His father's death... it affected him deeply. These documents represent his pain more than they represent policy."

Lucas felt Zara's hand on his shoulder. The warmth traveled through fabric and bone.

"She's good," Zara said quietly. "Better than good. She's turning your revolt into pathology."

On-screen, Helena fielded questions with the practiced grace of someone who had spent decades converting crisis into opportunity. She acknowledged "administrative failures" while promising "comprehensive reform." She spoke of "healing" and "accountability" in ways that made both concepts sound like items on a foundation budget.

"You're saying your son's allegations stem from grief rather than evidence?"

"I'm saying my son needs help." Helena's voice carried the authentic crack of a mother watching her child disappear into dangerous delusion. "Professional help. The kind of care we should have provided months ago."

The broadcast cut to analysis—three talking heads in a studio designed to suggest impartial deliberation began the process of converting Lucas's evidence into Lucas's breakdown.

"Turn it off," Lucas said.

"We need to see what we're fighting." But Zara's finger was already reaching for the power button.

Black screens. The room exhaled. The safe house returned to the sound of traffic three floors below, and servers humming in the next room, still seeding truth into a digital ecosystem that Helena was learning to poison in real time.

Lucas stood, walked to the narrow window overlooking a Johannesburg street he didn't recognize. Twelve years in London and he'd forgotten how the city looked when you couldn't afford to see it from the twenty-seventh floor. Down there, people moved with a purposeful rhythm of lives too busy for political theater—jobs, children, rent, realities that made the Brandt family saga feel like entertainment for people with the luxury of abstract moral concern.

"How long before they find us?" he asked.

"Here? Maybe a day." Zara's fingers moved across keys with the mechanical persistence of someone who knew stopping meant dying. "Maybe less if Darren's people are as good as everyone says they are. But we're not trying to hide forever. We're trying to stay alive long enough for the truth to take root."

"And if it doesn't?"

Zara's typing paused. "Then we become a footnote in someone else's story about how democracy died quietly while everyone was looking the other way."

Lucas turned from the window. On the folding table, documents formed neat stacks—bank records, shipping manifests, the photographed pages from Anton's vault that proved Helena had personally authorized Grace Mdluli's murder. Evidence that would have ended careers and toppled governments in a country where evidence still mattered.

But this wasn't that country. They were in South Africa, where truth was just another resource to be extracted, refined, and sold to the highest bidder.

His phone buzzed. Unknown number.

"My boy." Helena's voice, velvet threaded with command, through the receiver like smoke shaping itself into reason. "This has gone far enough."

"Has it?" Lucas kept his voice flat, but his free hand found the edge of the table and gripped until his knuckles went white. "Feels like it's just getting started."

"You're hurting yourself more than you're hurting us," Helena said, and the pronoun hung in the air like a blade: Us. The family that had decided he was no longer part of it. "The media is already losing interest. Tomorrow there will be another crisis, another scandal. By next week, people will barely remember your name."

"They'll remember Grace's."

"Grace Mdluli was a sad woman who died of a heart attack," Helena said with the finality of someone editing history in real time. "The suggestion that anyone in this family would harm her is... well, it's the kind of thing people say when grief makes them forget the difference between guilt and conspiracy."

Lucas looked at Zara, who had stopped typing and was listening with the expression of someone watching a master class in psychological warfare.

"I have the documents," Lucas said. "Your signature. Your authorization codes. The clinical notes that prove—"

"You have photographs," she paused, "of papers anyone could print between lies." Helena's interruption was surgical. "Documents without chain of custody. Evidence without verification. The kind of material that desperate people fabricate when they want to believe their delusions are reality."

She was right, and they both knew it. Truth wasn't what you proved; it was what you made people believe. And Helena had spent forty years learning how to make people believe exactly what served her purposes.

"Come home," she continued, her voice softening into the register she'd used when he was small and afraid of the dark. "Let us get you the help you need. The country will forgive you. I will forgive you. But only if you stop this now, before it becomes something we can't repair."

Lucas closed his eyes, and saw himself twelve years old, standing in Anton's study while his mother explained why he could never tell anyone what he'd overheard at dinner. Secrets, she'd said, were how families protected themselves. Truth was a luxury they couldn't afford.

He'd believed her then. He'd spent twelve years in London trying to forget what believing her had cost.

"Lucas?" Helena's voice carried a note of genuine concern that made him hate himself for recognizing it as genuine. "Are you there?"

"I'm here," he said.

"Then come home. Let me fix this."

Lucas opened his eyes and looked at the evidence spread across the folding table. Grace Mdluli's life condensed into bank records and shipping manifests and clinical notes that proved her murder had been budgeted like office supplies.

"You can't fix this," he said. "Because this isn't broken. This is exactly what you built it to be."

He ended the call and let the silence sit.

For a long moment, the safe house was quiet except for the sound of traffic and the distant hum of servers distributing truth to mirrors that Helena's people were already learning to kill.

Zara resumed typing. "She's going to come for us now."

"I know."

"Really come for us. Not just Darren and his people. Everything she has."

"I know."

"Good." Zara's fingers quickened. "Because in about six hours, every major news outlet in the world is going to receive a package that makes your vault data lock like a rough draft."

Lucas sat back down at the folding table. "What package?"

"Grace's insurance policy," Zara said without looking up from her screen. "The one she uploaded to fourteen international servers before they killed her. Bank records, communication logs, video footage of meetings that never officially happened. Everything she collected over five years of watching them destroy people like it was just another day at the office."

"You've had that this whole time?"

"I've had pieces. It took your vault data to fill in the gaps." Zara's smile was sharp enough to cut glass. "Helena taught you that secrets protect families. Grace taught me that secrets are weapons, and sometimes you have to use them to stop the people who taught you that lesson."

On the laptop, progress bars climbed. Fourteen servers, forty-seven mirrors, eighteen languages. Truth learning to replicate faster than lies could kill it.

Lucas watched the numbers climb and thought about inheritance. His father had left him money, property, and the machinery of organized forgetting. His mother had tried to teach him that survival required complicity.

But Grace Mdluli had left him something neither Anton nor Helena had ever understood: the knowledge that some truths were more important than the people who tried to bury them.

Outside, Johannesburg continued its ancient work of eating secrets and excreting lies. But in a safe house that smelled of instant coffee and exhaustion, two people sat in front of computers and fed truth into a digital ecosystem that was learning, finally, to prefer signal over noise.

The choreography had begun—only not to Helena's rhythm.

***

Helena stood in Anton's study and calculated the precise degree of force required to break a crystal decanter without damaging the carpet beneath it. Forty years beside a man who preferred metaphorical violence had taught her this: destruction satisfies most when it serves more than one purpose.

The decanter shattered against the fireplace with the crystalline note of expensive things learning they were not as permanent as their price tags suggested. Whiskey spread across stone like blood on marble, the scent filling the room with the ghost of Anton's evening ritual.

She felt better. Not much, but enough to think clearly about next steps.

On her desk, three phones buzzed with the synchronized urgency of an emergency that required coordination across multiple time zones. Beijing wanted assurance that certain shipping manifests would never see courtroom scrutiny; London needed confirmation that banking relationships established during the transition years would survive whatever media attention Lucas's tantrum generated; Washington required detailed projections about political stability in a region they considered strategically important.

Helena picked up the red phone first. "Phoenix confirmed," she said, in Mandarin that carried only the faintest trace of accent. "Activate Protocol Seven. Full-spectrum response within six hours."

She switched to the blue phone. "Tiger Seven operational. Banking exposure minimal. Political containment proceeding according to established parameters."

The black phone required no identification protocols. "The boy has become a problem that requires permanent solutions. Authorization confirmed. Implement immediately."

Three conversations. Three languages. Three promises that would reshape tomorrow's headlines as efficiently as today's revelations had reshaped this morning's. Helena had learned from Anton that power was just information moving at the right speed in the right direction. Lucas had forgotten that lesson somewhere in his London exile. She would remind him.

Her secure laptop chimed with the arrival of files that would change the context of every piece of evidence Lucas thought he'd revealed. Banking records that proved Grace Mdluli had been stealing from the foundation she claimed to serve. Communication logs that showed her selling information to foreign intelligence services. Video footage of meetings where she negotiated payments for industrial secrets that would have destabilized the region's energy sector.

All fabricated. All but undetectable. All backed by digital signatures and timestamps that would satisfy any forensic investigation maintaining even minimal professional standards.

Truth Helena had learned from watching Anton work was just consensus achieved through superior information management. Lucas had revealed facts. But facts were just raw material until someone with better resources shaped them into narrative.

She opened a secure connection to the media management firm that had turned Anton's funeral into a celebration of democratic values and his obituaries into love letters to pragmatic leadership. Within an hour, every major outlet would receive an exclusive package explaining how a grieving son's mental health crisis had made him vulnerable to foreign manipulation.

The evidence would be overwhelming. The psychology would be convincing. The alternative—that a family like the Brandts could have spent forty years committing murder with the casual efficiency of a construction company laying pipe—would seem absurd by comparison.

Her personal phone buzzed—Darren. His name appeared on the screen with the mechanical inevitability of bad news learning to travel at the speed of light.

"It's done," he said without preamble.

It was the same script he'd tested months ago in focus groups—now finally field-ready.

"Which part?"

"All of it. The journalist's apartment was a tragedy—initial findings say gas leak. These old buildings, you know how it is. Very sad. Her laptop was destroyed in the explosion, unfortunately."

Helena felt something that might have been grief if she'd had the luxury of emotions that didn't serve strategic purposes. Zara had been a good journalist. Under different circumstances, Helena might have enjoyed watching her build a career.

"And Lucas?"

"Still missing," Darren said. "Body hasn't been recovered, but he was inside when it happened. For now, the authorities are calling it an accident. Once the dust settles, our contacts will shape it as a murder–suicide—grief, guilt, all the familiar motives. It'll hold."

Helena closed her eyes and allowed herself thirty seconds to mourn the son she'd tried to save from his own conscience. Lucas had been beautiful as a child—curious, brave, willing to believe that truth and justice were more than convenient fictions used to manage public opinion. She'd loved that innocence even while teaching him to abandon it.

He'd never learned. Even twelve years in London hadn't taught him that survival required flexibility about reality.

"Clean up any loose ends," she said. "I want this contained before the next news cycle."

"Already handled. By tomorrow morning, Lucas Brandt will be remembered as a troubled young man who couldn't cope with his father's death." He sounded pleased. "Very sad. Very human. Very explainable."

Helena ended the call and poured herself a glass of whiskey from a replacement decanter that had materialized on her desk with the efficiency of grief-management protocols she'd established years ago. She toasted the empty room, the broken crystal on the hearth, and the son who'd forced her to choose between family and survival.

She chose survival. She always did.

Outside, Johannesburg exhaled the day's heat and inhaled tomorrow's possibilities. The city had survived apartheid, transition, and forty years of democracy that looked increasingly like oligarchy with better marketing. It would survive the loss of one troubled young man and one idealistic journalist.

Some stories ended with revelation and justice—Helena had spent forty years learning the difference.

***

But across the city, in a basement server room where the air tasted of electricity and determination, mirrors seeded truth faster than lies could kill it. Grace Mdluli's insurance policy had survived her murder, just as her evidence was surviving Helena's attempts at revision.

Some codes were built to break. Others to replicate.

The truth was learning to multiply—ready for the lights.

And above ground, beyond the basement's humming sanctum, the first digital heartbeat of tomorrow's performance began to pulse—camera shutters syncing with server rhythms, signal rising toward the surface where truth would learn to perform.

Chapter 10 – Continuity of Power

SEVENTY-TWO HOURS AFTER THE BROADCAST

By the time the world turned Helena's tragedy into a battleground, she had already learned the cover story wouldn't hold.

Surveillance gaps. Missing bodies. Inconsistent heat signatures—details Darren dismissed—but Helena never ignored.

Lucas Brandt was alive. And if he was broadcasting, she would answer.

***

From reinforced glass, Lucas watched the city divide itself—armored vehicles taking positions three blocks south, too far for assault, close enough to carve territories. Different truths, competing for dominance.

Helena's counterattack arrived with Swiss precision. Dawn brought international outlets running stories: "foreign manipulation," "digital evidence fabrication." By noon, three European banks questioned documents that twelve hours earlier had triggered emergency meetings. Frozen accounts.

Within hours Helena was everywhere—screens, feeds, front pages—as if grief itself had a publicist.

"She's good," Zara said. Her tablet cycled through feeds like vital signs. "Better than good. She's turned your truth into proof—proof that truth itself can't be trusted."

Lucas sat at the folding table. Grace Mdluli's insurance files, arranged like tarot cards predicting uncertain futures. Three days seeding evidence across networks, faster than Helena's people could kill mirrors.

Speed, they learned, was no match for institutional authority; not when that authority knew how to perform grieving motherhood for cameras.

"Foreign Intelligence Services Exploit Family Tragedy," he read—each capital letter another incision. A credible byline. Respected. Completely convinced Helena Brandt was victim to elaborate disinformation designed to destabilize regional stability.

"The Chinese signatures are perfect," Zara said, scrolling through technical analysis: proof beyond reasonable doubt—the vault documents were digitally manufactured. "Whoever built this frame understood forensic analysis."

Lucas thought of servers humming in the next room. Still broadcasting truth to audiences learning, in real time, that truth was performance. Helena taught him power was making people believe what served your purposes.

He'd never understood how efficient belief is as a weapon, not until he watched his evidence transform into proof of delusion.

His phone buzzed. Unknown number.

He let it ring twice.

"My boy." Helena's voice carried warm exhaustion—someone who'd spent sleepless nights trying to save her child from himself. "This has to stop."

"Which part?" Lucas kept his voice flat. His free hand found the table edge, gripped until knuckles whitened. "The truth about Grace? Evidence of your authorization codes? Or the part where you convinced the world I'm a mentally unstable foreign asset?"

"You're my son." Helena's voice cracked—authentic mother watching her child disappear into dangerous delusion. "Nothing you do changes that. But you're hurting people who don't deserve it. Foundation staff, scholarship recipients, communities we serve—they're paying the price for your crusade."

Lucas looked at Zara. She'd stopped scrolling, her face tight with the quiet fury of someone who'd studied this performance before and refused to be fooled twice.

"Grace Mdluli deserved better than a heart attack."

"Grace Mdluli's death was a medical event, nothing more," Helena said, her tone now clipped, tired of having to repeat the lie.

"The reports are clear. Anything else is fiction invented by people who need martyrs more than facts. Conspiracy theories your handlers built around her death are exactly the kind of inflammatory fiction designed to make you feel heroic while you're being manipulated."

She was right about one thing: someone was being manipulated. But the puppet master wasn't in Beijing or Moscow.

She was in Anton's study, speaking in the voice she'd used, when he was small and afraid of thunder.

"Come home," Helena continued. Her tone softened into the register that had once made him believe monsters could be reasoned with. "Let me get you the help you need. Medical attention. Security assessment. The world will forgive you—if you admit you were deceived."

Lucas closed his eyes. Saw himself at twelve, standing in that same study while his mother explained why secrets were how families protected themselves.

Truth, she'd said, was a luxury they couldn't afford.

"I have the medical reports. Your authorization. Clinical notes that prove you ordered her murder."

"You have expertly crafted forgeries that took advantage of your grief," Helena interrupted. "The kind of material foreign intelligence services create when they want to destabilize strategic relationships. They studied you, Lucas. Learned your psychology. Built lies that would feel true to someone with your particular vulnerabilities."

The worst part was how plausible it sounded. How easily his revolt could be reframed as victimization. His evidence as manipulation. His courage as careful psychological exploitation.

"The shipping manifests. Communication logs. Video footage of meetings that never officially happened."

"Digital fabrications. Deep fakes." Helena's voice carried patient authority—someone explaining basic facts to a confused child. "Technology exists now that can create any evidence serving any narrative. Your handlers chose their forgeries carefully. Made them compelling because they studied what you needed to believe."

Lucas opened his eyes. Looked at evidence spread across the folding table.

Grace Mdluli's life's work—murder disguised on paper as a heart attack—condensed into bank records and shipping manifests and clinical notes that might—if Helena was right—be nothing more than sophisticated lies, designed to manipulate his grief into geopolitical advantage.

But he'd been in the vault. Opened Anton's safe with codes only the family knew. Breathed stale air of secrets preserved for decades.

"You used your birthday," he said quietly.

Helena paused. "What?"

"The vault combination—fourteen oh two fifty-two. Valentine's Day. The year you were born."

Silence stretched, thin and sharp.

Helena's breathing changed—shallower, more controlled.

"Anton built his empire around you," Lucas continued. "Every code, every lock, every secret built on possession. Even after he died, you kept it. You still live inside his mythology."

"Because legacy matters," she said.

"Because control matters," Lucas answered. "You've spent your life preserving what he built—every lie, every ledger. Grace tried to change that. You killed her for it."

"Grace Mdluli died of a heart attack."

"And my father?"

A pause.

Then Helena's voice softened again, sliding into the register that had once made him believe storms could be calmed.

"Come home, Lucas. Let me explain what really happened—to Grace, to your father, to me. Let me show you the real files—the ones your handlers didn't want you to see."

"I've seen enough files."

"Then let me show you the recordings," she said. "Your father's voice. His actual words. The real reasons he did what he did."

Lucas felt something that might have been hope if he'd had the luxury of emotions that didn't serve strategic purposes. "You have recordings?"

"I have everything, my boy. Anton never threw anything away. Come home, and I'll play them for you. All of them. Including the ones that explain why she had to be stopped."

The admission hung in the air like gunpowder waiting for a spark.

"She had to be stopped," Lucas repeated.

"She was going to destroy everything your father built. Everything we've protected for thirty years. Everything that keeps this country from tearing itself apart." Helena's voice carried the weight of old justifications. "He chose ideology over stability. I chose survival."

Lucas looked at Zara, who was typing furiously. Recording every word through the phone's speaker.

"You chose yourself," he said.

"I chose the future. The same future I'm offering you now. Come home. Listen to what your father actually said before he died. Then decide if you want to repeat his mistakes."

Lucas ended the call.

For a long moment, the safe house was quiet except for traffic and the distant hum of servers distributing truth to mirrors that Helena's people were learning to kill with increasing efficiency.

"She has recordings," Zara said without looking up from her screen.

"She has something," Lucas agreed. "Whether it's authentic is another question."

"You want to hear them."

"I want to know what really happened to Grace—and how deep the Foundation's hands go in the deaths they call accidents." Lucas sat back. "But I don't trust Helena to tell me the truth about what I had for breakfast, much less about murder."

Zara's fingers moved across keys with mechanical persistence. "The upload is ninety-three percent complete. Grace's files will be fully distributed within the hour. Whatever Helena has, we'll have insurance against it."

"And after that?"

"After that, we decide whether to go home and face whatever trap she's prepared, or disappear into a world where people like us don't get to ask questions about people like her."

Lucas watched the progress bar climb toward completion. Thought about inheritance.

Anton had left him money, property, and the machinery of organized forgetting.

Helena had tried to teach him that survival required complicity with comfortable lies.

But somewhere in the Johannesburg night, servers hummed with evidence that some truths were more important than the people who tried to bury them.

Grace Mdluli had died for that principle.

Anton Brandt had died trying to outlive it.

The question was whether Lucas Brandt was brave enough to live by it.

***

Helena stood in Anton's study, her hand resting on the phone as if weighing its usefulness. After four decades beside a man who translated cruelty into metaphor, she'd learned that endings mattered most when they achieved more than silence.

The call to Lucas had gone exactly as planned. He'd revealed his knowledge of the vault combination, his understanding of his father's death, and most importantly, his willingness to come home if offered the right bait.

The recordings existed, of course. Helena never bluffed with cards she didn't hold.

But the recordings wouldn't show what Lucas expected them to show.

On her desk, three phones buzzed with synchronized urgency—an emergency requiring coordination across multiple time zones. Beijing wanted confirmation that the digital evidence trail would survive forensic analysis. London needed assurance that banking relationships could weather another forty-eight hours of international scrutiny. Washington required detailed projections about regional stability in the wake of what they were calling the Brandt Crisis.

Helena picked up the red phone first. "Phoenix confirmed," she said in Mandarin, carrying only the faintest trace of accent. "Target is moving toward acceptable resolution. Advance to protocol nine, activate final protocols."

She switched to the blue phone. "Tiger Seven operational. Exposure contained. Advance to phase two—political narrative achieving desired trajectory."

The black phone required no identification protocols. "The prodigal son is coming home. Prepare the family reunion."

Three conversations, three languages, three sets of promises that would reshape tomorrow's headlines as efficiently as today's revelations had threatened to expose yesterday's crimes.

Helena no longer needed Anton's lessons to remember them. Power was still information—only faster, cleaner, more precise than he'd ever imagined.

Anton taught the principle. Helena perfected the execution. Soon, Lucas would understand the difference.

Interpol accepted the forensics. Expert testimony from MIT, Cambridge—Beijing followed. The vault documents showed clear signs of state-level manipulation. Metadata analysis proved the files had been created using Chinese-manufactured servers and Russian encryption protocols.

All fabricated, of course. But fabricated by professionals who understood that the best lies were built from small truths arranged in convincing patterns.

She opened a secure connection to Darren's tactical operations center. Within thirty minutes, the safe house's location would be compromised in what investigators would later call a structural collapse.

Tragic. Predictable.

But not until after he came home.

Not until she'd played him the recordings that would explain everything he thought he knew about truth, justice, and the price of moral courage.

Her personal phone buzzed. Lucas's name appeared with the mechanical inevitability of a trap closing around prey that had never learned the difference between bait and food.

"I'll come home," he said without preamble. "But I want to hear the recordings. All of them."

"Of course," Helena said, letting maternal relief color her voice. "I've been waiting thirty years to share them with you."

"And I want Zara there. Whatever you're going to show me, she witnesses."

Helena felt something that might have been admiration if she'd had the luxury of emotions that didn't serve strategic purposes. Lucas had learned some things during his exile.

Not enough, but some.

"If that's what you need to feel safe," she agreed. "Bring her. Bring anyone you want. Truth doesn't fear witnesses."

She didn't mourn this time. Mourning was for mothers; strategy was for survivors. She had taught Lucas the difference, even if he'd refused to learn it. Love, she reminded herself, was just another form of continuity—the kind that endured by any means necessary.

But he was coming home.

And home was where Helena Brandt had spent forty years learning how to make love look like its opposite, and its opposite look like the only choice that mattered.

Some lessons were best taught in the room where the student could hear his own echo.

***

Across the city, in a basement server room where the air tasted of electricity and determination, Grace Mdluli's insurance policy achieved full replication.

One hundred and forty-seven mirrors across sixty-seven countries. Each one a small victory against organized forgetting.

But in the Brandt estate's master suite, Helena was selecting the dress she would wear to welcome her son home. Black silk, cut with the precision of someone who understood that mourning was performance.

Some codes were designed to break. Others were designed to reveal exactly what their programmers intended.

The truth was learning to serve many masters.

Chapter 11 – The Table of Lions

The overhead lighting in The Continent newsroom buzzed like failing electronics. Pale shadows crossed empty desks where Zara's colleagues had once hunted truth with predatory focus. Now those workstations sat dark and abandoned—their screens reflecting nothing but the ghostly outline of a woman who might be the last journalist standing in a war most people didn't know was being fought.

Zara Mokoena pressed her headphones tight against her ears. Samuel Mashaba's terrified whisper filled the spaces between her ears and her conscience. This was the third time she'd played the recording—each repetition revealing new layers of terror in the whistleblower's voice: the careful monotone of a man who knew his words might serve as his own eulogy.

"They're moving the shipments through Nkomazi again." Samuel's voice crackled through digital static that crackled like ice breaking. Zara did the math—he must have recorded this weeks before the mining story went live. "Same route. Same protection. But now they're not bothering to hide it. The customs officers have been told to look the other way. Anyone who asks questions gets transferred—or worse."

She paused the recording. Her fingers trembled not from fear but from the weight of months spent cataloging lives erased by paperwork. Transfer notices that read like obituaries—each line of bureaucratic text enough to make a person vanish. The coffee beside her had gone cold hours ago—another casualty of obsession. Around her, the newsroom's ghost-white walls reflected the pale glow of her monitor, transforming the space into a mausoleum for dead stories and silenced voices.

The detritus of a dying newspaper surrounded her like evidence from a crime scene. Unpaid invoices stacked in towers that leaned like accusatory fingers. Legal threats printed on letterhead expensive enough to intimidate. The quiet desperation of a truth-telling machine slowly grinding to a halt under the weight of forces that treated journalism like an infection requiring surgical removal.

Grace should have been here—should have been the one to break this story—to witness vindication of months spent mapping corruption that stretched from dockside customs sheds to cabinet-level briefing rooms where human lives were discussed in the language of profit margins and acceptable losses. Instead, Grace existed only in the residue of her own investigation—digital breadcrumbs left behind for someone else to follow down a path that led inexorably toward the same violent silence that had claimed its original architect.

Grace Mdluli—murdered for daring to ask questions—was still shaping the story through every encrypted note she had left behind.

The Cypress files spread across Zara's desk told a story that newspapers were no longer allowed to print, their pages revealing a shadow economy so sophisticated it made traditional organized crime look like children playing with toy soldiers: shell companies laced through offshore accounts like filigree—delicate, decorative, and impossible to untangle without breaking the whole design; bank transfers that moved with clockwork precision, always just below the reporting thresholds that would trigger official scrutiny. And at the center of it all, names she recognized from society pages and government directories. People who smiled for cameras while orchestrating a marketplace where weapons and silence were traded with equal facility.

Her phone buzzed against the metal desk with the particular urgency reserved for institutional death sentences. The message from Mthembu carried the brevity of a man who had learned to deliver bad news: "Board meeting tomorrow. They're pulling the plug. I'm sorry, Zara. Get out while you can."

She stared at the words until they blurred. Understanding that this wasn't just about losing her job. The paper had been their last independent voice—the final platform for stories that powerful people preferred to keep buried beneath layers of legal intimidation and economic pressure. Without it, journalists like her would be reduced to freelancing for publications that survived by asking only the questions whose answers were already known and approved.

Grace had seen this coming with the clarity of someone who understood that state-sanctioned murder didn't require bullets. Just the patient application of financial pressure until truth became economically unviable. "They don't have to kill all the journalists," Grace had said during one of their final meetings, her voice carrying the weight of prophecy. "They just have to kill the journalism."

Zara opened her laptop's camera app. She positioned it to frame herself against the newsroom's empty expanse. The fluorescent light was unforgiving—highlighting exhaustion that had carved new geography around her eyes—but she needed Lucas to see the truth. Not just hear it but witness the human cost of official silence. The camera became her confessor, the digital lens a window into a soul that had been ground down by months of carrying other people's secrets.

This wasn't about him anymore, she realized as she stared into the camera's unblinking eye. This was about Grace. About Samuel. About every source who had risked everything to get information to people like her—the designated carriers of society's most dangerous cargo. This was about the promise she'd made to Grace in the weeks before her disappearance. A vow that had become the organizing principle of her life: that the story would get told, no matter what price was demanded from its messenger.

"Lucas." She began speaking directly to the lens, stripping away every layer of pretense until only exhausted honesty remained. Not "hey" or "listen"—just his name, weighted with all the accumulated trust and betrayal that had defined their professional relationship. "I'm not sure what the rules are anymore. Every day, someone moves the goalposts. We report a scandal, and by the next week it's already standard operating procedure. You expose a network, but the network's just a symptom. The system—"

She stopped. Shaking her head at the futility of trying to capture systemic rot in words designed for individual stories. Behind her, a whiteboard still bore the remnants of their last editorial meeting. Story assignments that would never be written. Source protection protocols that no longer mattered. Deadlines for a paper that would never print again. The institutional memory of investigative journalism was being erased in real time. Each deleted assignment another small victory for forces that preferred their crimes to remain unobserved.

Grace's name was still up there, listed under "Active Sources." Someone should have erased it months ago, but none of them had possessed the heart to acknowledge that particular finality. Her name had become a shrine to the dangerous optimism that drove people into journalism. The belief that truth possessed some inherent power to protect those who served it faithfully.

"The system can't be shamed." She continued, her voice gaining strength as understanding crystallized into words. "It can only be replaced, or burned down. You know what scares me? It's not the Brandts. It's not Katz, or even you. It's how easy it becomes to accept the story they're selling. How simple it is to keep playing the game, even when you know the rules are designed to ensure you lose."

Through the newsroom's windows, Johannesburg's lights stretched toward the horizon like scattered embers from a civilization learning to burn quietly, one compromise at a time. Somewhere in that collection of ambition and survival, Grace was hiding—or had been transformed into something that could no longer be found by conventional methods of investigation. Somewhere else, the next shipment was being loaded onto trucks that would never be inspected by officials who had learned to develop strategic blindness when their salaries depended on not seeing.

Grace would have fought this official decay with the ferocity of someone who understood that surrender was just another form of collaboration. She would have found another way—another angle, another source willing to trade safety for the possibility of redemption. Grace never accepted that any story was impossible to tell—she just believed that some stories required more courage than their narrators initially possessed.

Zara looked directly into the camera lens. Seeing her own reflection in its dark circle of glass. The woman staring back looked like a soldier reporting from a battlefield where casualties were measured in silenced voices rather than body counts. "If you ever find a way out—don't come back. Not for me. Not for any of this. Just go, and don't look back long enough to see what we become without witnesses."

She reached toward the camera. Her hand momentarily blocking the lens like an eclipse of accountability. The screen went dark. The recording stopped automatically. Silence rushed in to fill the spaces where truth had briefly taken residence. She saved the video, encrypted it with a password Lucas would recognize, and uploaded it to their secure cloud—one more message in a bottle cast into uncertain seas.

Around her, the newsroom's hush felt absolute. Heavy with the accumulated weight of stories that would never be told. Even the building's mechanical systems seemed to hold their breath—as if understanding they were witnessing the end of something that could never be rebuilt with the same naive faith in journalism's power to illuminate rather than merely document darkness.

Then she began the work of institutional erasure. Hard drives wiped with military rigor. Source lists encrypted and hidden across a dozen different systems. Contact databases scrubbed clean of any evidence that journalists had once asked dangerous questions and received answers that proved fatal to both questioner and questioned. By morning, there would be no proof that The Continent had ever investigated Operation Cypress. No evidence that reporters had once believed exposure was a form of protection rather than an invitation to violence.

But Grace's files would survive—hidden across servers that couldn't all be erased. Grace had taught Zara that

redundancy was the purest form of faith: a way to ensure
that what mattered most outlived those who carried it. Zara
deleted her own traces one by one, not out of despair but
design, turning disappearance into strategy. Grace's story
would wait—preserved like a fossil of truth until someone
braver dug it free.

⁎

Helena had not invited him back to the estate after all.
The meeting place changed overnight—Helena's private art
gallery in Braamfontein, neutral ground disguised as culture.
Helena never allowed confrontation where the walls might
remember too much.

Helena's private art gallery occupied the top floor of a
converted warehouse in Braamfontein. Its soaring ceilings
and exposed brick walls providing the perfect backdrop for a
collection assembled not for aesthetic pleasure but for
strategic leverage. Each piece told a story—not of artistic
vision, but of institutional obligation. The Monet had been a
gift from a mining minister who'd needed certain
environmental reports to develop permanent amnesia; the
Rothko marked a pharmaceutical executive's gratitude for
expedited drug approvals that bypassed inconvenient safety
trials. Every canvas on these walls represented a transaction
where art served as currency and silence as the commodity
being purchased.

Lucas arrived precisely at noon. Punctuality serving as
the last gesture of respect he would ever offer his mother.
The gallery's security system recognized him immediately—
facial-recognition software trained on family photographs
dating back decades. Artificial intelligence, programmed to
grant access to bloodline rather than character. The elevator
rose in mechanical silence, carrying him toward a
confrontation he'd been avoiding since his return to
Johannesburg. Each floor marking another level of descent
into the moral architecture his family had constructed over
generations.

But today felt different. The revelation about Grace's vanishing—under suspicious circumstances—had crystallized something in him. A hardness that replaced the constant oscillation between guilt and duty that had paralyzed him for months. He wasn't here to be lectured about family loyalty or recruited into their machinery of organized forgetting. He was here to study the enemy. To understand the infrastructure of systematized evil before he began the work of dismantling it from within.

Helena stood with her back to him. Studying a Jackson Pollock that had been purchased with proceeds from an arms deal that armed both sides of a civil war—the perfect metaphor for a business model that profited from conflict regardless of its resolution. She wore white—the calculated white of someone who understands color's power to suggest purity while concealing stains.

Near the far wall, beneath a muted Rothko, a small plinth held a reel-to-reel deck—Anton's old apparatus, restored and labeled in his hand. A single spool turned quietly, the tape running like a heartbeat. The recordings— the thing Helena had promised—sat in plain view.

Lucas let her play the first spool. Anton's voice came through: steady, paternal, the cadence Lucas had known his whole life. But the sentences had been trimmed and rearranged; pauses stitched to create implication, phrases repeated to suggest intent that hadn't been there. The voice of the man who'd taught him how to be private had been turned into sermon. Helena's voice followed, soft and explanatory, filling the gaps with the right nouns and the right excuses. By the time the tape clicked to an end, Lucas felt less enlightened than enraged. He had come for evidence; he had found curated absolution.

Somewhere else, servers continued to mirror Grace's files; the city's information arteries were changing while they spoke.

"You've been busy," Helena said without turning. Her tone carried the unhurried control of someone who'd already rewritten the morning's headlines. "Your little broadcast has done more than embarrass us, Lucas. The vault files and their mirrors—your stunt—have rattled markets, frozen credit lines, and forced three ministers to deny they ever met your father. Our donors are calling. Governments are asking questions. The Foundation is triaging reputational hemorrhage even now."

She turned then, smooth and deliberate, the white of her dress catching the gallery's light. "You think you've exposed truth. What you've done is hand a map to chaos to people who prefer chaos to accountability. That isn't courage; it's negligence dressed as idealism."

"I've been learning." His response carried none of the defensive anger she'd expected. No trace of the uncertain heir who had fled to London rather than confront uncomfortable truths about his inheritance.

"Learning what? That your father was human? That power comes with costs?" Helena moved through the gallery with the confidence of someone who owned not just the art but the space itself. Every conversation here occurring in a location that officially didn't exist. "You think you've discovered something shocking, but you've simply stumbled onto the basic arithmetic of influence."

He watched her shoulders tense at his tone. Not the reaction of someone anticipating familiar patterns, but something colder and more purposeful. She turned to face him, her expression carved from the same moral marble that lined the Brandt estate's halls. Beautiful and unyielding in its refusal to acknowledge the suffering required to maintain its perfection.

Lucas let her circle him like a predator establishing dominance. Noting how she used the gallery's architecture to frame herself as both patron and protector of culture. Even this confrontation was being staged for maximum psychological impact.

"The Cypress operation. The weapons shipments. The murdered customs officers. That's not arithmetic—that's genocide by installment. And people are dying because of your ledger."

Helena's laugh was silk wrapped around razors. Beautiful and dangerous in equal measure. "Genocide? You've been reading too much Zara Mokoena. This is business, Lucas. We provide services to people who need them. We facilitate agreements between parties who might otherwise resort to more... dramatic solutions."

"Services?" Lucas felt the familiar Brandt rage begin to build in his chest, but this time he channeled it into clarity rather than confusion. "You're arming militias. You're bribing officials. You're making civil wars profitable by ensuring they never end definitively enough to threaten ongoing revenue streams."

"I'm preventing them from becoming unprofitable." Helena corrected with the patience of someone explaining basic economics to a child. "Power is like water, Lucas—it finds its level regardless of human sentiment. We simply ensure that level doesn't drown everyone in the process."

She stopped before a Basquiat that had been acquired during the artist's final year, when his work was still considered transgressive rather than investment-grade. The painting's aggressive energy seemed at odds with the gallery's sterile atmosphere. A raw scream preserved in a space designed for whispered conversations about the price of silence.

"Your father understood this fundamental truth." Helena continued, her voice taking on the rhythm of someone delivering doctrine. "The world is not a democracy—it's an auction. And in an auction, the highest bidder sets the rules that everyone else pretends are natural law."

Lucas studied his mother's profile. Noting the surgical precision of her makeup. The way her posture never wavered even when making statements that should have required shame. But now he saw something else—the performance of it. The careful construction of authority that required constant maintenance to prevent its artificial nature from becoming apparent.

"And Grace? The customs officer who asked too many questions? Was she part of the auction?"

For the first time, something flickered in Helena's expression. Not regret, but the kind of calculation that preceded necessary unpleasantness. "Grace Mdlul was a patriot. She believed in institutions that no longer exist in any meaningful form. Her tragedy wasn't her honesty—it was her naïveté about how honesty functions in systems designed to reward strategic blindness."

"Her tragedy was trusting people like you."

"Her tragedy was trusting anyone at all." Helena's voice hardened, revealing the steel that had always lurked beneath her maternal facade like a blade concealed in velvet. "Grace thought she could expose the Cypress network and walk away into comfortable retirement. She thought truth was protection. That public outrage would shield her from the practical consequences of threatening institutional stability. She was wrong about the nature of both truth and protection."

The admission hung in the gallery's recycled air like incense from a black mass. Lucas realized he was looking at the architect of Grace's disappearance. Not Darren with his crude operational approach. Not some shadowy military contractor motivated by mere profit. But his own mother— discussing murder with the casual efficiency she might apply to arranging flowers for a charity luncheon.

"You killed her." The words fell like stones into still water, sending ripples through a silence that had grown accustomed to accommodating structured evil.

"I made a business decision." Helena replied with the matter-of-fact tone of someone who had long since made peace with the price of power. "Grace had become a liability to operational security. Liabilities are addressed promptly, or they metastasize into existential crises. Your father taught me that lesson very early in our marriage—usually while demonstrating its practical application."

Something shifted in Lucas then. A tectonic movement deep in his chest that felt like the last vestige of the dutiful son dying quietly, replaced by something harder and infinitely more dangerous. He wasn't just observing this conversation anymore. He was calculating. Measuring distances and vulnerabilities. Building a mental map of the infrastructure he would need to abolish.

"This is what you're inheriting, Lucas." Helena moved to the gallery's floor-to-ceiling windows, gesturing at the city that stretched to the horizon like a testament to human ambition and the compromises that made such ambition possible. "Not just money. Not just companies. But responsibility for maintaining equilibrium in systems that would collapse into chaos without careful management. We are not the disease—we are the treatment that prevents societal sepsis."

Lucas let her words land, then answered from a place that no longer wanted to beg for permission. "You're arguing for a system that monetizes death. You call it management; I call it murder. And those files—what Zara has done—have already started to undo the quiet you built."

Helena's smile did not falter. "Which is why you needed to hear my side. The recordings show context; they refract your outrage into complexity rather than conspiracy. People will prefer a tidy explanation that spares them guilt and saves their investments. We can make them prefer it."

He heard the subtext in the neutrality of her phrase— we can make them prefer it—and for the first time every polite thing his parents had taught him about civility sounded like collusion. He had come in search of answers and was leaving with the shape of the enemy.

Lucas felt the trap closing around him with elegant precision. Each word carefully chosen to frame his choice as one between responsible leadership and selfish abandonment of duty. But for the first time since returning to South Africa, he wasn't panicking at the approach of planned pressure. He was planning. Calculating the angles of attack that would bring maximum damage to the structure she was inviting him to join.

"And if I say no?"

Helena's smile was winter sunshine. Beautiful, cold, and ultimately illusory in its promise of warmth. "Then you'll discover that some inheritances don't require acceptance. They simply exist. You can resist them temporarily, but you cannot escape their eventual influence on your trajectory."

She walked toward the elevator with the clicking rhythm of a countdown timer. Her heels marking time against polished concrete. "Dinner is at eight. Darren will be there, along with several Foundation board members whose names you'll recognize from newspaper headlines and government press releases. We'll be discussing your transition plan—the carefully structured process by which you'll assume responsibility for operations your father spent decades developing. I trust you'll find it educational."

The elevator doors closed behind her with the soft finality of a vault sealing. Leaving Lucas alone among stolen masterpieces that had been purchased with blood and hung on walls built from the bones of people who had asked too many questions. But instead of feeling trapped by the weight of his inheritance, he felt something else entirely: the clarity that came with finally understanding the game being played around him.

Helena thought she was managing him. Maneuvering him into position like a chess piece whose moves were predetermined by the board's configuration. What she didn't realize was that he'd stopped playing her game entirely. The rules she was operating under assumed he still cared about family loyalty. Still felt obligated to honor his father's legacy. Still believed that power came with responsibilities that transcended personal conscience.

He was starting his own game now. One where the objective wasn't preservation but destruction. Where victory would be measured not in accumulated wealth but in the completeness of the reckoning that was coming.

***

The Brandt dining hall did the work of intimidation in three neat moves.

A chandelier that made faces small.

A table polished so perfectly it reflected conscience as a gloss.

And seating arranged like a tribunal—each chair calibrated to the temperament it would contain.

Lucas entered at eight not as an heir seeking comfort but as a man taking measure. Helena presided at the head with the practiced serenity of a woman who owned the room's angles. Darren took the other end with the casual entitlement of someone who considered the world a set of negotiable commitments.

They were not joined by a parade of types so much as by a handful of gestures that said everything the biographies would have tried to explain. A retired general polished a fork he never ate with—turning the metal as if the motion itself kept him ready for a different kind of violence. A philanthropist dabbed the margin of a contract with a napkin, an almost affectionate gesture that erased the stain of an agreement no one would read.

Servers moved like rehearsed silence; wines were chosen not for taste but for their ability to declare cost. Conversation slid from civility into strategy with no audible seam. The threat in the room never needed to be named—it lived in the way hands hesitated over envelopes, in the pause before toasts, in the casual facts rehearsed as if this were merely charity work.

A dry voice near the middle of the table cut the air.

"You don't invite arsonists to strategy dinners."

The laugh that followed was thin as tissue, polite as self-defense.

Helena's smile didn't waver. "We invite those who need reminding what's at stake," she said, the syllables lacquered in calm. "That is how a family repairs itself."

The air adjusted but never softened. Conversations resumed in the key of controlled contempt. Lucas caught fragments: the finance director murmuring about donor withdrawals, another board member mentioning compliance raids in Nairobi and Geneva. They spoke of "liability management" as if it were a new cuisine. Someone asked, not quite sotto voce, whether the prodigal was here to apologize or negotiate his ransom.

He sat without acknowledging any of it. His composure became its own provocation.

Darren Katz commanded the opposite end with the confidence of someone who had never doubted his right to reshape the world according to his preferences. His expensive suit and predatory smile suggested a man entirely comfortable with his role as civilization's most charming monster—someone who could discuss mass murder with the same enthusiasm other people brought to sport.

"Lucas." Darren's voice carried the warm familiarity of shared complicity. "We were just discussing the Foundation's expansion into conflict mediation. Fascinating work—we're discovering that most civil wars are really just market inefficiencies waiting to be corrected through proper application of economic incentives."

The line drew laughter, brittle but sincere. The finance woman's pen tapped the menu like a metronome. "He's burned half our donors' faith in forty-eight hours," she said to no one in particular. "Sites are freezing funds; compliance teams are circling. This isn't theatre—it's cash-flow triage."

Helena let it stand. The rebuke served her better than silence.

Lucas nodded with apparent interest while mentally cataloguing names, connections, and the subtle hierarchies that governed this particular collection of institutional predators. The first course arrived with theatrical precision. Servers who moved like ghosts through spaces designed to make wealth appear weightless. Dishes crafted for visual impact rather than nourishment. Wines selected not for their taste but for their ability to signify the kind of casual expense that made ordinary people feel appropriately inadequate.

Dr Naledi Langa, the Foundation's newly appointed ethics advisor, raised her glass in a toast that managed to sound both celebratory and vaguely threatening. "To clean hands," she said. "The most expensive commodity in today's market."

The laughter that followed was genuine—the sound of people who had long since abandoned the burden of pretending their sins were accidental rather than strategic. Lucas joined the toast, noting how the wine's color resembled blood when held against the chandelier's prismatic light. His own glass trembled slightly in his hand—not from fear but from the effort of maintaining composure while surrounded by the architects of Grace's murder and countless other deaths transformed into line items in budgets approved by committees that met in rooms like this one.

Around the table, conversation flowed with the lubricated ease of people who understood that dinner was simply business conducted in more comfortable chairs. Each exchange of pleasantries concealed negotiations about the price of human life and the most efficient methods for making inconvenient people disappear.

But Lucas was no longer a passive observer absorbing lessons about the sophisticated application of institutional violence. He was memorizing details, filing away admissions, building a mental map of the network that had killed Grace and countless others whose names would never appear in any official record.

Helena watched him from across the distance of the table. Her eyes measured posture and breath, calibrating his restraint like a clinical test. Every movement—each pause of his fork, each delayed response—fed the quiet machine of her analysis. She believed she still knew the variables that governed him; she had built most of them.

"The transition plan." Her voice carried the authority of someone calling a board meeting to order. "We've prepared a comprehensive proposal for Lucas's integration into the Foundation's leadership structure. Beginning with a strategic consulting role that will allow him to understand our operational methodology. Advancing to direct oversight of specific projects. Culminating in succession to the chairmanship within eighteen months."

The language of restoration disguised as opportunity.

She handed him a leather portfolio that felt heavier than its contents should have warranted—as if the papers inside carried the weight of every life sacrificed to build and maintain the system they documented. Inside, he found organizational charts that read like war plans, budget projections with line items for "consensus building" and "narrative management," and a mission statement that used words like stability and partnership to describe acts that would have been crimes in any honest court.

Lucas studied the documents with apparent interest, but his mind operated on another level. He was cataloguing names, mapping reporting structures and financial flows, identifying every thread he would need to pull when the time came to unravel everything.

Darren leaned forward, evangelical in his enthusiasm for the work of methodical repression disguised as humanitarian aid. "This is about stewardship, Lucas. The Foundation exists because people like us understand that democracy is a luxury most societies can't afford without careful management. We provide structure. Guidance. The necessary interventions that keep civilization from collapsing into the kind of chaos that makes business impossible and human suffering inevitable."

The retired general nodded approvingly, his weathered face fixed in the expression of someone who measured success in problems eliminated rather than lives preserved. "Consider it civic duty dressed in better suits and conducted in more comfortable environments."

The portfolio's final document was a contract that would impress Mephistopheles with its comprehensive approach to moral compromise—signing bonuses calculated in millions, operational authority across three continents, and legal immunities that rendered its signatories untouchable. All he had to do was accept responsibility for managing the careful application of violence that kept their world stable.

Helena watched him read. She had practiced this silence in courtrooms and boardrooms alike: the patience of power waiting for capitulation. In that quiet, the chandelier hum sounded almost ecclesiastical, a hymn for control.

Lucas let his fingers trace the contract's edge, appearing thoughtful while buying seconds to memorize detail. He was calculating time, resources, and which of these people might be turned against the others when the demolition began.

"The beauty of the modern approach," Darren continued, "is that we've moved beyond the crude methods of earlier generations. No more midnight disappearances that create martyrs. We simply make truth economically unviable. Outbid conscience with properly structured incentives. Outlast anyone naïve enough to believe moral clarity can compete with capital."

Helena watched his face with the calm of a clinician. "The Grace Mdluli situation was regrettable," she said, her voice carrying just enough sympathy to sound human while remaining fundamentally cold. "But it demonstrated the risks of operating outside established protocols. Had she accepted our initial offer—a very generous package, incidentally—she'd be living comfortably in exile rather than becoming a cautionary tale."

"What was the offer?" Lucas asked, voice steady despite the pressure building behind it.

"Relocation to Canada," Dr. Langa replied with the precision of a case file. "New identity, tenure-track university position, and enough money to ensure comfort for her and her family. All she had to do was sign a nondisclosure agreement and disappear for ten years."

"She preferred martyrdom to pragmatism," Darren added, puzzled. "We've learned from that experience. Future offers will include more... compelling incentives for compliance."

Helena folded the thought back into calm. "Which brings us to you."

Her tone shifted—no longer maternal, not yet merciful. "You've done damage, Lucas. Real damage. But narratives heal faster than finances, and both can be repaired with the right confession. Withdraw the allegations. Explain that you were misled by falsified files and foreign agitators. Apologize for the disruption, and we stabilize the markets, protect the scholarships, and restore the Brandt name. Refuse, and those same channels we control will show the world a reckless heir manipulated by extremists, a boy who tried to burn down his father's legacy for attention. That's the difference between heir and exile."

He looked around the table and saw heads incline in near-unison—an orchestrated gesture of consensus. They were already writing the statement in their minds, drafting his redemption as press release and public theatre.

The final course arrived as Helena delivered what was clearly intended as closing argument. "You have twenty-four hours," she said, laying out the arithmetic as if it were a charity budget. "One statement: acknowledge you were deceived, apologize for the harm caused to the Foundation and its beneficiaries, and accept our transitional remit. We restore order; you keep what protection family can buy. Say no, and the protections evaporate—donors will demand resignations, regulators will insist on hearings, and the machinery that keeps inconvenient narratives from spreading will isolate you. That is the choice: reprise with us, or face a legal and reputational winter none of us can thaw for you."

The chandelier's light fractured across glass and silverware.

Around the table, faces that had smiled throughout dinner now revealed their true nature. Patient predators who had extended an invitation functionally indistinguishable from an ultimatum. Lucas realized he was being offered a choice between complicity and war, with no middle ground for those who preferred neutrality in conflicts between endorsed power and individual conscience.

Helena's gaze lingered as the others began to rise. "You'll make the right decision," she said, soft as a benediction, sure as command. "You always wanted to protect the family."

He met her eyes long enough for the silence to curdle. "I still do."

But they had made a crucial mistake in their assessment of his character. They had shown him exactly how their machine worked—who operated its levers, where its vulnerabilities lay, how its components depended on each other for continued function. They thought they were recruiting him. Instead, they had handed him their blueprints.

The dinner ended with handshakes that felt like signed contracts and pleasantries that carried the weight of implicit threats disguised as friendly advice. As guests departed into the Johannesburg night, their expensive cars disappeared down the estate's circular drive like a convoy of well-dressed predators returning to their lairs.

The hall fell quiet, its grandeur receding into aftertaste and static. The chandelier's light swayed fractionally, scattering pale outlines across the walls like ghosts of every compromise ever brokered here.

Lucas remained seated at the table that had witnessed his father's rise and would now oversee something far more consequential than his own fall. He folded the portfolio, slid it into his jacket, and left the hall with their maps in his head—each name a coordinate; each chart, a seam he had learned to open.

Chapter 12 – Echoes and Evidence

Anton's study looked like a stage set for the respectable. Leather-bound books shelved for display rather than use. A desk vast enough to host cabinet meetings. And a portrait of the first Anton Brandt—an engineer who'd arrived with mining expertise and a moral flexibility that became the family trade.

Tonight, Lucas did not move through it as a son remembering. He moved through it as an operator who had finally learned the instrument he'd inherited.

The safe's combination remained unchanged: 14-02-57. The numbers were Helena's birthday—Valentine's Day—, the date she'd always called her real independence day. Each digit felt like a pulse under his fingertip as he entered them. Each beep was a memory striking metal.

Inside, documents lay wrapped in acid-free paper, like relics cataloged for reburial. He unwrapped a sheet marked with a magistrate's initials—the same symbol he'd seen in Grace Mdluli's archived files—proof the pipeline ran through every courtroom in the province.

He thumbed forward and saw a journalist's name crossed out and replaced with "consultant." A budget spreadsheet listed "parliamentary theater" with line items specifying committee chairs and retainer amounts.

Those concrete entries carried an implication the chapter had no need to declaim: money bought rulings, appointments, silence. The ledger didn't preach—it annotated transactions. Next to each name, Anton's script assigned the cost of quiet. Sometimes a pension. Sometimes a transfer. Sometimes a grave.

The proof was in the detail: a bank account number typed next to a judge's initials. A courier receipt with a ministry stamp. The spreadsheet cell where an annual "education fund" entry diverted into a named shell company.

He found photographs next. Surveillance stills, grainy and relentless: handshakes blurred by telephoto lenses.

Envelopes exchanged under the table. Men from the Foundation standing beside militia leaders with the polite ease of people arranging a contract.

One image showed the Foundation's private gallery—Helena and Darren and Dr. Langa seated beneath the Basquiat, the painting now a mute witness to the transactions that had always taken place in front of it.

He photographed each damning page with methodical calm. Not the frantic scatter of someone exposing wrongdoing, but the deliberate logging of intelligence. This was work: gather, catalog, secure. He indexed names and dates. Made a secure copy on a drive he slid into his pocket. And noted the few loose ends that could be followed—shipping manifests, port timestamps, a recurring attorney whose initials threaded through contracts.

The ledger's composition showed a system built less by accident than by blueprint: networks of small corruptions added until institutions bent toward the Foundation's needs. Courts, media, committees, customs. The pattern read in specific examples, not in slogans: the magistrate's initials. The "consultant" appointment. The retainer for a committee chair. The photo of an envelope on a lap. Each item suggested the rest.

He paused at a small, folded page, inked in his father's hand. Anton's note was appalling in its clarity: "The Foundation is not a legacy—it is a living thing. It feeds on crisis, grows through conflict, and reproduces by creating the very problems it claims to solve. You cannot reform it. You cannot control it. You can only choose whether to be consumed by it or to burn it down before it consumes everything else."

Lucas folded the note carefully. Slipping it into his pocket alongside the key to the safe and the drive he'd duplicated—a final package not of wealth or authority but of instruments: receipts, account numbers, and surveillance. Anton had spent a life building the machine and, in the same hand, drawing its map.

He replaced the portrait. Shut the safe. And walked to the window. Johannesburg spread below like a field of small bargains: lights, late-night traffic, decisions made in rooms that smelled of polish and profit.

He had the evidence. He had patience. He had the levers, cataloged and dated. For now, he would wait—sequence, time, exposure—measured acts rather than declarations.

He did not imagine a single heroic act. He imagined sequences—timed disclosures, legal wedges, people flipped by exposure—an unmaking measured in steps rather than rhetoric. He turned off the study light and the portrait's eyes went back to a painted calm. Outside, Johannesburg hummed. In his pocket, the ledger settled like a verdict.

What came next would be measured, not announced.

***

The Brandt estate's conservatory had always been Helena's stage—glass, orchids, and the scent of control. She'd chosen it for tonight's broadcast: a live statement to stabilize markets and reassure donors after the leak. Lucas was there because absence would have looked like defiance. He played his part—the dutiful heir still deciding.

Zara arrived under another pretext entirely. The Foundation's communications division had requisitioned outside technical support to stabilize encrypted feeds; Lucas had insisted on the contractor, citing prior experience. The guards scanned her credentials, never realizing the signature embedded in the clearance codes came from Helena's own late-night authorizations.

Zara's "rig" was smaller than the ones she'd used in the field—a relay kit nested in a travel case marked satellite redundancy. She'd spent years making cameras disappear into décor. By the time Helena entered, nothing looked out of place.

Helena stood beneath the canopy of orchids, light spilling across the marble like stagecraft. The cameras were live, the script loaded on the teleprompter—a statement meant to calm investors, steady markets, and reassert control.

Lucas stood beside her, the loyal heir performing obedience. Across the set, Darren hovered by the control rig, monitoring the outgoing feed.

"Our family has always believed in managed transition," Helena began, voice smooth, rehearsed. "That reconciliation requires order, not spectacle."

Then she saw Lucas's face—and something in her composure cracked.

"But there are debts," she said, turning from the prompter. "Debts no reconciliation can erase. To Grace Mdluli."

Darren froze. His hand darted toward the console. "Cut the feed," he hissed to the comms techs.

Security moved instinctively. The first burst of gunfire was chaotic—an overreaction to movement near the control panel. Darren went down, his headset skittering across the marble.

Helena didn't flinch. She stepped toward the lens. "We built prosperity on disappearance," she said. "We called it necessary. I was wrong."

A second gunshot followed—suppressed, clean, deliberate. It didn't come from security. The orchids trembled, petals falling through dust and static. Helena collapsed mid-sentence, blood threading down the glass panels behind her.

The feed stayed live for seven more seconds—long enough for Zara's relay to archive every frame.

The shot had been fired from the service corridor behind the fern wall. That corridor was Foundation-security access only; outside crews—Zara's included—weren't cleared past the broadcast perimeter.

By the time the estate's tactical team breached the doors, the shooter was gone.

No one in the room spoke. The Foundation's board hadn't needed to send a message in words. The act itself was language enough.

They didn't kill Lucas or Zara. They didn't need to. Witnesses were useful while their narratives could be managed. The footage would surface, yes—but in pieces, redacted, reframed. Two survivors under supervision made the story credible; two martyrs might have made it dangerous.

***

The conservatory's shattered glass caught the morning light like scattered accusations. Each fragment reflected a different angle of the violence that had ended Helena's reign.

Lucas stood among the orchids and blood, watching forensic technicians photograph evidence that would never reach a courtroom. Official narratives were already being crafted—tragic family dispute, foreign manipulation, the inevitable cost of institutional stress during democratic transition.

Darren's body had been removed within an hour. Processed with the efficiency of someone whose death had been anticipated and prepared for by multiple agencies. The board had voted unanimously, they said.

Operational security required aggressive management of liabilities. Helena had become the greatest liability of all.

But Lucas had expected that outcome. What he hadn't expected was the gunshot that had taken Helena herself, delivered by someone who had entered the conservatory while tactical teams secured the perimeter. Professional. Clinical.

Fired by someone who understood that some secrets required permanent burial.

The tactical team leader approached with the measured stride of someone delivering a briefing that had been rehearsed multiple times before being deemed acceptable for witness consumption. Major Hendrik Botha, according to his identification, though Lucas suspected that name would prove as temporary as every other official detail surrounding this operation.

"Mr. Brandt." Botha's Afrikaans accent carried the mechanical precision of someone who had learned to deliver bad news in multiple languages. "I need to inform you that your safety remains a priority concern. The individuals responsible for this incident may have additional operational objectives that require protective measures."

Translation: Lucas was now a witness to institutional murder disguised as family tragedy. His continued survival depended on his willingness to accept whatever narrative would be constructed around Helena's death. The protective custody being offered was indistinguishable from house arrest—supervision designed to ensure his public statements aligned with whatever story would serve institutional interests.

"Protective measures," Lucas repeated, studying the blood patterns on the conservatory floor that told a story of execution rather than confrontation. "Against whom, exactly?"

"Foreign elements," Botha replied without hesitation. "Individuals and organizations with strategic interests in destabilizing regional democratic institutions through targeted elimination of key leadership figures."

The lie was elegant. And simple. Helena's murder transformed from institutional housecleaning into proof of international conspiracy. Her death reframed as evidence that hostile foreign governments were targeting South African business leaders who posed threats to their geopolitical objectives.

Zara emerged from the estate's eastern wing. Her laptop secured in a tactical case that had survived four days of manhunt and now contained the complete digital record of their confrontation. The global broadcast had reached over 200,000 viewers before the signals were jammed.

The damage was done. Helena's confession to multiple murders was already propagating across networks faster than any government could contain.

"The international response is immediate," she said, reading from secure messages that continued arriving despite the estate's communication blackout. "The ICC launches a formal investigation within six hours. Swiss authorities freeze all Brandt-related accounts pending review. The European Parliament calls emergency session on apartheid-era reconciliation failures."

Major Botha's expression tightened almost imperceptibly—the only sign that international attention was complicating whatever narrative management protocols had been prepared for this scenario.

"Ms. Mokoena," he said, his tone carrying the particular courtesy reserved for witnesses whose cooperation would be essential for maintaining operational security. "Your broadcasting equipment will need to be examined by technical specialists. Standard procedure for incidents involving potential foreign-intelligence operations."

"Potential foreign-intelligence operations," Zara repeated, her voice carrying the exhausted irony of someone who had spent years documenting the efficiency of institutional lying. "Is that what we're calling Helena's on-air admission—her own words about Grace Mdluli, recorded before your people cut the feed?"

"We're calling it a sophisticated disinformation campaign designed to exploit family grief and personal trauma for geopolitical objectives," Botha replied without missing a beat. "Initial technical analysis suggests advanced audio-manipulation techniques that created false confessions implicating prominent South African figures in historical crimes."

Lucas felt the familiar architecture of institutional immunity rebuilding itself around yesterday's revelations. The mechanical efficiency of a system that had learned to process moral challenges as routine maintenance.

Truth transformed into opinion. Evidence converted into entertainment. Revelation reframed as the predictable consequence of psychological manipulation by hostile foreign intelligence services.

"And domestically?" Lucas asked.

"Ministry of Justice claims foreign interference," Zara said, continuing to read from messages that painted a comprehensive picture of institutional response. "Says Helena was coerced into false confessions by international conspirators seeking to destabilize regional development partnerships. They're preparing charges against us for treason, terrorism, and economic sabotage."

The irony was perfect. Exposing state-sanctioned murder would be prosecuted as an attack on state security. Truth transformed into betrayal with the stroke of a ministerial pen.

Lucas walked to the conservatory's destroyed eastern wall, where tactical teams had entered with explosive precision designed to ensure no witnesses survived to contradict whatever official version would be released to media outlets.

Through the gap, he could see Johannesburg spread below like a circuit board. Lights that marked lives Helena had never considered worth preserving. Streets that carried people who would never appear in Foundation promotional materials. Communities that existed beyond the moral mathematics of managed transition.

The city continued its work of converting human aspiration into economic statistics, apparently unchanged by the revelation that its most prominent charitable foundation had been operated by someone who discussed murder with the casual efficiency of routine business decisions.

"Grace's family," he said, turning back to face Major Botha's carefully neutral expression. "They need to know what really happened."

"Grace Mdluli's family has been notified of recent developments," Botha replied with the clinical precision of someone reading from prepared talking points. "They've been informed that criminal elements exploited her memory for propaganda purposes, and that appropriate authorities are investigating foreign interference in domestic reconciliation processes."

"Already arranged," Zara said, showing Lucas her secure phone where messages confirmed contact with Grace's sister in Cape Town, her brother in Durban, the community organizers who had spent months demanding answers about her disappearance. "The recordings are being distributed through channels Helena's people can't monitor or intercept."

Grace Mdluli's voice would finally reach the audiences she'd died trying to inform. Her evidence about Cypress operations, the shipping manifests that proved weapons trafficking, the digital signatures that connected Foundation charities to militia financing—all of it would survive the people who had killed her to protect it.

But survival, Lucas was learning, was not the same as acceptance. Truth was just information until it found audiences willing to act on it. Those audiences existed within political systems that had learned to process revelation as entertainment rather than evidence requiring institutional response.

"And the Legacy Protocol?" Lucas asked.

"Activated six hours before Helena died," Zara replied, her fingers moving across her keyboard with the mechanical precision of someone who had learned to work while being hunted. "Grace's insurance policy was more comprehensive than any of us understood. Automatic distribution to every major media outlet, legal system, and human rights organization in the world. Triggered by specific events— including violent deaths of key witnesses."

Major Botha's expression remained neutral, but Lucas caught the slight tension around his eyes that suggested this particular development had not been anticipated by whatever contingency planning had prepared for Helena's elimination. International distribution of evidence complicated the narrative management protocols that depended on controlling information flow through domestic channels.

Lucas realized they were looking at something more sophisticated than revenge. Grace had built a dead man's switch that converted her murder into evidence distribution. Her silence into a chorus of revelation that would outlive everyone who had tried to silence her.

But the people who had killed her had also learned from her example, developing their own dead man's switches designed to ensure that exposure would be processed through legal and political systems that could transform moral challenges into administrative problems.

"Helena knew," he said with sudden certainty. "She knew about the Legacy Protocol. That's why she tried to manipulate me with those recordings—her own voice repurposed as moral leverage. She was gambling that family loyalty could override moral judgment."

"She was wrong." Zara's voice carried the finality of a verdict thirty years in the making. "Helena died believing she could still shape your conscience. You proved she couldn't."

Through the conservatory's ruined walls, helicopters moved against the morning sky with the purposeful coordination of a media operation designed to shape tomorrow's headlines. Lucas recognized the choreography— official statements, expert commentary, the patient application of narrative pressure that would transform yesterday's confessions into today's conspiracy theories.

But the mathematics had changed in ways that even Helena's contingency planning had not fully anticipated. Her empire had been built on the assumption that truth could be managed, contained, edited into acceptable shapes. Grace's Legacy Protocol operated on different principles: redundancy, persistence, the kind of digital immortality that made cover-ups impossible and institutional murder counterproductive.

"The phone logs we pulled," Lucas said, scrolling through the list. "Beijing, London, and Washington. She was activating contingency protocols."

Zara nodded, still typing with mechanical persistence as global responses continued flooding their secure communications. "International response teams, designed to discredit evidence and eliminate witnesses. But they're learning the same lesson everyone learns eventually—some information achieves critical mass. After that, suppression becomes amplification."

Major Botha stepped forward with the measured authority of someone whose job was to ensure that critical mass never translated into actionable consequences.

"Mr. Brandt, Ms. Mokoena, I need to inform you that your safety requires immediate relocation to a secure facility pending completion of the investigation. Standard protective protocols for high-value witnesses in cases involving foreign-intelligence operations."

"Protective custody," Lucas said. "Containment by another name."

"Essential security measures," Botha corrected. "Recent events have demonstrated that hostile foreign elements are willing to use extreme measures to eliminate individuals who pose threats to their geopolitical objectives. Your survival is a matter of national security."

The trap was closing with bureaucratic efficiency. Lucas and Zara would be protected from the consequences of their own revelations by being isolated from audiences who might act on those revelations. Kept safe from retaliation by being kept silent until the news cycle processed their evidence as historical curiosity rather than contemporary scandal.

Lucas looked at the blood on the conservatory floor, at the orchids that had cost more than most people earned in a year, at the tactical residue of violence designed to look like the inevitable consequence of institutional stress. Helena had died believing she could control the narrative even from beyond the grave.

She was wrong about control. But her death had served one final purpose: it had proven that even the architects of organized forgetting could be forgotten, erased by systems they had helped create when those systems decided their continued existence threatened operational efficiency.

***

Far below Johannesburg's central business district, the underground server room hummed with the mechanical persistence of digital resurrection. Fifty meters down, Grace Mdluli's evidence continued its global propagation. Each mirrored copy another small victory against the machinery of organized amnesia.

The facility operated with the sterile efficiency of a medical laboratory, though its purpose was preserving information rather than life. Banks of servers lined reinforced walls, their cooling systems breathing with mechanical regularity as they processed the constant flow of data that connected legal systems across six continents.

LED indicators blinked in synchronized patterns that spelled out upload statistics in colors that meant nothing to human observers but everything to the algorithms that managed global evidence distribution.

Banks of monitors displayed upload statistics that climbed with relentless precision: ninety-four percent complete, ninety-six, ninety-eight. Within hours, every piece of evidence Grace had collected during five years of investigating state-sanctioned murder would be distributed across servers scattered across multiple continents. Backed up on systems designed to survive nuclear war and institutional collapse.

The Cypress files alone would generate prosecution cases for decades—arms trafficking, money laundering, assassination for hire—the complete infrastructure of democratically sanctioned violence.

But distribution, the system made clear, was not the same as prosecution. Legal frameworks that processed moral challenges as administrative problems required more than evidence—they required political will that could withstand the kind of sustained pressure institutions like the Foundation had perfected over decades of practice.

Printouts of shipping manifests waited in archives: documentation of weapons flowing to militia groups across the region, payment authorizations signed by officials who appeared regularly on television promising peace and reconciliation, customs declarations edited to hide the movement of materials designed for one purpose—making civil conflicts profitable by ensuring they never ended decisively.

Anton's vision lived on in data tables and budget lines. Managed chaos. Conflict maintained at levels that generated revenue without threatening the stability required for business operations.

Helena had refined it, adding deniability and psychological components—narrative management, truth weaponization, the transformation of evidence into entertainment that could be dismissed by audiences trained to prefer comfortable lies.

Air conditioning breathed with mechanical regularity, processing the heat generated by machines that had learned to think faster than human institutions could adapt. Through reinforced walls designed to withstand both physical assault and electromagnetic interference, the distant rumble of traffic vibrated faintly—a reminder that the city above continued converting human aspiration into economic statistics reviewed by boards that specialized in not asking inconvenient questions.

Yet something in that work had changed, even if the change was invisible to casual observation. Grace's evidence was already generating responses from prosecutors who had spent years waiting for documentation comprehensive enough to survive legal challenges mounted by defendants who could afford the kind of representation that specialized in making evidence inadmissible on technical grounds.

Bank accounts were being frozen across multiple jurisdictions, though the freezes affected only assets not transferred to domestic institutions hours before Helena's death. Weapons shipments were intercepted by customs officials who suddenly possessed the paperwork required to ask dangerous questions, though the interdictions reached only operations not redirected through alternative routes weeks before exposure.

The Foundation would survive; institutions like it always did. They evolved, adapted, found new operators who understood the necessary compromises. But they would survive transformed—operating under scrutiny that made their previous methods impossible, watched by audiences who had learned to recognize the difference between reconciliation and organized forgetting.

In backup drives and encrypted vaults, fragments of Helena's handwriting were archived beside Anton's contracts: instructions about navigating between principle and pragmatism without losing one's soul. She had died believing that change was possible from within—that someone with the right understanding could transform systems of evil into something approaching justice.

She had proven instead that institutional power was stronger than individual conscience, that systems built to perpetuate themselves would consume anyone who threatened their continued operation—even their own architects when necessary, even witnesses whose testimony might complicate whatever narrative would later be constructed around their elimination.

Status indicators climbed toward completion, indifferent to any witness. Grace's Legacy Protocol achieved full activation. Evidence that had cost lives to collect was now beyond the reach of any single authority to suppress or destroy.

The knowledge encoded here was more permanent and more dangerous than property or inheritance. Truth itself had become a weapon in conflicts between power and accountability, and weapons could be turned on anyone who wielded them—even those who had learned to wield them with surgical precision.

Somewhere beyond the concrete, helicopters moved across the sky—media aircraft documenting the revelation, or tactical teams preparing for whatever came next. The sound was identical. The difference existed only in the observer's faith in the distinction between information and surveillance, between documentation and targeting, between preservation and elimination.

"Legacy Protocol complete," the system announced in synthesized English that carried no emotion, no understanding of the human cost required to collect the information it was preserving with mechanical efficiency. "All primary and secondary servers operational. Redundancy achieved. Mission successful."

Grace Mdluli's voice would never speak again. But her evidence would continue speaking for generations, carried by networks that had learned to preserve information more efficiently than human memory could preserve the people who had died to collect it.

Whether that preservation would translate into accountability depended on audiences who had not yet learned to distinguish between truth and entertainment, between evidence and opinion, between justice and the performance of justice for people who could no longer afford to ask inconvenient questions.

By the following morning, protective custody had become performative. The files were public, the servers untouchable, and keeping their witnesses contained served no purpose beyond optics. A call from the Minister's office authorized quiet release "pending further inquiry." No cameras, no statements—just the bureaucracy correcting itself in silence.

When Lucas stepped back into the Johannesburg daylight, the city was already rewriting its narrative. Headlines called him both traitor and reformer. Neither title mattered. Freedom, like truth, had become a form of surveillance.

***

The Rand Club's dining room maintained its atmosphere of institutional dignity even as the world outside reorganized itself around evidence of institutional corruption. Old men in expensive suits discussed market volatility over meals they could no longer taste. Each conversation a careful dance around admissions that might be recorded, analyzed, and transformed into additional evidence by prosecutors who had learned to think like intelligence analysts.

The club's membership had learned to conduct business in languages designed for deniability. Speaking in conditional tenses about hypothetical relationships that might or might not have involved activities that could theoretically be construed as problematic by observers who lacked proper understanding of how regional stability was maintained through carefully calibrated applications of economic pressure.

Lucas sat alone at a table overlooking Johannesburg's financial district, watching buildings that housed the infrastructure Grace had spent five years documenting. Bank towers where weapons purchases had been disguised as infrastructure investments. Corporate headquarters where militia financing had been processed as charitable donations. Government offices where murder had been authorized with the casual efficiency of routine administrative decisions that required no more moral consideration than approving office supply requisitions.

His phone buzzed with messages from lawyers who specialized in defending institutional operations against individual conscience. International firms that had learned to navigate the gap between moral law and practical necessity. Their partnerships spanned jurisdictions in ways that made prosecution technically difficult and politically expensive.

They offered services with names like "crisis management" and "reputation protection," though their actual function was transforming evidence into opinion and accountability into administrative procedure.

But the mathematics had changed in ways that even the most sophisticated legal representation could not fully control. Helena's empire had operated on the assumption that revelation could be managed, contained, processed through systems designed to transform scandal into acceptable cost of doing business.

Grace's Legacy Protocol had proven that some information achieved escape velocity—becoming too distributed, too documented, too witnessed to be suppressed by conventional applications of legal and financial pressure.

German industrialists discussed futures that never quite reached the present, speaking in clauses built for plausible deniability.

Chinese investors allowed grammar itself to blur, their English bending conveniently when numbers turned political.

American diplomats perfected a style of disclosure that revealed everything except accountability.

Lucas recognized the performance from years of participation in similar conversations, where responsibility was distributed across so many participants that individual accountability became mathematically impossible. The language of institutional immunity, where moral challenges were processed as technical problems requiring administrative solutions that could be implemented by committees whose membership rotated frequently enough to prevent anyone from accumulating dangerous knowledge about systematic operations.

But Grace's evidence had changed those mathematics in ways that made traditional approaches to legal protection technically more difficult and politically more expensive. Names, dates, amounts, authorizations—documentation comprehensive enough to support prosecution across multiple jurisdictions simultaneously. Evidence that connected individual decisions to institutional outcomes in ways that made legal immunity require increasingly sophisticated and increasingly visible applications of political influence.

"Mr. Brandt." A voice interrupted his reflection—Dr. Naledi Langa, the Foundation's former ethics advisor, whose resignation had been processed within hours of Helena's death. She approached with the careful precision of someone who understood that every conversation might be monitored by audiences that had learned to interpret silence as admission of guilt requiring immediate investigation.

"Dr. Langa." Lucas gestured to the chair across from him, watching her calculate whether association with him served her strategic interests or threatened her legal position in ways that could not be mitigated through conventional applications of legal representation.

She sat with deliberate casualness. Ordered coffee with the studied normalcy of someone who had learned to perform routine behavior while everything familiar collapsed around her—according to protocols designed by people who knew that institutional survival depended on appearing calm amid ruin.

"The board met this morning," she said, her voice carrying the clinical precision of someone delivering information that had been carefully reviewed by legal advisors who specialized in ensuring that truthful statements could not be construed as admissions of institutional liability. "Unanimous vote. The Foundation's operations are suspended pending comprehensive legal review conducted by independent specialists whose qualifications have been verified by appropriate authorities."

"Suspended," Lucas repeated, noting how efficiently the language transformed institutional murder into administrative procedure requiring technical review by experts whose independence would be verified by the same systems that had authorized the original crimes. "Not terminated."

"Institutions like ours don't terminate," she replied with the matter-of-fact tone of someone describing natural law rather than human choice. "They hibernate. Reorganize. Emerge under new management with improved public relations and enhanced legal protections that incorporate lessons learned from previous operational challenges."

The admission carried no shame, no defensive justification—only the clinical precision of someone who had spent decades studying the resilience of systematic corruption against legal and political systems that had been designed to make such corruption technically difficult to prosecute successfully. Institutions that generated profit from managed violence had learned to evolve faster than legal frameworks could adapt to contain them, developing new methods that incorporated whatever challenges had threatened their previous configurations.

"And the evidence?" Lucas asked, though he already knew the answer would demonstrate the sophisticated techniques available to organizations that could afford the kind of legal representation that specialized in making comprehensive documentation appear inadequate for supporting criminal prosecution.

"Will be challenged in every jurisdiction simultaneously," Dr. Langa replied with the confidence of someone who had observed similar challenges succeed in transforming evidence into opinion through patient application of technical analysis. "International teams of forensic specialists will discover irregularities in digital signatures that suggest sophisticated manipulation by hostile foreign intelligence services. Expert witnesses will testify about advanced audio fabrication techniques available to governments seeking to destabilize regional democratic institutions. Media campaigns will raise questions about the psychological motivations of witnesses who appear to benefit financially from international attention generated by their accusations."

Lucas felt the machinery of institutional immunity rebuilding around Grace's evidence—a system that treated moral challenges as maintenance, solved by procedure. Truth blurred into opinion, evidence into spectacle, revelation into the convenient pathology of a compromised mind.

"Some of it will stick," he said, the words carrying more hope than conviction as he watched Dr. Langa's expression confirm that sticking was not the same as penetrating, that individual prosecutions could be processed as proof that the system worked rather than evidence that it was fundamentally corrupted.

"Some of it always does," Dr. Langa agreed with the weary authority of someone who had observed this process multiple times over decades of institutional service. "Individual prosecutions designed to satisfy public demand for accountability without threatening the fundamental infrastructure that makes continued operations possible. Symbolic consequences that demonstrate system responsiveness while preserving operational continuity through enhanced security protocols."

She finished her coffee with the unhurried precision of someone who had nowhere urgent to go and nothing pressing to accomplish—the rhythm of institutional exile, where former operators waited to discover whether their previous loyalties would be honored or their continued silence would require additional incentives delivered through methods that maintained plausible deniability.

"Grace's children will receive scholarships," she said finally, her voice carrying the tone of someone delivering good news that had been carefully structured to serve multiple institutional objectives simultaneously. "Full university education, postgraduate opportunities, professional placements that ensure comfortable futures. The Foundation's final act of charity before operational suspension pending legal review."

"Purchased silence," Lucas translated, understanding how efficiently moral obligations could be processed as financial transactions that served everyone's interests while acknowledging no one's responsibility for creating the circumstances that made such transactions necessary.

"Practical recognition that some losses require appropriate compensation," Dr. Langa corrected with the precision of someone who had learned to transform guilt into policy through careful application of administrative language. "Grace Mdluli died believing that exposure would lead to accountability. Her children will live believing that their mother's sacrifice generated meaningful change that improved institutional oversight. Everyone gets the narrative that serves their psychological needs while preserving operational continuity."

Lucas realized he was looking at the future of Grace's legacy—not the systematic dismantling of institutional corruption, but its careful management through improved public relations and enhanced legal protections that incorporated lessons learned from previous exposure. Her evidence would generate prosecutions that would be celebrated as proof that justice was possible, while the fundamental systems that had killed her continued operating under new names with more sophisticated methods for preventing future exposure.

The Rand Club's dining room continued its work of civilized conversation conducted in careful euphemisms that transformed moral challenges into technical problems requiring administrative solutions. But through its windows, Lucas could see protesters gathering in the financial district—people carrying signs with Grace's name, demanding accountability that their legal system was constitutionally incapable of delivering through conventional prosecution of individual defendants rather than systematic reform of institutional operations.

Some codes were designed to break under sufficient pressure. Others were designed to adapt, survive, and continue operating under modified protocols that incorporated whatever challenges had threatened their previous configurations.

The bloodline code had learned to evolve, processing moral pressure as administrative feedback that could be used to improve operational security while maintaining fundamental objectives.

Grace Mdluli's legacy would outlive the people who had killed her. But it would outlive them, in forms they had learned to manage, contain, and process through systems designed to transform moral challenges into evidence that such challenges represented threats to democratic stability rather than attempts to strengthen democratic accountability through exposure of systematic corruption.

Chapter 13 – The Legacy Gambit

Three seals stared back. Three agencies. The international arrest warrant arrived via encrypted diplomatic channels at precisely 6 a.m.—their "expertise" braided into a framework that turns evidence into "foreign manipulation." Lucas read his name in official typeface while drinking coffee in a safe house that overlooked Johannesburg's financial district. The warrant rasped under his thumb. Issued less than a week after the first leak, stamped with an international seal that felt like exile made official.

Wanted for treason, terrorism, economic sabotage. Each piece of documentation they'd released reframed as intelligence gathered through illegal surveillance, each revelation reclassified as material obtained through unlawful conspiracy with hostile foreign governments seeking to destabilize regional democratic institutions.

Irony didn't miss him. The legal language converted courage into collaboration, moral clarity into mental instability exploited by international conspirators.

Beneath that rhetoric, the same buildings that had housed Helena's empire still translated human aspiration into statistical data—unchanged by the revelation that their architects had been systematically murdering witnesses to state-sanctioned torture.

The Brandt Foundation's offices maintained their regular hours. Staff arrived with briefcases and purposeful expressions—as if institutional murder was just another quarterly challenge requiring strategic adjustment. Through high-powered binoculars borrowed from the safe house's tactical equipment, Lucas could observe the morning routine that had continued uninterrupted despite global exposure of the organization's true function. Coffee steam rose from windows. Business as usual.

Security had been enhanced—he counted twelve additional personnel positioned at entry points, their earpieces and coordinated movements suggesting military training rather than civilian protection services. But the enhancements appeared designed to manage public relations rather than operations, ensuring that media attention would be controlled while fundamental activities continued under improved security protocols.

Zara emerged from the communications room. Her laptop displayed news feeds that competed to frame yesterday's revelations as today's conspiracy theories. The transformation had occurred with breathtaking speed: Helena's confession morphing from evidence of institutional murder into proof of sophisticated psychological manipulation by foreign intelligence services who had exploited family trauma for geopolitical advantage. The screen's glow painted her face blue.

"Twelve hours," she said, reading from secure messages that continued arriving despite official claims that their sources had been "compromised by foreign actors." "That's how long it took them to convert your evidence into proof of international manipulation designed to destabilize regional democratic institutions through targeted disinformation campaigns."

Crisis managers with badges. Agencies in tow. Academics to certify the seam work—specialists deployed in concert with government agencies, media consultants deploying psychological frameworks that recontextualized evidence as the product of mental instability combined with foreign exploitation. The speed demonstrated institutional capabilities that exceeded anything Lucas had anticipated.

Lucas studied the warrant more carefully. Digital signatures were analyzed by forensic specialists who discovered manipulation techniques available only to state-level intelligence operations. Audio recordings were examined by experts who identified fabrication methods that exceeded civilian capabilities. Financial documents were reviewed by analysts who traced funding sources to accounts controlled by foreign governments with strategic interests in regional destabilization. Each piece of evidence they'd released was addressed systematically, noting the sophisticated legal architecture that had been constructed around their revelations like scaffolding around a demolition site.

"Helena's contingency protocols," he said—understanding finally penetrating the layers of preparation that had anticipated even this scenario. "Even in death, she's rewriting the narrative according to plans that were developed years in advance."

Through the safe house windows, helicopters moved across the morning sky. Patient predators who had learned that surveillance was more effective than violence when applied systematically over extended periods. The aircraft weren't hunting—they were documenting, recording, building comprehensive visual records that would transform Lucas and Zara from whistleblowers into central figures in an international conspiracy to destabilize democratic institutions through sophisticated disinformation operations. Rotor wash echoed off glass towers.

Zara reviewed upload statistics showing Grace's evidence spreading across global networks faster than any single authority could contain. "Six continents, forty-seven countries, every major human rights organization and investigative network," she said. "Helena's confession lit the fuse, and the Legacy Protocol carried the proof beyond deletion—two signals converging until suppression became impossible."

Distribution isn't belief. It's bandwidth. Action needs oxygen. Truth was just information until it found audiences willing to act on it, and those audiences existed within political systems that had learned to process revelation as entertainment rather than evidence requiring institutional reform.

The global reach that had seemed like victory was being transformed into proof of conspiracy. International attention that should have generated accountability was being reframed as evidence of foreign interference in domestic democratic processes. The more comprehensive their documentation, the more sophisticated the conspiracy appeared to international observers who had been trained to recognize the signs of state-level disinformation operations.

"The European Parliament voted for sanctions," Lucas noted, reading from a secure news feed that tracked international responses in real time. "Asset freezes, travel bans, comprehensive investigation into apartheid-era business relationships that continue to influence regional political development. But the African Union expressed grave concern about foreign interference in domestic reconciliation processes."

Europe sanctions. Africa bristles. Same data, different weather. European institutions that had been designed to process accountability claims from post-conflict societies were responding exactly as anticipated—with sanctions, investigations, and legal mechanisms that would generate domestic resistance rather than cooperation. African institutions that had been designed to resist external pressure were responding with defensive nationalism that framed international attention as imperialism rather than support for justice. The continental divide revealed the sophisticated nature of Helena's final gambit.

"Which means what, practically?" Zara asked—though her expression suggested she already understood the implications that were becoming visible as international responses developed according to patterns that someone had studied and anticipated.

"It means Helena understood the game better than we did," Lucas replied, feeling the weight of inherited naïveté settling into his chest like a stone that would remain there permanently. "International pressure generates domestic resistance through mechanisms that transform external support into internal opposition. The more foreign governments condemn South African institutional corruption, the easier it becomes for those institutions to frame accountability as imperialism requiring patriotic resistance."

The safe house's communication systems buzzed continuously. Incoming messages from lawyers, journalists, and human rights advocates who had spent the week analyzing Grace's evidence and Helena's confession revealed the sophisticated challenges of prosecuting systematic corruption in legal systems that had been designed specifically to make such prosecution technically difficult and politically expensive. Static filled the pauses between alerts.

International law operated through frameworks that required either domestic cooperation or Security Council authorization. Both could be blocked through diplomatic mechanisms that had been refined over decades of practice. Domestic law operated through frameworks that could classify international evidence as foreign interference requiring investigation rather than prosecution. The legal architecture that should have supported accountability had been designed to make accountability dependent on political cooperation from the same institutions that would be threatened by genuine accountability.

"ICC preliminary examination approved," Zara read from an encrypted message whose source would need to remain anonymous to prevent retaliation against international legal professionals. "But jurisdiction requires either government cooperation or Security Council referral. South African government claims domestic legal system remains adequate for addressing historical grievances through existing reconciliation mechanisms."

The bureaucratic language concealed a simple reality: international justice required domestic permission that would never be granted by institutions whose survival depended on preventing international justice. Security Council authorization required political consensus that could be blocked by any permanent member with strategic interests in regional stability rather than regional accountability.

"Swiss authorities froze Brandt Foundation accounts," Lucas added, continuing to monitor international responses that demonstrated both the reach and the limitations of global financial oversight. "But discovered that most operational funds had been transferred to domestic banks hours before Helena died. Almost as if she knew exactly when to trigger final asset protection protocols."

Asset transfers reveal preparation. Not just exposure—but the specific timing of that exposure, suggesting coordination between Helena's death and financial protection mechanisms that had been developed as part of comprehensive contingency planning. Someone had calculated exactly when international attention would peak and had positioned resources accordingly.

They were experiencing institutional immunity in real time. Even comprehensive evidence, even global distribution, even international attention could be processed through legal and political systems that had learned to absorb moral challenges without allowing them to threaten fundamental operations. The machinery of justice had been designed to require more political consensus than the machinery of injustice required to continue operating.

"Grace's children," Lucas said quietly—his voice carrying the weight of conversations that would shape lives he would never see develop. "Have they been contacted?"

Zara nodded. Her expression carried the accumulated weight of conversations that had required her to explain that their mother's vindication would arrive in forms that bore little resemblance to conventional understanding of justice or accountability. "Dr. Langa's arrangement through the reconstituted Brandt Foundation stands," she said. "Full scholarships, priority placements in the Foundation's humanitarian programs once they're of age, and trust-funded medical support. International NGOs are supplementing it, but the framework came from the Foundation's board after Helena's death—Langa made sure her empire paid something back."

The support was comprehensive, permanent, and carefully structured to operate independently of whatever domestic political developments might affect local attitudes toward Grace's legacy. But it was also a form of exile—protection that required accepting that justice for their mother would come from international institutions rather than the South African legal system that should have been responsible for prosecuting her murderers.

"Purchased comfort," Lucas translated—recognizing the patterns that Helena had taught him to identify in other people's compromises.

"Practical recognition that systematic change requires generational thinking rather than immediate gratification," Zara corrected, though her voice carried more determination than conviction. "Grace died believing that exposure would generate immediate accountability through existing legal mechanisms. Her children will live with the understanding that justice operates on timescales that transcend individual lives, demanding patience measured in decades, not court proceedings."

Through the safe house walls, they could hear the distant sound of protests. Voices calling for accountability that their legal system was constitutionally incapable of delivering through conventional prosecution—Grace's name had become a rallying cry for people demanding truth and reconciliation that actually reconciled something, but those demands would be processed through institutions that had learned to transform moral pressure into administrative procedure requiring technical solutions rather than systematic reform. Chants echoed off concrete, then faded.

The protests would continue for weeks. Media attention processed as evidence of democratic vitality rather than democratic failure. The demonstrators would eventually return to jobs and families that required their attention more urgently than political activism that produced no measurable results, while the institutions they were protesting would incorporate their demands into enhanced public relations protocols while maintaining operational continuity.

"The Foundation board meeting is today," Lucas said, checking his secure phone for messages that continued arriving despite official claims that he was operating under foreign intelligence guidance. "Emergency session to address leadership transition following Helena's death and recent security challenges."

Succession planning, prepared in advance. Board members whose qualifications had been verified by appropriate authorities would elect new leadership whose independence had been confirmed by enhanced background investigation protocols. The selection process would be transparent, documented, and entirely controlled by the same networks that had authorized Helena's original appointment. The meeting had been scheduled with remarkable speed—suggesting that contingencies had been planned years before they became necessary.

"They'll elect a caretaker," Zara predicted with the weary authority of someone who had observed similar transitions manage public relations challenges while preserving operational continuity. "Someone clean enough to manage international media attention but connected enough to maintain institutional relationships that preserve essential capabilities."

Reform, modernization, enhanced accountability measures. The new leadership would represent everything designed to prevent future exposure while maintaining the fundamental activities that made the Foundation profitable—tightened security, stronger legal review processes, updated public relations strategies. But the core mission would continue under improved management.

Lucas realized they were witnessing something more sophisticated than cover-up: institutional evolution in real time. Helena's death had triggered protocols designed to ensure that the machinery she'd operated could continue functioning under new management that had learned from the mistakes that had led to exposure while preserving the fundamental systems that made such mistakes profitable rather than costly.

"We won," he said—the words tasting like ashes mixed with medicine that might cure the disease but couldn't restore what the disease had already destroyed. "Grace's evidence is global. Helena's confession is preserved on servers that can't all be compromised simultaneously. Erasure wasn't an option anymore."

"And the corruption will continue," Zara said. Her fingers moved steadily, each keystroke an act of defiance in a system that treated documentation as procedure, not resistance. "They'll be more careful next time—better lawyers, fewer witnesses, cleaner exits."

The arrest warrant trembled in Lucas's hands. He understood the true scope of Helena's final gambit—which had anticipated not just exposure but the specific forms that exposure would take and the institutional responses that would neutralize exposure while appearing to embrace transparency and accountability. She had died knowing that her confession would transform Lucas into a symbol of foreign manipulation rather than domestic accountability, that international attention would generate nationalist resistance rather than legal consequences, that the systems she'd operated would survive by incorporating the lessons her exposure had taught about improved operational security.

"Some codes are designed to break under sufficient pressure," he said, remembering Anton's words from the ledger that had started their investigation into systematic corruption that operated through charitable foundations and reconciliation commissions. "Others are designed to evolve, incorporating whatever challenges threaten their continued operation."

The safe house's tactical equipment included monitoring systems that tracked multiple news feeds simultaneously. Real-time construction of competing narratives about Helena's death, Grace's evidence, and Lucas's mental state displayed across screens like surveillance footage of their own destruction. Professional crisis teams were working with government agencies to ensure that international attention would be processed as evidence of foreign interference rather than domestic accountability requirements.

Academic experts provided technical analysis that discovered sophisticated manipulation techniques in Helena's confession, suggesting that advanced psychological operations had been deployed against family members who were vulnerable due to unresolved trauma and inherited guilt. Media specialists deployed psychiatric frameworks that recontextualized Lucas's courage as the predictable consequence of mental instability combined with foreign exploitation of personal vulnerabilities.

Narrative construction happened faster than they could monitor. Much less counter. Professional teams that specialized in crisis management were implementing protocols that had been developed through years of experience managing similar challenges to institutional reputation—the same expertise that had been used to manage apartheid-era revelation was being applied to post-apartheid accountability claims.

"Grace died believing that truth was protection," Lucas said—understanding finally penetrating his inherited assumptions about the relationship between evidence and justice. "Helena died knowing that truth was just another weapon that could be turned against the people who wielded it."

***

THE BRANDT FOUNDATION BOARD MEETING

Surveillance sweep, three times in six hours. Paranoia—mostly theatrical. The Brandt Foundation's emergency board meeting convened in a conference room that had been swept for surveillance devices, though every conversation was being monitored by multiple intelligence services, each one building evidence for competing narratives about whether the Foundation represented institutional corruption or institutional victimhood requiring protection from foreign interference.

Expensive furniture suggests financial competence. Artwork demonstrates cultural sophistication. Technology proves operational efficiency. The conference room's design reflected the institutional aesthetic that had been carefully cultivated over decades of operation, but the atmosphere carried new tension that reflected recent challenges to organizational reputation that required careful management through enhanced security protocols.

Dr. Naledi Langa had been recalled within days and took her seat at the head of the mahogany table with the composed authority of someone who had spent decades preparing for moments when leadership required navigating between accountability and survival. The promotion from ethics advisor to interim chairman represented institutional continuity rather than reform—she had been selected precisely because her previous role demonstrated commitment to moral oversight while her continued employment proved that such oversight could coexist with operational requirements.

Around her, board members who had learned to measure success in terms of problems managed rather than problems solved waited for guidance. How to process the transformation of their organization from charitable foundation to international symbol of systematic corruption—the men and women seated at the polished table represented expertise in law, finance, public relations, and international development, all disciplines that had learned to navigate the gap between moral principles and practical necessities.

"The immediate challenges," Dr. Langa began, her voice carrying the clinical precision of someone conducting surgery on a system that had to continue functioning during the operation, "are legal, financial, and reputational. International assets frozen pending investigation, domestic operations suspended pending enhanced legal review, media attention that treats every administrative decision as evidence of ongoing conspiracy rather than institutional reform."

Through the conference room's bulletproof windows, protesters carried signs with Grace Mdluli's name.

Demanding justice that their legal system was designed to process as administrative procedure rather than criminal prosecution—the demonstration was peaceful, organized, precisely the kind of moral pressure that institutions like the Foundation had learned to absorb without allowing it to threaten fundamental operations.

Genuine moral concern that could be acknowledged, processed, incorporated. The protesters represented something that could be transformed into enhanced public relations strategies without requiring changes to fundamental operational methods—their demands for accountability would be met through symbolic responses that demonstrated institutional responsiveness while preserving operational continuity through improved security protocols.

"The Helena recordings," said Marcus Webb—the Foundation's security director whose expertise had been developed through years of managing challenges to organizational reputation that required both legal and extralegal responses—"are being analyzed by forensic specialists from six different countries. Initial assessment suggests sophisticated audio-manipulation designed to create false confessions that implicate institutional leadership in historical crimes."

Technical analysis by experts whose qualifications had been verified by appropriate authorities. Independence confirmed through enhanced background investigation protocols. Their preliminary findings suggested that advanced psychological operations had been deployed against Helena, exploiting her grief and guilt to create recordings that appeared authentic but contained subtle indicators of foreign manipulation.

The lie was elegant in its simplicity and comprehensive in its technical support: Helena's confession transformed from evidence of institutional murder into proof of sophisticated psychological warfare conducted by hostile foreign intelligence services. Her death reframed as elimination of a witness who had discovered foreign infiltration of domestic reconciliation processes rather than elimination of an operator who had become a liability to organizational security.

"Lucas Brandt," Dr. Langa continued, consulting documents that had been prepared by legal specialists whose expertise included managing similar challenges to institutional reputation, "is now wanted for treason in cooperation with international conspirators seeking to destabilize regional democratic institutions through targeted disinformation campaigns. His claims about family involvement in historical crimes appear to be the product of psychological manipulation by foreign intelligence services exploiting his grief and inherited guilt."

Expert psychological profile. Extensive experience analyzing mental states of individuals targeted by foreign intelligence operations—Lucas's breakdown following his father's death, combined with his isolation during twelve years in London, had created vulnerabilities that made him susceptible to manipulation by hostile actors seeking to exploit family connections for geopolitical advantage.

His courage reframed as mental instability. His evidence reclassified as foreign disinformation. His moral clarity converted into proof that international conspirators would exploit even family trauma to advance strategic objectives that had nothing to do with justice or accountability.

"And Grace Mdluli?" asked Sarah Chen—the Foundation's new ethics advisor, a woman whose appointment demonstrated institutional commitment to enhanced moral oversight while her background in international development proved that such oversight could coexist with operational requirements that transcended conventional understanding of ethical limitations.

"Remains a tragic victim of the political violence that characterized the transition period," Dr. Langa replied with the measured authority of someone whose statements had been reviewed by legal advisors who specialized in ensuring that truthful information could not be construed as admission of institutional liability. "Her death was investigated by appropriate authorities and determined to be the result of criminal activity unrelated to her journalistic work. Recent claims to the contrary appear to be part of the same foreign disinformation campaign that has targeted her memory for propaganda purposes."

Comprehensive transformation supported by technical evidence. Multiple independent experts had reviewed—Grace's murder reframed as criminal violence rather than institutional elimination, her evidence reclassified as foreign manipulation rather than domestic documentation, her legacy converted into proof that international conspirators would exploit even the deaths of innocent journalists to advance geopolitical objectives.

Her name would continue to be associated with truth and reconciliation. But truth and reconciliation that had been protected from foreign interference through appropriate institutional responses rather than truth and reconciliation that required accountability from domestic institutions whose operations transcended conventional legal frameworks.

"Operational continuity," Dr. Langa announced, moving from historical challenges to future protocols with the efficiency of someone whose leadership style had been developed through years of managing complex organizations under enhanced security requirements, "requires immediate implementation of enhanced security protocols designed to protect institutional integrity from future foreign interference attempts."

Background investigations for all staff. Enhanced legal review for all programs. Improved coordination with government authorities—the security enhancements would include specialists whose qualifications had been verified by appropriate authorities, independent experts whose independence had been confirmed through proper channels, authorities responsible for protecting democratic institutions from foreign interference operations.

Translation: the Foundation would survive by becoming more sophisticated about legal protection, more careful about documentation that could be misinterpreted by hostile actors, more efficient about identifying and neutralizing threats before they achieved the kind of international visibility that made management problematic for institutional reputation.

"The scholarship programs will continue," she said, her voice carrying genuine warmth as she discussed the Foundation's most visible charitable activities—which had been designed to demonstrate institutional commitment to educational development while providing practical mechanisms for managing potential sources of future opposition, "including the new Grace Mdluli Memorial Scholarship for investigative journalism—a program designed to honor her memory while supporting the kind of independent media that strengthens democratic accountability through appropriate professional channels."

A wreath that files minutes. Grace's name transformed into endorsement for the same Foundation that had authorized her elimination, her legacy processed into charitable programming that would train the next generation of journalists to pursue accountability through institutional channels that could manage such pursuit without threatening operational continuity. The irony was perfect and entirely intentional.

Professional standards that emphasized verification through official sources. Legal frameworks that required evidence to meet technical standards that exceeded civilian capabilities. Ethical guidelines that discouraged speculation about institutional motivation when official explanations were available through appropriate channels—the scholarship recipients would learn exactly what the Foundation needed them to learn.

"Motion to approve temporary operating protocols pending completion of comprehensive legal review," Dr. Langa announced, preparing for a vote that would restore institutional functionality while maintaining enhanced security measures designed to prevent future exposure of sensitive operations. "All in favor?"

Unanimous, as anticipated. Board members whose qualifications had been verified by appropriate authorities had selected protocols that had been developed by legal specialists whose expertise included managing similar challenges to institutional reputation—the Brandt Foundation would continue its work under new management that had learned from Helena's operational mistakes while preserving the fundamental infrastructure that had made those mistakes profitable rather than costly.

Grace's evidence would be processed as foreign disinformation designed to destabilize regional democratic institutions. Helena's confession would be dismissed as sophisticated fabrication created through advanced psychological manipulation. Lucas's courage would be reframed as mental instability exploited by hostile intelligence services for geopolitical advantage.

The system had learned to survive transparency by incorporating it into enhanced security protocols, to process accountability as administrative challenge requiring technical solutions, to transform moral pressure into evidence of foreign interference in domestic democratic processes that required patriotic resistance rather than institutional reform.

The systems hadn't broken; they'd absorbed the lesson. Exposure was just another variable in their design.

***

SUNSET OVER JOHANNESBURG

Copper and gold skyline. City lights like stars in a constellation designed by people who understood that beauty could coexist with systematic evil if managed with sufficient sophistication and appropriate security measures. Lucas stood on the safe house balcony, watching aircraft move across the evening sky with the purposeful coordination of surveillance systems that had learned to document rather than pursue direct confrontation.

Financial district. Government complex. University. The view encompassed the buildings where Helena's empire had operated through charitable foundations and development programs, where domestic legal frameworks processed international accountability claims as foreign interference requiring investigation rather than prosecution, where academic experts provided technical analysis that supported whatever narrative served institutional security requirements.

His phone buzzed with a message from the one lawyer who had agreed to represent him despite international arrest warrants and domestic treason charges that had been supported by comprehensive technical evidence: "Asylum applications submitted to twelve countries with appropriate legal frameworks for processing political persecution claims. Response time estimated at 18–24 months pending completion of background investigations by relevant security agencies."

Eighteen to twenty-four months. Backgrounds, verifications, the slow hum of permission. Long enough for the news cycle to process their revelations as historical curiosity rather than contemporary scandal requiring immediate response, long enough for the institutional systems they had challenged to implement improved security protocols while maintaining operational continuity through enhanced management techniques, long enough for Grace's name to be converted from symbol of resistance into symbol of the need for enhanced protection against foreign interference in domestic reconciliation processes.

Humanitarian concerns: balanced with security requirements. The asylum process itself would be managed by legal frameworks that had been designed to ensure that political persecution claims were processed through appropriate channels while preventing abuse by individuals whose activities might threaten regional stability through coordination with hostile foreign intelligence services.

"The University of Cape Town wants to establish a Grace Mdluli Research Chair," Zara said, reading from messages that continued arriving despite official claims that their communications were monitored by intelligence services whose capabilities included real-time interception and analysis of encrypted transmissions, "endowed by international human rights organizations whose independence has been verified through appropriate investigative protocols."

Full academic freedom to investigate post-apartheid institutional development. Scholarly methods that emphasized peer review, technical verification, and coordination with appropriate authorities responsible for protecting sensitive information that might be misused by hostile actors seeking to destabilize regional democratic institutions—the research position would provide exactly the kind of controlled investigation that served institutional interests.

"Academic freedom to investigate anything except the institutions that would control the research budget and determine publication protocols," Lucas translated—understanding how efficiently moral commitments could be processed through administrative frameworks that maintained the appearance of independence while ensuring operational control through financial and legal mechanisms.

Through the safe house windows, they could see the Brandt Foundation building. Lights burning late as staff worked to implement the enhanced security protocols that would ensure their organization's survival through adaptation rather than elimination—new leadership whose qualifications had been verified by appropriate authorities, improved legal protections developed by specialists whose expertise included managing similar institutional challenges, more sophisticated methods for managing threats before they achieved international visibility.

The building looked exactly the same as it had before Helena's death, before Grace's evidence achieved global distribution, before Lucas's courage had been reframed as mental instability exploited by foreign manipulation. The continuity was intentional—designed to demonstrate that institutional operations could incorporate moral challenges without requiring fundamental changes to operational methods or strategic objectives.

"We exposed everything," Zara said, her voice carrying the exhaustion of someone who had spent a week learning that exposure was not the same as accountability when processed through legal and political systems that had been designed to absorb moral challenges without allowing them to threaten fundamental operations. "Helena's confession is global. Grace's evidence is mirrored across jurisdictions. Anyone can see it; only power can pretend not to."

"And the corruption continues," Lucas replied, watching the Foundation building through tactical binoculars that revealed staff working late to implement protocols that had been developed by specialists whose expertise included managing similar challenges to institutional reputation, "operated by people who've learned to be more careful about creating documentation, more sophisticated about legal protection, more efficient about eliminating problems before they become international incidents requiring enhanced crisis management."

The arrest warrant crumpled in his hand. He understood the true scope of what they had achieved—not the destruction of institutional corruption, but its evolution into forms that could survive transparency, accountability, and international attention by incorporating those challenges as administrative problems requiring technical solutions rather than systematic reform.

Moral courage converted into criminal collaboration. Evidence into foreign disinformation. Love for Grace's memory into proof that international conspirators would exploit even personal grief for geopolitical advantage. The warrant's legal language required comprehensive technical support that demonstrated institutional capabilities that exceeded his previous understanding of how power operated through legal frameworks designed to process moral challenges as security threats.

"Grace died believing that truth was protection from institutional violence," he said—understanding finally penetrating his inherited assumptions about the relationship between evidence and justice in legal systems that had been designed to require more political consensus than individual courage could generate, "Helena died knowing that truth was just another weapon that could be turned against the people who wielded it through appropriate application of enhanced security protocols."

"And we live knowing that some battles are won by losing them in ways that preserve evidence for audiences still learning the difference between accountability and procedure," Zara said. She kept typing—slow, deliberate, as if endurance itself were the only protest left.

Above them, the stars emerged one by one. Indifferent to human struggles that played out in cycles too brief for cosmic attention but too long for individual lives that operated on timescales measured in decades rather than institutional planning cycles that measured success across generations. But in basement server rooms across six continents, Grace Mdluli's evidence continued its digital reproduction, each mirrored copy another small victory against the machinery of organized forgetting that had learned to incorporate memory as administrative challenge.

It wasn't the code that endured, but the questions it kept alive—proof that every system carries the seeds of its own remembering.

Some codes were designed to break under sufficient pressure applied through legal and political channels. Others were designed to endure whatever force was applied to destroy them—preserving testimony for audiences not yet ready to tell truth from entertainment, accountability from procedure, justice from its performance.

The legacy gambit had succeeded, but not in the way they had hoped when they began their investigation into systematic corruption that operated through charitable foundations and reconciliation commissions. Not through immediate accountability that would satisfy their desire for justice, but through patient preservation of evidence that would outlive the people who had killed Grace while being processed by institutional systems that had learned to manage moral challenges without allowing them to threaten operational continuity.

Grace's truth would outlive the people who had killed her. But it would outlive them in forms they had learned to manage, contain, and process through systems designed to transform moral challenges into evidence that such challenges represented threats to democracy rather than attempts to strengthen democratic accountability through exposure of systematic corruption that operated through enhanced security protocols.

The bloodline code had not just survived exposure—it had adapted. What had once processed moral pressure as feedback now absorbed resistance itself, translating outrage into new algorithms of control, refining the very systems it was meant to dismantle.

Chapter 14 – Clean Hands Coup

ONE WEEK AFTER THE CONSERVATORY

Thirty floors above Sandton, the media-operations suite gleamed—white walls and chrome under artificial light that never dimmed. At 6:47 a.m., the city below pulsed with morning traffic and the low electrical hum of servers that never slept.

Crisis Protocol Theta had been live since Helena Brandt's broadcast and the gunfire that ended it. The star was gone; the narrative wasn't. The speed of the machine told everything about how long they'd prepared for this moment.

The Control Room

Annelise Fourie stood before monitors cycling through polling data and social feeds—each refresh was another artificial heartbeat of manufactured consent. Behind her, three operatives worked in silence, fingers moving with surgical precision across glass and keyboard—Darren Katz's playbooks running on rails, the voice of a dead strategist whispering through code.

"The numbers shifted overnight," one analyst murmured. "Helena's approval up eleven. Lucas down eight."

Momentum was no longer a statistic—it was an infection curve.

Darren's lessons lingered like residue: Never fight sentiment; redirect it. Annelise had memorized that line, tracing it in the margin of his old notebooks the night they pulled his body from the conservatory.

She turned toward the data wall. "Keep the sympathy surge high but volatile. Too stable, and people start asking who benefits."

"Understood."

Graphs flickered in blues and grays. Riots muted into vigils, vigils into trending hashtags. The machine knew grief had a half-life; her job was to recycle it before it decayed.

"Run the Helena package," she said.

The central monitor bloomed to life: Helena Brandt, immaculate under studio light, speaking about legacy, reconciliation, courage. The footage had been recorded three weeks before the conservatory, back when she still believed she could control the timing of her confession.

Annelise watched the lip movements sync perfectly with the freshly inserted captions. The illusion was near flawless—breathing sweetened, pauses tightened, every imperfection sanded away by algorithmic empathy filters.

"She looks alive," one tech said softly.

"She is," Annelise replied. "Just not in the way she planned."

Helena's eyes stared from the screen—bright, certain, weaponized. The woman had built an empire on the conviction that appearance was proof of truth. Now appearance was all that remained.

"Segment two: Clean Hands Protocol," another operative announced.

The anchor on-screen spoke with casual authority, smile never quite touching her eyes. The phrase had been seeded months earlier through think tanks and policy blogs until it sounded like common sense. Now it captioned the posthumous redemption of a murderer.

Annelise allowed herself the smallest nod. "Push the long-form explainer to the European feeds. Keep Africa on the human-interest cut. Opposite sides of the same coin."

She turned to the window. From this height, traffic looked choreographed, pedestrians like figures in a simulation of real life. Darren's words echoed from memory: Power isn't about control—it's about choreography.

He'd been right. Even dead, he conducted the rhythm.

***

Annelise lingered at the glass wall until her reflection blurred into the skyline.

For a moment she imagined what Darren might have said if he'd lived long enough to see this version of his creation—the refinement of propaganda into pure algorithm.

He would have approved the metrics, adjusted a headline, then asked her if she still believed in conscience.

She no longer answered questions like that, even privately.

Working under Dr. Langa had taught her that morality and efficiency were not opposites but tools calibrated to circumstance. Ethics were just operational settings—change the input, change the virtue. Every institution eventually learned this truth; the successful ones admitted it early.

The suite hummed around her. Screens plotted outrage in real time. A line on the far wall mapped global reaction to Helena's death—a soft upward curve labeled Engagement/Empathy Index. Human sorrow, quantified to two decimal places.

She thought of her first month at the Foundation, when she'd written an internal memo arguing that transparency should have measurable goals. Darren had written a single comment in the margin: If it can be measured, it can be monetized.

Now his handwriting lived in her head like scripture.

The dead man's doctrine guided her through the living's confusion.

***

The conference table gleamed beneath recessed lights. Screens embedded in the surface displayed fragments of strategy—hashtags, projected audience sentiment, lists of journalists to cultivate or starve.

"Legacy narrative?" asked the young operative seated nearest her, eyes flicking nervously between columns of numbers.

"Consolidated," Annelise said. "Anton Brandt remains the necessary villain; Helena becomes the reformer who died too soon. Lucas stays undefined until public opinion demands definition. Undefined men can't be prosecuted."

A ripple of muted laughter. Relief disguised as professionalism.

"Any sign of the original footage?"

"Still sealed under investigation. We own the investigation."

They would, of course. The Brandt Foundation's board—now chaired by Dr. Naledi Langa—had positioned itself as both subject and supervisor of the inquiry. Independence verified by appropriate authorities, oversight confirmed by enhanced background checks—the vocabulary of legitimacy performing its usual miracle.

Annelise gestured toward the glass wall overlooking the newsroom floor. "Remember the rule. Every revelation becomes proof of foreign interference unless proven otherwise. Every doubt is patriotism."

She paused, scanning their faces for hesitation. None. They'd learned quickly; survival was an excellent tutor.

She dimmed the lights. Helena's face reappeared—re-edited, color-graded, luminous.

"The beauty of clean hands," she said quietly, quoting Darren's old memo, "is that everyone wants to believe in them. Even when they're covered in someone else's blood."

The operatives waited for instruction.

"Run it again," Annelise ordered.

The video looped—Helena smiling, apologizing, forgiving the world for what it had forced her to do. Somewhere inside the machine, empathy indexes rose by measurable degrees.

Downstairs, the system moved without its architect—smoother, faster, stripped of conscience.

***

Downstairs, the edit bay pulsed with blue light. Dozens of drives labeled ARCHIVE H/PR/LEGACY lined the shelves like tombstones. A young producer scrubbed through raw footage of the conservatory broadcast—the uncut chaos before the network feed switched to black.

"Skip past the gunfire," Annelise said from the doorway.

"Ma'am, that's where the confession starts—"

"We've all heard it."

She stepped closer. The image froze on Helena mid-sentence, eyes wide not from fear but recognition: the exact instant she realized control was gone.

Annelise studied the frame. "Cut from here to her earlier statement on responsibility. Blend with B-roll of the orchid wall. Overlay Darren's last audio file."

"The one marked Aftermath Directive?"

"Yes."

The producer hesitated. "That file... it's dated twelve hours before the shooting."

Annelise met his gaze. "Then he knew what was coming."

She left before he could ask anything further. In the corridor, she paused beside a window overlooking Sandton's skyline—sunlight hitting glass like confession reflected back. Two bodies gone, she thought, and still the building hums.

In the early years, she had believed systems died with their founders. Now she understood the opposite: people were the expendable components; the machine was immortal.

***

Board   Feed—Internal

Timestamp: 8:12   a.m.

Source Brandt Foundation Secure Channel / Dr. Naledi Langa (Interim Chair)

Langa: International attention remains high. We continue to frame Helena's death as the price of courage. Mr. Katz's actions during the incident will be characterized as operational miscommunication pending legal review.

Board Member 2: Do we expect criminal charges?

Langa: None that will survive discovery. The Directorate has accepted our offer of cooperation.

Board Member 3: And Lucas Brandt?

Langa: Exile by reputation. He's already trending as "the reluctant heir." The more he speaks, the guiltier he sounds.

Board Member 1: Public sentiment?

Langa: Improving. People mourn Helena; they distrust her enemies. That's enough for stability.

The transcript ended. Annelise closed the feed and stared at the screen's reflection—her own face haloed by the Brandt Foundation logo.

Helena was dead. Darren was dead. The broadcast had killed two people and birthed a machine.

She whispered it to herself like liturgy, a reminder and a warning.

***

The suite dimmed again. Technicians prepared the composite: archive interviews, humanitarian footage, the final edited confession scrubbed of blood and noise.

The first cut began with a wide shot of the conservatory before the shooting—Helena among orchids, her smile composed, voice gentle: Reconciliation requires order, not spectacle.

Then came the dissolve: a child receiving medicine in a clinic, a solar pump turning, the Brandt logo discreet in the corner frame. A eulogy disguised as advertisement.

"Overlay the tagline," Annelise said.

Words appeared in white serif: CLEAN HANDS BUILD THE FUTURE.

She tasted bile. "Lower-third it. Never headline."

The junior editor nodded. "Audio?"

"Use the Grace track."

He frowned. "The journalist?"

"Her last voicemail. Keep the static."

They layered Grace Mdluli's trembling voice—half-broken, half-defiant—beneath Helena's image. Truth has a

224

memory, it said. The juxtaposition tested like art: compassion scored to confession.

Annelise listened once, twice. "Good. Loop it across six continents. Let outrage run concurrent with admiration."

"Won't that confuse the audience?"

"That's the point. Confusion's the perfect sedative."

***

The distribution stand-up began with the economy of a combat drill. No greetings, no names—just function

"South African broadcast partners?" Annelise asked.

"Primary networks confirmed—late-night replay blocks secured," the syndication lead said. "Local radio will run the clip packages with approved intros. Community outlets get the human-interest cut and a call-in prompt."

"Add a grief counselor to the radio pack," Annelise said. "Script two questions that ask for memories of Helena's philanthropy. No open mics."

"Done."

"Continental feeds?"

"East Africa prefers the scholarship angle; West Africa is testing the hospital footage. North Africa is running the governance frame—rule of law plus stability."

"Keep Europe on policy language," Annelise said. "Sanctions fatigue works in our favor there. Remind them corruption is complex and transition is delicate."

A junior on the far end raised a hand—hesitant, precise. "We're seeing a small spike of 'weaponized nostalgia' complaints. Users saying the montage is manipulative."

"It is manipulative," Annelise said, without heat. "That's why it works. Lower the music bed two decibels and cut a breath into the transition. People trust edits that let them breathe."

The junior nodded and typed.

"United States?" she asked.

The analytics lead didn't look up. "Polarized—predictably. Right-leaning outlets are amplifying 'foreign interference' tags; center-left is leaning on 'institutional reform' and 'courage to confront legacy.' We bought two think-tank newsletters on each side to 'converge' around the same conclusion: complexity."

"Good," Annelise said. "Complexity is consent's older sister."

On the wall, a heat map pulsed—a living body of sentiment. A pale vein ran through Johannesburg's northern suburbs, blue edged with ember. The caption read: Trust Drift—0.06/hr.

"Trust drift?" she asked.

"Slow movement," the analyst said. "Not toward belief, just away from anger. People still argue, but the stakes feel smaller."

Annelise let the numbers sit. Stake-shrink was one of Darren's favorite pressure valves. Lower the perceived cost of caring and you lower turnout. She could hear his voice delivering the lesson while he stood at a window just like this, a city just as compliant.

"Push the long read," she said. "The one that asks whether outrage culture harms reconciliation. Link to a podcast with a gentle host and a tireless yawn."

Soft laughter moved through the room like permission.

"What about the raw conservatory footage?" someone asked. "Not our cut. The one with the chaos."

"It will surface. It should," Annelise said. "Give people something to call 'the real one.' Then point out there are three 'real ones'—and none match. If reality is crowded, authority decides."

The phrase landed and stayed. Authority decides. It was the kind of sentence that could drive a lifetime or end one.

A producer at the back cleared her throat. "There's a thread gaining speed: 'Grace's files are being chopped up.' Do we address?"

"Of course they're being chopped up," Annelise said. "Everything is. Respond once from an expert account: 'Contextualization is standard editorial practice.' Then go quiet. If you argue with grief, you become the villain in your own story."

The producer wrote it down like a recipe.

"Language pack," Annelise said.

A copywriter swiveled his laptop toward the table. "Updated terms: curation, timed transparency, stability dividend, civic stamina. Retire moving forward—it's polling dead."

"Replace with continuing the work," Annelise said. "It implies progress without promising outcome."

On the heat map, the pale vein cooled by a shade.

"Last item," she said. "Counter-programming for tonight."

A scheduler clicked to a grid: sports finals, a celebrity breakup, a minister's minor scandal. "We're feeding friendly producers three mini-segments not about us. Audiences can only metabolize so much tragedy."

Annelise nodded. "Then give them something to metabolize."

The meeting ended as cleanly as it had begun. Chairs slid back. Screens changed shape. The room exhaled.

For a moment, nobody moved. They were listening—to the hum of the building, to the slow click of a thousand scheduled posts going live, to a ghost of a voice that had once told them this was simply professional excellence in the service of public calm.

Annelise pressed a palm against the glass. Below, lanes of traffic braided and unbraided with the grace of practiced obedience.

"Run the package," she said again, softly. "Let it teach them how to feel."

The tech at the console didn't ask which cut. By now, the machine knew.

***

Annelise turned back to the monitors. On one, Helena smiled eternally; on another, stock footage of Johannesburg at dawn; on a third, live metrics tracking the acceleration of belief.

The numbers climbed.

Outside, the sun cleared the skyline. The city glittered with the cruel beauty of systems that could not feel remorse.

∗∗∗

The safe house was small and deliberately anonymous—the kind of place where a journalist could disappear between stories.

The television's blue light washed over the walls like static prayer; every few seconds a new broadcast replaced the last, looping the Helena Package across networks as if repetition could become truth through endurance.

Zara sat on the edge of the couch, laptop balanced on her knees, eyes fixed on Helena's edited smile.

The broadcast carried all the refinements of postproduction: background hum reduced, light softened, pauses timed to the heartbeat of empathy.

It looked live. It looked sincere.

The anchor introduced Helena as "the visionary reformer whose courage cost her life."

Footage of the conservatory shimmered briefly—glass and orchids before the violence—then faded into charity footage and institutional logos.

Zara muted the sound and let her gaze rest on the crawl of metrics beneath the image.

Audience engagement up nineteen percent. Positive sentiment trending.

The machine had learned to mourn profitably.

Her phone buzzed with a new message from an encrypted channel she didn't recognize.

Stop chasing ghosts. You already published them.

She deleted it. She'd received dozens like it since the conservatory—each one written in the same clipped syntax that could have come from anyone with clearance high enough to monitor her transmissions.

The Helena narrative wasn't merely surviving; it was multiplying.

Zara opened a new window and began tracing packet routes through anonymized relays.

Half the addresses resolved to content farms in Singapore and Bratislava, the other half to a Johannesburg law firm that claimed to specialize in intellectual-property arbitration. She followed the legal trail until it looped back to the Brandt Foundation's media-licensing arm. Every path ended at a subsidiary designed to look independent.

She saved screenshots, hash-stamped the files, uploaded them to an offshore vault. Proof didn't matter anymore, but habit was survival.

An encrypted ping blinked in the corner of her screen.

V MOKOENA: Still breathing?

Z MOKOENA: Breathing. Not sure for how long.

V MOKOENA: The footage's source node moved. They're laundering it through satellite mirrors. You'll never prove authorship now.

Z MOKOENA: Maybe proving isn't the point.

She closed the chat and stared at the static face of Helena on the monitor. The woman had become pure content—indestructible because she was no longer human enough to contradict herself.

Zara whispered, "You win by being everywhere and nowhere."

Then she added another line to her notes: Omnipresence is the final privilege of the powerful.

Zara closed the terminal and leaned back.

The room hummed softly—refrigerator, hard drive, heartbeat. Then a new window opened on its own—no ping, no command. A gray interface filled the screen, stamped with the Brandt Foundation seal and the words INTERNAL TRAINING FEED – VERIFIED SOURCE.

She almost closed it, then stopped.

Curiosity, that oldest occupational hazard.

The feed resolved into a polished recording of Dr. Naledi Langa standing at a lectern in a sound-treated studio. Behind her, the Foundation's insignia rotated like a halo.

"Welcome to this quarter's Ethics and Information Stewardship module," she began, voice low, deliberate, motherly. "Our responsibility is to guard not merely truth, but trust. Data is never neutral—it carries the emotional architecture of those who believe it."

Zara froze.

The speech was framed like a university seminar, but the subtext read like counter-insurgency doctrine.

Langa continued:

"Transparency requires discernment. Not all revelations serve reconciliation. Some truths, when released prematurely, create harm greater than the secrecy they replace. The ethical practitioner therefore curates information with empathy. To protect people is not to hide the truth—it is to time it."

Slides appeared beside her: smiling employees, foundation clinics, schoolchildren beneath solar panels. Beneath each image ran small text—phrases that sounded innocuous until repeated aloud:

Perception management as humanitarian safeguard. Compassion through calibration.

Zara scribbled notes, though she knew the feed was probably logging every keystroke.

Langa's voice flowed on, precise and persuasive.

"Our late founder understood that facts are fragile. Mishandled, they become weapons. Managed responsibly, they become bridges. The difference lies not in content, but in control."

A ripple of applause followed from an invisible audience.

Then a second speaker appeared—one of the younger communications officers. She recited a case study on "narrative contamination," explaining how digital fragments of Helena Brandt's final broadcast had been "misinterpreted" by hostile networks.

Her closing line drew polite laughter: "Even truth benefits from editing."

Zara felt the air thicken around her.

This wasn't an internal pep talk; it was doctrine being minted in real time.

The Foundation had learned to convert catastrophe into curriculum.

Langa's voice returned for the conclusion.

"Remember," she said, hands clasped, eyes steady on the camera, "the public hungers for certainty more than accuracy. Give them certainty, and they will forgive the delay of truth."

The feed froze.

A line of white text scrolled across the bottom:

This training material is confidential. Unauthorized redistribution constitutes a breach of reconciliation protocol.

Zara exhaled slowly.

Her laptop fan kept spinning, like a tiny engine processing disbelief.

She copied the cached file to a hidden directory—not to release it, not yet—but to remind herself that moral vocabulary was the most efficient disguise for corruption.

When she finally looked back at Helena's looping smile on the muted television, the message played differently.

It wasn't confession anymore; it was compliance.

Even the ghosts were taking the course.

She whispered to the empty room, "They've made ethics the new censorship."

Every network carried a version optimized for its audience—human-interest profiles for Africa, moral-redemption arcs for Europe, think pieces about legacy management for North America.

Grace Mdluli's evidence still surfaced in fragments across the deep web, but every time it did, a verified account appeared to "contextualize" the leaks: foreign manipulation, malicious editing, deep-fake contamination.

Zara replayed the Foundation's statement once more.

Helena's voice—polished, haunting—spoke of reconciliation and rebirth.

It was the voice of a woman who had already been buried, resurrected by algorithm.

The irony twisted in Zara's throat. They killed her twice, she thought. Once with a bullet, once with perfection.

She opened her laptop and began typing, the motion automatic.

Headlines filled the screen—each article dissecting the tragedy, each analysis quoting officials whose affiliations led back to the same corporate nodes.

The Brandt Foundation had transformed guilt into governance, crime into policy.

In her notes she wrote:

THE MACHINE HAS NO CONSCIENCE—ONLY CONTENT.

Then beneath it:

Truth is not erased. It's overwritten.

A knock sounded at the door. Too soft for police, too punctual for neighbors. She didn't answer.

Instead she whispered into her recorder:

"They're burying Lucas alive. Not with dirt, but with irrelevance. And the beautiful thing is—they're making it look like mercy."

She saved the file under a random filename and sent it to a dead drop Victor had once configured for her—one of those old intelligence addresses buried in cloud architecture.

Seconds later, the transmission confirmed: Delivered.

Zara exhaled. Somewhere, Grace's voice still lived in servers they couldn't reach. Maybe that was enough.

She shut the laptop. The screen went black, and for a moment her own reflection looked like a witness statement—flickering, incomplete, but still breathing.

***

The rooftop of the safe house stretched like a slab of poured concrete beneath the Johannesburg sky, its edges

232

hemmed by a low parapet that offered no comfort to those who lingered there. Lucas lit a cigarette. He hadn't smoked in years; the first drag tasted like memory and ash, steadier than sleep.

He stood at the railing, cigarette burning down between his fingers, watching the city's lights pulse with the rhythm of consumption. Below, the building murmured with anonymous tenants and the static buzz of power lines. Inside, muted televisions replayed Helena's reconstructed confession. Her death had been edited into advertisement; her voice now sold forgiveness by the hour.

Lucas scrolled through the day's coverage on his phone. Each headline repeated the same mantra: Helena Brandt— Architect of Renewal. Commentators described him as the grieving son withdrawing from public life. He wasn't withdrawing; he was being written out.

He lit another cigarette and stared into the night. The ember's glow reflected in the glass railing—a private composition.

Someone had texted him earlier from an encrypted number: Tomorrow's headlines are already written. Last chance to write your own. He'd deleted it without answering. Darren's tone—impossible, since Darren was dead, but the cadence unmistakable. The man's systems still spoke through automated outreach, predictive responses built to impersonate initiative. Even in death, Darren's voice managed the conversation.

He remembered the conservatory's chaos—the gunfire, the orchids trembling under pressure waves, the smell of cordite and cut flowers.

He remembered Helena collapsing mid-sentence, the blood halo blooming behind her.

And he remembered Zara's face illuminated by laptop light as the feed continued to broadcast. Every second archived. Every frame replicating across encrypted servers faster than any authority could erase it. They had all survived the broadcast except the ones who mattered. Now the living cleaned the mess with narratives the dead had left behind.

He opened the secure folder on his phone—files Grace had entrusted to Zara, mirrored once more to him through the Legacy Protocol. Each document bore timestamps, signatures, invoices—proof of the machinery beneath philanthropy. He knew releasing them again would accomplish nothing; the data was already public, absorbed, neutralized by overexposure. Transparency had become camouflage.

He closed the folder and recorded a message instead. "They think they've won because they control the story. But stories change. When this one changes, I want to be holding the pen." He attached the audio to a new encrypted packet and sent it to a relay address Zara would recognize by pattern, not by name. Then he deleted every trace of it and watched the smoke drift toward the skyline. The city glittered—beautiful, complicit, alive. He could almost believe it didn't care who ruled it, so long as the lights stayed on.

Inside the apartment, televisions cycled through Clean Hands Protocol retrospectives—analysis panels, orchestral soundtracks, polished anchors. Helena smiled eternally from every screen. Her voice promised reconciliation while data crawlers harvested the metrics of forgiveness. Lucas poured himself a drink—whiskey, neat, the kind Anton had reserved for victory nights. He raised the glass to no one. "To the survivors," he muttered. "To the ghosts that pay dividends."

He thought of Darren's meticulous planning, of Annelise Fourie—the new communications director he'd only read about—now executing his scripts without hesitation. He imagined Dr. Langa chairing the Foundation board, delivering statements about reform while budgets rerouted through identical channels. The system hadn't died; it had molted.

From the open window came the city's steady exhale—sirens, laughter, a passing helicopter's low thrum. It sounded like a creature digesting its meal. He placed the glass on the railing and watched the reflection split the night sky: one world above, one below. Maybe that was the truth of it—

two reflections feeding each other, light bouncing endlessly until no one remembered which image was real.

He whispered, "Grace was right. Truth has a memory. But memory forgets who told it first."

His phone vibrated again: a single notification from an unknown address. Packet received. No signature. No words. Just confirmation. Somewhere, Zara had opened it. Lucas smiled faintly. That was enough.

He leaned against the parapet, cigarette ember falling like a tiny meteor through the dark. From this height he could see the Brandt Foundation tower glowing across the city—the skyline's cleanest lie. Every window burned as though conscience could be measured in lumens. He knew inside those offices Annelise and Langa were preparing the next wave of outreach, the next recalibration of guilt into gratitude. Helena's holographic projection would open tomorrow's symposium. Darren's algorithms would supply the talking points. The dead would keep working.

Lucas whispered to the night, "Then so will I."

He turned toward the stairwell. Each step echoed against concrete, drumbeats announcing a different kind of war—the quiet one waged with evidence, with patience, with the stubborn insistence that the truth deserved witnesses even if it never earned justice.

At the landing he paused and looked back once more at the city—its towers shining like circuitry, its streets pulsing with encrypted traffic. He thought of Grace's children, of the scholarships now bearing her name, of the cost of being remembered correctly. If the system wanted stories, he would give it one it couldn't digest.

Night pressed against the glass as though testing the strength of conviction. Some codes were designed to break under sufficient pressure. Others were built to adapt, absorbing resistance until resistance became fuel. But there were a few—rare, dangerous—that learned to outwait the systems that created them.

Lucas exhaled the last of his smoke. "It's not the code that endures," he murmured, "but the question it keeps alive."

He turned off the light.

Outside, the servers of Johannesburg hummed, carrying Helena's voice, Darren's algorithms, Grace's evidence— millions of fragments of confession drifting through fiber and cloud. Each copy another heartbeat in a machine that mistook persistence for morality. And somewhere among those signals, one packet carried a new voice. Not a confession, not a plea—just the promise he'd sent, whispered now into circuitry.

This time, I'm the one writing the story.

The night accepted it without argument. Stars burned indifferent above, and in the windows across the skyline, the screens kept glowing. Some codes were meant to be broken. Some stories were meant to survive.

Chapter 15 – Roots of the Truth

The red lamp flickers—steady, deliberate. Each flash, a heartbeat against the concrete hush. It illuminates nothing beyond a shallow circle of blood-warm light, but it's enough. Enough to spike her pulse and remind her how far she's pushed. The lamp's crimson pulse marks time between revelation and ruin.

The air feels thicker now.

Overhead fluorescents hum with mechanical indifference. Their pallid glow pools across strewn files, battered hard drives, machines in the corners gathering dust. Stale odors cling to the air: cold coffee, accumulated sweat, the metallic tang of her anticipation. The workspace breathes exhaustion. Sleepless nights, burned bridges—each surface a witness to months of careful investigation and dangerous discovery.

Grace had trusted her to finish what truth began—a simple, impossible inheritance Zara now carried alone.

This wasn't a repost of the Cypress dump. This was the second wave—Grace's ledger, the pieces held back until the world finished swallowing the first hit and Annelise Fourie had finished muddying the water.

Zara's gaze never strays from the monitor.

Grace had been careful. Too careful. Even her disappearance felt rehearsed. They never found her body—just a classified file and, months later, a fraudulent certificate that turned disappearance into paperwork. But the deeper Zara dug, the more questions multiplied like viral code. Grace's name still tastes like ash—bitter, incomplete.

They'd all moved on too quickly. Accepting the official narrative with suspicious ease. Zara hates that she almost had, too. The absence carved a void no amount of evidence could fill—a reminder that in this war between truth and power, casualties weren't always what they seemed.

The timing had been too perfect. Too convenient. Grace disappears just as her investigation reaches critical mass, just as she's about to expose the Cypress network's deepest connections. The kind of timing that suggested careful orchestration rather than tragic coincidence. Someone wanted Grace gone. Dead—or only silent?

In Zara's experience, the most effective silencing doesn't need a corpse. It needs a ghost.

She touches the corner of her monitor where Grace's contact photo once sat—a ritual of remembrance performed each night before diving into the files. "I'm still listening." Her whisper to the empty workspace, barely audible above the electronic hum that serves as the soundtrack to her crusade. "Wherever you are."

Grace would have laughed at the setup. Working in shadows to expose people who thrived in them. If you're going to fight monsters, she'd said once, make sure you don't become one. But monsters, Zara had learned, were just people who'd forgotten the weight of consequences.

Grace never forgot. Grace carried every cost, every casualty, every choice that led to someone else's suffering. That's what made her disappearance so suspicious—Grace would never have simply run. She would have left breadcrumbs. Clues. Some way for the truth to survive even if she couldn't.

The outside world—Johannesburg, simmering under a humid sky—vanishes beyond thin glass. Here, time slows to revelation's pace. Each discovery a step deeper into corruption's labyrinth, stretching back decades. She's chased leads like this before. Each one a high-wire act against powers that bury inconvenient truths.

Two schools sabotaged. Three newsroom offices raided. Expulsions and blacklists.

Yet she's survived. So have her sources—most of them.

Scars mark her memory—late nights handcuffed to keyboards, dodging bribes from spooked informants, sifting through patchy code. But hunger for truth drives her past fear and safety alike. That same hunger had driven Grace, right up until the moment she vanished into the bureaucratic ether that swallows inconvenient people in post-apartheid South Africa.

Tonight's haul shimmers on screen like a dark array.

None of this appeared in the Cypress files. This was the rebuttal: hard receipts and provenance keys. Signatures. Timestamps. The chain of custody that turns outrage into evidence.

Payment logs tied to shell companies. Chain-of-command cables whispered through back channels. A battered photo of Anton Brandt clasping the former president's hand above an off-limits mine shaft. Each document is a star in guilt's galaxy, connected by invisible threads of complicity and greed.

But threaded through it all are anomalies. Patterns that suggest someone on the inside had been documenting everything, preparing for this exact moment of exposure.

Grace's work. It had to be.

Not just more of the same—corroboration. Cross-checks the algorithms couldn't shrug off, the kind of redundancy built to survive injunctions and press conferences.

Metadata signatures. Careful chronology. Files encrypted with keys only Grace could have generated. She hadn't just been investigating the Cypress network—she'd been building a case that could survive her elimination. The question was whether that elimination had been permanent. Or whether Grace was still out there, waiting for the right moment to resurface.

Zara inhales. Exhales slowly enough to keep tremor from leaking into her voice. Beneath that measured breath, her heart hammers—in her throat, behind her eyes, in the metallic taste at the back of her tongue. Each new file represents another secret liberated from darkness. But also another piece of evidence that Grace might still be alive, somewhere in the shadows between official death and underground survival.

She shifts—hips cracking—and tilts back in the swivel chair that's become both throne and prison over sixteen hours. Fingers hover over keys, taut and ready.

She recalls nights spent cursing dead-ends. Bribed ex-contacts whose witness relocation agreements collapsed. Endless decryption loops that nearly smoked her rig. Rusty servers in abandoned warehouses that might as well have been booby traps. But also nights when phantom messages appeared in encrypted channels. Unsigned documents materialized in secure drops. Intelligence that came from nowhere and led everywhere.

The Cypress USB, polished and cryptic, finally surrendered its contents after she threatened legal channels the suppliers couldn't deny. But the real breakthrough had been recognizing the handwriting in the margin notes—Grace's distinctive script, commenting on financial flows and operational timelines with the precision of someone building a case for posterity.

At 3:00 a.m., the breakthrough. Exhaustion cracked the encryption like a lock picked by fatigue itself. Inside the USB: a roadmap to hell paved with good intentions and lined with blood money. Banking records show funds flowing from mining operations to political campaigns, from campaign coffers to private accounts, and from private accounts to offshore shelters where money launders itself clean in tropical jurisdictions that ask no questions and keep no records.

But it wasn't just money.

The drive contained communications—encrypted emails revealing institutional greed's human cost. Conversations about "acceptable losses" and "necessary sacrifices." Discussions of environmental impact reports buried before ink dried. Medical studies suppressed when they revealed mining operations' true cost on surrounding communities. Each message was a window into souls that had sold themselves so thoroughly they no longer remembered what integrity felt like.

And woven through it all, like a golden thread in a tapestry of corruption, were Grace's annotations. Subtle marginalia that revealed patterns the original actors hadn't seen. Connections that transformed isolated incidents into systematic oppression.

Grace had seen fragments of this before her disappearance. She'd mapped the edges, traced the connections, understood that what they were uncovering wasn't isolated corruption but systematic architecture. She vanished knowing the scope of it. Vanished trying to build a case that would survive her apparent elimination.

The evidence cascades across multiple screens now—banking records, encrypted communications, photographs showing handshakes worth millions. Each document threads through corruption's web stretching from the goldfields of the Free State to Parliament's marble halls. The Brandt name appears again and again, woven through decades of impossible deals. Profitable arrangements leaving environmental disasters and silenced whistleblowers in their wake.

But so does Grace's signature methodology. The careful documentation of sources. The cross-referencing of dates and amounts. The patient construction of irrefutable cases.

She opens another file containing geological surveys never meant for daylight. The reports detail environmental damage requiring generations to heal—if healing were possible at all. Groundwater contamination. Soil depletion. Air quality measurements that would have shut down operations if anyone with authority had bothered reading them.

But authority was purchased. The financial records made that clear. Regulatory blindness was carefully itemized, each bribe documented with business-expense meticulousness.

A photograph stops her scrolling. Anton Brandt, younger but no less predatory, standing beside a mine shaft that no longer exists according to the metadata. Image quality is poor—shot in secret—but the faces are unmistakable. Beside Anton stands a man in government uniform, insignia marking him as a mine safety inspector. Between them, a briefcase sits open, revealing currency stacks catching camera flash like dirty snow.

The timestamp predates the Hartbeespoort disaster by six months. Grace couldn't have been more than twenty-three—sharp-eyed, unshaken, already chasing corruption before it learned to hide in plain sight.

In the corner, barely visible, are Grace's initials—GM—marking this as one of her photographic intelligence collections. Grace had been there. Documenting corruption before it crystallized into tragedy. Building evidence for prosecutions that never came.

Zara's breath catches. This wasn't about covering up the past. It was about buying silence before disaster ever struck. Grace had been right—the corruption wasn't reactive, cleaning up after accidents. It was preemptive, ensuring that when people died, their deaths would be deemed acceptable from the start.

And Grace had documented it all. Creating a paper trail that led directly to the Brandt empire's heart.

Her secure phone buzzes. Vibration sharp against the desk's metal surface. A message from Lucas: "Found something in the files. Can't discuss over phone. Meet tomorrow?"

She stares at the message, pulse quickening. After months of careful investigation, following breadcrumbs and dodging threats, they're finally close to the center of it all. The Brandt family's secrets. Grace's disappearance. The systematic silencing of anyone who asked wrong questions—it's all connected, and evidence is finally within reach.

But more than that. The evidence suggests Grace might have been preparing for exactly this moment. Building networks and safeguards that could operate even in her absence.

But as she prepares to respond, something shifts in shadows outside her workspace window. Movement that doesn't belong in the city night's ordinary rhythm. Two figures press against the opposite building, their stillness too deliberate for casual observation. Professional surveillance has a quality distinguishing it from casual observation—predatory patience setting it apart from passersby's random glances.

She freezes. Hand hovering over the phone. Every instinct screams danger.

The movement is too deliberate, too coordinated for randomness. Someone is watching. Grace had described this feeling in her final weeks—the sense of being observed, cataloged, measured for elimination. "They don't just kill you," she'd said. "They study you first. Learn your patterns, your habits, your weak points. Then they strike when you can't defend yourself."

But Grace had also said something else. Something Zara only remembered now in the adrenaline clarity of immediate danger: "If they're watching you, it means you're close to something they can't afford to lose. Don't back down—double down. Make the cost of silencing you higher than the cost of letting you speak."

She doesn't turn toward the window. Instead, she continues typing. Fingers moving across the keyboard in what she hopes appears normal work. But peripheral vision tracks the shadows, noting their positions, their stillness. Predators, not passersby.

Her screen reflects the window behind her. In that distorted mirror she catches a glimpse of a figure pressed against the opposite building. No features visible, just someone's outline who has learned to become invisible while remaining present. The kind of watcher who documents everything and reports to people paying for anonymity. The same kind of surveillance that had preceded Grace's disappearance. The careful cataloging that preceded action.

A second shadow joins the first. Then a third.

They're not just watching anymore—they're positioning for something more active than observation.

Zara's mouth goes dry. One watcher might be paranoia. Three suggests something organized. Something imminent. She saves work to multiple encrypted drives, each hidden elsewhere. If they're coming tonight, they won't find all evidence in one place.

Grace had taught her this too—distribute the risk, never keep all the evidence in one location. "If they get you," Grace had said, "make sure they don't get the story too."

But as she implements Grace's protocols, a new thought strikes her with the force of revelation: What if Grace had done exactly that? What if the disappearance hadn't been an elimination but an extraction? What if Grace was still out there, still fighting, still building the case that would eventually bring down the entire network?

The fluorescent light above her desk flickers once. Twice. Then dies, leaving the air humming like a held breath.

She tells herself it's just the wiring.

In sudden darkness, lit only by monitor glow, Zara realizes she's no longer the hunter. She's become the hunted. But maybe, just maybe, she's not hunting alone.

The red lamp's pulse seems louder now. More urgent. Each beat marks time running out, seconds stolen from a clock counting down to something she can't see but knows is coming. She reaches for the lamp's switch. Hesitates. Then leaves it blinking.

Let them know she's aware. Let them understand she's not hiding anymore.

She opens her secure messaging app and begins typing: "If something happens to me tonight, the files are already distributed. Grace's work won't be the last thing they have to explain."

As she hits send, she could swear she hears something through the workspace's electronic hum—the faint sound of typing from somewhere else in the building. As if someone else were working late. Following the same protocols. Building the same case.

The ghost in the machine, still fighting long after official records declared the war over.

⁕

The power hadn't failed again; the bulb had simply burned out. The threat, for now, remained outside.

Later that night, in the safe house, the encrypted recording app glows on her phone screen like a confession booth window in darkness. The space feels smaller than usual—walls closing in under the weight of accumulated secrets and the certainty that her enemies are no longer content to watch from shadows.

They're moving. She can feel their approach like a storm front building on the horizon.

She sits on the edge of the narrow cot, shoulders curved inward. The day's revelations pressing down like a physical thing. The room is silent except for distant Johannesburg traffic—a city that never quite sleeps, never quite stops watching. Through thin plasterboard, she hears other tenants shifting in the corridor—footfalls, a door latch, the indifferent sounds of a building that keeps its own counsel.

But tonight, the silence feels different. Occupied.

As if the same watchers from outside her workspace had tracked her here. Taking up positions in stairwells and service corridors. Weaving a net of surveillance that would close when they received the signal. The paranoia should be crippling, but instead it sharpens her focus. Grace had lived with this same pressure in her final weeks. And Grace had used it to fuel her most important work.

Her thumb hovers over the record button. She's done this a thousand times—organizing findings, preparing stories, whispering truth into the digital void. But tonight feels different. Tonight, the words wanting to come aren't for publication. They're for Grace—wherever she might be.

This is what Grace would have done. In her final weeks, when the surveillance had become obvious and the threats explicit, Grace had kept recording. Kept documenting. Kept building a record that would survive her apparent elimination. Not for posterity, but for the people who would continue the work after she was gone.

She presses record.

"Grace?" Her voice cracks on the single syllable. The name carrying more weight than her vocal cords can bear. She clears her throat, tries again. "Grace, I know you're out there. I know you're listening, somehow. The files, the annotations, the way evidence keeps appearing in places I didn't expect—that's you, isn't it?"

The admission hangs in the air like smoke from a cigarette she'll never finish. The certainty grows stronger as she speaks, fed by months of anomalies that only made sense if Grace were still operational. Still fighting from whatever shadows she'd managed to find.

She stands abruptly. Paces to the window overlooking the city's sprawl of lights. Each light represents a life. A secret. A truth waiting to be revealed—or a person who has learned to survive in the spaces between official reality and underground resistance.

Her reflection stares back—hollow-eyed, exhausted, wearing the perpetually hunted's uniform: dark clothes, hair pulled back severely enough to keep it from her face when she runs. The woman in the window looks like a soldier. Perhaps that's what she's become.

Grace's war. Their war. A campaign that had never really ended, just gone underground.

"I found them, Grace. I found the bastards who made you disappear." Her voice drops to a whisper, as if walls themselves might be listening. The paranoia isn't irrational anymore—it's operational security. "And you know what the worst part is? They're not monsters. They're not some shadowy cabal in expensive suits. They're just... people. People who decided your questions were worth less than their answers."

The simplicity makes it terrifying. No grand conspiracy, no elaborate plot—just institutional indifference weaponized into elimination. Grace hadn't vanished because she'd uncovered some massive conspiracy. She'd vanished because she'd asked questions that inconvenienced people grown comfortable with their lies.

But Grace had understood that too. Had seen the banality of the evil she was fighting. The way it disguised itself as necessity, efficiency, pragmatism. "The worst part," Grace had said during one of their final conversations, "isn't that they're monsters. It's that they're humans who've convinced themselves they're still good people."

Her hands shake now. But it's not fear—it's recognition. Recognition of the pattern Grace had seen. The systematic machinery of organized forgetting that ground up truth-tellers and called it progress. But also recognition of something else: the way Grace had prepared for exactly this moment. Building networks and protocols that could operate even after she was officially gone.

She watches her hands tremble in the window's reflection. Remembers Grace's steady fingers on keyboards, always sure, always careful. Grace who never let fear creep into her voice during late-night strategy sessions. Grace who believed truth could set them all free, right up until the moment her freedom was officially revoked by someone who preferred slavery to uncertainty.

"I'm scared." She whispers into the dark. The words feel like betrayal—like treason against everything she's built her career on. "Not of dying. I made peace with that a long time ago. I'm scared of failing you. Of letting them win. Of becoming a footnote in someone else's war."

But as the words leave her lips, she realizes something else: she's not alone in this fear. Somewhere out there, Grace is dealing with the same terror. The same weight of responsibility. The same knowledge that failure means more than personal destruction—it means institutional victory, systematic triumph, the permanent eclipse of accountability.

The fear is real. Visceral. A living thing that has taken residence in her chest and feeds on doubt. But it's not paralytic fear—it's strategic fear. The kind keeping soldiers alive in combat zones and journalists breathing in police states. Fear that sharpens rather than dulls. Clarifies rather than confuses.

Grace had been scared too, in the end. Had admitted it during one of their final meetings, when the surveillance had become impossible to ignore and the threats had escalated from implicit to explicit. "I'm terrified," she'd said. "But I'm more terrified of what happens if we stop."

Now Zara understands: Grace hadn't stopped. She'd just learned to fight from deeper shadows. To build cases that could operate independently of their original architect. The evidence flows, the careful documentation, the way certain files appeared at exactly the right moments—Grace's invisible hand, still moving pieces on a board her enemies thought they'd cleared.

She bites her lip hard enough to taste blood. Sharp pain anchoring her to the moment. Behind her, the phone continues recording, capturing every breath, every pause, every weak moment she can't afford to show the world. Some truths are too sharp for even paper to carry. But some confessions create connections across impossible distances.

"They think they can control the narrative by controlling the narrators. Eliminate the journalist, eliminate the story." Her voice steadies. "But they don't understand us, do they, Grace? They don't understand that the story lives in evidence, in connections, in truth itself. And truth doesn't die just because the person telling it officially disappears."

Her reflection straightens in the window. Jaw setting into the hard line that's become her signature expression. The transformation is subtle but complete—from mourner to warrior in a breath's space. The fear remains, will always remain, but it's no longer the dominant emotion. Beside it grows something else. Something harder. Something forged in loss's fire and tempered by months of careful investigation and the growing certainty that she's not fighting alone.

"Tomorrow, I publish everything. Every document, every photograph, every secret they've killed to protect." The decision feels inevitable, like gravity or sunrise. "And when they come for me—because they will come for me—

they'll find I'm not the same frightened girl who watched her mentor disappear into bureaucratic silence."

No choice remains. Just recognition of what has always been necessary. Grace's disappearance made it personal. The evidence has made it possible. The certainty of Grace's continued operation makes it unstoppable.

Grace would have done the same thing. Would have made the same choice, accepted the same risks, pursued the same reckoning. That's what partnership meant in this business—not just sharing sources and strategies, but sharing the burden of consequence. The weight of necessary choices that no one should have to make alone.

But Grace had made sure Zara wouldn't have to make them alone. The protocols, the distributed evidence, the careful preparation for exactly this moment—Grace's gift to the future. Her way of ensuring the war would continue even if individual soldiers fell.

She turns from the window. Moves back to the cot where the phone waits. For a moment, she considers keeping the recording, adding it to the digital archive of evidence that will outlive them all. Instead, she saves it to the encrypted partition Grace had taught her to build. The one that synchronizes with servers she can't identify. Networks that operate beyond the reach of official surveillance.

Let Grace hear it, wherever she is. Let her know the work continues. The partnership endures. The promise survives.

Grace would have understood the choice being made in this small room. The decision to transform personal loss into public reckoning. That was the promise they'd made to each other—that the work would continue. That the truth would survive. That neither of them would disappear for nothing.

The city outside continues its restless rhythm, unaware that in a small room at its heart, a woman has just chosen steel over surrender. Lights in surrounding buildings flicker like votive candles in a corrupted cathedral, each representing someone who has made their own accommodation with power.

But not her. Not tonight. Not ever again.

And somewhere in those same lights, Grace was making the same choice. Preparing for the same war. Building toward the same inevitable moment of reckoning.

In a few hours, the world will know the truth about the Brandt empire. About Grace's investigation. About the price of asking wrong questions in a country built on profitable silences. The evidence will speak for itself, but it will do so in two voices—Zara's and Grace's. Living and disappeared. Visible and invisible. Fighting the same fight from different sides of official reality.

She opens her laptop. Fingers moving across keys with new certainty. The story writes itself, each paragraph a kept promise. Each revelation a debt paid to the missing.

She packages the evidence bundle—article, data sets, custody logs, signatures. She flags the release: SECOND WAVE—GRACE PROTOCOL. Not a confession. A proof set.

Outside, Johannesburg sleeps fitfully, but in this small room, a woman sits with her ghosts and prepares for war.

The red lamp on her desk blinks once more, then goes dark. The waiting is over. The war begins.

Grace's war. Zara's war. Their war, fought with truth as ammunition and partnership as armor. The enemy had made a crucial mistake—they had assumed that making the messenger disappear would silence the message.

But some stories outlive their storytellers. Some partnerships transcend physical separation. Some truths are too vital to bury with their witnesses. Tomorrow, Grace Mdluli will speak from the shadows, and the living will finally have to answer for their crimes against the disappeared.

Outside, Johannesburg's first light presses against the glass. Inside, morning means judgment—and Zara is ready.

A status light—the ghost in the machine—pulses once, acknowledging receipt of the message, confirming what Zara has begun to suspect: some disappearances are strategic retreats, and the best fighters are the ones their enemies think are already dead.

By sunrise, the mirror servers that once belonged to The Continent will carry everything—receipts, provenance, custody logs. By noon, the injunctions will start again.

Chapter 16 – The Tipping Point

Zara's hands trembled as she pressed play for the third time.

The voice that emerged from her laptop speakers was barely a whisper—fractured by static and terror.

"My name is Samuel Mashaba. I work—worked—in customs enforcement at the Nkomazi border crossing." A pause. The sound of papers rustling. "They told me to look the other way. Said it was mining equipment. But I saw the manifests. Weapons. Military-grade communications gear. Enough to arm a small militia."

Through her flat's thin walls, Johannesburg's nighttime symphony leaked in—taxi horns, distant sirens, the persistent hum of a city that never quite slept. But Samuel's voice cut through it like a clean frequency.

"The signatures on the transport documents … bloody hell, they go all the way up. Cabinet level. The Brandt Foundation is listed as the primary recipient, but the end destination …" His voice broke. "Listen, I've got a family. Two daughters. But I can't live with this anymore. The blood on these contracts—"

A siren wailed somewhere below, distant and indifferent, pulling her back to the room.

Static swallowed the rest.

She checked the metadata—recorded eight days before the Brandt leak. Grace must have had it first.

Grace must have had it first.

Which meant she was alive, then. Alive, and still feeding the chain.

Silence pressed against her eardrums—cotton-thick.

Zara stared at the audio file's waveform—peaks and valleys mapping one man's journey from complicity to conscience. She poured another whiskey, her third since midnight, and watched shadows crawl across her cracked walls like living things. The amber liquid caught the laptop's glow, transforming into molten light that reminded her of Grace's last known smile: bitter and knowing, captured in a surveillance photo taken weeks before her official disappearance.

The timing of that disappearance still bothered her.

Too clean. Too convenient.

Grace vanishing just as her investigation reached critical mass, just as she was about to expose the deepest connections in the Cypress network. The kind of timing that suggested careful orchestration rather than tragic elimination. Someone wanted Grace gone—but the question remained whether they wanted Grace dead or simply invisible.

Her phone buzzed.

Unknown number:

We know about Samuel. We know about you. Stop digging or join him.

The message deleted itself as she watched—a faint haptic thrum in the quiet. Her pulse thudded at her wrists.

They're closer than I thought.

Zara set down her glass with deliberate care, her journalist's mind cataloging details even as her survival instincts screamed. The timing wasn't coincidental. They were monitoring her communications, tracking her sources. Samuel's recording had been a trap—or a test. Either way, she'd already failed it.

She opened her voice-memo app and began recording, her voice steadier than she felt.

"Lucas, if you're listening to this, we're blown. My source at Nkomazi—Samuel Mashaba—he's either dead or disappeared. They're moving faster than we anticipated." Her words came measured, controlled. "The weapons trafficking through the border isn't just corruption. It's preparation. For what, I don't know yet. But the Brandt connection runs deeper than we thought."

She paused, listening to the building settle.

Every creak might be footsteps. Every shadow might conceal a watcher. The whiskey burned in her stomach, adding its own heat to the fear crystallizing in her chest.

"I'm accelerating the timeline. We publish everything we have, or we lose it all. Contact me through the usual channels, but assume they're compromised. Trust no one else."

She ended the recording and encrypted it.

Outside the window, a car had been parked across the street for the past hour. Engine off. Someone moving inside. In her line of work, paranoia wasn't a diagnosis—it was survival.

But as she prepared to send the message, another thought struck her—one that had been building since she started seeing anomalies in Grace's files. The careful documentation, the precisely timed intelligence drops, the way certain evidence appeared exactly when she needed it most. What if Grace's disappearance hadn't been elimination but extraction? What if she was still out there, still fighting, still building the case that would eventually expose the entire network?

The possibility should have been comforting—but instead it sharpened her fear.

If Grace was alive and operating from the shadows, then the danger was even greater than she'd imagined. And if Grace was dead, then Zara was truly alone against forces that had already proven they could make inconvenient people vanish without trace.

Zara pulled the curtains closed and double-checked her door locks. The metal was cold against her palm—solid, but somehow insufficient protection against enemies who could delete messages with electronic precision.

Tomorrow she would force the issue.

Tonight she would prepare for war.

***

The Continent's newsroom felt like a mausoleum—one with invoices.

Empty desks stretched under harsh fluorescent lighting. Computer screens—dark. Phones silent. Even the coffee machine had been unplugged, a faint ring of dried milk marking where the carafe used to sit.

254

Zara hadn't expected anyone to still be here. Yet in the editor's office, amid boxes of archived files and unpaid bills, Ronald Mthembu sat behind his old desk as if habit could resurrect a newsroom. A half-packed cardboard box rested at his feet, the ghost of a headline curling at the top of a discarded proofs stack.

"We're not running the story." He didn't look up.

"We?" she asked quietly. "There is no we anymore."

"Then call it reflex," he said. "A letter came in this morning. Cease and desist. Not to the paper—it's gone—but to me. To anyone still holding fragments. They don't want notes, drafts, or backups finding daylight."

Zara set a flash drive on the desk. "Listen first."

"I don't need to listen to anything." His voice had the weight of a man who'd fought too many battles and lost too many wars. "They're warning that if I share a single file, they'll bury the rest of my life in litigation."

She studied him—the loosened tie, the nicotine-yellow fingertips, the exhaustion etched deeper than wrinkles. "We used to call that censorship."

He gave a dry laugh. "Receivership calls it risk management. The liquidator has orders to cooperate. The moment I tried to copy the archive drives, the passwords were revoked. Even the off-site backup company suddenly discovered 'billing discrepancies.' " He gestured to the heaps of paperwork. "They've mapped every vein that used to carry oxygen through this place and sealed them shut."

The air smelled of dust and stale toner. Old press passes hung like memorial ribbons from cubicle walls. She remembered when this room had been alive—ringing phones, shouted copy edits, the smell of ink and adrenaline. Now it felt like the aftermath of faith.

"So we fight back," she said. "Expose the intimidation."

"With what?" His laugh was bitter as burnt coffee. "There's no budget. No staff. The keys don't even open half the doors anymore."

Zara moved to the window. From twenty-two floors up, Johannesburg shimmered in midday heat—the city's noise muted by glass. "Then it's just us."

He rubbed his eyes. "You think I haven't asked myself why I stayed? Maybe I thought the press card still meant something. Maybe I wanted to be the last one to turn out the lights."

They weren't losing the story; the story was being starved—of witnesses, of bandwidth, of nerve.

"What about your legacy, Ron? Forty years of fearless journalism."

"My legacy," he said slowly, "is keeping the archive intact long enough for someone outside this jurisdiction to use it. I won't feed anyone else to the machine."

He leaned back, eyes roaming the empty room. "You remember the smell of the presses? The vibration through the floor when the first run started? That was a kind of prayer. Now the presses are scrap metal somewhere outside Germiston."

"It won't get buried if we publish."

"It will if we're all dead."

He said it softly, without drama—just a line of arithmetic that no longer balanced in favor of courage.

On the wall, a front page from '94 had slipped in its frame: riots, smoke, a boy in a school blazer staring into a future no one had promised. Ron crossed the room and straightened it with two careful taps, like righting a picture could steady a world.

"You think I don't hear Grace every time I turn a light off?" he said. "I do. I also hear the accountant. And now the liquidator."

Zara let the silence stretch. The fluorescent tube above them flickered, caught itself, and held—the light thin, stubborn, barely enough. A thread of cobweb swayed in the updraft, twisting like something alive that refused to break.

Maybe, somewhere in the city's electronic networks, Grace's ghost was still working—still building cases, still fighting wars the living had been forced to abandon.

"Then I'm not asking for The Continent's backing," she said. "I'm asking you to look the other way while I do what needs to be done."

He replaced his glasses and regarded her as though seeing a younger version of himself. "You're talking about going freelance. Burning your career for a story that might never see daylight."

"I'm talking about honoring Grace Mdluli's work."

He sighed, a sound that carried both affection and surrender. "Grace is gone," he said. "You don't have to join her."

Gone—but not necessarily dead. If Grace was still operational, still building cases from the shadows, then this wasn't martyrdom. It was succession.

Zara turned to the door, then paused. "When they write the history of this moment, they'll note who stood with the truth and who stood aside. Choose carefully which list you want to be on."

He didn't answer. Behind her, the newsroom remained silent except for the hum of the dying light—an epitaph written in electricity.

Zara left him sitting among the ruins of one of the last independent papers in the country, another casualty in a war most people didn't even know existed. Down the corridor, her footsteps echoed off linoleum and glass, fading into the hollow belly of a building that had once printed truth by the ton.

She stepped out into the warm afternoon air, the echo of Ron's defeat following her. Her phone vibrated once—from an encrypted number she hadn't seen since Grace disappeared. Five words: Same place as before. Midnight.

***

The parking garage beneath the Carlton Centre reeked of petrol and decay.

Zara descended through levels of increasing darkness, footsteps echoing off concrete walls marked with graffiti that ranged from political slogans to desperate prayers. This was where journalism came to die—or to be resurrected by those willing to risk everything.

She found her contact in the deepest level, standing beside a rusted sedan with mismatched tires—a man she knew only through Grace's old network. James Maseko had been Grace's final known source—a civil servant who'd fed information to investigative journalists for two decades without ever being caught. Tonight, he looked like a man who'd already written his own obituary.

"You shouldn't have come." His whisper barely carried over the garage's ambient noise. His eyes darted to every shadow. "They know about our connection."

He studied her face for a moment, as if measuring her against Grace's descriptions, then nodded once. "She said you wouldn't stop. She was right."

The use of past tense stung—but Zara had learned to read between lines. Grace had prepared for multiple contingencies, built networks that could operate even if she was officially eliminated. The question was whether those networks were still active, still receiving intelligence from sources who believed Grace might somehow still be listening.

"Then why did you text me?"

He handed her a flash drive, hands shaking so badly he nearly dropped it. "Because Grace's work has to survive. These are the customs records from Nkomazi. The real ones, not the sanitized versions that go into official reports."

Zara pocketed the drive. "What's on it?"

"Proof the border shipments weren't what they claimed. The manifests show weapons and surveillance gear moving under humanitarian permits—cabinet signatures, the Foundation fronting the paperwork." His voice cracked. "The routes end at decommissioned mines—places cleared of residents, fenced, and reclassified as restricted zones."

"To hide what?"

"Preparation," he said quietly. "Something coordinated. They're building capacity, not profit."

A car engine echoed from the upper levels.

James flinched as if shot—a full-body reaction that spoke of weeks living on pure nerves.

Up close, she saw how his collar had been cut and resewn—a quick repair with mismatched thread, the kind you do in a motel with a sewing kit and a deadline. His wedding band had a new scratch, bright and raw, as if it had met concrete in the last twenty-four hours.

"They're using the side gates at night," he whispered, voice thinning. "Two trucks at a time—no weighbridge, no cameras. The guards look away together, like they practiced."

"How do you know?"

James angled his head toward the ceiling. A drop of water fell from a pipe and burst on his cheek. He didn't flinch this time. "Because I taught them to do it, before I remembered who I wanted to be."

He pressed his palms flat against the sedan's roof, leaving damp handprints that steamed in the cold. "You don't outrun this. You outlast it. Make them spend more to silence you than it costs to let you speak."

The advice sounded like something Grace would have said. The phrasing, the strategic thinking, the understanding of power as an economic equation. It was possible James was simply channeling Grace's methodology—but it was also possible he was passing along more recent instructions.

"I have to go. My family's already been moved to a safe house, but if they find me here ..." He pressed a piece of paper into her hand. "That's an encrypted email address. Someone overseas who can verify the documents. Trust no one else."

"James, wait—"

But he was already moving, disappearing into the maze of concrete pillars like a ghost returning to the underworld. Zara stood alone in the darkness, clutching evidence that could topple governments—or get her killed before sunup.

She unfolded the paper.

A Gmail address and a single word: Conduit.

The word sparked recognition. Grace had mentioned a Conduit once, during one of their final meetings. A backup system, she'd called it. Insurance against institutional failure. At the time, Zara had assumed it was metaphorical. Now she wondered if Grace had been more literal than anyone had realized.

Above her, the parking garage's entrance glowed like the mouth of a tunnel back into a world where people could pretend none of this was happening. Zara took a breath that tasted of metal and fear, then began the long climb to the surface.

If Grace was dead, then this evidence was her final gift to the living.

If Grace was alive, then it was the next move in a game that was far from over.

Either way, Zara had work to do.

***

In a rented back room two suburbs away, Zara worked with the methodical precision of someone preparing for war. The curtains were drawn tight, the air stale with the scent of old smoke and cheap detergent.

She copied files, compressed folders, and organized the evidence into narrative threads that could survive her disappearance. The customs records from Nkomazi painted a picture of systematic militarization—weapons and surveillance equipment flowing to remote locations under the cover of humanitarian aid.

She cross-referenced shipping manifests with mining company records, property transfers, and population displacement data. The pattern was unmistakable: communities were being cleared, infrastructure weaponized, and private security forces equipped for something that looked disturbingly like occupation.

But woven through the data were anomalies that suggested someone else had been building the same case— someone with access to sources and systems that even James couldn't reach. The metadata signatures, the careful chronological organization, the way certain files had been pre-sorted for maximum impact—Grace's invisible hand, still moving pieces on a board her enemies thought they'd cleared.

Her laptop cast pale light across stacks of printed documents, backup drives, and handwritten notes mapping connections that spanned decades. This wasn't just corruption—it was preparation for a conflict that hadn't been declared yet. And if Grace was still out there, still fighting from whatever shadows she'd managed to find, then the conflict might be closer than anyone realized.

Zara drafted an email to the address James had given her:

Subject: Grace Mdluli's Legacy

I have documentation of weapons trafficking, population displacement, and systematic preparation for armed conflict in South African mining regions. The operation involves cabinet-level government officials and traces back to the Brandt Foundation. Grace Mdluli disappeared investigating this story. I may be next.

Attached you'll find shipping manifests, customs records, financial transfers, and photographic evidence. If I don't respond to messages within twelve hours of your receiving this, assume I've been compromised and publish everything.

The people deserve to know what's being done in their name.

— Z. Mokoena

She scheduled the email to send automatically in eighteen hours—enough time to collect the remaining fragments she needed, to stitch the narrative so tight they couldn't unpick it. If nothing changed, it would go out. If she was gone, it would go out faster. And if Grace was still alive, still monitoring the networks she'd built, she would know that the work was continuing, that the promises they'd made to each other were being kept.

Her cursor hovered over *Schedule send.*

Once she pressed it, there would be no going back. She would be committed to a path that led either to justice or to joining Grace in whatever realm awaited journalists who asked too many questions.

She scheduled it.

Her phone buzzed immediately—another unknown number.

We gave you a chance to walk away. You chose poorly. Check your email.

Her blood turned to ice water. She opened her personal account and found a message containing photographs: the building's entrance, the rented room's door, her car in the designated parking space. The final image, shot through the room's window, showed her sitting at this very desk, taken less than an hour ago.

The photographs captured everything—the angle of her laptop screen, the whiskey glass at her elbow, even the way her hair fell across her left shoulder. Someone had been watching with telephoto precision, documenting her every movement. They'd been here all along.

The message continued: You have twelve hours to eliminate all evidence and disappear. Or we'll do it for you.

Zara closed her laptop and moved away from the window. Her hands were steady now—fear crystallizing into focus. They'd shown their hand too early, revealing their surveillance capabilities while she still had time to respond. Professional intimidation, but imperfect execution. A mistake Grace would have exploited mercilessly.

She pulled the service pistol from its lockbox and checked the ammunition. Six rounds. Not enough for a firefight, but sufficient for a last statement if things went badly. She tucked the weapon into her jacket and began packing essentials into a go-bag: cash, backup drives, encrypted phones, and Grace's original notes.

The rented room felt different now—not like a safe house, but like a stage set where the final act was about to begin. Every familiar object had become evidence of a life she might have to abandon: the coffee mug Grace had used during their last known meeting; the awards that lined her bookshelf; the photographs of stories that had toppled corrupt officials.

She knelt by the coffee table and laid the items out in rows the way Grace had taught her—not for aesthetics, for certainty. Cash in rubber-banded stacks. Two encrypted phones, batteries out. Drives labeled in her shorthand no one else would read. A metro card with three remaining trips. A single earring Grace had left in her car after a late interview, its pearl scuffed smooth by years of glove-box weather.

"Always pack the thing that reminds you you're a person," Grace had said, back when they still believed being a person could protect you. But Grace had also said something else—something that carried new weight in light of recent discoveries: "Sometimes the most important work happens after everyone thinks you're dead."

Zara added a paperback with split spine and underlined margins, then paused, listening.

The building's pipes clanked like an old man clearing his throat. Somewhere a baby cried, then thought better of it. But underneath the ordinary sounds of urban life, she could swear she heard something else—the faint electronic whisper of data moving through hidden networks, of systems operating beyond official oversight, of ghosts in machines that refused to stay dead.

She zipped the bag.

The sound was clean, decisive—the only line she was willing to draw tonight. If they came early, they would find a room; they would not find her. And if Grace was still out there, still fighting from the spaces between official reality and underground resistance, she would know that the work continued, that some promises transcended physical elimination.

All of it would mean nothing if she didn't survive the next twenty-four hours. But survival was just one variable in an equation that included justice, truth, and the possibility that some disappearances were strategic retreats rather than final defeats.

Zara turned off the lights and sat in darkness, listening to the city breathe around her.

Somewhere out there, powerful people were making decisions about her life based on spreadsheets and risk assessments. They'd calculated that her death would be cheaper than her continued existence.

They were probably right.

But Grace had taught her something important: some truths were worth dying for, especially when your death would make them impossible to ignore. Martyrdom was another form of journalism—a final story told in blood and justified by the changes it inspired.

And if Grace was still alive, still building cases from the shadows, then martyrdom might not be the only option. Sometimes the most effective fighters were the ones their enemies thought were already dead.

Zara checked her watch.

Eighteen hours until the switch tripped—no further action required. Once it left her outbox it would be public. If she canceled it before then, the distribution would be stopped; if she didn't, the work would be set loose.

She would spend these hours gathering everything else she could find, building an archive so comprehensive that her silencing would only amplify its impact.

The war had already begun. Her survival was optional. The truth wasn't. And somewhere in the electronic darkness of Johannesburg's hidden networks, the ghost of Grace Mdluli continued its work—patient and relentless and utterly undefeated by official death.

The revolution, Grace had once said, wouldn't be televised. It would be digitized, distributed, and made immortal by the very technology their enemies used to monitor and control. Tonight, in a small room overlooking the city's sprawl of secrets, that revolution continued its quiet advance toward an inevitable reckoning.

The city pulsed with electronic life, and in that pulse, Zara could hear the heartbeat of something larger than individual survival—the survival of truth itself, archived, distributed, made immortal by the love between friends who refused to let death have the final word.

She pulled the air-gapped case from under the bed. By dawn, there would be clean copies, sharded kits, and a plan that didn't depend on anyone surviving the night.

Chapter 17 – Ashes of Inheritance

After Zara's encrypted message, they'd revived their old newsroom dead-drop protocol—no calls, no lingering contact, only timed movements and fail-safe codes. She would wait two streets over as overwatch while he breached the estate. Earlier that evening at Checkpoint Two, she'd slid him a sealed pouch—three microSD kits and an encrypted thumb drive built from her air-gapped set. He would place the physical redundancies while she lit the digital fuse.

Anton's security system ran an hourly maintenance mask—ten minutes when the perimeter feeds cached instead of streamed. The old duress code Helena once used for contractors still silenced the alarms. Lucas had the gardener's gate key he'd never returned; he slipped through the side path and in by the study casement he'd learned to lift at twelve, the house inhaling him like memory.

The candlelight flickered across the ledger's yellowed pages like fingers of accusation. The wax had burned low through hours of solitary reading. Each shadow danced with thirty years of buried secrets. Lucas sat in his father's chair, the leather still holding Anton's shape, still exhaling the faint scent of tobacco and guilt. Outside, Johannesburg sprawled beneath a sky the color of old brass. Surveillance drones threaded between glass towers like mechanical vultures.

N. Langa—R2.5M—Pipeline approval. D. Mahlangu—R800K—Evidence suppression. M. Sibeko—R1.2M—Sentence reduction. Each entry signed with Anton's initials and a small triangle bisected by a vertical line—the symbol that meant "above reproach."

Memory. Sharp. Sudden.

He remembered the first time he'd seen the mark in the wild. Twelve years old, lost in a boardroom that smelled of lemon oil. Men in gray suits talked in shorthand while waiters ghosted in with silver coffee pots and cakes cut into immaculate wedges. Anton tapped a contract with his pen, the nib clicking softly against the paper like a metronome.

"Never sign what you can symbolize," his father said without looking up. "A signature is a promise. A symbol is an ecosystem. It says the same thing to those who already know."

The triangle appeared in the margin of a draft—nothing but geometry to anyone outside the room. Inside, it was a lock. His father folded the page in half, then quarters, until only the mark remained visible. "You don't need to teach a loyal man to read." He slid the square of paper across the table to Lucas as if it were a mint.

Lucas had kept it in a shoebox for years, thinking it meant membership. He understood now it meant containment.

A lie engraved in ink. Authority disguising complicity.

Sitting there, the hesitation he'd carried since childhood felt suddenly juvenile—the careful distance he'd maintained from his father's world. He wasn't the frightened boy who'd fled to London twelve years ago anymore. The evidence before him demanded action, not analysis.

But as he turned each page, documenting corruption that stretched back decades, one name appeared with troubling frequency in the margins—Grace Mdluli. Not as a victim, but as someone who had been systematically gathering intelligence; building cases; creating a parallel archive of evidence that mirrored Anton's own meticulous documentation.

The timestamps on her entries were wrong, though. Several were dated after her official disappearance, after the hospital records showed her presumed death. Either Anton's chronology was confused, or Grace's elimination hadn't been as final as everyone believed.

Then, near the back, Lucas found something that froze his blood.

The paper felt warmer than it should have, as if the secrets inside had their own pulse.

Night Horizon—operational parameters established— see supplementary files.

The entry was dated three months ago. Whatever Night Horizon was, Anton had been actively involved until weeks before his death. But as Lucas read deeper, the pattern became clear. Night Horizon wasn't Anton's first attempt at political elimination—it was the culmination of decades of smaller operations, a final evolution that consolidated all his family's shadow networks into a single, lethal instrument.

But threaded through the Night Horizon files were annotations in a different handwriting—notes that revealed someone else had been tracking the operation, documenting its personnel and methods with the precision of an investigative journalist building a case. The handwriting looked familiar, though Lucas couldn't immediately place it.

The candle flame guttered in a sudden draft; shadows jumped along the study walls. The bisected triangle appeared more frequently in recent entries, as if Anton had been marking time toward a final reckoning.

This isn't business. This is war.

His eyes burned from hours of reading by candlelight. He pulled out his phone—the screen's blue glow harsh against the flickering flame. A search revealed fragments: military contractors, private security firms, "political asset management." He threaded through aggregators and scrapers and old procurement PDFs that read like prayer books to violence. Line items for "nonstandard logistics." Shells for "post-incident remediation." He found a Canadian patent for a modular silencer stamped to a Namibian LLC, then a Romanian invoice for "archival services" that billed by the hour for fire. The same P.O. box surfaced three times—a harmless slot in a mall outside Pretoria, photographed by a hobbyist for a stamp collectors' blog.

The chatter on a legacy forum for private contractors was worse—men arguing about "angle discipline" like fishermen comparing lures. Two posts from six months apart mentioned a Johannesburg outfit that paid double if you never asked who signed the transfer. The handle that vouched for those jobs had since been deleted from the forum. The replies remained: job done, clean scene, no local press pickup beyond the day it happened.

Every breadcrumb curved toward the same blank space on the map. Night Horizon didn't advertise. It curated belief through absence. But Night Horizon itself remained a phantom—whispered on forums where mercenaries and arms brokers traded euphemisms.

The house settled with a groan of old timber. Somewhere in the distance, a security patrol's radio crackled with coded exchanges. He stood and crossed to the window, careful with the curtain so the gap looked accidental. The lawn lights threw pale cones across the grass—each halo a calculation. Lux levels set to wash faces without blinding cameras, enough spill to silhouette bodies against the hedges. Anton had paid obsessive attention to illumination, to angles, to the choreography of seeing.

A moth battered itself against the glass, throwing a frantic shadow on the paneled wall. Beyond the perimeter, a delivery scooter burred past, the rider's helmet mirror-black. Lucas knew, because Anton had taught him, that real watchers didn't lean against lampposts or idle where you could spot them. They enrolled the world in their work and let it carry them along—contracted guards in ordinary boots, neighbors paid to be curious, a utility van from a company that had been dissolved last year but kept its logos for precisely this reason.

The house wasn't only a sanctuary. It was a machine for recording who tried to enter. Even here, in his father's sanctuary, he was being watched—cataloged, measured for elimination.

Turning to the final pages, Lucas flipped where his father's handwriting frayed. Phase 3: authorization pending. Political targets: confirmed. Executive action protocols: activated. Understanding hit like ice water. Night Horizon wasn't a venture—it was a kill list. Names, addresses, methodologies. Politicians, journalists, activists. Anyone who threatened the network his family had built.

At the bottom of the last page, in Anton's careful script, *Lucas must never know the scope. The boy lacks the stomach for necessity.*

But below that, in different handwriting—the same annotations that had appeared throughout the Night Horizon files—someone had written: *Archive complete. Extraction Protocol successful. Ready for phase two.*

The second notation was dated two weeks after Grace's official disappearance.

His pulse hammered against his collar. The flame seemed to beat in time with his heart. The boy his father described was gone. What remained would make choices that rippled far beyond this room.

But as he prepared to act, another possibility struck him—one that reframed everything he thought he understood about Grace's fate, about the investigation he and Zara had been pursuing, about the nature of resistance itself. What if Grace's disappearance hadn't been elimination but extraction? What if she was still out there, still building cases, still fighting from whatever shadows she'd managed to find?

He reached for his phone. This time, he didn't hesitate.

***

Zara sat in the idling car two streets from Anton's house, the windows darkened with anti-surveillance film. The dashboard light glowed faint blue across her face, the only illumination inside. Signal jammers hummed under the passenger seat, and three secure handsets blinked in standby on the console.

The encrypted line chimed once. She answered.

"It's worse than we thought." Lucas's voice carried a certainty she hadn't heard before—no longer the conflicted heir, but someone who'd chosen a side.

"How much worse?"

"Night Horizon. It's real, and it's active."

Somewhere beyond the windshield, the choreography still ran on clockwork—different dancers, same steps.

Something cold settled in her stomach. She'd chased whispers of Night Horizon for months—a private military operation that made problems disappear. High-value targets eliminated with surgical precision; deaths staged as accidents, suicides, random violence in a country where violence could hide anything.

"What do you have?"

"Names. Targets. Methodologies." Steel in his voice now.

"There are journalists on this list, Zara. People we know. People who got too close."

He paused, then, softer: "But there's something else. Evidence that Grace might still be alive. Annotations in the files, dated after her disappearance."

Zara's breath caught. She'd been finding anomalies in Grace's files for weeks—intelligence that arrived exactly when she needed it, as if someone unseen were still feeding the case. If Grace had faked her death and gone underground, everything changed.

"Are you sure?"

"The handwriting matches her articles. The method is hers."

Zara opened the rugged laptop balanced on the center console. Air-gapped drives blinked awake, mapped to dark-web mirrors and dead drops across Johannesburg. She compiled clean copies of Anton's pages and her own research, then sharded them to release nodes. The physical kits she'd handed Lucas mirrored these shards—offline twins for when power failed or fire came too soon. Grace's teaching guided her fingers—proof must be modular, able to survive the loss of any single node.

"We leak everything," she said. "Multiple sources, multiple platforms. Make it impossible to contain."

"They'll kill us."

"They're going to try anyway. At least this way we take them with us."

She typed fast, routing contact bursts through London, Berlin, New York. "We fragment the data, stagger releases, set a schedule."

"Tell me what you need."

"Minibus taxi ranks in Soweto—too public and chaotic for clean tailing. Old Wits library basement—academic networks they haven't fully penetrated. A rooftop in Hillbrow—visual confirmation of handoffs, multiple exits."

"How long do we have?"

"Eighteen hours to full cascade. Wave one in six."

Her burner phone buzzed. *Recording this conversation. Suggest you reconsider.—A friend.*

Outside, an engine turned over—too deliberate, too timed. The jammer's hum faltered, then steadied.

"They're listening," she said.

"Then we move faster." No panic in his voice, only calculation. "End the call. Location Three. One hour."

The line went dead. Zara wiped the devices, activated backup protocols, and grabbed the go-bag from the footwell—cash, IDs, encrypted drives, Grace's original notes. For the first time in months, she felt it: not fear, but momentum. The careful plan had become a race, and for once, it was a race toward hope rather than away from despair.

***

The minibus taxi rank downtown lived in controlled chaos that made surveillance nearly impossible. Heat rolled up from the engines like breath. Conductors slapped the sides of minibuses with open palms—three quick strikes for Soweto, straight, a rapped-out rhythm that meant go now or lose your seat. Vendors hawked vetkoek and airtime. Two women argued about change with the ferocity of trial lawyers. Somewhere a battery speaker gave itself to a gospel track that made a whole queue sway.

Cameras hate this kind of movement. The lens wants patterns, repeatable paths, not fifty bodies crossing, doubling back, pausing to greet an auntie while a trolley of oranges shudders by and rearranges the frame. Lucas let himself be carried by the current, his speed governed by a stranger's elbow and the snap of a boy's plastic sandals.

He bought a sachet of water he didn't need because the vendor's eyes were watching for something else: men who didn't sweat, men who wore the wrong shoes, men who never looked lost. He made change slowly, not caring when he overpaid. Credibility had a price.

Lucas moved through the crowd with new purpose. Designer clothes marking him as an outsider while his gait insisted otherwise. His coat said Sandton. His body language said Soweto. The trick was confidence: walk like you belong; conduct your business like it's legitimate.

This wasn't the hesitant prodigal anymore. This was execution.

But as he moved through the carefully choreographed drops, Lucas found himself looking for signs that Grace was still operational—still watching from whatever shadows she'd managed to find. The mysterious intelligence that had been appearing in their investigation, the way certain evidence had surfaced at exactly the right moments—if Grace was alive, she would know about these operations. She might even be coordinating them.

***

The pouch in his coat held three identical microSD kits: one for community radio, one for the hackers' shard farm, one as a moving decoy. Zara's schedule would push the digital releases; his job was to seed the physical proof.

The first drop: a newspaper stand run by a grandmother whose eyes missed nothing and whose mouth stayed shut for the right price. Lucas bought three papers, slid a microSD between the pages of *The Star,* and left it on the counter. She would know. Her grandson ran with a community radio station that specialized in stories the mainstream wouldn't touch.

But as he completed the transaction, the grandmother leaned forward slightly. "Your friend," she said quietly, "the one who used to come here. She says hello."

Lucas's heart stopped. Grace. The grandmother was talking about Grace, and speaking in present tense. Alive. Still operational. Still fighting.

"Tell her," he said carefully, "that the family reunion is almost ready."

The grandmother nodded once. Understanding passing between them like current through a wire.

Drop Two.

The second drop took on new urgency: the old Carlton Centre—once Africa's tallest, now a vertical city of informal economies. He took the service elevator to the thirty-second floor, where a collective of hackers and digital activists kept a hidden server farm humming on stolen electricity and stubborn hope.

He found them in a former executive office, windows black-painted against lenses. Banks of computers hummed in the dark, their LEDs a tight arrangement of data. A young woman with intricate facial scarification looked up, a thumb idly rolling a worn brass token across her knuckles.

"You're early."

"Timeline's accelerated." He handed over a sealed envelope—the second kit. "Everything goes live in six hours, regardless of what happens to me."

She slid the envelope into a scanner that would shred, image, and shard it across a dozen encrypted servers. "Payment?"

He pushed the transfer. Offshore hops, then home. Clean money, untraceable. He'd learned when to think like his father—and when to turn that logic against him.

"Your journalist friend," the young woman said as he prepared to leave. "The one who disappeared. She left something here for you."

She handed him a small encrypted drive. "Said to give it to you when the fight went public."

Lucas stared at the device, understanding that Grace hadn't just survived—she'd been planning for this moment, building networks and safeguards that could operate even if she remained officially dead. The drive was warm in his palm, carrying the weight of promises kept and partnerships that transcended physical separation.

Drop Three. Nearly fatal.

As he crossed a Hillbrow rooftop, a sniper's round passed so close it kissed heat along his ear. Lucas dove behind a concrete lip as masonry spat into the night. Found him. Despite their precautions, the network was inside the operation.

A second shot sparked off a fire escape. Professional— herding, not harvesting. They wanted him alive. Containment, not closure.

No fear. Just anger. They still saw the conflicted heir, not the adversary.

He rolled left, using ductwork and vents for cover, working toward the roof's edge. Below, the city grid glowed like a circuit board. The pickup point: a garbage truck that would pass beneath in four minutes, the driver one of Zara's people.

Another shot, closer. He sprinted; Italian leather slipped on rain-slick concrete. He jumped. Air tore the breath from him. He hit the truck's open bed hard, ribs cracking against steel, then tumbled into shadow among industrial waste.

The truck never slowed. By the time the shooter reached the parapet, Lucas was three blocks away, hidden in the offal of a city that made art from its own decay.

As adrenaline burned off, copper bloomed on his tongue and his ribs screamed with each breath. The smell of refuse wrapped him like a baptism

into the world he'd chosen—ugly, necessary, real.

But as he lay among the garbage, he clutched Grace's encrypted drive like a talisman. Somewhere in its data was proof that the resistance had never been broken, that some disappearances were strategic retreats, that the war he and

Zara thought they were starting had actually been continuing all along.

He was still here. Still fighting. And now he wasn't fighting alone.

***

Lucas returned to his father's study near midnight, moving like a ghost haunting its own past. The ledger waited where he'd left it; the candle had guttered to a thin, stubborn flame. He sat in Anton's chair and felt not the weight of inherited sin, but the lightness of impending freedom.

The room was exactly as Anton had kept it—books aligned, surfaces polished, secrets cross-referenced. Not a study, he realized, but a mausoleum. A shrine to power built on graves.

But before he acted, Lucas inserted Grace's encrypted drive into his laptop. The files that bloomed across his screen were a revelation—not just evidence of Night Horizon's operations, but a complete parallel investigation that had been running for months. Grace hadn't just faked her death; she'd used her disappearance to access sources and intelligence that would have been impossible to reach as a living journalist.

The scope of her operation was breathtaking. Financial networks mapped across three continents. Communication intercepts revealing government complicity at the highest levels. Personnel files on Night Horizon operatives that read like a rogues' gallery of international mercenaries and assassins.

And woven through it all, a message for Lucas specifically—coordinates for a meeting, instructions for activating what Grace called the "Legacy Protocol," and a simple notation: *The family reunion is ready. Bring everything you have.*

Grace wasn't just alive. She was ready to resurface, to step out of the shadows with evidence that would make the Brandt ledger look like a practice exercise. But she needed the physical documentation Lucas had found, the original records that would corroborate her digital intelligence.

He hit record. His hands were steady; his voice clear.

"My name is Lucas Brandt. I am the son of Anton Brandt, heir to an empire built on blood money and systematic corruption." A breath. Stronger now. "For thirty years, my family hid behind legal protection and institutional power, believing wealth could insulate us from consequence."

He looked at the ledger—three decades of documented evil. The boy who'd feared these pages was gone. Truth was a weapon, not a burden.

"Tonight, that protection ends. Tonight, the truth comes out—regardless of the cost to my family or myself."

He took up a silver lighter engraved with the Brandt crest—a lion devouring a snake, *Virtus et Industria* curling beneath. The irony wasn't lost on him.

"They call it Night Horizon," he said, voice gathering heat. "A private military operation specializing in political assassination. Funded by my family's mining empire and protected by a lattice of corrupt officials, from local police to cabinet ministers."

He opened to the first page. Anton's hand neat across yellowed paper. Secrets waited to be judged.

"This ledger records everyone who took our money, looked away, or helped turn South Africa into a marketplace for violence. Keeping these secrets doesn't serve justice—it serves the perpetrators." He swallowed. "It ensures the cycle doesn't break."

But before he lit the flame, Lucas looked directly into the camera. "This exposure is not the end of our investigation. It's the beginning. Because some people who were thought dead are very much alive. And tomorrow, the world will learn that resistance doesn't die when resisters disappear—it adapts, it evolves, and it returns stronger than ever."

He held the flame close. The paper warmed, edges curling. This wasn't panic or penance. It was choice.

"The only way to break the cycle is to burn it all down—the protections, the lies, the comfort that lets evil live in shadows." He thought of his mother, thought of Grace, thought of the courage required to disappear in order to fight more effectively. "Some truths are worth dying for. Others are worth living underground for."

Ignition. Transformation.

The page ignited. The past began to burn, but the future was being born from its ashes.

The first curl of smoke smelled of dust shaken from old curtains. Then the ledger found its deeper register and the air thickened with the sweetness of cooked glue. Lucas held the lighter away, letting the paper choose its paths. In school they'd taught him that fire needed three things—heat, fuel, oxygen—and he thought how often his family had provided all three to worse blazes than this: a rumor warmed into a scandal; a rival fed with false leads until he choked; a courtroom supplied with just enough air for their lawyer to bloom.

Ink went last, the strokes resisting until the page buckled. Names he had whispered in fear blackened to lace and then to nothing. He realized, with a calm that surprised him, that he did not want to keep a single strip as souvenir. He wanted absence—the kind that didn't ache when you prodded it.

When the spine cracked and folded in on itself, he felt the house release a held breath. It might have been the draft. It felt like permission.

Flame raced across dry paper with hungry efficiency. The study filled with the acrid smell of old secrets set free. Each page that curled and blackened was another chain undone.

It wasn't destruction—it was transformation. As the ledger burned, digital copies were already moving—sharded and mirrored across networks no single power could contain. And somewhere in those networks, Grace was waiting with her own evidence, her own networks, her own plan for final justice.

The fire was ritual. The decision was real. But the revelation would come from multiple sources, multiple voices, multiple witnesses who had been presumed dead but were very much alive.

***

He messaged Zara: "The blaze is lit. Grace is alive. Tomorrow we finish this together."

Across the city, in a safe location, Zara received the text and felt hope surge through her veins like electricity. She began final preparations, but now they weren't preparing for a suicide mission. They were preparing for a reunion—with Grace, with justice, with the possibility that some wars could actually be won.

As flames climbed higher, consuming three generations of Brandt secrets, the last of the weight lifted. Lucas wasn't Anton's conflicted son anymore. He wasn't the uncertain heir to an empire of blood.

***

He was Lucas Brandt—an agent of disclosure. And tomorrow, he would stand beside Grace Mdluli as they brought down the system that had tried to destroy them both.

For the first time, it felt like destiny, not defiance.

The study door stayed shut as the ledger collapsed into ash. Outside, the city's night went on. Inside, something fundamental had changed. The bloodline code that protected the Brandts had finally broken—not by coercion, but by one man's choice: truth over safety, revelation over silence, action over complicity.

But more than that, it had been broken by the understanding that resistance could take many forms—including the courage to disappear in order to fight more effectively, the wisdom to fake death in order to build unassailable cases, the love between friends and allies that transcended physical separation.

279

✳✳✳

As the blaze sank to embers, Lucas planned for first light. They would come—that was certain. But they would not find the boy who fled to London twelve years ago. They would find a man who knew the difference between legacy and destiny—between being born into power and choosing what to do with it.

And they would find him standing beside a woman who was supposed to be dead, holding evidence that would prove some truths are too powerful to bury with their witnesses.

✳✳✳

The war was only beginning. For the first time since returning to South Africa, Lucas Brandt was ready to fight. Ready to win. And ready to discover that he had never been fighting alone.

Chapter 18 – The Black Ledger

He hadn't meant to go back. The ledger collapse felt like a sacrament, ashes and absolution, the past finally reduced to something the city's gutters could swallow.

But when the ashes cooled he found, tucked under the spine where Anton had once pressed a folded square of paper, a penciled coordinate and a phrase he'd half-remembered from childhood: behind the portrait. It was the kind of detail Anton loved—small, private, a secret within a secret.

Before two in the morning Lucas was back in the study, fingers raw from prying and searching, because the book he'd just burned was the public ledger. This was something else: the archive Anton had never meant anyone to know existed.

The room had the soft stink of cooked glue and old paper. Ash freckled the desk like scripture written in a dead language. Lucas did not sit. The chair remembered someone else.

Anton's study bore the scars of last night's burning— scorched marble where the ledger had fed flames that devoured forty years of documented murder. The smell clung to velvet drapes and oil paintings: leather binding reduced to carbon, secrets transformed into smoke that had long since merged with Johannesburg's indifferent sky. But some proof outlived fire by design, hidden where even Anton's paranoia had provided redundancy.

Lucas moved through the room like a curator of catastrophe, cataloging what remained when institutional memory met flame. The main safe stood open, emptied of its obvious contents—bank records, property deeds, the surface documentation of a mining empire built on systematic elimination. But his father had been thorough about backup protocols, paranoid about single points of failure.

The grandfather clock in Anton's study struck two with the precise, clockwork certainty of a countdown.

Lucas stood before his father's portrait—the official one, where Anton wore the expression of a man who had never apologized for anything—and felt the weight of inheritance press against his chest. A physical force.

He moved to the portrait with surgical precision. His fingers traced the frame's ornate molding until he found the hidden release mechanism Anton had shown him years ago—a brief, clinical demonstration that felt now like a deathbed confession. The portrait swung inward on silent hinges, revealing the safe that had been hidden behind Anton's watchful gaze for decades.

The steel door was unmarked except for a single brass nameplate: "A.J. Brandt – Estate Archive." The electronic lock glowed red in the darkness, waiting for the eight-digit code that would release whatever truths Anton had deemed too dangerous for public consumption.

Lucas's hand hovered over the keypad, mind blanking against the eight red digits waiting to be summoned. He tried to think like Anton—not as a father but as a strategist. The first safe had yielded to Helena's birthday—a personal code, intimate and mocking. This one felt colder. Public.

His gaze drifted across the study until it caught on a frame half-hidden between law tomes and obsolete annual reports. The certificate gleamed beneath glass, its gilt border catching the lamplight: *Brandt Mining Limited – Initial Public Offering, Johannesburg Stock Exchange, 1983.*

Lucas remembered the night Anton had shown it to him—brandy on his breath, the boy not yet twelve. *This, son, is when we stopped playing at wealth and started owning it.* Property is fragile. Mining rights can be revoked. But once the public buys your story, they defend it with their pensions. *An IPO isn't money. It's immortality.*

The date stared back at him from the embossed type: 07-11-1983. November seventh—the day Anton ascended from private fortune to untouchable dynasty. His fingers moved before fear could catch them: 07111983.

The lock beeped, each digit a resonance of Anton's lesson in power. With the final press, the red glow shifted to green. A whisper of hydraulics followed. The steel door unsealed, exhaling the stale air of secrets preserved for decades.

Inside: cassette tapes in labeled boxes, microfilm canisters arranged with archival precision, and a weatherproof envelope marked in Helena's distinctive script—*Black Ledger Archive—Emergency Protocols Only*. Her handwriting carried the particular confidence of someone who believed contingencies were just another form of control.

Truth had a pulse.

Lucas lifted the envelope, weighing proof that had outlived its creators. Inside, photocopied pages organized with efficiency: *Night Horizon* operational charts that read like corporate flowcharts, Cypress privatization contracts that converted torture into consulting, TRC witness-management protocols that transformed reconciliation into amnesia. At the bottom, a Dictaphone wrapped in anti-static film—Helena's voice preserved for purposes she hadn't lived to oversee.

He pressed play, watching the tape wheels turn like a countdown to revelation.

"Secondary archive protocols, revision 14-A (post-Anton schema)."

Helena's voice emerged from the tiny speaker, clinical and measured as surgical instruction.

"If this recording is accessed, primary containment has failed and Phase Three implementation must proceed under crisis parameters."

Papers rustled in the background—the sound of someone organizing catastrophe into manageable categories.

"The Clean Slate Protocol encompasses four operational phases. Phase One: elimination of problematic witnesses, completed per established parameters. Twenty-three targets eliminated, seven successfully extracted via false-termination protocols for future asset deployment."

Lucas stopped breathing. Extracted. Not eliminated.

"Phase Two: neutralization of investigative threats, proceeding within acceptable variance. Media management operational, legal containment functional, political insulation maintained through established channels."

He watched the tape turn, measuring the confession in millimeters of magnetic ribbon.

"Phase Three: installation of controlled successor. Lucas positioning proceeds according to established frameworks— subject remains unaware of operational nature, believes resistance represents autonomous choice. Emotional-manipulation protocols show ninety-three percent effectiveness in similar demographics."

The words hit like physical objects, each syllable rewriting his understanding of choice versus script. Even his rebellion had been choreographed, his moral conscience cultivated like a crop that would someday feed the machinery of institutional amnesia.

"Phase Four: historical-narrative consolidation, projected duration approximately eighteen operational cycles. Truth Commission findings will be recontextualized as transitional necessity, witness elimination reframed as security operations, systematic capture presented as unfortunate bureaucratic failure rather than institutional design."

Helena paused, and Lucas could hear her breathing— the sound of someone reviewing the architecture of organized forgetting.

"Note: Grace Mdluli extraction successful, asset remains viable for controlled deployment. Recommend maintaining presumed-death status until operational requirements necessitate resurrection. Her survival provides valuable leverage over emotional vectors within resistance networks."

The tape ended. Silence pressed against the study's mahogany walls, heavy as judgment deferred too long.

Lucas gathered the scattered documents, his hands moving without conscious direction. Bank records that traced murder as line items, shipping manifests that documented weapons disguised as mining equipment, communication logs that proved coordination between government ministries and private elimination contractors. Evidence comprehensive enough to collapse the entire infrastructure of managed reconciliation—if it survived long enough to reach public consciousness.

But more than institutional proof, the archive contained something Helena had never anticipated: Grace Mdluli's marginalia. Her handwriting appeared in corners and on yellow sticky notes, corrections and cross-references that revealed months of infiltration while officially dead. Grace had been inside the system, documenting its operation with the methodical precision of someone building a case that would survive systematic suppression.

"G.M. access verified," Helena's notation confirmed what the marginalia suggested. "Asset cooperation proceeding per extraction parameters. Counter-intelligence value significant."

Grace hadn't just escaped the attempt on her life; she'd turned her official death into operational advantage, becoming a ghost in the machine Helena had built to rewrite accountability as managed historical revision.

Lucas closed the archive and spoke to the study's expensive silence. "The Black Ledger."

Not melodrama. Classification.

***

Two streets away, Zara Mokoena sat in the borrowed Honda, watching packet traffic ripple across her screen—confirmation that the mirrors were alive.

The air-gapped machine no longer built the truth; it guarded it, a silent bodyguard humming against her knees.

She monitored transfer logs with exhausted precision. She knew the hardest part of revelation was keeping it breathing once it escaped.

The ritual kept her functional: unwrap stick of Wrigley's Spearmint, three breaths through nose, count streetlights visible through windshield. Fourteen. Count again to verify. Still fourteen. Numbers mattered when everything measurable was the only anchor against forces designed to make reality negotiable.

She'd learned the routine from Grace during those final weeks at *The Continent*, when paranoia had stopped feeling like pathology and started feeling like survival instinct properly calibrated. "Trust the count," Grace had said, watching Zara's hands shake as they reviewed photographs of Samuel Mashaba's border-crossing documentation. "If numbers stay consistent, you're still attached to what's real."

Real was eighteen hours until the dead-man timer released everything. Real was six server farms across three continents, each carrying an identical payload designed to survive coordinated attack. Real was Grace Mdluli's voice, captured on encrypted audio that proved some disappearances were strategic retreats rather than final defeats.

Her phone buzzed. Text from unknown number: "Recording this conversation. Suggest immediate reconsideration."

Standard intimidation protocol, but the desperation leaked through the phrasing like blood through bandages. Whoever had inherited Helena and Darren's operation was working from crisis-management playbooks, not strategic-planning documents. They were reacting, not controlling—a fundamental shift in operational dynamics that suggested opportunity rather than threat.

Zara traced the message origin through proxy chains that led to a server farm in Sandton, memorized the IP array, then crafted her response: a single image of Grace Mdluli's press credentials, timestamp-verified and cryptographically signed. Below it, four words: "Some deaths don't stick."

The reply came within minutes, faster than institutional protocol should have allowed: "Verification required."

She didn't respond. Fear was more useful than information, and whoever was monitoring communications had just revealed they weren't entirely certain Grace was dead—which meant they weren't entirely certain their elimination protocols had succeeded.

Her laptop chimed with a new file upload—Lucas, sharing Helena's Dictaphone confession. Zara listened once, twice, parsing clinical language for operational details that confirmed what Grace's marginalia had suggested. Helena's voice carried the particular confidence of someone who believed enemies were either dead or controlled, recorded when the Clean Slate Protocol still seemed inevitable rather than increasingly desperate.

But woven through Helena's certainty were Grace's corrections—handwritten notes that revealed systematic infiltration of the very network designed to eliminate her. Grace hadn't just survived the attempt on her life; she'd turned survival into intelligence gathering, becoming operational asset within the machinery built to guarantee her silence.

Each annotation carried the dry precision Zara remembered from newsroom collaboration: "Cypress privatization complete—see attached contracts." "TRC manipulation documented across seventeen commission meetings." "Lucas emotional management proceeding per H.B. directive, subject unaware of scripted nature."

Grace's marginalia read like field reports from deep cover, documenting systematic corruption while everyone believed her eliminated. The extraction protocol hadn't been rescue—it had been strategic repositioning, transforming apparent defeat into operational advantage that Helena's successors still didn't fully comprehend.

Zara's secure phone vibrated against her ribs. Incoming call, number blocked but recognizable pattern: five rings, disconnect, immediate callback. Grace's old signal from when paranoia was just professional caution rather than survival requirement.

She answered on the first ring.

Static, then: "Proof must be modular. If one falls, three stand."

Grace's voice, unmistakable despite electronic distortion that turned familiar warmth into digital cold. Alive. Operational. Ready.

"Where—" Zara began.

"Not where. When. Coordinates follow—midnight, previous arrangement. Bring everything including Lucas's inheritance."

The line died. Coordinates appeared via encrypted message seconds later: Rand Club, smoking room, the location where South Africa's most successful criminals had spent a century discussing atrocity as business development.

Zara stared at the screen until numbers burned themselves into retinal memory. A reunion then. The living and the dead, the visible and the invisible, converging on the moment when accumulated truth finally outweighed the machinery built to contain it.

She began final preparations, hands moving across keys with renewed purpose. The work was almost finished. Everything else was just implementation details.

***

The phone call lasted thirty-seven seconds. Grace's voice, distorted by encryption that turned conversation into electronic whisper, carried instructions that felt like benediction after months of fighting shadows without confirmation that shadows could fight back.

"Helena's confession changes operational parameters," Grace said, her words compressed into digital packets that reassembled into something approaching hope. "Her successors are working from outdated playbooks, managing crisis instead of controlling narrative. Window of opportunity approximately seventy-two hours before they adapt."

Lucas held the phone between them, studying Zara's face as she processed implications. Seventy-two hours to release everything, survive retaliation, and trust that public exposure would generate sufficient outrage to overwhelm institutional suppression. Not much time for transforming forty years of systematic murder into accountability that might survive the news cycle.

"The archive is comprehensive?" Grace's voice carried the particular precision of someone reviewing tactical assessments.

"Complete," Zara confirmed. "Helena's confession, Anton's financial records, operational directives spanning three decades. Plus your marginalia—proof of infiltration and ongoing documentation."

"Sufficient for Phase One exposure. Release protocol should cascade across multiple platforms simultaneously, overwhelming capacity for coordinated suppression. Timeline critical—they're already mobilizing countermeasures."

Lucas watched rain streak the Honda's windshield, each drop catching streetlight like evidence scattered across dark glass. "What about collateral damage? Staff, sources, people who didn't choose this war?"

"Already calculated," Grace replied, and something in her voice suggested calculation had cost more than tactical advantage. "Minimal exposure for non-combatants, maximum impact on institutional infrastructure. Some battles require accepting imperfect outcomes to prevent worse ones."

The call terminated automatically—thirty-seven seconds, exactly as Grace had trained them during those final weeks when paranoia felt like the only rational response to systematic gaslighting. Below the time limit that triggered automated surveillance flags, long enough to coordinate strategy without creating prosecutable evidence of conspiracy.

Lucas and Zara sat in expensive silence, watching rain transform Johannesburg's night landscape into something that looked like grief processed through neon and streetlight. The city pulsed with electronic life that carried their evidence through networks designed to monitor and control but now serving distribution and verification.

"She's different," Zara observed, studying Lucas's expression for confirmation of what they'd both heard in Grace's voice.

"Six months of presumed death will change anyone," Lucas replied, but the words felt inadequate for describing what survival under those conditions might have cost. Grace's voice had carried operational confidence built on foundations deeper than optimism—the particular clarity that came from accepting that personal survival was optional but mission completion was not.

"Midnight," Zara said, checking her watch. "Four hours to finalize everything."

"Four hours to end forty years of systematic murder," Lucas corrected, feeling the weight of family name transform from inheritance to choice. "Some deadlines are worth meeting."

They began final preparations in silence heavy as judgment deferred too long.

***

The Rand Club at midnight resembled a gentleman's crypt—mahogany polished to a dark shine, antelope glass-eyed on the walls, leather armchairs arranged like confessionals for men who never confessed. The smoking room held a hush that tasted of tannin and old tobacco, a curated quiet for private verdicts.

Zara set the rugged laptop on the table between them. The screen threw a pale square onto glass and brass and the fine dust that settles in places where power rests. Lucas stood instead of sitting.

"Mirrors are awake," Zara said. "Six primaries, ten hot standbys. HMACs check clean."

"Say it," Lucas replied. He needed the ritual—the liturgy of due procedure before the sacrament of exposure.

She ticked them off like a rosary: "Primary in Berlin; shadow in Reykjavík. Primary in Nairobi; shadow in Mombasa. Primary in São Paulo; shadow in Montevideo.

Three domestic seeds, two university relays, four hobbyist clusters who don't sleep. Dead-man in eighteen." A beat. "And a mechanical timer—clockwork, not code—because sometimes you can bribe electricity."

He watched her fingers move. He had learned to hear time inside keystrokes: the quarter-beat hesitations when she verified signatures, the clean triplets when she wrote to multiple drives. Calm hands on a night designed to vaporize calm.

"Verification," he said.

Zara slid the drive into the air-gapped port. The screen populated with blocks of green text—hashes, signatures, the cryptographic equivalent of fingerprints pressed into wet cement.

"Ledger scans match. Anton's ledgers, Helena's tapes, Cypress privatization contracts, the witness-management directives. Grace's marginalia digests compiled and salted. Nothing moves without two-of-two, and the salts aren't here."

"Where are they?"

She didn't look up. "Not in this room."

The grandfather clock in the corner marked the minute with a softened chime. Not the hour. Not yet.

The phone on the table vibrated once. A number without a number; a caller ID that looked like a shrug. Zara put it on speaker and leaned back so the microphone wouldn't catch breath as confession.

Static. Then a voice ironed flat by encryption into something that had warmth buried inside it like a live coal in ash.

"Proof must be modular," the voice said.

"If one falls, three stand," Zara answered, and caught Lucas's quick glance—the look of a man hearing a voice both familiar and altered, the timbre he had kept in a box inside his chest, now run through circuitry and necessity.

"Checksum delta Kilo-Two-Seven?" the voice asked.

Zara recited the last four of the ledger digest. "Seven, three, nine, A." She paused, the old newsroom habit of letting the other side fill the silence. "Your turn."

"Cypress chain-of-custody, third handoff. Name on the loading dock."

"D. Mashaba," Zara said softly, and the name reached across months and morgues. "Alive long enough to sign

. Dead long enough to be useful."

Static scaled down to a fine fizz. "You're inside the room?"

"Yes," Lucas said. He kept his voice level. "We brought what you asked for."

A breath, almost a human sound under the encryption. "Helena's dead," the voice said. "Darren too. That leaves infrastructure without a navigator. They'll still mount countermeasures. It will feel like weather. Ignore weather. Read pressure."

Lucas thought of the study at home—char on the hearthstone, secrets cooked to air, the way the house had exhaled at the first lick of flame. "We're ready."

"Ready isn't a feeling," the voice said. "It's a map." The sentence landed with the familiar cadence of Grace's training: you don't soothe a reporter; you brief them. "Listen carefully. We run the cascade in three waves. Wave One is administrative—shell corps, tax filings, the polite paperwork of indecency. It buys you thirty minutes of plausible deniability while platforms argue with themselves. Wave Two is financial—payments, transfers, the route money took from ore to obituary. Wave Three is human—witness statements, taped authorizations, Helena's confession. No redactions. You can't negotiate with a flood."

Zara's fingers hovered over the keys. "Mirror thresholds?"

"Use audience as ignition," the voice replied. "One thousand unlocks money. Ten thousand unlocks method. Fifty thousand unlocks names and the tape. Each threshold notarizes itself—we piggyback signatures from live viewers. The crowd becomes our PKI."

"Crowds are noisy," Zara said. "Noisy breaks."

"That's the point," the voice said, and in the flattened tone there was something like tired humor. "Noise is weather. We need climate."

The clock breathed its soft breath into the room. Somewhere above them a floorboard answered—it was that kind of club, where nothing creaked that didn't mean to.

"Countermeasures?" Zara asked.

"They'll start with procedural—copyright complaints, terms-of-service theater," the voice said. "When that fails, you'll see volumetric—DDoS through prestige clouds. Then surgical—targeted injunctions, a judge who owes a golf debt. After midnight, they'll switch to personnel. That's you."

"Let them," Lucas said.

"No," the voice answered, flat. "Let them after the threshold. You don't get paid for dying early."

He almost smiled. It sounded like Grace—the dry instruction, the refusal to romanticize loss. He wondered what she had had to empty out to speak like this and remain herself.

"You kept the cadence," he said, more to himself than the phone.

"Cadence is an instrument," the voice said. "We've tuned it for broadcast."

Zara tapped a hotkey. A quiet heartbeat of drives spinning up answered. "Wave One staged. I'm giving the bots something to chew: board minutes, beneficiary registers, five sanitized consultancy agreements."

"Put the Savile Row invoices on top," the voice said. "It comforts them to drown in silk."

On the screen, the first mirrors lit—a patient pattern: Berlin, Reykjavík, Nairobi, Montevideo—each reporting healthy and seeded. Zara checked HMAC again, then again, then stopped herself. "We're green."

"Zara," the voice said, softer. For a moment the encryption couldn't bleach all the human out of the sound. "You know what this costs."

Zara breathed in through her nose, counted three, tasted mint and metal. "I knew when we started."

"Lucas?"

"I'm here," he said.

"You stop being a son tonight," the voice said. "That was always the price."

He looked at the window—his own face ghosting in the glass, Johannesburg's lights below like solder points on a circuit. "I stopped last night," he said. "Tonight I become something else."

A small silence. Approval lived there, spare and exact.

"Begin," the voice said.

Zara launched Wave One. The browser stack rolled the administrative scaffold into daylight: incorporation documents, trust registries, two letters to auditors with polite verbs that meant *don't look too closely*.

The first viewers arrived—curiosity, then hunger— pulled by the smell of paper that ought not to exist.

Comments bloomed like mold. Some accused, some denied, some simply said names out loud the way you say a spell. Mirrors reported load, shrugged it off. Exfiltration lines watched the first automated takedown request arrive, stamped it with a form letter, and slipped it into a circular file in the cloud.

"Next," the voice said.

"Threshold," Zara answered. "We use math here."

Numbers climbed. 1,000. 2,000. 7,000. 10,000.

Wave Two dropped like a mezzanine collapsing: payment schedules, transfers routed through shell companies whose articles of association read like parables, invoices with euphemisms that wouldn't survive translation—nonstandard logistics, post-incident remediation. A line item for fire. A line item for silence.

Berlin burped under load. Nairobi steadied it. Reykjavík took a bite it could handle and passed the rest to hobbyists with opinions about capturable truths.

"Volumetric," Zara said, watching the dashboards. "They've put a faucet on us."

"Open more pipes," the voice said. "Make their bill painful."

She spun new relays into existence—the kind that ran under stairs and behind radiators, paid for by enthusiasm and bad coffee. The attack redistributed itself, frustrated by amateurs who were professionals at being amateurs.

"They'll escalate," the voice said. "Keep your posture low."

"Posture's on the floor," Zara said. Her eyes shone, hard as cut glass. "It's staying there."

Lucas felt the room thicken with the low hum of consequence. He thought of Helena's voice on the tape, the precise way she'd made necessity sound like mercy, strategy like fate. He saw himself at twelve in a chair that smelled of lemon oil, learning how a handsome lie sounded when you gave it a Latin motto.

"Fifty thousand," Zara said.

"Wave Three," the voice said.

She armed the final lattice. The tape queued. The ledger exhaled. A thousand hands on a thousand mice became a single lever. Zara clicked.

Helena spoke into the city—clinical, tempered, chemical-clean. Phase One, Phase Two. The count of dead with the digits filed off. The phrase "extraction via false termination" delivered in the learned serenity of someone describing weather fronts.

The comments sobered. A few jokes tried to float. They sank.

"Personnel time," the voice said. "You need to move."

"How?" Zara asked.

"Leave by two different doors at three-minute offset," the voice said. "Lucas first. You're the bright object. Zara, you're the payload. East stairwell is cold and blind for ninety seconds on the quarter-hour. That's your window. The car two blocks east has a quarter tank and a full trunk. Do not open the trunk. Drive four blocks and turn left on a red road with no lanes."

"What's in the trunk?" Lucas asked.

"Replacements," the voice said. "Of you. If we must."

Zara closed the lid of the laptop. The room seemed to inhale.

"Grace," she said, the name finally allowed into the air.

A pause. Not denial. Not confession. A line between them that could be both.

"Modular proof," the voice said. "If one falls—"

"Three stand," Zara finished, and caught her reflection in the window—someone who had learned to wear the weight so it didn't show.

"Go," the voice said.

The call clicked off. The old room returned to its curated quiet, but the quiet wasn't the same. Outside, Johannesburg vibrated—routers singing, servers sweating, people turning their screens toward a ledger that had learned how to live without paper.

Zara slipped the laptop into the bag. Lucas stayed a second longer, palm pressed to the table as if blessing or apology.

"Ready?" she asked.

"Ready is a map," he said. "We follow it."

They left at three-minute offset—Lucas down the broad stair with portraits that watched him like creditors, Zara through the service door that smelled of soap and secrets— two departures mapped against a city waking into a new shape of truth.

The clock released a single chime when the door fell shut, a clipped amen to whatever they had started.

Behind them, the mirrors multiplied. Ahead, the road with no lanes waited.

Chapter 19 – Phase Two

The rooftop didn't offer distance anymore; it offered exposure.

Wind lifted grit and carried it sideways, a dry scrape against glass and skin. Far below, intersections flashed red-blue-red as if the city were trying to cauterize itself with light. The sirens had changed timbre since midnight—less panic, more choreography. Somebody had begun giving orders again.

Zara's laptop muttered the last of its confirmations. The progress bars were already history—mirrors handshaking with mirrors in places whose laws didn't understand the word injunction. She closed the lid gently, as if quiet would keep the traces thinner than the light.

"Traffic's peaked," she said. "Half the country's trying to read at once."

Lucas kept his eyes on the grid below—block by block, a pattern of road closures and "random checks" knitting a net nobody cared to name. He felt the old familiarity he hated: the choreography of power expressed as logistics. You can hide a raid by routing it through the language of safety.

A door clanged open behind them.

Lucas turned, already cataloguing threat: the angle of the arm, the shadow of a weapon, the balance in the hips that meant speed. What stepped into the rooftop glow disobeyed all that math. Grace Mdluli. A scar like a seam sealing a second life. Hair rain-plastered. Eyes bright, not theatrical.

"Not a ghost," she said. "Stop looking at me like one."

Zara didn't move for a beat, the body catching up to the miracle. Then she crossed the space quickly enough to make wind of her. "You—"

"Later," Grace said, the word gentle enough to count as mercy. She set a heavy duffel on the parapet and unzipped it with the brisk hands of someone who no longer performed fear for anyone. "We need to move. And you need to see this first."

The bag held three kinds of proof arranged with the calm of things that didn't need to shout to be believed: a nest of hard drives in waxed cloth; a flood-soaked USB sleeved in rubber and epoxy; a narrow notebook mummified in duct tape. Each had a small white label written in the cramped clarity of a woman who had done this too often to indulge flourishes.

"Physical chain of custody," she said. "Customs gate footage from Nkomazi, two serial loops matched to shell-company manifests, and a ledger cross-check in a hand the courts will recognize."

"Helena's?" Lucas asked, the name a reflex that didn't stab as much as it used to. Death was not forgiveness; it was classification.

Grace tilted her head, a quiet concession. "From 2019, when she still signed off reconciliations by hand because she didn't trust digital witnesses. There's enough variance to prove it's not a copy-and-paste job. And enough context to make it perjury-proof."

Wind picked up, tasting of tar leached from the roof. A helicopter dragged a cone of light across a line of buildings to the east, then doubled back and took its time tracing air that should have remained private.

Zara's breath misted thin and quick. "How did you get all this out?"

"By staying officially dead," Grace said. "Paperwork is the most obedient weapon. The living have schedules. The dead have corridors."

Lucas found himself smiling without pleasure. "We were told you were a martyr."

"They tried to make me one," Grace said. "Then discovered martyrs talk too much when their files survive. We'll debrief in a room with fewer edges. For now— questions you'll be asked before breakfast: yes, the footage's hash matches the export I seeded in the vault last week; yes, the serial loop has an external witness; no, the notebook never touched your hands until now."

Zara glanced toward the stairwell. "We're not alone."

"Not for long," Grace said. "They'll triangulate your uplink to this building and then improvise legality on the way up the stairs." She nodded to the duffel. "We walk that. Nothing electronic left on except your heartbeat."

"My upload routes are clean," Zara said, insult knocking softly. "No direct—"

"This isn't about clean," Grace cut in. "It's about stubborn. The Clean Hands system is on rails. It doesn't need truth to locate you—just inertia. We go."

Lucas scooped the notebook and drives back into the bag. The USB slid into his jacket pocket, cold and real against his ribs like the memory of a key.

They took the service stairs, iron complaining the way old infrastructure does when asked to sprint. The building had been a hotel long enough to forget who slept where; half the floors were ghosted with scaffolding and plastic sheeting slapped by wind.

On the fifteenth landing, Grace stopped. She pulled a wafer-thin phone from her jacket, popped the back, and fed the battery to her pocket like a magician swallowing a coin. "Everything that pings is betrayal."

"Even the dead?" Lucas said.

"Especially," she answered. "Dead people shouldn't carry reception."

They pushed into a maintenance corridor that smelled of mop water and tired electricity. Fluorescents buzzed. The rhythm wasn't quite human.

"Garage," Grace said. "Sub-level. There's a government-era maintenance tunnel under the ramp that opens near Fox Street if they haven't welded it shut."

"They?" Zara asked.

"The kind of people who give welders good pensions."

They moved. A humming grew with them—the particular, expensive sound of rotor wash lapping at concrete. Somewhere above, a loudspeaker insisted the public remain calm. Calm is the first thing you demand when you intend to remove its cause.

Grace led them down a ramp slick with a film you couldn't name without a microscope. The tunnel mouth was a rectangle of dark unpromised by code. Cold air moved out of it as if the building had decided to breathe through underground lungs.

Inside, the narrow passage had walls lined with conduits and old paint. Their footsteps doubled back at them. The echo made it sound like the kind of company you only get in tunnels: yourself, multiplied.

Halfway down, Lucas crouched, two fingers pressed to dust. "Tracks."

Grace's light skimmed tire prints that weren't theirs. "We're late to our own escape."

Voices reverbed from the garage—at first abstract, then carrying words: "Clear the north ramp." "Thermal shows three." "Negative on civilians." The last was bureaucratic comfort: if they're not civilians, we don't need to talk about the law.

Grace killed the light. "Twenty meters, right-hand niche," she whispered. "Breathe like you've got secrets to conserve."

They slipped into a shallow alcove where a utility panel gaped open, wires like nerves. A torch beam slid across the tunnel entrance, paused, withdrew, returned with interest. Radios spoke in rhetoric—units, vectors, confirmations— language you use when nouns are expensive.

Zara's shoulder pressed against Lucas's. The duffel cut into his shin, banal pain that kept him from listening too hard to his pulse.

The beam passed a third time, slower. Boots receded. A door slammed. Silence crept back like a cat that pretends it owned the room all along.

Grace waited ten counts longer than Lucas would have. "Move," she mouthed, not bothering with sound.

The tunnel climbed. At the end of its modest ambition, it opened into a maintenance substation: low ceiling, naked bulb in a wire cage, graffiti professing loyalties that would not survive adulthood. A fuse box waited like an apology.

Grace popped it and stripped a pair of wires with a thumbnail. The bulb died. The tunnel behind them inhaled darkness. Somewhere above, a siren choked mid-note. Panic hates blackouts; choreography hates them more.

Zara eyed the improvised sabotage. "You used to be a customs officer."

"I still am," Grace said. "It's just that my customs have changed."

Fox Street took a minute to happen. Rain had begun again—not drama, just persistence. They emerged at the mouth of the tunnel like people exiting a thought experiment and finding weather.

"Car?" Lucas asked.

"Working on it," Grace said. She scanned the block without moving much. "Driver should flash once."

On cue, a headlight winked from under a billboard whose product had updated more frequently than the city's conscience. The sedan looked like a memory of three different models stitched together. An honest car because it didn't pretend.

Inside, the driver had the relaxed posture of someone paid to be forgettable. He passed back three disposable phones with their backs pried open. A paper envelope lay between the front seats like evidence awaiting jurisdiction.

"You expecting anyone else?" the man asked, eyes forward.

"If we are, we shouldn't be," Grace said.

They slid in. The car pulled away with the sureness of a plan practiced by people not paid enough to discuss it later. The wipers moved like a metronome teaching endurance.

Lucas watched the city adjust to its new weather. Screens glowed behind curtains. At a bus stop, a man angled his phone to show three others a clip. The group nodded in the shared way men nod when the story confirms a thing they wanted to be true. Truth had become something you could subscribe to monthly.

Zara broke the silence. "Grace—what is Phase Two?"

"A dead woman's last useful gift," Grace said. "Not Helena's hands—her protocols. Schedules that fire when certain thresholds trip. Numbers don't mourn."

"Who's pressing the buttons?" Lucas asked.

"The buttons press themselves. But Annelise is watching the lights."

The driver made three left turns and a hesitation that would have shaken a tail if one existed. Twice, Lucas thought they had one. Twice, the maybe-vehicle chose a different lane at the last second and became a coincidence.

They pulled into a warehouse whose windows had learned to be opaque. Inside, air smelled of dust that remembered furniture. Someone had painted a name in letters taller than a person. The paint had dripped like honesty.

The driver cut the lights. "Your second car's under the tarp," he said. "Key's on the visor. Don't use the freeway. Don't come back."

Grace found the hatchback where it should be: beige insisting on anonymity. She checked the wheel wells and the seam beneath the trunk liner. Her hand came out with a small black rectangle. She toggled it. The device hummed at a frequency you felt in your fillings and your bones.

"Jammer?" Zara asked.

"Half-dead," Grace said. "Half is double what we had."

The envelope waited on the front seat of the hatchback. Grace slid a finger beneath the flap and removed a keycard, a printed address, and a small folded note in block letters that avoided personality: PHASE TWO. T–06:00.

Zara's jaw tightened. "From Annelise?"

"If it were," Grace said, "it would have come with etiquette and an alibi."

"Then who?"

"Someone who wants us to know the clock," Grace said. "Or someone who wants to change what we think time means."

Lucas felt the words settle in his chest like a new kind of gravity. "Six hours to what?"

"To a countermove already baked into the system," Grace said. "Helena is dead. Darren is dead. But the machine they built has a habit of living long enough to confuse the difference between mourning and management."

They switched cars. Beige replaced black. The city outside had decided to rehearse order—traffic cops at corners looking at papers that existed to be shown. Grace picked side streets with the precision of a woman who navigated by the absence of cameras.

"Where are we going?" Lucas asked.

"A place that remembers what it was before it became a place," Grace said. "And then another one after that. We never stay in nouns that can be guessed."

They stopped beneath a tangle of corrugated roof and wires that sang softly in the rain. Inside, the safe room was the kind of space bureaucracy forgets to collect rent on: concrete painted the color of better intentions, a table with a past life in a pub, two mattresses that had made peace with their stains. On one wall, a vent taped over with care that signaled practice. A baking tray sat on the table. It had never met food; it would be asked to meet phones.

"Batteries out," Grace said. "Even if they're already out, show me they're out."

They complied. The disposables lay open-backed in the tray like beetles mid-dissection. Grace set the jammer on a crate and dialed until the hum softened telemetry into a suggestion.

Zara hovered above the table, instinct tugging toward the laptop. "I can post a three-paragraph update—chain-of-custody exists, footage exists, timing to protect sources— keep the pressure without burning our clean arrows."

"Do it," Grace said, "but no numbers that lead anyone here. Say we, not I. If they can't isolate you, they try to isolate your verb."

While Zara drafted, Grace emptied the duffel with the intimacy of ritual. Polaroids slid into a line. The flood-sleeved USB went to a separate corner like a guest requiring both courtesy and distance. The notebook she didn't open yet. Objects that know what they are don't need to look at themselves.

Lucas watched the Polaroids without touching them. Each image was a page in an old ledger, the paper's fibers visible, ink absorbed with the slow authority of time. In the margin of one, a line of numbers in a deliberate, feminine hand—caught mid-calculation. He felt the familiarity like a bruise pressed to test its honesty.

"My mother," he said.

"Your mother's math," Grace corrected. "Her argument with a number at the moment before she made it obey. It places her in the loop formally. The prosecutors will call it corroboration; the defense will call it forgery. Your job is to not help either before we can clock provenance in a courtroom voice."

Zara read back her copy—clean as a scalpel:

At 22:43, The Continent received physical evidence corroborating chain-of-custody links between cross-border shipments and Brandt Foundation subsidiaries. The material includes gate footage, serialized cargo loops, and handwritten numerical reconciliations by a senior Brandt official.

We will publish in stages to protect sources and to give public agencies 48 hours they have requested to secure implicated sites. Mirrors hold if our systems go dark.

"Good," Grace said. "Add one line: Attempts to intimidate witnesses will be documented as part of the record. It's both a promise and a trap."

Zara typed, posted, leaned back. The room brightened by a fraction, the way rooms do when the world outside has been asked to pay attention.

They worked an hour without language that didn't serve a task. Grace drafted chain-of-custody sheets and signed like a person who expected to repeat her name to strangers for months. Zara cut stills from the gate footage—plates visible, timestamps blurred. Lucas made lists of names he wished were strangers and filed that wish under a heading called Later.

At 03:11, the light in the taped vent flickered—then held. Grace glanced up without moving her head fully. "Neighbor unit woke up," she said. "Could be a refrigerator. Could be a relay."

Lucas went to the sink, ran water so cold it disciplined his breath, and returned. The kettle on the hot plate tried to boil with the half-hearted will of old appliances; it gave them warm water that tasted like the idea of tea.

When the text came, it didn't so much arrive as reveal that it had been waiting for someone to look.

A faint vibration shivered the baking tray. The phones in it were disassembled, silent. Grace's eyes narrowed. She reached into the envelope they had tossed aside and drew out a fourth disposable—thinner, cheaper, designed to be forgotten. It pulsed again, a small animal heart.

She pressed the button. The screen lit blue-white. A single line of text without origin:

PHASE TWO. T–06:00.

Zara's voice found the flatness she used when everything useful in her wanted to panic. "She's dead. He's dead. Who's—"

"Nobody living," Grace said. "Schedulers and thresholds. Clean Hands isn't a press office. It's a climate."

Lucas's mind did the old work it had once done for men he no longer wanted to resemble. Six hours was either a bluff or a rhythm. Either way, the city would be beating to it by dawn.

"What does it buy them?" he asked.

"Reframing," Grace said. "Asset flight. Injunctions. A raid on the wrong storage unit at the right hour for cameras. Algorithmic grief pushed in six languages. They'll try to turn truth into an aftertaste."

The text didn't change. The room listened the way rooms do when they suspect they're being recorded for posterity.

Zara closed her eyes once, hard. "We need something thicker than a wall."

"Witnesses," Grace said. "Ones they didn't plan for. And one more thing."

She crossed to the taped vent, peeled it back, and removed a gray metal box the size of a lunch and twice as unassuming. She set it on the table and flicked a switch. A new hum braided with the jammer's lower drone. LEDs scrolled until they found a pattern.

"What is it?" Lucas asked.

"A listener," Grace said. "Not sound. Signature. The packet stream their engineers use when the system begins rewriting a narrative at the infrastructure level. I've seen it once."

"When?" Zara asked.

"The day my file changed categories," Grace said. "Living to dead."

The LEDs jumped. Held. Jumped again.

"There," Grace said softly. "They're warming up."

Lucas looked at the blue-lit phones, the gray box, the Polaroids, Zara's laptop, the taped vent, the thin mattresses in the corner. The room could have been any room in a city that loved concrete more than justice. But it was this one, and it had them in it, and the next six hours had chosen to happen here.

"We hold?" he said.

"We hold," Grace answered. "And we make them come inside if they want to change the weather."

She put the cheap phone back in the tray. It vibrated once more, as if pleased with itself.

The city outside adjusted its breathing.

"Welcome to Phase Two," Grace said.

* * *

By 04:07, the city had settled into its counterfeit calm. Sirens thinned into distance, traffic lights remembered to change again, and the drones of a hundred generators stitched Johannesburg back together one neighborhood at a time. The blackout Grace had caused three hours earlier had been absorbed into the noise floor of a nation built to metabolize crisis.

Inside the warehouse, the air carried the metallic sweetness of tired electronics. Zara sat cross-legged on the floor, laptop open in privacy-mode, building mirror nodes by hand. Grace paced between the table and the taped vent, counting under her breath. Lucas kept to the window, eyes tracing the street's geometry the way soldiers read weather.

He watched a sedan roll past twice within twenty minutes, different drivers, same rhythm. Surveillance didn't need imagination—just payroll.

"They're patterning the block," he said.

"They'll want to see who still moves after the upload," Grace answered. "Annelise is running the optics desk now. She'll need a villain with better bone structure than the last one."

"Me," Lucas said.

Grace didn't disagree.

Zara closed her laptop. "Mirrors seeded. Back-channels confirm replication across two educational servers and one faith-based network in Nairobi. Those won't fold under political pressure."

Grace nodded. "Religion and universities—both run on stubborn belief."

The gray box on the table whispered its static heartbeat. LEDs pulsed green-amber-green.

"They're escalating," Grace said quietly. "Packet signature just doubled. That means an automation loop came online—likely Phase Two rollout. Prewritten articles, scheduled talking heads, cleanup contracts, algorithmic grief. You'll see the hashtags in forty minutes."

Zara swore softly. "They're rewriting while we sleep."

"Then we don't sleep," Lucas said.

Grace looked at him. "You look like you already tried that experiment."

He smiled, an expression that didn't reach allegiance with joy. "It didn't stick."

The warehouse lights flickered once—grid voltage catching its breath. Grace adjusted the jammer's gain. The hum rose a half-tone, a new key for paranoia. "If we vanish from the net completely, people will assume arrest or death. Zara, you need to publish something small every hour. Nothing overt, just heartbeat posts—quotes, timestamps, a line of poetry, anything. It keeps us statistically alive."

Zara nodded. "Ghost proof."

"Exactly," Grace said. "Give them ghosts to chase so we can work."

***

At 04:31, a push notification fluttered through the VPN like a paper airplane that had flown through fire. Zara enlarged it. A headline bloomed on every major outlet simultaneously:

BRANDT FOUNDATION VINDICATED BY INDEPENDENT FORENSIC REVIEW

Digital forensics confirm manipulated files in so-called "Cypress Leak," clearing Brandt Foundation of wrongdoing.

Zara's jaw clenched. "Already?"

"Crisis Protocol Theta, automated sub-routine," Grace said. "They loaded that press kit months ago. The review body doesn't exist—it's a Brandt subsidiary folded last year. But headlines don't have audit trails."

Lucas skimmed the text. "They even quoted me— 'anonymous source within the investigation admits timeline inconsistencies.'"

"That's Darren's ghost," Grace said. "His language module writes better lies than most men tell in person."

Zara exhaled through her teeth. "Annelise's fingerprints?"

Grace shook her head. "Too disciplined. She's using the machine correctly. That's what makes her dangerous—she believes in structure, not ideology."

Lucas stepped away from the window. "How do we beat structure?"

"By forcing improvisation," Grace said. "Machines choke on that."

***

The clock advanced. They ate in fragments: stale protein bars, tepid water. Human maintenance disguised as strategy.

At 05:02, Zara's mirror monitor pinged—one node gone dark. "Server disconnect."

"Which one?" Grace asked.

"University of the Witwatersrand."

Grace frowned. "That's local. Legal order, not hack. Someone pulled plug authority."

Lucas met her gaze. "Annelise?"

"Or the State Security Agency doing her favors. Either way, they're folding witnesses back into silence."

Grace opened the notebook—Helena's handwriting dense and angled, the numbers domestic yet merciless. "We'll counter with provenance," she said. "You show them this page—handwriting, ink analysis, cross-reference to bank transfer ID in public records. Facts slower than rumor but harder to delete."

Zara scanned the page with her phone's back camera, no signal attached, saving locally to encrypted storage. She cropped, adjusted contrast. "If I post a blurred version—just enough of the handwriting—?"

"Do it," Grace said. "Caption: There is ink under the algorithms."

Zara smiled, grim and small. "You've missed journalism."

"I've missed verbs that still take human subjects," Grace said.

***

By 05:27, rain began again, thin and silver. It hissed through the cracks in the roof, a sound like data static scaled to weather.

309

Lucas lit a candle—power redundancy and comfort in one gesture. The flame bent toward the door draft.

Grace watched it. "When that moves wrong, we move."

"Define wrong," Zara said.

"When it goes out without reason," Grace said.

***

At 05:38, the phone in the tray vibrated once, twice. Grace flipped it facedown. The gray box answered with a flare of light. "Incoming burst," she said. "They're seeding the narrative overseas now—EU, US, Singapore. Automated hashtags in twelve languages. Six-hour rollout confirmed."

"So T–06:00 was literal," Lucas said.

"Within minutes," Grace said. "They'll drown evidence under sympathy and patriotic exhaustion."

Zara's eyes flicked to the clock. "One hour down."

"Five to go," Grace said. "Annelise won't need all six."

***

At 05:46, an unexpected sound threaded the night: children's voices. A choir recording, faint, echoing from the street loudspeakers the Foundation used for community alerts. "Nkosi Sikelel' iAfrika"—the national anthem, but slowed, stretched, its harmonies repurposed for grief footage.

Zara's skin went cold. "They're running memorial reels."

Grace moved to the window. Screens on the opposite building pulsed with Helena Brandt's image—her face framed in grayscale, eyes turned upward in digitally enhanced devotion. Below it, a banner:

HELENA BRANDT: THE LIGHT WE FOLLOW.

Lucas felt his stomach contract. "They canonized her."

"They're writing her saint-day," Grace said. "Martyrs simplify billing."

The anthem looped. Children's faces intercut with Helena's, the Foundation logo dim behind them like a watermark of benevolence. Across the bottom crawl: "A nation rebuilds through unity."

310

Zara closed the curtain. "I can't watch her become holy."

"You have to," Grace said. "It's data. Every frame tells you how they plan to bury the rest."

***

At 06:03, the first tactical message hit encrypted chatrooms: Anonymous group claims Brandt leaks a foreign psy-op. By 06:05, state outlets echoed it as a "developing theory." By 06:07, comment threads flooded with bot syntax—repeat lines, misplaced idioms, borrowed rage.

Zara's laptop pinged a system alert: traffic anomaly. She turned the screen toward them. "Botnets crawling my mirrors. Thousands of hits per second. They're running a denial-of-service on truth."

Grace's voice stayed calm. "Hold bandwidth open long enough for a public journalist to notice the pattern. They love stories about censorship. Feed them that."

"I thought we didn't trust journalists," Lucas said.

"I trust hunger," Grace replied. "Every outlet wants the exclusive on a machine war. We give them the preview."

***

At 06:21, Lucas's burner phone—a separate line, never connected—buzzed. He frowned, checked. No number, just a file name: R-04 Echo.mp4.

He hesitated, then pressed play. The screen filled with the Conservatory footage. Helena mid-speech, hand over heart, voice measured. Then the gunfire, the collapse, the scream that had rewritten policy. But this version didn't stop there. A new angle—unseen before—showed a woman stepping into frame seconds after impact, face half-lit, mouth forming a word the microphone never caught. Later, the world would know her name—Annelise Fourie.

Grace watched over his shoulder. "Where did that come from?"

"Someone wants us to see her hesitation," Lucas said.

311

"Or they want to remind you she's not done," Grace said.

Zara leaned close. "Freeze that frame—her mouth."

Lucas did. The shape of the word was distinct: Continue.

Grace's expression didn't change. "There's your confirmation. Annelise inherited everything—including her permission."

***

06:34. The gray box began to whine softly, higher pitch. Grace adjusted the dial. "They're rewriting DNS tables—trying to redirect archive links to Foundation servers. It's a full digital coup."

Zara typed fast, fingers bruising keys. "I can counter-route through mirror farms, but I need a clean node."

Lucas thought of one—an academic mirror Grace had mentioned earlier. "Nairobi Faith Network. They'll hold."

Grace nodded. "Send through them. Religion still believes in revelation."

Zara executed the command. Lines of code streamed. "Re-routed. Mirrors live again."

Grace exhaled. "That buys us thirty minutes."

***

At 06:52, power cut. The candle went first, then the city beyond. The hum of the jammer remained—a lonely frequency pretending to be courage.

Lucas stood, ears straining. A car door. Two more. Measured footsteps. "They're here."

Grace's tone didn't rise. "Let them be. We have our own broadcast."

She moved to the table, switched the gray box's secondary port, and connected it to Zara's laptop with a short cable. "We're live-streaming their approach—anonymous mirror, metadata scrubbed. Every step they take toward this door uploads to a dozen nodes. If they kick it in, the world watches."

Zara's throat tightened. "You think they'll stop for optics?"

Grace met her eyes. "Optics built this country."

***

The first knock came polite, bureaucratic. "Ms. Mokoena," a man's voice called. "Emergency Management. We need to check the premises."

Zara said nothing.

Second knock, harder. Lucas could see silhouettes through the frosted glass—three, maybe four.

Grace clicked record on her phone. "Remember," she whispered, "truth doesn't need to win, it just needs to survive."

The door shuddered. Hinges screamed. A boot found its argument. Dust rose.

Grace hit send on the stream. "And now the world knows who knocks."

The first figure breached—body armor, visor, no insignia. Flashlight beam cut across their faces. The man barked, "Down! Step away from the devices!"

Zara lifted her hands, palms up but voice steady. "You're live to the world."

The man hesitated. In his earpiece, someone yelled; they couldn't hear the words. He lowered the weapon fractionally, uncertain which manual covered this situation.

Grace spoke quietly, almost kindly. "Tell Annelise Fourie her weather pattern failed."

The man's jaw tightened. "You're under arrest for data terrorism."

"Not by their definition," Grace replied, voice flat. "Information is ordnance now."

Another flashlight swept the room, finding the gray box, the drives, the candle stub. Outside, engines idled, impatient.

Lucas stood motionless, every muscle coiled but language still intact. "Grace—"

She shook her head once. "We don't run anymore. We document."

Zara's stream window showed viewer count rising—hundreds, then thousands. Comments in ten languages, disbelief turning to fixation.

The officer's radio crackled: "Abort visual. Cut feed."

Too late. The feed was already mirrored, already impossible to kill without killing the net.

Grace smiled—barely a movement. "They built a world where nothing dies quietly."

Outside, the sirens started again, higher pitch, as if frustrated by daylight.

The clock on Zara's screen ticked 06:59.

***

The first flashbang flattened sound into light.

For three seconds the world was a photograph that refused to stay still—white, depthless, lawless. Then came the noise: boots, shouting, the metallic punctuation of objects meeting authority.

Lucas hit the ground before thought caught up, arm over Zara's head, grit in his teeth. The air smelled of magnesium and wet dust. Grace stayed upright longer than either of them, eyes half-shut, watching the lens of the nearest helmet-cam the way a diver watches the sun from the bottom.

"Keep filming," she said. It wasn't a plea.

One officer yanked the cable from Zara's laptop. Sparks spat; the screen went dark.

"Step back!" he shouted. "Hands visible!"

Grace raised her hands slowly. "You're already visible," she said.

The second officer hesitated, recognizing her face. The name had circulated for months—first as whistleblower, then as casualty, then as footnote. Seeing her alive made something in the choreography stutter. He gestured for the others to hold position.

"Orders were capture only," someone murmured over radio.

"Then capture your conscience," Grace said. "It's the only thing you'll lose clean."

The third officer swung the butt of his rifle toward the table. The blow cracked wood and shattered the glass jar of candle wax. Liquid flame bled across the surface before dying in the draft.

Lucas forced himself upright. "She's unarmed," he said.

"Not by their definition," Grace replied, voice flat. "Information is ordnance now."

Zara turned toward the door. Outside, the dawn had arrived unnoticed—pale and indifferent. Sirens faded. The world was too awake for secrecy to pass as duty.

The lead officer touched his earpiece, listening, then looked at Grace again. Whatever command came through, it wasn't the one he expected. He lowered the weapon.

"Stand down," he told his team. "We're to leave the evidence untouched."

"From who?" one asked.

"Higher than we reach," he said.

Grace smiled, not kindly. "Annelise."

The officers backed out without another word. The last one closed the door as if manners could erase history. Their engines receded into the architecture of traffic.

Silence returned, cracked at the edges.

Zara stood slowly. "That just happened?"

"It happened," Grace said. "But it didn't finish."

Lucas leaned against the wall, pulse still drumming. "Why pull back?"

"Optics," Grace said. "They realized the feed was live, mirrored, and multiplying. Arresting us now would make them authors of the footage."

"So we're free?" Zara asked.

Grace shook her head. "We're useful. Different thing."

***

They moved carefully, restoring the table to something like order. The gray box still blinked, wounded but operational. The drives survived; the notebook lay open to Helena's final reconciliations—ink ghosts under the fluorescent pulse.

Lucas looked at the handwriting. "She did this for herself," he said.

"No," Grace answered. "She did it because she couldn't stop keeping score."

Zara sat, fingers trembling around the mug that had survived the chaos. "I thought when we exposed them, the machine would stop."

"It did," Grace said. "Then the replacement booted."

Outside, the city sounded different—no longer frightened, just loud. Vendors unpacked. Radios played fragments of Helena's memorial coverage: government officials promising reform, CEOs pledging transparency, each speech perfectly calibrated to sound contrite at volume.

Zara listened, then turned the radio off. "They're already rewriting us."

"Of course," Grace said. "History's first draft used to be written by journalists. Now it's written by servers."

Lucas stared at the gray box. "Then we give them a second draft they can't delete."

***

At 07:12, a new broadcast began—shortwave, untraceable. Grace found it on the emergency band. The voice was synthetic but styled to sound human: calm, maternal, unflappable.

"This is the Clean Hands Continuity Channel. The Foundation mourns Helena Brandt. In her honor, we announce the Brandt Fellowship for Ethical Leadership—supporting young investigators dedicated to truth and nation-building."

Zara shut her eyes. "They turned her into a scholarship."

Grace killed the radio. "Crisis Protocol Theta completed its cycle. Now we live in its PR."

Lucas crossed the room, picked up the gray box, and set it near the window. "Does this still hear them?"

"It hears everything that talks too loudly," Grace said.

The LEDs trembled, then steadied. The hum thickened—subtle interference filling the space between breaths. "They're sweeping again," Grace said. "Digital perimeter, not physical. They'll trace who mirrored the feed."

Zara checked her laptop. "Too late. The footage's on independent servers already. Thousands of reposts."

"Then Phase Two failed," Lucas said.

Grace shook her head. "Phase Two never fails. It adapts. It will make your truth look like another product. That's survival disguised as defeat."

Zara looked up. "Then what do we do?"

"We outlast the news cycle," Grace said. "And build something that can't be licensed."

***

They packed what could be carried: drives, notebook, gray box. The rest they left—empty mugs, ash, a candle stub, a burned patch on the table that looked like punctuation. The sedan from earlier waited under the same billboard. The driver wasn't the same, but the posture was identical—paid neutrality.

Grace slid into the front seat. "Rand Club fallout still trending?"

Zara checked. "Number one for now. They're already framing you as rogue intelligence."

"Perfect," Grace said. "I'd rather be myth than mascot."

Lucas watched through the windshield as rain glazed the road ahead. "Where to?"

"Somewhere that doesn't believe in addresses," Grace said. "There's a contact north—retired systems engineer who helped build the first Brandt compliance modules. He owes me clarity."

Zara frowned. "You trust him?"

"No," Grace said. "But I trust his guilt."

The car merged into traffic that didn't yet know what it was carrying.

***

By 08:03, they reached the outskirts—the city thinning into warehouse districts, billboard skeletons, and the pale industrial fog that passes for horizon. Grace directed the driver into a service lane beneath a bridge. They transferred to another vehicle—a utility van with no markings and the smell of old engine oil.

Grace sat in the back beside the duffel. "Annelise will call a press conference before noon," she said. "She'll use the word stability three times. She'll promise independent oversight and announce that the Foundation is dissolving itself into a public trust. None of that will happen, but the promise will be archived. You can't indict an archive."

Zara stared at her. "You've already written the speech."

Grace met her gaze. "I wrote it three years ago. She'll just delete my name."

Lucas shook his head. "Then we can predict her next move."

"Not predict," Grace said. "Anticipate. Prediction's a luxury. Anticipation's survival."

***

The van climbed a narrow road into the ridges east of the city. From up there, Johannesburg looked smaller, less certain. Smoke from a power plant drifted sideways across the skyline, blurring the distinction between sky and consequence.

Grace pointed to a compound half-hidden by eucalyptus trees. "There."

It wasn't much—a low concrete structure, antennas like ribs against the morning light. A man waited by the door, early sixties, shoulders concave from years spent inside data

318

centers. He wore a jumper two decades old and the face of someone who once believed in systems.

"Grace," he said, voice a rasp. "You shouldn't be alive."

"Neither should your code," she said.

He hesitated, then opened the door.

***

Inside: dust, humming servers, maps pinned with cables connecting continents like veins. The man—Venter—moved with careful guilt.

"I heard about the Rand Club release," he said. "You detonated a history."

Zara stepped forward. "We detonated a lie."

"Same architecture," Venter said. "Different audience."

Grace set the duffel on a workbench. "You helped Helena build the Clean Hands shell. We need to know how to kill it."

He sighed. "You don't. It's self-healing. Every time you delete a node, it replicates elsewhere—state servers, private backups, embedded news feeds."

"There must be a root," Lucas said.

Venter nodded reluctantly. "There is. But it's not digital. It's legal—the charter filed when the Foundation registered its humanitarian division. It gives the system personhood. As long as that stands, Clean Hands has standing."

Zara's eyes narrowed. "You mean it can sue."

"And be sued," Grace said softly. "If we find the right jurisdiction."

Venter looked at her. "You'd take it to court?"

"I'd make it confess," Grace said. "In a place where records survive longer than reputations."

Venter laughed, small and sad. "You'll need counsel immune to fear."

Zara smiled thinly. "We know one editor who doesn't sleep."

***

By 09:24, data had begun flowing again—grayer now, slower. The machine had eaten its crisis and was digesting applause. Traffic stats dropped. Helena's memorial trended behind football and weather. The world's attention had already moved on.

Zara watched the numbers. "They forget fast."

"They have to," Grace said. "Otherwise, everything would hurt forever."

Lucas leaned against the doorway, eyes on the skyline. "So we start again?"

"No," Grace said. "We continue. Starting again is for people who think the past agrees to stay quiet."

She turned to Venter. "How many mirrors left uninfected?"

"Maybe a dozen," he said. "Mostly academic or religious hosts."

"Keep them alive," she said. "Feed them one verified proof a day. Slow truth is still truth."

Venter nodded. "You'll make enemies."

Grace's smile was brief. "I brought my own. We starve their spin with portion control."

***

Outside, light broke through the cloud deck—thin gold filtering across the highway's curve. The city shimmered under it, freshly laundered and none the cleaner. On a nearby digital billboard, Helena's face still lingered—grayscale, eyes heavenward, tagline THE PRICE OF COURAGE.

Zara stared at it. "Do we let them keep her like that?"

Grace studied the image. "She belongs to the lie now. Let them have her myth. We'll keep her math."

Lucas looked from the billboard to the horizon. "And us?"

Grace zipped the duffel. "We vanish correctly. Truth doesn't need monuments. It needs maintenance."

320

The van door slid shut; they rolled into the compound's garage. They cut the engine. Outside, the city kept broadcasting repentance to anyone still tuned in.

***

By noon, the press conference began. Annelise Fourie stood before a wall of microphones, immaculate, measured. The feed played on a monitor in Venter's lab.

"In honoring Helena Brandt's legacy," she said, "the Foundation will commit to transparency and cooperation. We denounce malicious actors spreading false narratives. The Brandt dream endures—clean, accountable, human."

Grace turned off the screen midway. "I wrote that line," she said.

Lucas met her gaze. "Then you can write the next one."

Zara closed her laptop. "What would it say?"

Grace thought for a moment. "History is what refuses deletion."

***

They stayed until evening, refining backups, cross-signing timestamps, building a lattice of survival.

When they finally stepped outside, the light was different—softer, forgiving nothing but pretending to.

From the ridge, the city looked like circuitry—streets glowing in patterns that might once have been prayer.

Somewhere beneath that electric sky, stories continued to rewrite themselves, always cleaner, never truer.

Grace watched the horizon darken. "They think this is over."

Zara adjusted the strap of the duffel. "It's never over."

Lucas nodded, the gesture heavier than hope.

The three of them crossed the courtyard toward the garage, where the van waited in shadow. Overhead, the first stars pushed through the haze like punctures in a blackout.

Chapter 20 – The Bloodline Code

It had taken three days, two generators, and every favor Mthembu still had to bring the newsroom back from the dead. The Continent's offices had been dark for months—licenses frozen, accounts seized, staff scattered to safer bylines. But when the files went live and the world began speaking their language again, the old glass-walled floor came alive too. Desks were hauled out of storage, cables scavenged, routers fed from car batteries. By dawn, the hum had returned—a pulse steady enough to fool the building into thinking journalism was still legal.

The newsroom had quieted into that particular hush that follows an explosion—the predawn fluorescents casting everything in morgue-light. Papers still drifting. Ears still ringing. Everyone speaking in lower voices, as if the air itself carried shrapnel. Nothing was ever silent after history had been forced into motion; there were always screens.

Hope was the most dangerous register—it made people forget the cost of speaking.

Jamal kept three of them up as evidence. On the left: a world map tattooed with pulsing dots, mirroring nodes in Reykjavík, Nairobi, São Paulo, and New Delhi—with a stray one winking from a university lab in Christchurch where some grad student had decided to house a copy for the sheer romance of it. In the middle: a tiled grid of progress bars that had already finished but continued to loop—blue filling to the brim and resetting like a heartbeat. On the right: the receipts—transaction logs, hash matches, checksum confirmations—blinking in a staccato language that said this really happened and if anyone asked, here is the math.

Today wasn't a hunt; it was an inheritance protocol— the files teaching the world how to keep them alive.

"It's done," Jamal whispered—the servers handshaking across continents like a pulse. "Mirrors stable. Hashes clean. If one goes down, ten inherit."

The wall clock read 10:42 a.m. They looked like people who had outlived the hour. Sleep was a rumor. There'd been a raid at dawn, a retreat, a regrouping. Now the newsroom was the only room left that felt like ground.

Lucas sat on the edge of a plastic chair that had never been designed to carry a family history. Elbows on knees, tie slackened, palms pressed together the way people hold a prayer they don't quite believe in. He had stared into a lens and unsealed the name that had paid for so many rooms like this one; now Brandt lived outside him—an organism under glass.

Across the bullpen, Grace worked at a terminal that officially didn't exist, her fingers moving across keys with the fluid precision of someone who had spent months learning to be invisible. She looked different than in the photographs—thinner, sharper, hair darker from months of careful anonymity—but her presence filled the room with the electric energy of resurrection. Every few minutes, she would glance up from her screen and catch Lucas or Zara watching her with the wonder of people who had learned to live with ghosts, suddenly finding themselves haunted by the living.

"The international networks are picking up the story," Grace reported, her voice raspier than before but carrying the same intelligence that had made her such an effective investigator. "BBC, CNN, and Al Jazeera. Clips from the dawn-raid live stream are looping every hour. Your father's name is trending in twelve languages."

"And yours," Jamal said from the screens. "Not a memorial. A byline."

Zara's monitor painted exhaustion across her face in thin blue strokes. She hadn't smoked in years, but her fingers kept traveling to the space where a pack would have been. Nicotine had always been a ritual more than a drug: something to do with hands when taking on the state with a laptop felt too easy.

Mthembu's voice carried from the glass-walled office even though he kept it low—the clipped cadence of a man who understood that delay could kill a story as thoroughly as bullets. "Yes, we've seen your injunction. No, we will not comment without counsel. Yes, you may send questions by email. No, we will not let you set the terms." He hung up, the handset gentler than the words.

"Trending already," Jamal said without glancing away from the panel. "Number one in South Africa. Number two globally. All three of your names are everywhere."

Lucas closed his eyes. Grace alive, Zara vindicated, himself finally free of inherited guilt. The algorithm knew enough to put them together as a story of resistance rather than tragedy.

Relief lasted seconds. If their names were everywhere, so were the targets on their backs.

Zara swiveled toward Jamal without standing, never taking her hands off the keyboard. "Build a static page: what we released, where the files live, how we verified. Pin it. Make it look like it belongs to someone the President can't bully."

"And the legal page?" Jamal asked.

"Plain language," she said. "No adjectives. The documents speak. We just teach people how to listen."

Grace looked up from her screen with the ghost of a smile. "The beauty of being officially dead," she said, "is that they can't serve papers to someone who doesn't exist. I can coordinate international distribution while they're still trying to figure out how to intimidate a ghost."

Mthembu stepped out of the office carrying three foam cups that used to be coffee and now were a promise to the body that warmth would arrive eventually. He handed one to Zara, one to Lucas, and offered the third to Grace with the kind of reverence usually reserved for saints.

"We've been served," he said, his voice pitched for the room. "High Court—ex parte. They're reaching for the State Security Act, plus a defamation claim—like salt and pepper. 'Interim relief to protect the integrity of ongoing investigations.'"

Zara snorted. "Investigations that start today."

"Investigations that start when evidence leaves the room they control," he said. "Counsel says prepare for a dawn hearing; they'll try the usual trick—seal it all 'for the public good,' and let us argue with a gag in our mouths."

Jamal pointed at the map. "They can gag us. They can't gag Reykjavík."

"And they certainly can't gag someone who's been legally dead for six months," Grace added, her fingers never pausing in their work. "I've been building networks they don't even know exist. Every contact I've made, every server I've established, every backup protocol I've created—it all operates independently of South African law."

"They don't have to," Mthembu said softly. "They just have to kill this newsroom for sport. Make an example. Warn every freelancer that courage is non-renewable."

The air conditioner clicked and gave up; a long fluorescent tube above the copy desk stuttered itself into steadier light. It made everything look more honest.

Zara took the cup and found the coffee cold. "Do we have counsel for dawn?"

"I've got three names," Mthembu said. "Two will take the case. One will take the case and then get disinvited from certain dinners. We need the third."

"Call him," Zara said. "Offer him something no dinner can give."

"Like?" he said.

"His name opposite the State," she said. "History pinned to his lapel."

"And if that doesn't work," Grace interjected without looking up from her screen, "remind him that officially dead journalists make excellent character witnesses. Hard to cross-examine someone who doesn't legally exist."

He almost smiled. "That worked on me when I still had hair."

Lucas's hands had not moved. He looked like someone trying to hold a metronome still, as if by stillness he could stop a song from playing. The chair groaned when he leaned back.

"Everything we have," he said quietly, "the whole archive—"

"—is not ours anymore," Zara finished with him, not unkind. "That's the point. You let it out of the room. You let it find people you can't control."

"And some of us," Grace added, finally looking up with eyes that carried the weight of months spent building cases in the shadows, "never let them control us in the first place."

The phrase made him flinch without moving. Control had been the family grammar. To choose the opposite tense felt like treason at the cellular level.

"Hey," Jamal said, not turning. "Z. He's topping searches in Mumbai. And Lagos. And Berlin. And there's a university in Chile telling people how to verify hashes on their own machines."

"Good," Zara said. "Teach them to read the ledger without us."

"Better than that," Grace said, her screen reflecting the global reach of their operation. "Teach them to read ledgers we haven't found yet. This isn't the end of the investigation—it's the beginning. Every other family, every other network, every other system built on organized forgetting—they're all watching to see if accountability is possible."

For a minute nobody spoke. The three screens kept narrating. Somewhere deeper in the building, a cleaner's cart squeaked past and then paused—the way people pause when they hear a foreign language and understand the subject if not the verb.

Lucas stood and the chair sighed with relief. He walked to the window as if the glass might have answers the servers did not. Outside, the street was a smear of wet light; Johannesburg was giving itself to morning's favorite trick— pretending this time would be different.

He said, not quite to the glass, "Now what?"

"Now," Mthembu said, "we stay awake."

"Now," Grace corrected gently, "we stay alive. All of us. That's the point of surviving your own death—you get to help other people avoid theirs."

It landed less like bravado than like a promise.

***

The room had been chosen for its acoustics, not its beauty. Sound died a quiet, polite death here; no echo survived long enough to carry meaning into the next minute. Phones vibrated on polished oak like nervous animals— foreign numbers blinking at cabinet ministers who had once believed their phones were domesticated.

The President did not sit until everyone else finished doing it. He stared at his reflection in a dark monitor as if a word might appear on his face and tell him what to do.

The minister of transport muttered, scrolling like a penitent through PDFs he had signed with a flourish only to see that flourish now turned into a blade.

The minister of state security slammed his fist lightly—a gesture calibrated to read as anger on camera if any camera had been allowed. "How did it get out? We had the archives under lock. We had layers."

"You had men who were paid to believe locks mattered," the justice minister said without lifting his eyes. "Now the world is reading about how you audited the locks and declared them robust."

The finance minister cleared his throat. "Markets will be unhappy."

"We are not a market," the minister of state security shot back.

"We are, when we call the IMF," the finance minister said, too quickly, and then looked at the president as if to be rescued.

The president said nothing long enough to make silence a tactic. His eyes traveled the ring of tired faces—the men who had helped him build the appearance of stability around an economy that preferred collapse. He had always believed in tempo: outlast the panic, and panic becomes mood.

"We do not contest," he said finally. "We defer. We call it foreign interference. We call it a narrative coup. We say the documents are real but context is weaponized. We say we will investigate, and then we appoint a judge with the right kind of caution."

"Sir," said the minister in charge of his party's fortunes, braver—or more frightened—than the rest, "and the Brandts? Their name is the headline. If they fall, donors dry up. If donors dry up—"

"Then we make sure they fall slow," the president said. "Slow buys time. Time buys silence."

"Helena Brandt will not be allowed to fall—not in the memorial they're writing with her," the minister of state security said.

The president allowed the hint of a smile to crease his face without landing. "No. She has become useful precisely by being gone. Annelise Fourie is coordinating Clean Hands from the media ops floor. She'll handle narrative containment."

"And the son?" the justice minister asked. "He is useful to someone. He thinks he is useful to himself."

"Frame him as naïve," the president said. "A reckless conscience who stumbled. A boy returning from London with a bag full of guilt. The street loves a penitent. We'll teach him which sins they are allowed to forgive."

"And the journalist?" the minister of state security asked. "Zara Mokoena?"

"Frame her as foreign-funded," the president replied. "A useful idiot for powers that want to destabilize Africa's success stories."

"Sir," the justice minister said carefully, "there's a complication. Grace Mdluli."

The room went silent. The name hung in the air like an accusation that had learned to speak.

"Grace Mdluli is dead," the minister of state security said, but his voice carried uncertainty.

"Grace Mdluli appeared on a live stream during the dawn raid six hours ago," the justice minister corrected. "Standing beside Lucas Brandt and Zara Mokoena. Very much alive. Very much operational."

The president's face went through several expressions before settling on the kind of calm that precedes either enlightenment or violence. "Explain."

"She faked her death six months ago. Has been building cases from deep cover. Tonight she emerged with evidence we didn't know existed, from sources we didn't know she had." The justice minister's voice carried the weight of someone delivering a terminal diagnosis. "She's legally dead, which means she can't be intimidated, arrested, or served. She's the perfect witness."

A digital clock on a sideboard clicked to a new minute. The sound was microscopic and rude.

"Full spectrum?" the minister of state security asked.

The president nodded once, but the motion carried less confidence than before. "Full spectrum," he said. "But understand—we're not just fighting three journalists anymore. We're fighting a ghost who's learned to be more dangerous dead than alive."

The men understood which spectrum that was: coordinated injunctions; friendly anchors hand-fed exclusive concerns about "stability"; a task-team raid staged for prime time; traffic officers at the right intersections with "random checks" for the wrong cars; and a thrum of sirens that made people want someone, anyone, to promise order.

But they also understood something else: some fights become more difficult when your enemy includes someone who has officially ceased to exist.

A secretary entered, head down, a file balanced like contraband on her palms. The president signed without reading. He had learned long ago to sign for effect and keep the decisions elsewhere.

"Gentlemen," he said, letting the plural cover the room like a sheet. "Hold your nerve. Speak softly. Offer process.

Above all, let the Foundation's caretakers sell the saint they've made."

They nodded as if surprise were a sin. But surprise had already arrived in the form of a woman who had died to fight more effectively.

The room swallowed the sound.

***

Thirty floors above the city, the media operations suite glowed like a lab that had forgotten its purpose. Screens stacked three deep, each one whispering a different version of order. Annelise Fourie stood at the center of it—white blazer, hair pinned so tightly it could draw blood, posture calibrated to broadcast calm.

Helena's image cycled in grayscale across the main wall: a face edited for martyrdom beneath the caption THE PRICE OF COURAGE. Below it scrolled the crawl Annelise had approved twenty minutes earlier: The Brandt Foundation commits to transparency and reform following the tragic loss of its founder.

"Phase Two is live," an analyst said. His voice carried the respectful dread of someone addressing machinery that sometimes answered back.

Annelise didn't look away from the data wall. "Keep the memorial reels," she said. "Push stability across partner channels. Route the 'foreign interference' package to state broadcasters at :15 past the hour."

Another analyst pivoted from his console. "Ma'am, the raid live-stream is still mirrored. Faith-network and academic servers. Takedowns aren't holding."

"We don't need takedowns," Annelise said. "We need doubt. Seed it, then sell process. If people are arguing about legitimacy, they're not watching evidence."

She moved closer to the wall of graphs, eyes sweeping sentiment curves that climbed and dipped like vital signs. "Schedule the noon statement: The Foundation welcomes independent oversight. It's a sentence, not a promise."

A technician adjusted her headset. "Tiger Seven just checked in—State Security confirms escalation authority."

"Good," she said. "Protocol without panic. Keep it invisible."

The room hummed. Orders became packets; packets became weather. On the lower ribbon, Lucas Brandt's face appeared beside a headline that toggled between reckless conscience and traitor. Annelise selected the softer option; redemption tested better in morning focus groups.

"Retag Grace Mdluli as 'former investigator linked to foreign NGOs,'" she said. "Add a question mark to the line about her death. Questions travel faster than answers."

"Understood."

An intern leaned forward timidly. "Ma'am, the President's office is asking whether we confirm her resurrection."

Annelise allowed herself a small breath that might have been amusement. "We confirm confusion. Say the Foundation mourns her loss and welcomes clarification."

Across the suite, the server hum shifted pitch—the sound of algorithms retraining on live input. Annelise closed her eyes for half a second, listening. The machine was grieving efficiently.

"Cut sentiment feed on channels showing fatigue," she said. "Hope content in rotation B."

"Hope?" an analyst asked.

"School scholarships. Children quoting Helena. Give them the hymn before anyone notices the words."

On another screen, Grace's face froze mid-sentence, pixels trembling under compression. Annelise studied it: the composure, the defiance, the inconvenient life.

"You don't erase a witness who's already been erased," she murmured. "You erase her context. Make her miraculous—then unbelievable."

The technician nearest her hesitated. "Should we draft something for the noon statement—regarding Ms. Mdluli directly?"

"Not yet," Annelise said. "Let the system argue with itself first. When the noise peaks, we'll offer coherence. People mistake coherence for truth."

A courier entered carrying a sealed folder. She signed receipt without reading; habit. Inside were overnight polling summaries—confidence down twelve points, but trust in Helena Brandt as symbol up twenty-four. The dead were performing better than the living.

"Good," she said softly. "Let them believe in her. Belief metabolizes guilt."

The junior analyst who had spoken earlier cleared his throat. "And Mr. Katz's legacy code—do we still deploy automated counter-hashtags?"

"Deploy," she said. "But limit aggression. We're shepherds now, not wolves."

He hesitated. "Darren Katz would've preferred wolves."

"Darren Katz," she said, still facing the wall of light, "preferred himself. He's gone. We're what remains."

For a moment nobody moved. Outside the windows, Johannesburg pulsed—billboards looping Helena's smile, drone cameras mapping sympathy, taxis idling in manufactured calm. The city looked airbrushed by guilt.

Annelise turned to the room. "At noon we go live. If anyone asks about the Brandt family, the line is continuity with accountability. If anyone asks about the leaks, say national healing requires context. And if anyone asks about Grace Mdluli—" She paused long enough for the silence to obey. "—say nothing. Let her haunt them."

She dismissed the team with a nod. The analysts returned to their stations, eyes blue with artificial daylight. The machine inhaled again.

Annelise remained still, watching the curve of public sentiment rise toward acceptable faith. When she finally spoke, it was to herself. "Legacy management," she whispered. "Not damage control. The Brandt name survives by becoming a memorial. The rest is maintenance."

She exhaled, and the suite resumed its rhythm—screens cycling, graphs pulsing, empathy scheduled in quarter-hour blocks.

***

Behind The Continent, the alley smelled of oil and last night's rain. Floodlights from the TV van still flattened the front entrance into daylight—reporters who had called Zara reckless now stretching microphones toward anyone she'd ever shared a coffee with.

They went out the side door—Lucas, Zara, and Grace moving with the practiced caution of people who'd learned to trust one another precisely because trust had been lethal. Damp air gathered on their faces. Their shoes echoed on wet pavement. None spoke until the corner, where a streetlamp flickered like a verdict reconsidered five times a second.

"It's out," Zara said finally, though they all knew naming a fact sometimes made it bearable. "Everything Anton built is crumbling."

Lucas's jaw tightened as if a thought had teeth. "It's out," he said. "And now it's not ours. It belongs to whoever edits it fastest."

Grace turned just enough to take them both in. Sodium light outlined her face like a study of someone who had learned to exist in the space between life and afterlife. "You expected relief," she said, not unkindly. "Relief doesn't live here."

"Relief is just exhaustion in a fresh shirt," Lucas said. He tried a smile and abandoned it.

A sedan drifted past with windows darker than regulation. They all stiffened—muscle memory meeting fresh habit—eyes flicking to plates and silhouettes they'd remember in sleep.

"Do you regret it?" Zara asked.

Lucas shook his head. "No. I regret not knowing what comes next."

"What comes next," Grace said, certainty born of exhaustion, "is the hardest part—staying alive long enough for the truth to matter."

They stood longer than the city's patience allowed. Rain resumed, indifferent. Grace's voice found the tone of instruction again. "The three of us—we're not just witnesses anymore. We're proof that resistance is possible. That some people can't be silenced, even when you kill them."

"Especially when you kill them," Zara said. "You've become something they never planned for—a dead investigator who kept investigating."

"The ultimate source protection," Lucas observed. "They can't threaten someone who's already officially gone."

Grace smiled; for a moment she looked like the woman Zara remembered—brilliant, relentless, completely unafraid of consequence. "Exactly. Death, it turns out, is excellent job security for journalists."

They moved toward the safe house, three silhouettes against Johannesburg's tungsten glow, carrying between them the weight of a nation's secrets and the possibility that some truths were too stubborn to stay buried.

***

In Hillbrow, a crowd gathered around a battered television in a shebeen—the broadcast bleeding through static. Men in work shirts leaned too close to the screen; women with backs that had carried too many years squinted when the crawl ran too fast.

"They finally said it," one man exhaled, as if proof had weight and he'd been allowed to set it down. "And that woman—Grace—she came back from the dead to say it."

Another spat into the bucket and didn't aim. "Coming back from the dead is one thing. Staying alive after—that's the trick."

In Sandton, in bars with glass walls, whisky-glassed men whispered without lowering voices. Phones buzzed with instructions from banks that never slept. Account numbers crossed oceans faster than auditors could fasten their shoes. A woman laughed too loudly—the sound edged with the hysteria money gets when it meets its own reflection.

"Grace Mdluli," someone said. "Supposed to be dead six months. Now she's everywhere."

"Dead journalists," another replied, "are the only kind you can't buy."

In Khayelitsha, a spaza-radio rasped between a talk show and a weather report. Callers said the same country couldn't keep asking the poor to forgive what the powerful refused to name. The host stopped one caller to ask them to breathe. It didn't help.

"What do you think," the caller wheezed, "about this Grace woman coming back?"

"I think," the host said carefully, "that some people are harder to kill than others think."

On WhatsApp, the files became screenshots that had lost their metadata—truths turned into slogans. On Twitter, hashtags flowered like invasive species: #BloodlineCode, #BrandtFiles, #GraceReturns. A rumor outran its correction and earned a parade.

At OR Tambo, a customs officer refreshed a feed and found designer ads standing politely beside evidence. On the cargo apron, a man in a neon vest read Grace's name and wondered if anyone really died anymore—or if they just learned to fight differently.

In Canary Wharf, a junior analyst highlighted a paragraph in a weekend supplement that had guessed too close by accident, forwarded it to a thread titled RISK-SSA, and wrote: exposure, not default. P.S.—Grace Mdluli is alive. His boss deleted the mail and picked up a phone. Deleting was theatre.

Washington adjusted its tie. A deputy assistant secretary drafted a statement about steadfast partnerships that said nothing and meant "we're counting votes." Two floors down, an NSC staffer wrote a memo asking where the debris would fall if the Brandt scaffolding collapsed—and whether dead journalists staying dead was a policy the U.S. should have an opinion about.

Berlin parceled worry into procedure; Paris shrugged and called the bank. In Beijing, a quiet apparatus waited for phone calls about port concessions that might need laundering by a better metaphor.

By morning, someone had printed the first meme of Grace as a saint—halo made from a typewriter. It was beautiful and effective; beauty travels faster than truth.

The city was awake and deciding what the evidence meant. The files said what had been done; the crowd would write who did it—and why the answer mattered. And Grace Mdluli, officially dead for six months, was helping them write it.

***

He didn't remember the drive. The body will sometimes bring you home on its own motor and leave the mind to arrive later.

The apartment offered no refuge; light did its best to stage calm and failed. He put the USB on the table the way you place a relic from a dangerous excavation—carefully, admiring its ordinariness with a touch of fear. The files had already detonated elsewhere; the object had become theatre.

He filled a glass with water and did not drink it. Surface tension made a lens of his face—the features warped into a man he recognized more comfortably than the one above the glass.

He thought about Anton's study, about the ledger, about the sigil that had corralled a generation of brave men into obedience. He thought about Helena, who had spent a lifetime making sacrifice look like taste. He thought about Darren, who had turned pity into a weapon and called it framing.

He thought about Grace—alive when the world thought her dead, building cases when everyone else thought the investigation was over. The truth was out. The Brandts

336

were still awake. But now they faced something they had never planned for: a witness who had survived her own elimination and learned to fight more effectively from the shadows.

He pressed both hands flat on the table as if to tell it what he weighed. "What holds this together now?" he asked the room.

His phone buzzed. A message from Grace: Now we finish what we started. Together. The living and the officially dead.

From the street below came sirens, rain, and the sound of a city learning that some stories outlive their storytellers, some witnesses transcend their own deaths, and some truths are too powerful to bury with the people who discover them.

***

Helena did not return because history doesn't allow second funerals. But her image did—the curated martyrdom looping on every broadcast. Three screens in the media suite still carried her smile while Annelise Fourie watched sentiment graphs flatten toward equilibrium.

"Containment achieved," an analyst said.

Annelise nodded, though she knew the word was fragile. Containment was never permanent; it was only pause.

She leaned closer to one monitor where a clip from the dawn-raid stream replayed in slow motion: Grace stepping between two officers, eyes clear, voice audible even through distortion—You can't arrest the dead.

Annelise paused the frame. The phrase had gone viral, embroidered on T-shirts before breakfast. "Whoever writes the slogans," she said softly, "wins the day."

A technician approached. "Tiger Seven confirms secondary escalation ready if needed."

"Stand by," she said. "We've used enough thunder for one morning."

She muted the feed and studied her own reflection in the black glass where Helena's face had been. The system lived; the architects didn't. That was inheritance of a kind.

"Legacy maintenance," she whispered. "Always forward, never free."

Outside, a billboard rotated to a new campaign: The Brandt Foundation—For a Cleaner Future. The irony pleased her less than it used to.

***

By mid-morning the newsroom felt like a bunker someone had forgotten to bury. Phones rang until they became a kind of weather. Nobody said the word victory; even optimism felt like a provocation.

Zara worked the way surgeons do when they know relatives are watching: steady, efficient, meticulous enough to matter but not enough to look like art. She had a spreadsheet open that wasn't for editors—it was for courts, watchdogs, citizens. Documents cross-referenced to invoices, to GPS pings, to diaries in neat handwriting that would get the men who wrote them in more trouble than their signatures ever had.

Grace worked at the terminal beside her with the focused intensity of someone making up for six months of official non-existence. Her resurrection had galvanized the entire floor; even the most cynical reporters found themselves writing with a kind of belief that embarrassed them.

Mthembu moved through the room with two phones and a list in his head of people he used to admire. He looked like a man performing optimism and settling for stamina.

"We've been served a follow-up injunction," he said when he reached their desks. "High Court—ex parte. They want us gagged under the State Security Act and, because irony is a national resource, they added defamation and 'ongoing investigations.' Counsel can get a hearing in two hours if he eats his gown on the drive."

"Grounds?" Zara asked, hands still moving.

"That we are dangerous," he said. "That truth is dangerous when it's inconvenient. And that Grace Mdluli is somehow violating the law by being alive."

"Can they do that?" Zara asked. "Prosecute someone for not staying dead?"

Grace looked up from her screen, smile sharpened by months in legal grey zones. "They can try. It's hard to serve papers to someone who officially doesn't exist. Harder still to intimidate someone who's already endured the worst they can do."

"True," Zara said, managing a small smile. "They'll try to make us the story."

"They already are," Mthembu said. He lowered his voice. "And they're driving to people's houses. Durban. Pretoria. Plain cars, un-plain men. They'll call it 'proactive engagement.' Your phones—"

"Our phones are lanterns," Grace said. "They make us visible, not safe. But visibility's its own protection."

On Zara's screen, a new message blinked from an unknown number. Five words: Your brother's name is next.

Her skin changed temperature. She showed Mthembu and Grace because secrets are expensive—you must choose when to spend them.

They read, both blinking once. "Go," Mthembu said. "If they're going to knock on a door, better yours be the one already open."

"I'll come with you," Grace said. "Official advantage of being dead—I can provide protection without paperwork."

"This is the job," Zara said, as if refusing would insult every dead journalist who hadn't gotten to come back.

"The paper will be here—or in court—by morning," Mthembu said. "Either way, the story's too large for this room now."

Jamal drifted over with a printout and the kind of grin you only allow yourself out of superstition. "Mirror in Iceland posted their own verification guide," he said, as if announcing that a stranger had volunteered to guard your child. "And the Kenyans turned the ledger into a searchable archive without the victims' names. They're teaching people to be careful."

"Good," Grace said. "Out there is where safety lives—in distributed truth, replicated evidence, knowledge that belongs to everyone and therefore to no one."

Zara stood, grabbed the go-bag that had learned the weight of a life, and looked once at Lucas across the room. He saw her this time and nodded—the kind of nod that meant they were all in this together, living and officially dead alike.

***

By dusk, The Continent's website showed three updates: A guide to verifying hash chains. A legal explainer in plain language. A single line that read: Attempts to intimidate witnesses will be documented as part of the record.

The post went viral not for its defiance but for its clarity. Even the algorithms hesitated before trying to bury something that clean.

Across the city, billboards still displayed Helena's sanctified face. In the feeds beneath, users counter-posted a different image: Grace Mdluli mid-sentence, captioned The Dead Don't Lie. Within hours the two images began to merge—one martyr polished, one resurrected raw—opposite sides of a country arguing with itself.

Lucas watched it from his apartment window. The skyline pulsed like circuitry remembering its design. He whispered the words Grace had written in her message: Together. The living and the officially dead.

Outside, thunder rolled east toward the mines. The air smelled of iron and coming rain.

In the newsroom, Mthembu poured two cups of cold coffee, left one on Grace's desk, and said to no one in particular, "Hold your nerve."

340

Grace looked up from the keyboard, eyes rimmed red but alive. "That's the job," she said.

The servers hummed, mirrors breathing across continents. Johannesburg exhaled into the dark. Somewhere a phone vibrated with a new upload; somewhere else a firewall fell. The bloodline code was breaking, line by line, checksum by checksum—and this time the world was watching.

Epilogue

Three weeks after the sworn testimony—and the words he spoke on those courthouse steps, which brought down his family's empire—Lucas Brandt sat in a safe house overlooking Johannesburg's sprawl. He watched the city wake to headlines he'd helped ignite.

Some nights the glass still caught the ghost-light of old servers, a faint pulse beneath the silence.

The safe house was anonymous—rented under a false name, paid in cash: beige walls and borrowed furniture. A place designed to be forgotten. Through the rain-streaked window, the Carlton Centre rose like a concrete tombstone against gray dawn, its abandoned floors catching first pale light.

A train horn drifted up from the station below: one long note dissolving into rain.

But he wasn't alone in this exile.

Grace Mdluli sat at the kitchen table—officially dead on paper for seven months, very much alive in headlines. Most of the country knew she'd survived; kids in Braamfontein wore knockoff tees quoting her line about how being dead could be safer than being alive. Her laptop displayed satellite feeds from mining operations across three provinces. She'd learned to use the bureaucratic fiction of her death as leverage: able to investigate without interference, document without detection, build cases that survived every attempt to silence them—even as her name trended like a warning.

Zara worked at a second laptop near the window, fingers moving across keys with practiced efficiency. Someone who had learned to change the world one carefully verified fact at a time. The three of them had become an unlikely partnership—the disgraced heir, the relentless journalist, and the ghost who refused to stay buried. Grace's voice threaded through their nights like static, reminding them that ghosts make the best witnesses.

The television flickered in the corner, volume low but insistent. "BRANDT EMPIRE IN RUINS," scrolled the news ticker. "LEAKED FILES SPARK GLOBAL INVESTIGATION." Lucas didn't need to hear the words anymore. He'd memorized them over weeks of sleepless nights—the same phrases repeated across channels like a mantra of destruction.

Street vendors had already learned the economy of aftermath—selling umbrellas, knockoff press passes, and shirts stenciled with Grace's dead-better-than-alive line in four fonts and two spellings.

On the table beside Grace, a moth fluttered against her laptop screen. Drawn to the digital glow that had become their collective obsession. The creature's wings beat frantically against glass, seeking something it couldn't understand, couldn't reach. Grace watched it—the quiet patience she reserved for all persistent creatures.

"Still tracking the Mozambique shipments," she said without looking up from her screen. Being officially dead had given her access to sources that living journalists could never reach. Customs officials who shared information with ghosts they could never admit to meeting. Port workers who documented evidence for someone who couldn't be intimidated because she didn't officially exist.

Lucas had been watching old footage of Anton—archived interviews, board meetings, the public face of a man who'd taught his son that power was inherited like blood type. On screen, his father gestured confidently at a podium, explaining why certain mining accidents were "statistical inevitabilities." The younger Lucas had stood in the background, dutiful and silent—complicit by proximity.

"Some codes," he'd told Zara on those courthouse steps, "are meant to be broken." But breaking codes, he was learning, was like shattering glass. The pieces cut everyone, especially the one who held the hammer.

His phone buzzed. Another encrypted message from a journalist in London, asking for comment on the Hartbeespoort settlements—thirty million rand, distributed among forty-seven families. It wouldn't resurrect the dead, but it would send children to university, pay for medical care, rebuild lives that empire-building had crushed. Justice, incomplete but tangible.

"Answer it," Grace said, not looking up from her screen. "Mrs. Sibeko called this morning. Her grandson starts university next month because of that settlement. She wanted to thank you."

Grace's ability to maintain contact with families affected by the mining disasters remained one of the stranger advantages of her official death. Everyone knew she wasn't a ghost—there were interviews, slogans, a public afterlife of clips—yet the systems that mattered still listed her as deceased. That clerical invisibility let her visit, interview, and document without creating legal complications for anyone involved. The dead, it turned out, made excellent investigative journalists—especially when everyone knew they refused to stay buried.

Ronald Mthembu—Grace's editor—had started a hand-distributed newsletter, *The Johannesburg Truth*, printed on cheap paper and paid for in rand coins and trust. Circulation: 847 subscribers. Sometimes the smallest resistances proved most durable.

Lucas looked at his phone, then at Grace's encouraging nod. He began typing a response. Learning to use his name as a tool rather than a burden, to turn inherited guilt into inherited responsibility.

***

Rain intensified, drumming against the window like time itself—steady, relentless, indifferent to human schemes. Below, Johannesburg stirred to life. Commuters hurried through puddles, newspapers tucked under arms, carrying his family's shame in their briefcases and backpacks. The Brandt name had become synonymous with corruption—a cautionary tale told in headlines and courtrooms.

Helena was gone, her death at the Conservatory replayed endlessly across networks—half martyr, half villain, depending on the hour. Darren Katz was gone too, the strategist who had treated morality as a variable finally outplayed by the system he'd built. His lieutenants scattered like roaches when the lights came on—some to prisons, others to jurisdictions without extradition treaties.

The network his father had spent three decades building had collapsed in three weeks—brought down by USB drives and the testimony of a son who'd chosen truth over blood.

But truth, Lucas had discovered, was both poison and cure. It killed what it touched—including the one who administered it.

"The Bangkok node came through," Zara announced from her position by the window. "One of the offshore shells feeding the weapons network—we've got them."

Grace looked up from her screen with the kind of smile that had once terrified mining executives and customs officials across southern Africa. "Good. The families deserve to know how deep this goes."

A torn photograph lay beside Lucas's laptop, edges charred from the previous night's small fire—a ritual of his own making. It had shown the three of them at some corporate function—Anton commanding, Helena elegant, Lucas young and eager to please. He'd saved their eyes from the flames, cutting out the eyes with surgical precision before consigning the rest to ash. Even in destruction, he couldn't quite erase them completely.

The USB drive rested in a shot glass beside the whiskey, its edges blurred by amber distortion. It was the seventh copy he'd made—insurance against the insurance, backup to the backup. The others were already distributed through channels Zara and Grace had helped him establish: journalists in three countries, human rights organizations, government investigators with reputations for incorruptibility.

Truth had metastasized beyond his control, beyond anyone's control.

That was the point. That was also the protection.

His reflection in the rain-streaked window looked older than his thirty-two years—hollow-eyed and sharp-featured, like Anton in his final months. The weight of generational sin had settled into his bones, making him feel ancient despite his youth. He'd broken the cycle, but cycles, once broken, left jagged edges that cut both ways.

"You look like hell," Grace observed with the casual honesty of someone who had learned that life was too short for polite lies. "When did you last sleep?"

"Sleep is for people who aren't being hunted by international mining cartels," Lucas replied.

"Sleep is for people who want to stay sane long enough to finish the job," Zara corrected. "Grace, tell him."

Grace closed her laptop and fixed Lucas with the penetrating stare that had made her such an effective customs investigator. "The advantage of being officially dead is perspective," she said. "You learn what actually matters. And what matters is that we're winning. Slowly, expensively, but we're winning."

Truth was a weapon that wounded its wielder. Every revelation in those courthouse testimony sessions had carved something away from him—not just guilt, but the comfortable fiction that distance could equal absolution.

But truth was also a weapon that protected the people who wielded it together.

***

He lifted the USB drive from the whiskey glass, amber droplets clinging to its surface. Grace laughed at the irony—truth preserved in alcohol, the same substance that had numbed his father through decades of necessary compromises. Her laugh was sharp—the humor of someone who'd learned to find comedy in institutional failure.

"Anton would have appreciated the symbolism," she said. "Truth pickled in the same alcohol he used to drown his conscience."

The laptop chimed with another headline, this one from *The Financial Times*: "GLOBAL MINING CONSORTIUM FACES REGULATORY SCRUTINY FOLLOWING BRANDT REVELATIONS." Ripples were spreading beyond South Africa, beyond mining, into boardrooms and government offices where his father's influence had propagated over decades. Power, Lucas was learning, was not just inherited—it was infectious. Spreading through networks of complicity until entire systems became diseased.

"We've exposed the infection," Grace said, reading his thoughts with the eerie accuracy of someone who had spent months learning to anticipate everyone's reactions. "But exposure is not cure. It's merely the first cut of a surgery that will take years to complete."

A knock at the door made them all tense—muscle memory from weeks of living as targets. But it was only Mrs. Ndaba, the building's cleaner, checking if they needed anything. Grace had chosen this place partly for her. A woman who'd lost a husband to silicosis in the mines, who cleaned offices for apartheid-era executives, who understood that some justices came too late but still mattered.

"I saw the news, Mr. Brandt." Her careful English carried neither accusation nor sympathy—just acknowledgment. "Your father's people, they caused much suffering."

"We know," Grace said gently, appearing beside Lucas with the fluid movement of someone who had learned to navigate spaces without disturbing the air. "We're working to make it right."

Mrs. Ndaba studied Grace's face with curiosity but no surprise. In the weeks since they moved in, she had become a quiet legend on their floor—the woman who kept odd hours and asked careful questions—though no one knew her name. Officially, Grace Mdluli had died in a border accident months earlier. The woman who lived here was just another tenant with a careful smile and no forwarding address.

She studied their faces with the penetrating gaze of someone who'd learned to read truth in a country built on lies. Her eyes held the particular wisdom of women who had buried husbands and sons to feed other people's ambitions. Who had learned to measure apologies by the actions that followed them rather than the words that carried them.

"Sorry is not enough," she said. "But it is beginning."

"Beginning is all we can promise," Zara said. "But we can promise that."

***

After she left, Lucas returned to the window. The city sprawled below him like a circuit board, lights flickering in patterns that suggested order but concealed chaos. Somewhere in those patterns, families were reading about compensation payments that would never resurrect the dead but might salvage the living. Somewhere else, powerful men were calculating whether Lucas Brandt was worth eliminating or simply discrediting.

The game never ended. It just found new players, new rules, new ways to disguise the same fundamental transaction: human life for profit margin, conscience for competitive advantage.

"But the game has new rules now," Grace said, joining him at the window. "They can't kill me again—I'm already dead. They can't discredit Zara—her work speaks for itself. And they can't make you disappear without proving everything we've said about them."

On the television, a reporter stood outside Hartbeespoort, interviewing women whose husbands had died in Anton's mines. Their faces were tired but determined, weathered by grief but not broken by it. They spoke of justice delayed, of children who would now attend university, of medical care that might save the men still coughing up rock dust after decades underground.

"Mr. Brandt's testimony sealed the case." One woman's Afrikaans carried decades of loss. "We do not forgive him

348

for his family's crimes. But we thank him for his courage to speak truth."

Lucas watched her speak and thought of Grace in her decision to fake her death. Not the tortured woman who had supposedly died of a heart attack, but the customs officer who had walked into that warehouse knowing she might have to disappear. Knowing that someone needed to see what was hidden in those shipping containers. Grace had staged her death believing that official elimination would give her protection, that invisible investigation would provide armor. She had been right about both the protection and the necessity.

"I never felt courage on those courthouse steps," Lucas said. "Only the hollow certainty that silence would kill me more slowly than truth ever could."

"That's what courage is," Grace replied. "The moment when staying still becomes more terrifying than moving forward."

Courage. The word sat comfortably in Lucas's chest now—not as a burden but as a shared responsibility. He'd felt no courage on those courthouse steps as an individual. But as part of something larger, as one member of a team that included a brilliant investigator who had learned to fight more effectively from official death, courage became possible.

***

He remembered Grace's laugh—the sound she'd made when Zara had first shown her the encrypted files, when she'd realized the scope of what they were confronting. Not bitter, not desperate, but almost joyful. The laugh of someone who had finally found an enemy worth fighting, a secret worth disappearing to expose. Lucas no longer envied her that clarity. He was learning to find his own.

"You're thinking too hard again," Grace observed. She was back at her laptop, but her attention remained partially focused on the two people who had helped her learn that some battles could only be won by people working together.

The whiskey glass reflected the laptop screen's glow, turning the amber liquid into liquid light. Lucas lifted the whiskey glass carefully, feeling the weight of ritual in the simple gesture. The USB rested at the bottom, its casing dulled where alcohol had kissed it. The data remained intact—truth preserved in silicon and code, waiting for its next deployment.

"There will be a next deployment," Zara said, as if reading his thoughts. "The Brandt files revealed not just your family's corruption, but the architecture of systems that enabled it."

"Mining consortiums with government ministers on their boards," Grace added, her fingers never pausing in their work. "Defense contractors laundering money through apartheid-era channels that have never truly closed. Chinese state enterprises buying silence with infrastructure projects that enslave as much as they develop."

His father had been a node in a network that stretched across continents, through generations, into boardrooms where men spoke of acceptable losses and necessary sacrifices. Lucas had cut one node, but networks were resilient. They rerouted around damage, found new pathways, evolved new methods of concealment.

"The real war is just beginning," Grace said. "And somewhere in that new work will be the codename buried in Anton's ledger—Night Horizon—the deeper conspiracy in your father's files. The reason the next phase will be harder to survive."

"But we'll survive it together," Zara added. "The living, the officially dead, and everyone in between."

***

Rain continued to tap against the window like time's metronome, measuring moments in a rhythm older than empires. The city below pulsed with life that would outlast governments, outlast corporations, outlast the men who thought they could own nations like family heirlooms.

The moth found a gap in the window frame and escaped into a colorless morning, its brief captivity ended but its destination unknown. Grace watched it disappear into the rain, understanding finally why Anton had kept moths in his study, why he'd been fascinated by creatures drawn to light that could eliminate them.

"Power was like that light," she said. "Beautiful and necessary and ultimately fatal to those who flew too close. The difference was choice. Moths followed instinct. Men could choose to turn away."

"Lucas chose to burn," Zara observed.

"We all chose to burn," Grace corrected. "The difference is we chose to burn together."

Now they lived in the aftermath—not safe, not redeemed, but their own. The bloodline code had been broken, but bloodlines ran deeper than code. They ran through DNA and memory, through the accumulated choices of generations, through the stories children told themselves about who their fathers really were.

The television flickered to a new story—something about electoral reforms, about transparency initiatives, about the slow machinery of democracy grinding toward something that might eventually resemble justice. But justice, they were all learning, was not a destination. It was a practice, a discipline that required constant vigilance against the gravity of compromise that pulled everyone toward the comfortable middle ground where atrocity became acceptable if it was efficient enough.

Grace turned off the screen and they sat in the gray morning light, listening to the rain and the distant sound of traffic. The ordinary music of a city that would survive its own corruption because survival was what cities did. Johannesburg had outlasted the Randlords who had carved it from gold-bearing rock. It had survived apartheid and transition, state capture and resistance. It would survive the Brandts, too, and whatever came after.

"Together," Grace said simply.

"Together," Lucas and Zara agreed.

***

Lucas's reflection in the dark screen looked solid now, no longer ghostly. Lucas Brandt, thirty-two years old, unemployed heir to a dismantled empire, survivor of his own truth-telling and member of the most effective investigative team in South African history. Not a hero—heroes acted from courage, and he had acted from desperation until he learned to act from partnership. Not a villain—villains chose evil, and he had simply stopped choosing complicity.

Just a man who'd chosen his own name over his family's, his own conscience over their code, his own future over their past.

The whiskey glass sat empty on the table, amber residue catching what light filtered through the rain. Beside it, the USB drive waited for its next mission, patient as a bullet in a chamber. Truth was like that—it waited, accumulated pressure, found the weakest point in whatever tried to contain it.

He would carry Anton Brandt's genetics until the day he died. But he would not carry Anton Brandt's crimes. That inheritance, at least, ended here. And with Grace and Zara beside him, it felt like ending was the same thing as beginning.

In the distance, the Carlton Centre continued its slow decay, floor by floor, year by year. But decay, they were all learning, was not the same as defeat. Sometimes things had to fall apart before they could be rebuilt properly. Sometimes inheritance was about knowing what to break, not what to preserve.

Rain

was stopping. Through breaks in the clouds, sunlight began to filter into the room, warming the anonymous space into something approaching home. Lucas closed his laptop and stood, stretching muscles that had grown stiff from hours of stillness.

Somewhere in the city below, children were walking to schools his family's money had never reached. Somewhere else, miners were going to work with safety equipment his testimony had helped mandate. And somewhere, in boardrooms he would never see, powerful men were learning that acceptable losses were no longer acceptable—not when there were journalists who could investigate from beyond the grave, not when there were inheritors willing to burn down their own legacies, not when there were truth-tellers who had learned to work together instead of dying alone.

***

Grace walked to the window and looked out over Johannesburg—sprawling, scarred, stubbornly alive. The city breathed like a creature waking from anesthesia, wounded but finally aware of its injuries. From this height, she could see the patterns that connected wealth to poverty, power to powerlessness, the careful segregation that had outlasted apartheid because it served interests that transcended ideology.

But she could also see the spaces between those patterns, the gaps where people lived and loved and struggled without reference to the grand designs that claimed to govern their lives. Mrs. Ndaba, walking to work with quiet dignity. Children playing in streets that had no names on any official map. Families mourning and celebrating and surviving, indifferent to the institutional failures that obsessed men like Anton.

"Our city," she said. "Our country. Ours to help heal, if healing is possible. Ours to serve, if service is something we can still offer."

"Service is exactly what we can offer," Zara said, joining her at the window. "Documentation, investigation, truth-telling. The work of democracy."

353

On the table behind them, Lucas's laptop waited. A blank document was open, cursor blinking like a heartbeat. Not testimony this time, not confession, but something else—a letter to the families of Hartbeespoort, perhaps. Or a guide for other inheritors who might one day face the same choice between legacy and conscience. An accounting of what it cost to choose truth over blood, and why that cost was worth paying.

Lucas picked up his father's old Montblanc—the same pen that had signed so many elegant lies. He would write by hand first, the old way, letting thoughts flow through ink and paper before they became pixels and data. Some truths demanded that kind of permanence, that physical connection between mind and word.

The pen felt heavier than it should, weighted with the memory of every signature Anton had made with it. But weight could be useful. It reminded you that words had consequences, that every sentence carried the potential to heal or to harm.

As he began to write, a quiet thought settled in his mind—not a memory, not a plan, but a question that Grace had asked him just that morning: "What would you tell your children about this choice?"

***

He paused, feeling the pen's familiar weight, the slight texture of expensive paper beneath his palm. The Montblanc had written boardroom betrayals and ministerial bribes, but now it would serve a different purpose. Ink flowed dark and certain as he pressed the nib to paper.

I chose to be the ancestor my children can claim, not my father's son.

The words looked strange on paper, too simple for the complexity they tried to contain. But truth was often simple, even when its consequences were not. Especially then.

Grace read over his shoulder, her presence warm and encouraging. "Good," she said. "That's exactly right."

Outside, Johannesburg continued its ancient work of transforming minerals into money, hope into disappointment, suffering into stories that would outlast the suffering itself. The city would endure whatever came next—more corruption, more revelation, more of the cyclical struggle between justice and expediency that defined every attempt at human governance.

But for the first time since returning from London, Lucas felt like he belonged to something larger than his family's history. Not the city, exactly, and not the country—both carried their own burdens of complicity and compromise. But to the idea of accountability itself, to the stubborn belief that actions had consequences and consequences could be faced rather than hidden.

He looked at the words on the page—few so far, but honest—and continued writing. Mrs. Ndaba had been right: sorry was not enough, but it was beginning. There was no deadline for this confession, no editor waiting to shape his thoughts into publishable form. Just the slow work of understanding what he had done and why it mattered, of building a life from the rubble of inherited sin.

"Truth doesn't win outright," Grace said, settling into a chair beside him. "It only waits long enough to outlast the lies."

She'd been right about that, as she'd been right about so much else. Truth had waited thirty years to surface, and now it would outlast all of them.

"But truth doesn't have to wait alone," Zara added, pulling up a chair on his other side. "And it doesn't have to win alone, either."

The bloodline code was broken. The real work was just beginning. But they would do it together—the living, the officially dead, and the redeemed. A partnership that had learned to survive everything their enemies could inflict, including death itself.

Truth doesn't win outright. It just waits longer. But it waits in better company than it used to.

Teaser: Bloodlines of Power: Book Two – Dust and Empire

The email arrived at 3:47 a.m., routing through seven proxy servers and a mesh network that existed only in the shadows of the dark web. By the time it reached Zara Mokoena's secure terminal in her Johannesburg apartment, it had been encrypted, fragmented, and reassembled so many times that its original digital fingerprints were nothing but algorithmic ghosts.

She read it twice before the implications fully registered:

Z—They didn't all die in the mine. Three survivors, kept off the books for three decades. They're talking now. Location attached. Come alone. —A friend.

The attached coordinates pointed to a township north of Pretoria, a sprawling collection of tin shacks and cinder-block houses that had grown like a fungus around the remains of an old mining camp. Zara had driven past it a hundred times on assignment, never thinking to stop, never imagining that some of South Africa's most carefully buried secrets might be hiding in plain sight among the satellite dishes and laundry lines.

She printed the email, then fed the pages into her shredder and watched them become confetti. On her secure laptop, she pulled up the mining records from the Brandt trials—the official reports of the cave-in at Hartbeespoort that had killed twenty-three men in 1994. Twenty-three bodies were recovered and identified, families were told all were dead, twenty-three families compensated, and twenty-three graves were in the township cemetery outside Rustenburg, according to official reports.

Crisis Protocol Theta had been archived, but the algorithms never forgot.

But if the email was authentic, the math was wrong. Which meant the cover-up went deeper than even Lucas Brandt had imagined.

* * *

Zara Mokoena—an investigative journalist, and once Lucas's closest confidante—made coffee, strong and bitter, and sat in her kitchen watching the sun rise over Johannesburg's sprawling skyline. The Brandt trials had been her ticket to international recognition—a Pulitzer nomination, speaking engagements in London and New York, job offers from news organizations that had never returned her calls before. But they had also made her enemies, people with long memories and longer reach who considered her work a personal affront.

The smart thing would be to forward the coordinates to the NPA's Investigating Directorate (or the Hawks) and let official investigators handle whatever was waiting in that township. The safe thing would be to delete the email and pretend it had never arrived, to focus on the comfortable assignments that came with her newfound reputation.

Instead, she grabbed her keys.

* * *

The drive took ninety minutes through traffic that moved like congealed blood through the arteries of a city still learning to heal. As Johannesburg gave way to the Highveld's endless grasslands, Zara found herself thinking about Lucas—David now, according to the Christmas card she'd received from Mozambique, no return address but the handwriting unmistakably his.

He had vanished completely after the trials, disappearing into the kind of anonymity that only serious money or serious enemies could purchase. She envied him sometimes, the clean break he'd made with his past, the freedom to reinvent himself without the weight of expectation or the burden of other people's secrets.

But she was a journalist, which meant she was constitutionally incapable of leaving mysteries unsolved. The email had hooked her the moment she'd read it, its promise of hidden truth too tempting to resist.

* * *

The township appeared gradually, first as scattered shacks on the horizon, then as a dense maze of narrow streets and improvised architecture that spoke of generations of making do with whatever materials could be scavenged or stolen. Zara followed her GPS through a labyrinth that seemed designed to confuse outsiders, past hair salons operating out of shipping containers and mechanics repairing cars on plots of bare earth.

The coordinates led her to a community center, a low building of painted cinder blocks surrounded by a fence topped with razor wire. A hand-lettered sign in three languages advertised literacy classes and HIV testing, the mundane services that kept communities like this one functioning despite official neglect.

She parked and locked her car, acutely aware of being watched from doorways and windows, a woman in expensive clothes venturing into a world where such visitors usually brought bad news. Her press credentials might protect her, or they might make her a target—in places like this, the line between friend and enemy was often thinner than the metal of a reporter's badge.

Inside, the air was cooler than the street but heavy with the smell of disinfectant and the accumulated weight of human struggle. A young woman at a reception desk looked up from her computer. She took in Zara's appearance with the practiced assessment of someone who had learned to judge strangers quickly.

"I'm looking for someone," Zara said in English, then repeated it in her limited Afrikaans. "About the old mine. Someone sent me coordinates."

The receptionist's expression shifted, wariness replacing curiosity. She picked up a phone, spoke quietly in a language

Zara didn't recognize, then hung up and gestured toward a hallway lined with motivational posters in fading colors.

"Room seven," she said. "They're waiting."

* * *

Zara walked down the hallway, her footsteps echoing off concrete walls painted in cheerful yellows and greens that couldn't quite mask the institutional grimness beneath. Room seven's door was ajar, revealing a circle of plastic chairs and overhead lighting that hummed with electrical fatigue.

Three men sat waiting for her, their ages difficult to determine but their faces marked by the particular weariness that comes from carrying secrets too heavy for one lifetime. The youngest might have been fifty; the oldest looked as though he had been carved from mine-darkened stone and then forgotten by his sculptor.

"Ms. Mokoena," the middle one said, rising from his chair with the careful movements of someone whose bones remembered harder work than they were currently asked to perform. "We've been waiting a long time to tell this story."

Zara took the offered chair, pulled out her digital recorder, and set it on the metal table between them. "How long?"

"Three decades," the oldest man said, his voice carrying the rasp of lungs that had breathed too much dust and too little clean air. "Three decades of keeping quiet, of pretending we died with the others, of watching the families grieve for us while we hid like criminals."

The third man, who had remained silent, opened a battered briefcase and withdrew a stack of photographs. He spread them across the table with the deliberation of someone dealing cards in a high-stakes game. The images were grainy, clearly taken in secret, but they showed the aftermath of the cave-in with devastating clarity—and they showed something the official reports had never mentioned.

"The mine didn't collapse by accident," he said simply. "And we didn't survive by luck."

* * *

Zara leaned forward, studying the photographs. In one, men in mining gear emerged from what appeared to be a hidden tunnel, their faces obscured by dust and shadow. In another, official-looking figures stood near vehicles with government plates, their body language suggesting urgency and secrecy.

"Tell me," she said, activating her recorder. "Tell me everything."

The story that emerged over the next three hours was like a geological survey of buried corruption, each layer revealing new depths of institutional betrayal. The cave-in had been deliberate—triggered by explosives placed not to extract ore but to silence men who had discovered something far more valuable than gold in the depths of Hartbeespoort mine.

"They found it two weeks before the collapse," the youngest survivor explained. "A chamber, deep in the old workings, filled with equipment that didn't belong there. Communications gear, computers, files in languages most of them couldn't read. The kind of things that would interest certain government departments during the transition years."

Zara felt her pulse quicken. "What kind of files?"

The oldest man smiled grimly. "The kind that could start wars or prevent them, depending on who controlled them. Names, bank accounts, photographs of people in compromising positions. Information certain parties would pay anything to possess—or to bury."

"So they buried it," the middle survivor continued. "Along with anyone who might tell the story. Twenty-three men died to keep that secret, and we three were kept alive to provide the labor needed to remove everything from the chamber before the official investigation began."

* * *

Zara's mind raced, connecting these revelations to the network charts from the Brandt trials, the web of relationships that had seemed comprehensive but now revealed crucial gaps. "Who ordered it? Who was running the operation?"

The three men exchanged glances—the kind of wordless communication forged by shared danger and kept faith.

"The same people who protected the Brandts for so long," the youngest said finally. "But bigger. International. The kind of organization that doesn't appear on any government chart but has representatives in every capital from Washington to Beijing."

He reached into his jacket and set a flash drive on the table beside the photographs. "Everything we salvaged from that chamber before they sealed it permanently—recovered onto old drives back then, now copied here. Three decades we've been waiting for the right moment, the right person to tell this story."

Zara stared at the drive, understanding that accepting it would make her a target of forces that made the Brandt network look like amateur hour. But she also understood that some stories demanded to be told, regardless of the personal cost to their messengers.

"Why now?" she asked. "Why me?"

The oldest man leaned back, eyes reflecting the weight of years spent in hiding. "Because your reporting on the Brandts proved the truth can still matter, even against powerful enemies. And because we're old men now, tired of carrying other people's secrets to our graves."

"Besides," the middle survivor added with a bitter smile, "our graves are already dug. Have been for three decades. Might as well make them mean something."

* * *

Zara picked up the flash drive, feeling its weight—light as a feather, heavy as the world. Outside, the township continued its daily rhythm of survival and hope, unaware that the foundations of everything they thought they knew about their country's recent history were about to shift once again.

"One more question," she said. "The friend who sent me the email—was that one of you?"

The three men looked at each other and began to laugh, a sound that carried equal parts tragedy and relief.

"Ms. Mokoena," the youngest said, "you're about to discover that your friend David Santos is not as safely hidden as he believes. The bloodlines of power run deeper than any one family, and they have very long memories indeed."

Zara felt a chill that had nothing to do with the air conditioning. Somewhere in Mozambique, the man who had once been Lucas Brandt was about to learn that breaking one family's code of silence had consequences that stretched far beyond his father's sins.

The flash drive seemed to pulse with digital life in her palm, containing secrets that would reshape her understanding of power, corruption, and the price of truth in a world where information was the ultimate weapon.

She remembered what Grace says whenever a lead goes cold or a source pulls out: "Truth doesn't win. It just waits longer." Tonight, it had waited long enough.

* * *

As she prepared to leave the community center, one thought echoed in her mind: Lucas had destroyed his family's empire, but the empire had been part of something much larger—something that viewed his testimony not as justice served but as a declaration of war.

The real bloodlines of power were about to reveal themselves, and this time, there would be nowhere to hide.

To be continued in Bloodlines of Power: Book Two – Dust and Empire. Pre-order Book Two now.

Acknowledgments

To my wife, Lea-Anne—anchor, fire, compass. Every line I write remembers you. Every truth I chase carries your breath in its lungs.

To my parents—thank you for everything I could ever want, including a superlative education, and for the quiet, steadfast support that made all things possible.

To Ben Brooks, my high school principal at Redhill High School—thank you for teaching us that writing was both art and discipline. In Grade 12, it was our privilege to have you guide us through creative writing for an entire year. You showed us how language could cut glass and still hold light.

To the early readers who read between the lines and trusted what wasn't yet on the page—thank you. You saw the shadow before it had shape.

To the ghosts behind the glass: whistleblowers, journalists, survivors who paid in blood or silence—you're in every broken ledger, every whispered file, every name the world tried to forget. This book owes you more than words.

To Lucas and Zara—fictional, but real enough to bruise. You taught me that sometimes the cleanest truth is found in the dirtiest rooms. And that the cost of telling it is almost always personal.

To the invisible hands—editors, collaborators, machines made of code and care—thank you for sharpening the signal when the noise got too loud.

And to the ones watching quietly, always just outside the frame: I see you. I remember you. This book is stitched with your silence.

Some codes are meant to be broken. Some names deserve to be spoken. This was mine.

—J Buck
Buderim, Australia | 2025

Glossary

A selection of South African terms, acronyms, and locations referenced in *The Bloodline Code*. Definitions are offered for clarity and reader enrichment, not as strict translations.
(Listed alphabetically)

ANC
African National Congress. South Africa's ruling political party since the end of apartheid in 1994 Once a liberation movement, now a complex and often controversial political force.

Boet
Afrikaans slang for "brother." Used informally among men, similar to "bro" or "mate."

Braai
A traditional South African barbecue. More than just grilling—braais are social rituals, deeply woven into community life across race, class, and region.

Carlton Centre
Once the tallest building in Africa. Located in Johannesburg's inner city, now partially abandoned—a towering symbol of faded ambition and urban decay.

Hartbeespoort
A dam and mining region in North West Province. Site of industrial tragedies and cover-ups referenced in the Brandt family's past.

Hawks
Directorate for Priority Crime Investigation within SAPS. Handles organized crime, corruption, commercial crime, and high-priority cases; often partners with the **NPA** *(see NPA in glossary)*.

Hillbrow
A densely populated Johannesburg suburb. Once cosmopolitan, now known for overcrowding, crime, and resilience.

Indaba
A Zulu word meaning "matter for discussion." Widely used in business, media, and politics to describe meetings or conferences.

Investigating Directorate (ID)
A specialized unit within the **NPA** *(see NPA in glossary)* focused on complex corruption and state-capture matters. Works with the Hawks and other agencies.

Jozi
A popular nickname for Johannesburg. Also called Joburg or Egoli ("City of Gold").

Muti
Traditional African medicine. Often herbal, but can involve spiritual or ritual components.

NPA
National Prosecuting Authority. South Africa's independent prosecuting service. Brings criminal cases to court; houses specialized units.

Nkomazi

A key border post between South Africa and Mozambique. Frequently referenced in trade—and smuggling—routes.

Pollsmoor

A high-security prison near Cape Town. Formerly held Nelson Mandela; still operational.

Randburg

A northern Johannesburg suburb, historically white and affluent. Often contrasted with the decline of the inner city.

Rosebank

A vibrant Johannesburg district known for its hotels, offices, and shopping precincts. A common meeting place for business and politics.

SABC

South African Broadcasting Corporation. The national public broadcaster. Frequently criticized for political bias or state influence.

SAPS

South African Police Service. The country's national police force. Often under-resourced, politicized, and mistrusted.

Sandton

Johannesburg's financial capital. Known as "Africa's richest square mile," home to stock exchanges, banks, and elite enclaves.

Soweto

Short for "South Western Townships." A sprawling township hub on the city's edge—birthplace of resistance, struggle, and South Africa's democratic soul.

TRC (Truth and Reconciliation Commission)

South Africa's post-apartheid tribunal (established 1995) that heard testimony on politically motivated crimes from 1960-1994 and offered conditional amnesty. **Historical; not an active investigative body today**. Its reports (1998–2003) still inform public debates and cases.

Wits

Short for the University of the Witwatersrand. One of South Africa's premier universities, known for activism, investigative journalism, and political thought.

Coming Soon in the Bloodlines of Power Series

Book One: The Bloodline Code—*Released*
Lucas Brandt inherits more than an empire. He inherits a legacy of secrets too dangerous to keep… or expose.

Book Two: Dust and Empire—*December 2025*
When truth collapses an empire, the dust doesn't settle—it chokes. And the past comes hunting.

Book Three: Echoes in the Ledger—*January 2026*
Memory becomes a weapon as apartheid-era secrets rise from the vault to fracture the future.

Book Four: The Clean Hands Coup—*January 2026*
Power rebrands. Justice is staged. Lucas is framed in a media coup—and Zara strikes back.

Book Five: The Inheritance Clause—*February 2026*
The clause that crowns the next Brandt ruler. Lucas must choose: burn it all, or become what he hates.

Book Six: Redemption Protocol—*February 2026*
Final moves. Final betrayals. A coded legacy, a buried truth—and one last shot at redemption.

For future releases and series updates:
sandtonpublishing.com
sandtonpublishing.com/newsletter

About the Author

John Buck is a South African-born author whose fiction excavates the moral ruins of power, legacy, and betrayal. His work blends psychological depth with high-stakes thriller momentum, drawing on real-world experience in business, politics, and post-apartheid elite circles.

Before turning to fiction, Buck led multiple ventures across sectors, earned postgraduate degrees in business administration and finance, and witnessed firsthand how systems bend to those who write their own rules. His stories reflect that pivot—layered, noir-tinged investigations of truth under siege and the people trying to reclaim it.

The Bloodline Code is his debut novel and the first in a six-book series exploring the intersection of technology, generational guilt, and systemic corruption.

He lives in Australia with his family, where he is rebuilding, reimagining, and mapping the next great fracture in the architecture of power.

Also from Sandton Publishing

Sci-Fi Thrillers by Michael Hardy

Archive   of   Echoes

In a city where memories are currency, forgetting is a crime—and remembering can kill.

Book One: The Echo Thief – on Amazon & Kindle Unlimited, December 2025

Book Two: Signal Fracture – *Available January 2026*

Book Three: Ghost State – *Coming soon*

Book Four: Event Cascade – *Coming 2026*

Book Five: The Oracle Fault – *Coming 2026*

Book Six: Ouroboros Protocol – *Finale coming 2026*

Each novel delves deeper into the Archive—a neural blockchain where memories are traded, stolen, and weaponized.

Perfect for fans of Black Mirror, Blade Runner 2049, *and* The Peripheral.

* * *

Romantic Suspense by Lisa Hart

The   Ex-Wives   Club

Six women. One monster of a man. A boutique agency built from survival—and a chance at love after betrayal.

Book One: The Wife Before Me – Available on Amazon & KU December 2025

Book Two: The One Who Stayed – *Available December 2025*

Book Three: The Wife Who Lied – *Available January 2026*

Book Four: The Wife Who Vanished – *Available January 2026*

Book Five: The Fifth Wife – *Available February 2026*

Book Six: The Woman He Never Broke – *Available February 2026*

Sexy, suspenseful, and emotionally rich—these are survival stories disguised as second-chance romances. *For readers who love* Colleen Hoover, Nora Roberts, *and* Verity.

Join the Sandton Universe

Want behind-the-scenes intel, deleted scenes, and early access to **Book Two?**

Don't miss a thing.

Sign up now: **sandtonpublishing.com/newsletter**

Follow the story across platforms: **@sandtonpublishing**

(Facebook | Instagram | TikTok)

Explore the full author universe: **sandtonpublishing.com**

Be the first to know.

Stay one move ahead.